PENGUIN BOOKS

SHERLOCK HOLMES AND THE RED DEMON

Larry Millett is a writer for the *St. Paul Pioneer Press*. He is
the author of *Lost Twin Cities* and two other books dealing
with Minnesota's architectural history. He lives in St. Paul
with his wife and two young children.

Sherlock Holmes

and the

Red Demon

By John H. Watson, M.D.

[Edited and with an Introduction by Larry Millett]

PENGUIN BOOKS

PENGUIN BOOKS
Published by the Penguin Group
Penguin Books USA Inc., 375 Hudson Street,
New York, New York 10014, U.S.A.
Penguin Books Ltd, 27 Wrights Lane, London W8 5TZ, England
Penguin Books Australia Ltd, Ringwood, Victoria, Australia
Penguin Books Canada Ltd, 10 Alcorn Avenue,
Toronto, Ontario, Canada M4V 3B2
Penguin Books (N.Z.) Ltd, 182–190 Wairau Road,
Auckland 10, New Zealand

Penguin Books Ltd, Registered Offices:
Harmondsworth, Middlesex, England

First published in the United States of America by
Viking Penguin, a division of Penguin Books USA Inc. 1996
Published in Penguin Books 1997

1   3   5   7   9   10   8   6   4   2

Maps courtesy of the Hinckley Fire Museum, MN;
adapted for this work by the author.

THE LIBRARY OF CONGRESS HAS CATALOGUED THE HARDCOVER AS FOLLOWS:
Millett, Larry, 1947–
Sherlock Holmes and the red demon/by John Watson: edited and with
an introduction by Larry Millett.
p.   cm.
ISBN 0-670-87039-0 (hc.)
ISBN 0 14 02.5882 5 (pbk.)
1. Holmes, Sherlock (Fictitious character) — Fiction.   I. Title.
PS3563.I42193S48   1996
813'.54 — dc20   96–6723

Printed in the United States of America
Set in Cochin
Designed by Jaye Zimet

To my mother, Agnes Millett,
who would have enjoyed this adventure

Acknowledgments

✳

A number of people deserve thanks for helping with this book. The idea of sending Sherlock Holmes to the pineries first occurred to me after a tour of the Hinckley Fire Museum, where director Jeanne Coffey and her staff were unfailingly helpful. Later, I received invaluable assistance from James Hubbs, collection specialist at the University of Minnesota's Wilson Library. He introduced me to the library's superb Sherlock Holmes Collections and offered much useful information about other pastiches featuring the great detective.

John Camp, better known to the reading public as John Sanford, took time from his own busy writing schedule to read and critique the manuscript. Steve Thayer, another of St. Paul's literary lights, did likewise and was also kind enough to direct me to his agent, Al Eisele, who made a leap of faith and agreed to represent me. At Viking Penguin, Al Silverman provided expert editing and the encouragement that every author needs.

My wife, Stacey, was an early and enthusiastic reader of the manuscript, and her confidence in the project kept me going through many months of writing. Finally, I owe a debt of gratitude to my two youngest children, Lexy and Corey, whose remarkably reliable sleep schedules allowed me to complete this book with a minimum of disruption to family life. I hope that, one day, both will enjoy reading what their father wrote while they were sound asleep.

Introduction

The book you are about to read—a hitherto unknown Sherlock Holmes adventure—is in every respect an extraordinary document. Not the least of its wonders is the fact that for one hundred years it lay hidden in the massive walls of the James J. Hill mansion in St. Paul, Minnesota. How it came to be discovered there, in a secret safe, is a tale worthy of Holmes himself.

On July 20, 1994, James Parkins, a master electrician employed by a St. Paul contracting firm, was assigned to work in the Hill mansion.[1] One of his tasks was to install a new lighting circuit in the library, which had always been Hill's favorite room. As Parkins attempted to "fish" wiring through a wall behind a massive built-in bookcase, he struck solid metal. Further investigation revealed a large object embedded in the wall, and Parkins surmised—correctly, as it turned out—that he had found an old safe. Victorian tycoons such as Hill, fearing that proletarian armies might one day assault their ramparts, often equipped their homes with hidden safes. In fact, another safe on the second floor of the mansion had been found many years before. But the library safe—accessed, it was later learned, by means of a pivoting shelf—had held its secret for over a century until Parkins blundered into it.

Parkins reported his discovery to the administrator of the mansion, which since 1978 has been maintained as a public monument by the Minnesota Historical Society. Experts from the Society were called in at once to assess the situation. They soon decided to do the obvious, which was to open the safe and examine its contents.

Knowing that the safe might well contain highly sensitive documents, the Society chose not to publicize its find immediately. Instead, it was decided to open the safe in secret and let the contents determine whether any public announcement should be made. And so, on August 3, 1994, as a handful of trusted Society officials watched, a locksmith equipped with a cold chisel and blowtorch broke into the safe.

The contents turned out to be far more valuable than anyone expected. For among the safe's treasures was an astonishing manuscript entitled "Sherlock Holmes and the Red Demon," written by none other than Dr. John H. Watson.[2]

Besides providing the world with a new Sherlock Holmes adventure, the manuscript is noteworthy in several respects. It provides valuable insights into the life and times of Hill, the railroad tycoon who more than any other man created the vast inland empire of America's Northwest. Although readers today may find it odd that Hill would have reached all the way to England to hire Holmes, such a bold move was consistent with the Empire Builder's character. For all his rough-hewn qualities, Hill was a man of great strategic vision. When he perceived his larger interests to be at risk, he would go to any length and bear any cost in order to eliminate the threat. Hiring Holmes was, from Hill's point of view, merely a matter of good business.

More important, the manuscript sheds stunning new light on one of the great natural disasters of its era—the Hinckley, Minnesota, forest fire of 1894.[3] The cause of this deadly conflagration has long been the source of speculation. But if Watson's account is to be believed (and there is no reason to doubt its veracity), the fire was an act of mass murder.

Skeptical readers, or course, may think it unlikely, and perhaps even entirely unbelievable, that Sherlock Holmes visited faraway Minnesota in 1894. Indeed, when word of the manuscript's discovery spread through the scholarly community, several "experts" — without ever having seen the document — immediately pronounced it a fake. It was at this point, late in 1994, that I was engaged by the Society as a consultant to examine the handwritten manuscript and determine its authenticity or lack thereof.

The authentication of Dr. Watson's manuscripts is a scholarly task to which I have frequently applied myself, beginning in the late 1970s when I was able to untangle certain knotty questions involving early versions of *A Study in Scarlet*.[4] Since that time, I have collected a number of monographs into a volume that has come to be regarded in many circles as the definitive guide to Dr. Watson's manuscripts.[5] In the case of "Sherlock Holmes and the Red Demon," I am convinced, based upon the most thorough study possible, that the manuscript is absolutely authentic.

This conclusion is supported by evidence both internal and external. The internal evidence begins with the handwriting itself. Over the years, I have examined all of Dr. Watson's original manuscripts — now housed in the Watson Archives at the British Museum in London — and have come to know his handwriting as well as my own. That the manuscript found in the walls of the Hill mansion came from the hand of Watson, Holmes's longtime friend and companion, there can be no doubt. The good doctor, for example, formed his capital Qs in a highly distinctive manner, and the broad loop of his gs is equally unmistakable. Both characteristics are readily evident in the manuscript of "Sherlock Holmes and the Red Demon."

Watson also favored a distinctive type of foolscap writing paper manufactured by the Eynsford Paper Mills in Eynsford, Kent, England.[6] A watermark of the kind used by the Eynsford Mills between 1893 and 1900 is clearly visible on the manuscript pages of "Sherlock Holmes and the Red Demon." At least six other authenticated Watson manuscripts from this period bear the identical watermark.

There is one other crucial piece of internal evidence, which is that the manuscript was written with an early version of the Koh-I-Noor pencil. Introduced by the L. & C. Hardtmuth Company of Vienna in 1890, the Koh-I-Noor was in its day considered the Rolls-Royce of pencils.[7] Watson, it is known, fell in love with the Koh-I-Noor and always used the pencil for his first drafts, which were then typed by a secretary before being sent to the publisher. Made from Siberian graphite, the Koh-I-Noor leaves a unique microscopic signature. My analysis of the manuscript discovered in the Hill house shows conclusively that it was written with an early version of the Koh-I-Noor No. 2—perhaps the surest evidence of all that the work is authentic. It is likely, for reasons which will become clear later, that the manuscript was never typed and that it is the only copy Watson ever made.

The external evidence that points to the manuscript's authenticity is of a more indirect nature. First, there is the matter of timing. Could Holmes and Watson, based on the known historical record (a record provided exclusively by Watson's accounts of their adventures), have been in Minnesota in the late summer of 1894? The answer is a resounding yes.

As students of Holmes's career are well aware, it was in the spring of 1891 that he and his archnemesis, Professor Moriarty, fought to the death at the Reichenbach Falls in Switzerland. Watson's account of this episode, in "The Final Problem," first appeared in December 1893 in the *Strand Magazine*. At that time, Watson assumed—as did all the world—that both Holmes and Moriarty had plunged to their deaths over the gloomy cataract.

In the spring of 1894, however, Watson and the world learned otherwise. It was then that Holmes—who, fearing retribution from Moriarty's henchmen, had remained incognito for three years—made his triumphant return by capturing one of Moriarty's most sinister agents, Colonel Moran. Readers will find an account of this in "The Adventure of the Empty House."

Between 1894 and 1901, Watson went on to recount a dozen other Holmes cases, collected in 1905 in *The Return of Sherlock Holmes*. Watson did not always assign a year to these adventures, but the earliest date to be found in any of them is November 1894 (in "The Adventure of the Golden Pince-Nez"). In this adventure, not published until almost ten years after the fact, Watson made a point of noting five other cases in which Holmes had been involved in 1894. Curiously, none of these cases was ever committed to print, even though at least one—involving Huret, the Boulevard assassin—supposedly earned Holmes the Order of the Legion of Honor from the president of France.

It is my belief that these five cases are fictitious, cited by Watson as a way of disguising Holmes's real activities during the late summer and early autumn of 1894. The opening chapter of "Sherlock Holmes and the Red Demon" reveals that Holmes—far from being busy—was in fact idled by melancholy for several months after his return to England and the capture of Colonel Moran. Only when he went to the Minnesota pineries at James J. Hill's request in August 1894 did Holmes regain his old enthusiasm. And since the manuscript makes clear that Holmes and Watson had returned to London by mid-September, there is no conflict with the November date assigned to "The Adventure of the Golden Pince-Nez."

In short, the time frame established in "Sherlock Holmes and the Red Demon" does not in any way conflict with what is known of Holmes's activities between the spring of 1894 and November of that year. While all of this, of course, does not "prove" that Holmes and Watson were in Minnesota, it makes it difficult if not impossible to demonstrate otherwise.

Other external factors also support the manuscript's credibility. There is, for example, the matter of money. The manuscript reveals that Holmes was offered a tremendous sum to make the trip to Minnesota. That Hill could afford such a large payment is beyond doubt—he was by 1894 one of the richest men in Minnesota and well on his way to becoming one of the richest in America.[8] Perhaps more important, it can also be inferred that Holmes needed money badly at the time.

Watson, the soul of Victorian discretion, was never very forthcoming about finances and only once revealed how much Holmes earned—the six thousand pounds (worth about thirty thousand U.S. dollars at the time) he received from the Duke of Holdernesse, as documented in "The Adventure of the Priory School." But it can be assumed that Holmes's fees were often considerable, given the importance of his cases and the wealth of many of his clients. It can also be assumed that these fees were Holmes's major means of support, since he was not wealthy by birth. In fact, at the end of the "Priory School" case, Holmes even claimed to be a "poor man."

In any event, there is good reason to believe that the incident at Reichenbach Falls seriously drained Holmes's resources. It is known that he spent the years between 1891 and 1894 traveling (to Tibet and Persia, among other places) and that he relied on his brother, Mycroft, for financial assistance. Undoubtedly, upon his return to England, Holmes felt obliged to repay his brother and any other creditors who had supported him during his years of wandering. Thus it is highly believable that when he was offered a princely sum by Hill, Holmes made the decision to go to Minnesota.

Another piece of presumptive evidence lies within the character of Holmes himself. Although Holmes was an indifferent traveler—"neither the country nor the sea presented the slightest attraction to him," wrote Watson in "The Cardboard Box"—he thrived on new and exotic adventures. And as readers of "Sherlock Holmes and the Red Demon" will discover, the Minnesota pineries, despite their distance in both time and spirit from the gaslit world of London, presented the great detective with the most remarkable case—and brought him face-to-face with the most deadly villain—of his celebrated career.

A final note: Although it may seem implausible that a document as rare and valuable as a Sherlock Holmes adventure should remain hidden for a century, this unusual circumstance can, I believe, be readily explained. As readers will learn, Hill had good reason not to share the manuscript with the world, for it contains information of a highly explosive nature that could have severely (if perhaps unjustly) damaged his reputation. For this reason, it is likely that Hill, who controlled the purse strings and much else in the case, secured a promise from Watson that only one copy of the manuscript be made. That Watson lived up to his end of the agreement there can be no doubt. The doctor, after all, was a Victorian gentleman, and one can suppose that having given his word, he kept it.

By the same token, it is not surprising that Hill held on to the manuscript despite its disturbing revelations. Hill was an avid collector, a man who seems to have preserved every scrap of paper that ever came before him. In the end, I suspect, he could not bring himself to burn the manuscript, as many another man in his position might have done. For this, if for no other reason, the world owes a debt of gratitude to the Empire Builder.

And now, let the adventure of "Sherlock Holmes and the Red Demon" begin.[9]

Larry Millett

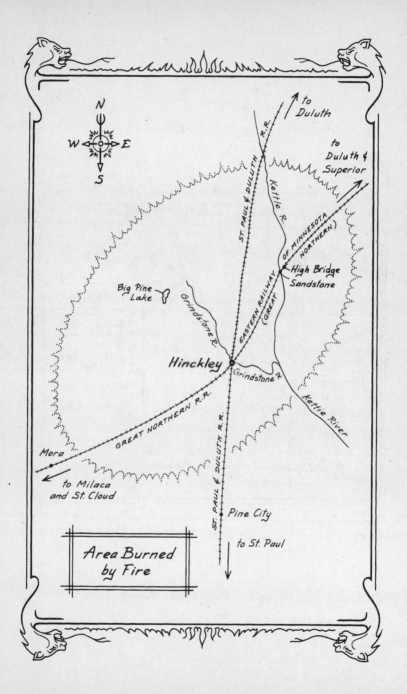

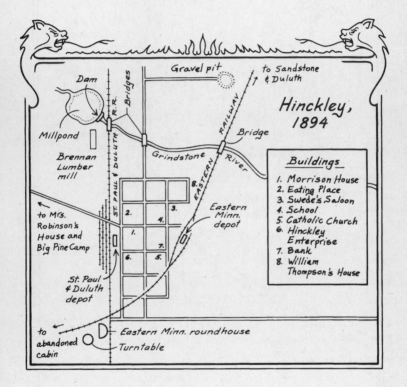

Hinckley, 1894

Dam

Gravel pit

to Sandstone & Duluth

Millpond

Bridges

Brennan Lumber mill

Grindstone River

Bridge

ST. PAUL & DULUTH R.R.

EASTERN RAILWAY

to Mrs. Robinson's House and Big Pine Camp

Eastern Minn. depot

St. Paul & Duluth depot

to abandoned cabin

Eastern Minn. roundhouse
Turntable

Buildings

1. Morrison House
2. Eating Place
3. Swede's Saloon
4. School
5. Catholic Church
6. Hinckley Enterprise
7. Bank
8. William Thompson's House

Chapter One

"How Is It Possible to Burn Down a Railroad?"

✵

Readers of *The Times* may recall the great fires which blazed across the forests of the American Midwest in the late summer of 1894.[1] For days on end, London and much of Europe followed with rapt attention the stories of death and destruction emanating from the remote pineries of the Upper Mississippi, where entire communities succumbed to the ravages of these wild infernos.

What is not known, and will be revealed here for the first time, is that my good friend Sherlock Holmes and I were in the very midst of the most lethal of all of these conflagrations, the Hinckley, Minnesota, fire. Holmes's unmasking of the malignant and cunning villain behind this catastrophe was in every respect the most remarkable achievement of his career.

Yet to this day, Holmes can hardly bear to speak of the case, which he regards—unjustly, I believe—as his greatest failure. As a result, I have been forced to rely exclusively on my own recollections in recounting the singular and tragic events of that summer. That Holmes should prefer a posture of silence is not surprising, for the "Hinckley Horror"—as he sometimes calls it—left him in a state of profound gloom from which he is only now recovering. I know that the awful scenes of devastation I witnessed in the pineries of Minnesota shall remain with me always like a painful scar across my heart.

Yet one other unforgettable image comes to mind when I think of our days in Hinckley. It is a picture of Holmes, standing on a high and lonely bridge, with fiery death all around him, confronting one of the purest madmen the world has ever known. Never, I believe, was Holmes more magnificent than he was at that moment, and it is only proper that posterity, regardless of what Holmes himself may think, should know the true story of his courage, tenacity and genius in confronting the Red Demon.

❋

The summer of 1894 was one of those periods of tedium which Holmes always found unbearable. The excitement attending his return and the brilliant capture of Colonel Moran had quickly subsided to a whisper, and London itself—damp and dreary under a protracted late summer chill—seemed to reflect Holmes's dismal mood. By August, he had lapsed into a state of melancholic torpor from which nothing, it seemed, could rouse him. He would often stay in bed until noon, refusing breakfast entirely, and would roam the streets from dusk to dawn like some poor wanderer lost in the fog. At other times, he played incessantly upon his violin, with each new melody more dirgelike than its predecessor. In hopes of restoring his spirits, I tried to engage his restless imagination in the more highly publicized crimes of the day, but even the curious affair of the two severed arms found in St. John's Wood failed to draw him out.[2]

"It is an inconsequential matter," he told me after I read him an account of the case in *The Times*. "The solution is so perfectly obvious that even Lestrade and his benighted minions at Scotland Yard should have no trouble perceiving the truth. No, my dear Watson, I am afraid the criminal element of London, which for so long provided me with problems of at least passing interest, has now entirely abdicated its responsibility. Dullness reigns, Watson. Bah!"

Such was the atmosphere on the morning of August 13, when there came a knock on the door of our flat at 221B Baker Street. On this particular day, Holmes had roused himself sufficiently to undertake one of his infernal experiments in chemistry, a field in which his knowledge was both wide and profound. He was investigating, or so he informed me, certain hitherto unknown properties of prussic acid. For this purpose, he had filled the laboratory table in the "chemical corner" of our apartment with beakers, retorts, test tubes and other apparatus in which various liquids bubbled above the blue flames of Bunsen burners. This work produced a most unpleasant odor, and I was about to escape for a walk when I heard the knock.

"Get the door, would you, Watson," said Holmes, engrossed in his work. "And whoever it is, kindly tell them to go away."

"Really, Holmes," I replied, "there is no need to be impolite." I put down *The Times*, where I had been following an account of the latest depredations of the anarchists then infesting London, and went to the door.

Upon opening it, I discovered Mrs. Hudson, the redoubtable landlady who maintained our flats and who tolerated, though not always happily, Holmes's peculiarities. "There is a man downstairs who wishes to see Mr. Holmes," she said, handing me his card. She sniffed the air as she spoke. "And what is that awful smell?"

"Another of Mr. Holmes's experiments, I'm afraid," I said as I glanced at the card, which identified our caller as J. G. Pyle, agent of the Great Northern Railway.[3] The name was unfamiliar to me. Given Holmes's unsociable mood, I suggested to Mrs. Hudson that our visitor might wish to return at a more propitious time.

"The gentleman is very insistent," she said. "He says it is a matter of the utmost urgency."

At that moment, Pyle himself appeared, bounding up the stairs with a tremendous display of energy. He was a compact, well-dressed man of forty or so, with broad smooth features, a firm chin and a handsome red mustache which curled up past his cheekbones toward his deep blue eyes.

"I am sorry to intrude," he announced, "but it is absolutely essential that I speak at once to Mr. Sherlock Holmes."

At the sound of Pyle's voice, which unmistakably identified him as an American, Holmes looked up from his experiment table, cocked his head to one side, and said: "Chicago."

"What was that you said, sir?" asked Pyle, still standing in the doorway and appearing confused by Holmes's abrupt manner.

Holmes smiled—the first time in a month I had seen him do so. "I simply mentioned that you are from Chicago, sir, that fabled city of gangsters, ward heelers and other species of American criminality. Am I correct?"

"Not exactly, sir," replied Pyle, adding: "I take it I am speaking to Sherlock Holmes."

The smile left Holmes's face. "You say you are not from Chicago?" he said, ignoring Pyle's attempt to secure an introduction. "I find that quite unbelievable."

Pyle turned to me with a questioning look. "I'm afraid, sir, that I do not quite understand what Chicago has to do with this. I was born in that city, to be sure, but I have not lived there for many years. Now, if this gentleman"—he gestured toward Holmes—"has some interest in the matter, I should be happy to discuss it with him at the appropriate time. At present, however, I would like to speak to Mr. Holmes."

Holmes, who had long prided himself on his ability to identify the most subtle nuances of the English language, let out a contented sigh. "Ah, Mr. Pyle, do come in and sit down. I am Sherlock Holmes. You have already met my friend, Dr. Watson. And this"—

he swept a hand toward Mrs. Hudson—"is the wonderful woman who, if there is no inconvenience in it, shall bring us some tea."

❉

Glaring at Holmes, Mrs. Hudson retired downstairs to attend to her duties while I ushered Pyle to a seat by the bay window overlooking Baker Street. Holmes, as was his wont, pulled up a side chair and turned it around, so that he sat with his elbows resting upon the back. He contemplated our visitor with the utmost interest.

"I fear that you have had an unfortunate encounter with our London pickpockets," he remarked casually as Pyle sat down and took off his bowler hat, which he held in his lap. "But then, I assume a newspaperman such as yourself is all too aware of the activities of the criminal class. Even in St. Paul, I imagine, crime is not unknown."

"My God," Pyle ejaculated, as though he had just witnessed an act of black magic, "how could you know these things?"

"It is a simple matter of observation, Mr. Pyle," Holmes responded. "As to the pickpocket, I note that your fob is slightly torn and, of course, there is no watch in it. Now, since you are a journalist by profession—a fact evident from the small notebook in your left coat pocket, a notebook of the peculiar sort every newsman carries—you naturally would regard a watch as essential. But you clearly have not had time to replace it, which leads me to conclude that it was stolen quite recently, probably within the hour.

"Moreover, it is likely that this theft occurred at a railroad station, since the crowds there always attract members of the light-fingered fraternity. And, of course, it is quite obvious that you have traveled here from far away. Your accent readily identifies you as an American, as does that fact that in your hat is a prominent label from a haberdasher located, if I read the label correctly, in St. Paul, Minnesota."

I had seen Holmes engage in such deductive exercises many times and had come to regard them as little more than parlor tricks. Pyle, however, was quite taken by the demonstration. He looked down at his hat and shook his head in amazement.

"It is all true, Mr. Holmes," he said at length. "My watch was stolen, at Victoria Station, I believe.⁴ And I am a newspaperman, presently employed by the *Daily Globe* in St. Paul."

"Quite," said Holmes. "Now, pray tell us, sir, what is the urgent matter which brings you all the way to London?"

Pyle responded with a question of his own. "Are you familiar, Mr. Holmes, with the name of James J. Hill?"

"An American railroad tycoon who recently completed, unless I am mistaken, a transcontinental line to the Pacific Ocean."⁵

Holmes's field of knowledge—so complete in some areas, so deficient in others—was a constant source of wonder to me, although I had been unaware until this moment that his expertise extended to the railroads of America.

"You are once again correct, Mr. Holmes," Pyle said. "Mr. Hill, for whom I have on occasion undertaken certain delicate missions, is indeed one of the leading railroad men of America. He is also a man who believes, as he has often put it to me, that 'only the best will do.' That is how he built his railroad and that is why it has flourished at a time when so many other enterprises have collapsed. That is also why he has sent me here, Mr. Holmes. It is his conviction that you are the greatest detective in the world and he would like to engage your services on a most important matter."

Holmes raised his eyebrows and glanced at me in that mocking, ironic manner to which I was so accustomed. Yet I could tell that Pyle's flattering words had not been without effect.

"Mr. Hill's sentiments," Holmes remarked, "are admirable, though I am sure not all the world agrees. Now, sir, what precisely is this 'important matter' to which you have referred?"

Pyle paused, leaned forward, and said: "Mr. Hill wants you to find the man who is trying to burn down one of his railroads."

❄

Mrs. Hudson chose this dramatic moment to arrive with three cups of tea, and the conversation momentarily came to a halt. After her departure, Holmes turned again to Pyle and said:

"Your request, sir, is indeed intriguing, but I should be pleased if you would first enlighten me on a number of points. What, for example, leads Mr. Hill to believe that someone intends to commit such a peculiar act of destruction? And why is this not a matter for the local police or detective agencies? The Pinkertons, as I recall, have done notable work for the American railroads."

"I will do my best to answer your questions," Pyle replied, meeting Holmes's eyes with a steady gaze, "although there are certain details that only Mr. Hill himself can reveal to you. However, I am at liberty to tell you that, over the past month, Mr. Hill has received letters of a most foul and provocative sort. These letters—at least three thus far—all contain similar threats against the Eastern Minnesota Railway, one of several lines controlled by Mr. Hill that connect to the Great Northern.[6] Now—"

Holmes interrupted: "Have you seen these letters, Mr. Pyle?"

"No. Mr. Hill, so far as I know, has shown them to no one other than the investigating authorities who were called in immediately upon receipt of the first of the letters."

"When was that?"

"Let me check, Mr. Holmes." Pyle removed a small notebook from his coat pocket—the same notebook Holmes had noticed earlier—and went rapidly through the pages. "Ah, here it is. The first letter was received July 16. The next came one week later. The third letter arrived on August 3."

"And all of these letters contained an explicit threat to do damage to the railroad in question?"

"That is correct."

Holmes stood up and began pacing about the room, a habit of

his when pondering a problem. Stopping by the window, he said: "Tell me, Mr. Pyle, why are these letters of such great concern to your employer? Surely a man of Mr. Hill's wealth and power is accustomed to receiving unpleasant letters. Extortionists are all too common, I fear. However, in my experience, few are prepared to carry out their threats."

"But that is the odd thing, Mr. Holmes. The person who wrote these letters has never asked for money. Worse, he has already acted upon his threats. Three days after the first letter arrived, a fire of highly suspicious origin broke out near the Eastern Minnesota depot in the town of Hinckley, about ninety miles north of St. Paul. Another, much larger fire ten days later was also the work of an arsonist, and only good fortune prevented it from becoming a general conflagration."

Holmes returned to his chair, where he propped up his elbows and cradled his head in his hands. His eyes, as was usually the case during moments of intense concentration, were closed. He said: "That is most interesting, Mr. Pyle. Now, I believe you said Mr. Hill turned these letters over to the local authorities. What did they make of them?"

"Nothing. The police in St. Paul were of no help. Their investigation, to Mr. Hill's mind, was desultory and incomplete. They finally informed him that they could deduce little from the letters and that, in any event, the problem was one for the local authorities in Hinckley."

"I see. And I presume Mr. Hill has gained no satisfaction in Hinckley either?"

"None whatsoever," Pyle said, leaving little doubt as to his contempt for the legal authorities in that village. "But this is not surprising, since the marshal there is a man of dubious reputation. Many suspect, in fact, that he has turned a blind eye to numerous crimes, and thereby lined his own pockets."

Holmes nodded. "I have been told that the American police are inclined toward corruption. That is most unfortunate. But, tell me, has Mr. Hill formed opinions of his own as to the identity of this arsonist? After all, a man in his position must have made many enemies."

"He has made his share," Pyle acknowledged. "The world of railroading is not a tender business. But to answer your question, Mr. Hill does indeed have certain theories about who might be responsible for the fires."

"Anarchists," I said. "That would be my thought. Why, just today there was a story in *The Times* about them. They are capable of the greatest outrages, as the recent murder of the French president attests."[7]

"My dear Watson," said Holmes, "I believe that if your soup arrived cold for lunch, you would see in this event the dark hand of the anarchist. However, I would be curious to know who Mr. Hill thinks is behind the assaults on his railroad."

Pyle, however, said he was not authorized to discuss the matter any further, except to say that Hill would be happy to share his ideas with Holmes at the appropriate time.

"Very well," Holmes said, "though I would imagine that the railroad workers' strike last spring, in which the Great Northern was no doubt involved, might bear on Mr. Hill's theories as to the arsonist's identity."[8]

Pyle grinned. "That is not a bad guess, but I would prefer that you hear any more of this matter directly from Mr. Hill."

Holmes shrugged, then said: "I am curious about one other thing. Why has Mr. Hill not hired detectives of his own to investigate these criminal acts?"

"Oh, but he has, Mr. Holmes. The day after the first fire, Mr. Hill dispatched his most trusted railroad detective, Thomas Mortimer, to Hinckley. Mr. Mortimer telegraphed a week later that he had uncovered some promising leads and expected to resolve the matter shortly. And then—"

Pyle paused, a troubled look upon his normally open and frank countenance.

"Go on," said Holmes impatiently.

"Well, the fact is that Mr. Mortimer, who was a good friend of mine, has not been heard from since. It is as though he vanished from the face of the earth."

"And it is believed he met with foul play?"

"I fear that is a possibility, Mr. Holmes."

"I see. Now, one more question, Mr. Pyle. How is it possible to burn down a railroad? I find it hard to imagine such a thing."

"I admit, Mr. Holmes, that it does seem strange. But you must understand that the Eastern Minnesota passes through one of the world's last great pineries. White pines grow thick and abundant along much of the main line, and there are places where the jacks are now taking eighty thousand board feet out of a single acre of forest."

"I take it that is a remarkable figure."

"Indeed it is. But this year, unfortunately, a great drought has occurred in the pineries. Where thirteen inches of rain would normally be recorded during the summer, less than an inch has fallen. Day after day of brutal heat has accompanied this drought. The result, as you might imagine, is that the pineries are now a veritable tinderbox. Thus far, only minor fires have occurred. But if a madman is intent on using fire as a weapon against the Eastern Minnesota, God help us if he should succeed! An uncontrolled fire in the pineries now could produce a vast conflagration that would not only destroy much of the Eastern Minnesota Railway but would also jeopardize the lives of hundreds and perhaps thousands of innocent people."

Pyle paused to let his words sink in. "And that, sir, is why Mr. Hill sent me here to try to persuade you to come to Minnesota. He believes you are the only man in the world who can find this arsonist and stop him before he causes untold damage and misery. I should add"—here Pyle's voice suddenly became more businesslike—"that Mr. Hill is prepared to pay you the sum of fifty thousand American dollars for your services."

※

Although his work as a consulting detective had earned Holmes a comfortable living, he was not a man in whom the desire for money burned brightly. Money for him was purely a means to an end, and I had known him to waive any fee whatsoever in cases where his client was of limited means. By the same token, no amount of money could interest him in a case that he considered beneath his abilities. Some years earlier, for example, he had turned down an offer of eight thousand pounds from a prominent figure in the London mercantile community who sought evidence of his wife's infidelities. Yet Holmes was by no means insensible to the value of money, and the sum offered by Mr. Hill, which amounted to ten thousand pounds or more, was indeed astonishing.

Holmes sat in silence for a moment after the amount was mentioned, giving no sign that the offer had heightened his interest in the case. Finally, he observed: "Mr. Hill obviously attaches great importance to this matter."

Pyle gave a solemn nod. "You must understand, Mr. Holmes, that millions of dollars are at stake. If the pineries burn, they will be lost forever, since the white pine does not regenerate itself. As for the Eastern Minnesota, it is now and for the foreseeable future utterly dependent on the logging industry, which accounts for the bulk of its freight. I cannot impress upon you too strongly, Mr. Holmes, the importance of this matter. Naturally, Mr. Hill is also prepared to pay your travel expenses to and from Minnesota, and he will put his private railroad car—which I think you and Dr. Watson will find most comfortable—at your disposal."

Without a word, Holmes stood and went to the fireplace mantel, where he kept his pipes. He selected one to his liking, filled its bowl with tobacco from the Persian slipper which hung nearby, then struck a match against the rough stone of the fireplace. The match flared instantly to life.

Gazing intently at the small yellow flame, Holmes said: "Fire is a most intriguing phenomenon, Mr. Pyle, a simple combination of fuel, oxygen and combustion that drives the great engines of our progress as a species. Our civilization could not advance without it.

And yet"—the match had now burned down almost to the tips of Holmes's fingers—"it can leap beyond our control, causing unspeakable horrors, especially if it is used for ill purposes."

Holmes extinguished the match and said: "You may not be aware, Mr. Pyle, that I have written a trifling monograph on the subject of pyromania.[9] In it, I—"

"You make the point that to solve the crime of arson one must first understand the mind of the arsonist. You also offer certain novel means of tracing a fire to its source by means of careful analysis of the pattern and extent of the burns."

"Mr. Pyle," said Holmes, momentarily taken aback, "you are quite full of surprises."

Pyle smiled. "I was referred to your work in this regard by Mr. Hill. He is not a man to enter into any situation without first learning as much of it as he possibly can. He was, I assure you, quite taken by your monograph, which he does not regard as trifling in the least. And now, Mr. Holmes, I must ask you. Will you come to America?"

Holmes tried to maintain an air of nonchalance, but I could see high excitement in his eyes, which glinted with an enthusiasm I had not observed in months. He turned to me: "Well, Watson, what say you? Are you up to an adventure in America?"

"Of course," I said, although the prospect of a journey to the American frontier was not entirely pleasing, since it would entail disruption of my practice, which I had only with the greatest labor built up in recent months. Still, I was heartened by the fact that Holmes, after weeks of paralyzing inactivity, seemed suddenly to have been revitalized.

"Then it is done," Holmes said.

Pyle fairly leaped from his chair and embraced Holmes. "You will not regret your decision, sir, for you will be doing a great service to humanity."

"But what about travel arrangements?" I asked, since that practical issue had not yet been addressed.

Pyle had anticipated the question. He said: "I have taken the liberty to book you and Mr. Holmes on the *Lucania*, which steams from Southampton tomorrow evening at six.[10] Once we have reached New York, we will board the first available train of the Pennsylvania Railroad for the trip to Chicago. There, Mr. Hill's private Pullman car will be available for the remainder of the journey to St. Paul. I trust these arrangements will not be inconvenient for you."

"Most thoughtful," said Holmes, a note of irritation in his voice. "And if our steamship founders, I am sure Mr. Hill will be waiting at the side for us, life preservers in hand. Now, Mr. Pyle, you will excuse us. We must go about our preparations."

"Certainly," Pyle said, appearing to take no offense at Holmes's sharp manner. "I shall see you in Southampton."

After our visitor had gone, Holmes went to the front window and looked out over the bustling noontime scene on Baker Street.

"Minnesota," he said, taking a long draw on his pipe. "I rather like the name, don't you?"

It was a sentiment he was never to voice again.

Chapter Two

"It Is a Perfect Atmosphere for Mischief"

✳

Of our journey to the New World, I shall provide only the briefest account, since a detailed travel itinerary is not the purpose of this narrative. We sailed as scheduled on the Cunard Line's handsome *Lucania*, and during the week of our Atlantic crossing Holmes was, I must confess, not the best of company. Immune to the sea's enchantments, he spent his days—and most evenings as well—alone in his stateroom. Only once did he venture out on deck, on the fourth day of our crossing, to watch a large iceberg, rare for so late in the season, that had floated into view off the starboard bow. He seemed fascinated by this great white object, noting that the bulk of its mass was hidden beneath the water.

"So it is with a criminal investigation, Watson," he said, "for what one sees at first glance is seldom the totality of the thing itself. There is always danger lurking beneath the surface of events. After all, that rather benevolent-looking piece of ice to our starboard would, I have no doubt, sink this mighty ship in a moment if we were to collide with it."

"Oh, it would take more than a little ice to send the *Lucania* to the bottom," I said with a smile. "Surely, even you would admit that."

"Perhaps," said Holmes, "but I should not count on it."[1]

After delivering this brief homily upon the treacheries of ice, Holmes returned to his room, where he spent his time reading from among a large collection of books and pamphlets he had brought along in a bulging brown valise. Many of these publications, which Holmes had obtained the day before our departure from my friend Lomax at the London Library, concerned either lumbering or railroading in America.[2] I also noticed several titles relating to the State of Minnesota, along with books and articles on the general subject of fire. While Holmes expanded his knowledge, Pyle and I enjoyed the fresh sea air and found the crossing to be a delightful experience.

We reached New York on the early morning of August 21, but were afforded no opportunity to view its wonders. Consulting his schedules, Pyle found that the Pennsylvania Special, fastest of that great railroad's luxury fliers, was due to leave for Chicago within an hour.[3] We hurriedly bade farewell to the *Lucania* and soon found ourselves bobbing across the Hudson River on a ferry, which took us to the Pennsylvania Railroad's magnificent new station in Jersey City.[4] There, an agent informed us, no tickets were to be had for that run of the Special, as all seats were taken. But Pyle, a man of the utmost resolve and enterprise, went to the stationmaster's office and emerged moments later with luxury accommodations for the three of us. How he accomplished this feat he would not say, but there can be little doubt that the mention of James J. Hill's name had much to do with our good fortune. We had barely settled into our Pullman sleeper when the Special, with two shrill blasts of its whistle, commenced the one-thousand-mile journey to Chicago.

The splendid scenery of the American continent was as lost on

Holmes as had been the bracing grandeur of the Atlantic. He remained buried in his books as we passed through Philadelphia and wound along the endless Pennsylvania valleys before breasting the Allegheny Mountains at the famous Horseshoe Curve near Pittsburgh.[5] Even that singular city, with its great pall of black smoke and its fiery mills so reminiscent of Manchester, failed to arouse Holmes's interest, and he kept at his reading as we thundered on through the night to Chicago.

It was only upon our arrival in Chicago, twenty-four hours after leaving New York, that Holmes at last took an interest in his surroundings. The gangsters of Chicago had long fascinated him, and he stared out the train window with a look of yearning as we approached the heart of the city, where tall buildings towered over the adjacent flatlands like great mountains of brick and stone.

But Chicago was also to be only a brief interlude on our journey. Within minutes of our arrival at the Union Station,[6] we transferred to a train operated by the Chicago, Burlington & Quincy Railroad. Here, Hill's palatial private car — or "private varnish," as Pyle called it — was waiting. Soon, Chicago was behind us as we hurtled west across the Illinois prairies in our luxurious apartment on wheels. Around noon, we reached that mighty Nile of American civilization — the Mississippi River. We then turned north and began the final leg of our journey, following the great river toward its head of navigation in St. Paul.

My next memory of the trip is being awakened by Pyle, who like Holmes seemed oblivious to the curative powers of repose.

"What is it?" I asked, glancing at my watch as I awakened. It was after five in the afternoon.

"Look out the window," Pyle said.

I did so and saw, up ahead, a line of white bluffs towering over a wide bend in the river. Atop this escarpment, tall buildings formed the unmistakable profile of a great urban center. A few minutes later, our train pulled into the station. We had reached St. Paul, after more than eight days of travel.

"Welcome to the Saintly City," said Pyle as he opened the door of the car and waited for a porter to assemble our bags. "If you have no objections, Mr. Hill would be pleased to see you at once."

✳

The depot in St. Paul proved to be quite small but extremely busy. The entire building, in fact, was a sea of mobile humanity, and it was only with some effort that we made our way to the front entrance and out into the street.

"A rather tempestuous place," Holmes remarked to Pyle, who led the way. "Is it always so?"

"It is, Mr. Holmes. Well over two hundred trains a day use this depot. Only New York and Chicago exceed those numbers."

Outside, more chaos awaited. A small army of dark-suited drummers with thick black bags and tired red eyes had assembled on the front steps, where they were being fought over by the roughest collection of hackmen this side of London. Upon spotting us, several of these untamed gentlemen of the road began offering their services. Before long, unseemly epithets filled the air as the competition for our patronage grew intense and disagreeable. I began to wonder how we might escape these wild men when Pyle once again came to the rescue.

"Follow me," he said, tossing a handful of change at the hackmen to divert their attention. He then took us up a steep, narrow street that led away from the river. Here, we passed several families of men, women and children dressed in the plainest of clothes and speaking a strange language.

"Swedish immigrants," Pyle explained, "on their way to the western wheat lands. Mr. Hill believes very strongly in settling the western lands. He believes it is good for America."

"And good for business, too, I should imagine," said Holmes, "since railroads are not known to thrive in wastelands."

After a short walk, we turned onto a large straight street lined with substantial brick and stone buildings that, to my surprise, were as tall or taller than anything of their kind in London. I was equally surprised to see, moving down this thoroughfare, an electrified streetcar, which struck me as a far more civilized conveyance than the smoking trains of London's abominable underground.[7]

I had hoped we might board this streetcar, but Pyle had made other arrangements. An elegant open carriage was parked nearby, safely away from the mad hubbub of the depot, and this provided our transportation to Hill's mansion.

Our ride took us through the center of St. Paul, which seemed to be a prosperous and well-built city, though still somewhat irregular as to the quality of its improvements.

"You must remember," Pyle told us, "that just thirty years ago St. Paul was a mere village in the wilderness. It still has much growing up to do."

Passing through the commercial district of the city, we reached the base of a commanding bluff, the crest of which harbored a number of palatial estates. It took but a few more minutes to ascend this promontory, and after a sharp turn we found ourselves on a wide boulevard called Summit Avenue. A short ride down this handsome thoroughfare, lined with imposing homes built for the city's merchant elite, brought us at last to the mansion of James J. Hill.

❋

This immense edifice, dark and rather forbidding on its magnificent hilltop site, was built with plain walls of deep red sandstone which suggested enormous power but avoided any hint of flamboyant excess. Its owner, we were soon to discover, possessed similar qualities.

Pyle directed our driver to a porte cochere in front of the house, and we were then escorted inside. After passing along a magnificent hallway decorated with Persian rugs, exquisitely carved woodwork and cut-glass chandeliers, we reached Hill's private study. And there, attired in a brown evening coat and seated with a book in his hand, was the fabled Empire Builder.

He stood to greet us, shaking my hand with an iron grip and repeating this ritual with Holmes. I had somehow expected a taller man, for Hill was rather below the middle height and appeared to have legs somewhat short in relation to his torso. Yet so massive was he through the shoulders and upper arms that he conveyed a sense of tremendous physical strength, which his handshake had only confirmed. What set him apart, however, was his great domed forehead, which rose over his white bearded chin, wide nose and deep-set eyes like a slab of smooth rock crowning a mountain. Beneath this extraordinary crag were the most intense gray eyes I had ever seen. Their gaze was confident, piercing, lordly. Here was a man accustomed to wielding great power and supremely secure in doing so.

It became instantly clear that he employed these penetrating eyes to take the measure of men, for as he and Holmes shook hands, I saw their gazes meet and lock. I had never seen the man who could stare down Holmes, but in Hill my friend met his match. They stood for several moments in a silent contest of wills, like two mighty tigers facing each other on a narrow jungle path. Finally, as though by some secret signal known only to themselves, they mutually agreed to look away.

"Please," said Hill," sit down." As we selected our seats, Hill drew on a bell cord and a servant appeared instantly at the door.

"Four brandies, Mr. Thomas, and cigars as well." The servant nodded and disappeared back into the hall. Hill then turned his full attention to Holmes and myself. "I trust your long journey was not too tiring, and that Mr. Pyle proved to be a capable guide."

Holmes, who was sitting directly across from Hill, responded that Pyle had indeed been most accommodating. "As for our travels, I am quite sure that my dear friend Watson found the scenery endlessly fascinating. I fear I do not care much myself for the view from a train window. I am more interested in observing the small details of life, which reveal so much."

"So I have been told," said Hill. "It is said you can tell much about a man simply by looking at him."

"That is true," said Holmes, who was never troubled by false modesty. "For example, in your case, Mr. Hill, I should imagine that you were a very young man when you lost your right eye. A hunting accident perhaps? And, of course, I am sorry to learn of your daughter's illness."

I could only sigh as Holmes undertook this latest feat of deduction. In my opinion, he had become entirely too fond of these little exercises, but there was nothing to be done about it, since Holmes delighted in displaying his peculiar gift. Hill, I must acknowledge, was taken off guard by my friend's pointed observations, and he shot a quick glance at Pyle, who protested his innocence with a shrug.

Fortunately, Hill was more amused than offended, for he slapped his knees, let out a bellowing laugh and said: "You are indeed the great detective, Mr. Holmes, though I am sure there is a simple explanation for these seemingly astonishing insights of yours."

There was, and Holmes happily revealed how he had arrived at his conclusions. Hill's blind eye, he pointed out, was readily apparent from the fact that the pupil did not dilate in response to light, a condition, I should add, that I too had noted.

Holmes continued: "In addition, I noticed a small scar directly below the eye, which naturally suggested an injury of some kind. But since the scar is only faintly visible, I surmised that the injury had occurred long ago, probably during boyhood, for it is during that reckless time that most such mishaps occur. And since it is well known that you are a great outdoorsman, the most logical conclusion was that the eye had been damaged in a youthful hunting accident."

"You are right," Hill said. "I was hunting with a bow and arrow when it happened."

Holmes bowed slightly in Hill's direction, then went on with his explanations: "As for your daughter being ill, I must confess this deduction was based on more flimsy evidence. You see, as we entered the house, I observed a servant girl carrying a doll in one hand and a bottle of castor oil in the other. It occurred to me that she might be on her way to minister to a sick child, undoubtedly a girl."

"It is little Gertrude," said Hill.[8] "A bad stomachache, I am afraid. But Mrs. Hill informs me it is nothing serious."

"I would be happy to examine the child to see if I could be of any assistance," I said.

"That is very kind of you, Dr. Watson, but I am sure Gertrude will be fine. She is a sturdy little girl."

As Hill spoke, the servant returned with our brandy and cigars. After these amenities had been passed around and enjoyed — though Holmes declined a cigar in favor of his pipe — Hill stood up and went over to a large window at one end of the room. The address which followed brought an abrupt end to the evening's social formalities.

"Mr. Pyle, I am sure, has explained to you in a general way why I have gone to the considerable trouble and expense of engaging your services," he began, fixing his magnetic eye on Holmes. "The situation in the pineries is growing more critical by the hour. We have had no rain in a month now and hardly any for the summer, the heat has been oppressive and continual, and the air in the woods is drier than anyone can remember. It is a perfect atmosphere for mischief, and that is why it is essential that the person threatening these acts of arson be apprehended at once. A large fire now — and it would not take much to start one — could cause immeasurable disaster."

Holmes nodded gravely and puffed furiously at his pipe, a sign that he was in the midst of deep thought. He said: "Such a disaster, if I am correctly informed, would have severe economic consequences both for the logging industry and your railroad."

"It would," agreed Hill, who then drew our attention to a large wall map of Minnesota, where he pointed out an area to the north of St. Paul. "If you will look at this map, you will see that the Eastern Minnesota Railway begins here, in the town of Hinckley, and then proceeds in a northeasterly direction eighty-five miles to

Duluth, at the head of Lake Superior. The countryside through which it passes is as yet undeveloped, but it contains especially fine stands of white pine. One estimate by a timber cruiser of the highest repute is that much of this area will yield forty thousand or more board feet of lumber per acre."[9]

"That is indeed impressive," Holmes remarked, "though not, I should think, quite up to the yields in Michigan."

I looked at Holmes in surprise. Where, I wondered, had he obtained this sudden expertise in American forestry? I then remembered all the reading he had done during our days of travel.

Hill's face also registered surprise. "You have done your homework, Mr. Holmes," he said in his usual forceful manner. "I admire that in a man. You are correct. Michigan had the best pine in the Midwest. But it is almost all gone now, and the largest remaining stands are in Minnesota. And nowhere in Minnesota is there better or more easily accessible pine than in the Hinckley area. On the market today, good-quality white pine lumber will fetch thirteen to twenty dollars per thousand board feet wholesale and an additional five dollars or more retail. It is but simple arithmetic to see how much could be lost if fire were to consume thousands of acres of this prime woodland. Certain business associates of mine who own substantial pine acreage near Hinckley would, in fact, be absolutely devastated by a general conflagration."

"And what of the Eastern Minnesota?" Holmes asked. "What does it stand to lose?"

"Hundreds of thousands of dollars in long-term business," Hill replied. "Lumber is now the railway's lifeblood. It is a steady and lucrative source of freight revenue. But if the pineries around Hinckley should go up in flames, it would take years for the Eastern Minnesota to recover. And, of course, the damage to railroad property itself would be enormous."

"Would not such a fire also be a great threat to human life?" I asked.

"It would," Hill acknowledged curtly.

Having delivered his economics lesson, Hill returned to his

chair, took a sip of brandy and leaned forward toward Holmes. All the massive power of his personality was now focused on my friend, and when Hill at last spoke his words were blunt, provocative and emphatic.

"I am informed, Mr. Holmes, that there is no finer detective in the world than yourself, and I expect you to prove it. Find this d--ned arsonist, sir, and find him quickly!"

※

Holmes was not used to the gauntlet being laid so strongly before him, but more than any man I have ever known, he relished a challenge. He replied: "I will find your man. Of that you may be sure."

"That is all I wanted to hear," said Hill. "Now, Mr. Holmes, what will you need to begin your investigation?"

"The facts. They are the foundation of all that will follow. Your man Pyle has ably described to us the general aspects of the case, but you are in a position to provide more particulars. Let us begin with the matter of your agent, Mr. Mortimer, who I am told disappeared shortly after being dispatched to Hinckley. I am safe in assuming he was a highly trusted agent?"

"Mr. Mortimer was a man in whom I had complete confidence. He had only one good leg, as I have but one eye, but that did not prevent him from being the Great Northern's most able and resourceful investigator."

"Very well. Now, when did you last hear from him and what were the circumstances?"

Hill obviously had anticipated the question, for he withdrew from his breast pocket a small piece of paper and gave it to Holmes. "This is the last message I received from Mortimer. As you will see, it is dated July 27. He had then been in Hinckley for seven days, I believe."

Holmes swiftly perused the document and handed it to me without comment. It was a telegram, sent on the Great Northern's own lines and addressed directly to Hill. Several words had been crossed out and replaced by others written above, indicating that Mortimer had used some kind of cipher. The message read: "Confidential. Am making progress on fire. Expect results by tomorrow if suspicions are correct. Believe we have been on the wrong track. Will wire details as available. Mortimer."

"A most tantalizing message," said Holmes. "What do you suppose Mr. Mortimer meant by suggesting that you had been, as he put it, 'on the wrong track'?"

"I have puzzled over that myself," Hill replied. "I can only suppose that he believed he had found some new avenue of inquiry beyond the obvious one."

"So it would seem. Now, Mr. Hill, just what is the 'obvious' avenue of inquiry?"

Hill gave out a great sigh, and his demeanor became grave yet curiously agitated. "It is not a thing I would like to believe, Mr. Holmes, but I greatly fear the arsonist could be an employee of the Eastern Minnesota. I have always paid my men a fair wage and treated them in the best manner possible, but the strike this spring—fomented by Debs and his crew of socialists—provoked much bitterness. There were also acts of vandalism all along the line, although I am convinced only a few troublemakers were behind these outrages."

"Who was the leader of the strike against the Eastern Minnesota?" Holmes asked.

"William Best," said Hill without hesitation. "But I cannot believe that he would be involved in this business."

"Why?"

"It is not in his character, sir," Hill said in a way that left little doubt he had no wish to discuss the matter further.

Holmes nodded. "I see. Nonetheless, I should like to meet Mr. Best. Could that be arranged?"

Pyle, after glancing at Hill and receiving a favorable signal in return, spoke up: "You will have no trouble finding William Best,

Mr. Holmes. He will be the engineer on your train to Hinckley tomorrow."

"How convenient. I shall make it a point to have a talk with him. Now, Mr. Hill, please tell me more about these fires. When and where were they set?"

Hill responded to Holmes's question with a quick, imperious nod in Pyle's direction.

"I can provide that information," Pyle said, turning to Holmes, "since I have kept a careful record of the situation at Mr. Hill's request. The first fire, at the Eastern Minnesota depot in Hinckley, occurred at four in the morning on July 19. Fortunately, our station agent there, who lives on the property, was awakened by the smell of smoke and managed to put out the fire before it could spread. Damage to the building was minor.

"The second fire, on July 29, was far more serious. It also occurred in the early morning hours and destroyed the railway's roundhouse in Hinckley, along with two locomotives inside. Only quick action by the local fire department prevented a catastrophe, and several men nearly lost their lives fighting the blaze. Both fires, it is certain, were deliberately set. Piles of brush and matches were found by the depot, while several cans of kerosene were discovered near the roundhouse.

"I should add that the railroad has since begun to build a new roundhouse, where watchmen are stationed twenty-four hours a day. Special guards have also been posted on other railroad property, but the extent of the Eastern Minnesota is such that not every building or piece of rolling stock can be protected."

Holmes took in this information with a nod and then abruptly returned to a previous line of inquiry. "I have one more question regarding Mr. Mortimer. What efforts have been made to locate him?"

Pyle once again provided the answer. "We have, of course, pressed the matter with all of the appropriate authorities in Hinckley, but to no avail. Three undercover Pinkerton agents were also hired, but they, too, failed to discover any traces as to Mortimer's whereabouts. All we know is that, after sending his final message, Mortimer was seen walking out of Hinckley on a road which leads to a number of logging camps. He has not been seen, or heard from, since. I greatly fear for his well-being."

"As well you might," said Holmes gravely. "Incidentally, how far is the closest of these logging camps from Hinckley?"

"Ten miles, I should judge," said Pyle.

"How curious," Holmes murmured. "How very curious."

✳

Holmes had many other questions for Hill, mostly relating to the town of Hinckley and the operations of the Eastern Minnesota, and it was nearly eight o'clock before he turned his attention to the most crucial evidence in the case.

Putting down his pipe, which had been constantly lit throughout the evening, Holmes casually remarked: "Perhaps it is time, Mr. Hill, to see the threatening letters."

"Of course," said Hill. Rising from his chair, he selected a key from a large ring attached to his belt and went over to a small secretary in one corner of the library. He unlocked the top drawer and removed several envelopes, which he then gave to Holmes. "Here they are, in the order in which I received them. Another one came today. It is on the bottom."

The library was lit by an incandescent table lamp of the newest kind, and Holmes began his examination by holding up the first envelope to this bright light. He then turned the envelope over and used his pocket magnifying glass, which he never failed to carry with him, to study the address and postmark. I was surprised to see that he also smelled the envelope.

When he had gone through this ritual with all four envelopes, he opened them and conducted a similar examination of the single sheet of paper which each contained. Finally, Holmes returned his magnifying glass to his inside coat pocket, calmly relit his pipe, and handed the letters to me.

Below, I have reproduced these fantastic documents—each of which was addressed in identical fashion to "J. J. Hill, Summit Avenue, St. Paul, Minnesota"—although for reasons of good taste I have censored a crude word found in all four letters:

July 14, 1894
Dear Hill of S---:
    You are warned. The fiery Flames of Hell shall reduse the Eastern Minnesota to ashes.
    The Red Demon

July 21, 1894
Dear Hill of S---:
    The Depot was but a begining. The grate Conflagration is near & it shall ingulf the Eastern Minnesota in a great Storm of Fire.
    The Red Demon

Aug. 1, 1894
Dear Hill of S---:
    You can not stop the Burning, nor can your Agents. Soon, the Pineries shall be ablaze with the Work of Vengeance. The Fires will find You & your acursed Railway. Watch your Bildings, watch your Tracks, watch your Locomotives, watch Everything.
    The Red Demon

Aug. 20, 1894
Dear Hill of S---:
    Now comes the Day of Judgement. Ruin shall rain down on you like the Rath of God. Day shall become Night, the very Air shall catch Fire & the Eastern Minnesota shall be consumed.
    The Red Demon

"It is a curious name he uses—the Red Demon," Holmes remarked. "Am I correct in assuming that he has borrowed this rather colorful term from the newspapers?"

"That is my assumption," said Hill. "The newspapers here, and Mr. Pyle's *Globe* is no exception, have a habit of referring to fire of any kind as the 'red demon.' "

"I have always found that good metaphors make for good circulation," explained Pyle with a grin.

"Very well, we know from whence came the Red Demon's name," said Holmes. "But what do we know of the person behind this strange appellation? You've had a chance to read the letters, Watson. Tell me, what do you think?"

"They are the work of a demented mind," I said at once. "It is my opinion that we are dealing with a madman!"

"My dear Watson, your command of the obvious is, as always, nonpareil," Holmes said in a mocking manner which I did not find amusing. "Of course, the person who would write such letters is quite mad. But the world is full of madmen, and the problem before us is this: What do these letters tell us about this particular madman?"

"I am not sure," I confessed, "though I would note he is a poor speller."

"Ah, now we are getting somewhere, Watson. The peculiar spelling in these letters is extremely informative."

"How so?" asked Hill.

"What is intriguing is that the spelling is poor in a very inconsistent and artificial way. Note that the writer appears to have trouble with simple words—'reduce,' 'buildings,' and 'wrath' are three examples—yet has no trouble spelling 'conflagration,' 'vengeance' or 'locomotives,' all of which are more difficult. Also note that in the second letter, 'great' is spelled correctly in one place and incorrectly in another."

"I get your drift, Mr. Holmes," Pyle said. "You're saying that whoever wrote these letters was trying to make himself appear less educated than he is."

"Precisely. There is another indication of this as well. The letters, despite their spelling errors, are perfectly grammatical and are properly punctuated. Good grammar and punctuation invariably indicate a well-educated person, for among the lesser classes these literary virtues are almost unheard of."

"But what is the significance of all of this?" Hill asked with a note of impatience.

"The significance is that it gives us the beginning brush strokes of a portrait, Mr. Hill. It tells us that our letter writer is an individual of some educational attainment. And since the village of Hinckley, as it has been described to me, is not, dare I say, an Oxford among the pines, it undoubtedly shelters but a small number of well-educated citizens. Moreover, the writer's spelling tricks indicate that we are dealing with a person who possesses a high degree of cunning and calculation."

"I see your point," Hill said. "Now, do these letters provide you with any other clues as to their author? The paper, for example. Could it be traced?"

Holmes shook his head. "I fear not. Both paper and envelopes are of the commonest variety. I do not pretend to be an expert on American stationery, but I should not be surprised to find a dozen stores in St. Paul where paper of this sort could be purchased. The ink, which I inspected as well, is also of a very ordinary and inexpensive variety. Nor does there appear to be anything unusual about the stamps or postmarks on the envelopes. No, I am afraid these letters will not tell us a great deal more, other than the fact, which I am sure must be obvious to all of you, that they were written by a woman."

※

Had Holmes stood up and thrown a bomb in our midst, he would not have produced a greater surprise than this revelation.

"A woman?" said Hill incredulously. "Why, the very idea is absurd!"

"I think not," Holmes responded coolly. "I have made a study of handwriting, which is most instructive as to a person's character and, I am convinced, gender.[10] A woman's handwriting can be distinguished from that of a man by several readily apparent features. The woman's hand will be more delicate in the application of ink to paper, which is to say the lines will be thinner. It will also display wider loops for many of the letters. And most important, the slant of the script will lack the forward momentum of the typical male hand. Now, Mr. Hill, if you would be so kind as to examine these letters closely, you will see that such feminine characteristics are quite obvious."

I passed the letters over to Hill, who examined them with a reading glass he had taken from his vest pocket. "I am not convinced," he said, tossing the letters down on a table beside his chair. "The handwriting looks no different from that which I see daily in my business correspondence. Besides, I do not believe any woman could write something as foul and disgusting as these letters."

Holmes responded with one of those quick and penetrating smiles which always signaled he was about to provide a demonstration of his superior intelligence. "Tell me, Mr. Hill, would you account it remarkable if I told you I could tell the writing of a left-handed man from that of a right-handed man?"

"No. I imagine they would be quite different."

"Exactly. Then why do you find it hard to believe that men and women, who are far more different from each other than the left-handed man is from the right-handed, should have distinct styles of handwriting?"

"It's not the same thing," Hill responded, "and there is no reason to belabor the point. Still, I do not see how you can possibly believe that the arsonist, and the author of these vile letters, is a woman."

"Oh, but I do not believe that, Mr. Hill. No, what I am suggesting is that a woman wrote these letters on behalf of a man."

"But why would the arsonist want a woman to write his letters for him?" The question came from Pyle.

Holmes smiled once again. "Ah, Mr. Pyle, you have put your finger on the essential question. Why indeed? There are any number of possibilities that come to mind, but I will not trouble you with them at present."

Hill, meanwhile, sat in his chair, shaking his head. "Well, I believe this whole theory of a woman is nonsense. As I told you before, Mr. Holmes, I am not convinced."

"Very well," Holmes said. "You are not convinced. Let me refer you, then, to the last letter, the one dated August 20."

Hill, making no effort to disguise his skepticism, picked up the letter in question from the pile and examined it with his reading glass. "All right, Mr. Holmes, I have done as you asked, but I fail to see your point."

"Put the letter to your nose, if you would. Do you smell anything?"

"Really," Hill said, "this is ridic—." Suddenly, his visage changed, the skepticism so visible a moment before now replaced by intense curiosity. Holding the letter directly beneath his nostrils, he sniffed several more times, and the sight would have been comic were it not for the gravity of the circumstances. "My God," he said at last, "it smells like—"

"Perfume," Holmes interjected. "The odor, I agree, is very faint but nonetheless quite unmistakable. Now, tell me, Mr. Hill, among those business correspondents you spoke of a few moments ago, are there a great many who use perfumed stationery?"

"I see I have been unwise to doubt you," Hill said matter-of-factly, for like all truly large-minded men he was not afraid to admit his own mistakes. "It will not happen again."

"Do not trouble yourself with the matter any further. It so happens, as my friend Watson will attest, that I have always had perhaps a greater sensitivity than the average person to the testimony of the senses."

This was true. Holmes's senses were far more acute than those of other men. Whether this was a gift of nature or simply a useful skill Holmes had taught himself, I cannot say. But I recall a number of instances—the curious case of the missing Lyons chocolatier comes to mind—when Holmes's heightened sense of smell proved crucial to the outcome of an investigation.[11]

It was to be the case again now, for Holmes had already formed some definite ideas as to the nature of the perfume in question. He expanded upon this in response to a query from Pyle, who wanted to know whether Holmes could identify the scent.

"No," he said, taking another whiff of the letter, "it is not one with which I am familiar, though it has a distinctive lavender bouquet, with perhaps a touch of rosemary, lemon and sandal.[12] But I can tell you that it is not a cheap perfume of the kind used by women of the lower classes. Unless I am mistaken, Mr. Pyle, this is one of the better French perfumes, the market for which, I suspect, is not large in Minnesota."

Turning to Hill, he asked: "Is there a shop in St. Paul where a woman of taste might buy authentic French perfume?"

Hill, though a married man, was obviously not well acquainted with items of a feminine nature, and he responded to Holmes's question with a hearty laugh and a shrug of his great wide shoulders. "I buy railroads, Mr. Holmes, not perfume."

Pyle, however, came to the rescue. "There is only one place I know of in St. Paul that sells such fancy goods. Schuneman's, on Sixth Street."

"Good," said Holmes. "We shall visit that establishment in the morning before our departure for Hinckley."

"But first, gentlemen, you must visit the dining room," said Hill, rising from his chair. "I see that it is nearly half past eight and Mrs. Hill will not suffer us to be late for dinner."

Chapter Three

"Let Us Begin with Our Noses"

✳

" Watson, come along! The game is afoot."

So spoke Sherlock Holmes early on the morning of August 23, 1894, the date which marked the beginning of our extraordinary adventure in the Minnesota pineries. I had intended to arise earlier, but the comforts of Hill's spacious guest room, and the attentiveness of his servants, had allowed me to slip into a deep and dreamless sleep brought on by the fatigue of our long journey to St. Paul. Holmes, however, seemed utterly unaffected by the rigors of the trip, for he mentioned that he and Hill had already spent two hours over breakfast discussing the Hinckley situation. Hill, a notoriously early riser, had then gone off to his office to conduct the business of his far-flung railroad empire.

"Mr. Hill and I have agreed upon a strategy," Holmes said as I changed into proper attire, "and you now have a new name."

"A new name?" I remonstrated. "Whatever for?"

"For the very simple reason that, even in the wild woodlands of Minnesota, the names of Sherlock Holmes and Dr. John Watson are not unknown. That is your penalty, Watson, for publishing accounts of our adventures in the American magazines."[1]

"I will not apologize for acquainting the world with the achievements of Sherlock Holmes," I responded rather hotly. "If you do not wish me to continue my literary efforts, you have only to say so."

Holmes smiled and put a hand on my shoulder. "My dear, dear Watson, I should never think of depriving you in that regard. And besides, where would I be without you? Who would be the sounding board for my ideas? Whom would I rely on in moments of crisis? Who else would so ably assist me in every endeavor? But we have before us now a most unusual and, I fear, dangerous investigation, and that is why we must travel incognito."

"Of course," I said, mortified that I had snapped at Holmes. "It is the only thing to do. What are our new names to be?"

"You, my friend, will henceforth be known as Mr. Peter Smith, a common but not unattractive name."

"And what of you, Holmes?"

"I am now Mr. John Baker, of London, a traveling correspondent for *The Times*. My assignment is to provide English readers with an overview of life in the wilds of the American Northwest. Naturally, this must include some account of logging and railroading, both of which are so important to the region's development. You, Mr. Smith, are my associate. I think this arrangement will serve us well once we reach the pineries."

Holmes then told me that, upon our arrival in Hinckley, we were to meet with Benjamin Cain, the Eastern Minnesota's agent there and an employee who enjoyed Hill's complete confidence. Although our true identities would not be known to Cain, we had been represented to him as English acquaintances of Hill's.[2] Cain had therefore been instructed to provide us with "the lay of the land" and to offer any additional assistance we might require.

"There is one other item of which you should be aware," Holmes said, handing me a small pocket-sized notebook bound in leather. The logotype of the Great Northern Railway and the word "Confidential" were stamped in gold on the front cover.

"What is this?"

"This, Watson, is the code book for the commercial cipher used by the Great Northern Railway. Mr. Hill has insisted, and I am in complete agreement, that we must encode all of our messages so as to maintain the secrecy of our mission in Hinckley."

I examined the notebook, which resembled a small dictionary, with lists of words in two columns. "How does it work?"

Holmes sighed. "I am afraid it is extremely primitive — a simple substitution cipher. For example, the word 'linguist' is actually a code for 'legislature,' 'zone' means 'winter,' 'shrine' means 'taxation' and so forth. There are also letter substitutions that can be used to form words not listed in the code book. It is, unfortunately, a cipher which even the poorest amateur cryptographer could break with ease, provided he had a sufficient amount of text to work with. But it will have to do, since Mr. Hill seems convinced it is foolproof. Naturally, had I been consulted, I would have suggested a far more secure code."[3]

"And we must use this code in all telegrams to Mr. Hill?"

"That is his wish, Watson, and it will be something of a bother, for Mr. Hill has made it clear that he expects frequent reports from us while we are in Hinckley."

"And how long do you suppose that will be?" I asked, for it was not clear to me how Holmes intended to proceed.

"That is hard to say. But there is already one suggestive feature of this case, which is that the Red Demon, as he calls himself, has chosen a member of the fair sex to pen his messages. If we can find the woman, then we shall find the man."

"But how shall we do that?"

"Let us begin with our noses," said Holmes. "I am of a mind to buy some perfume."

❈

After I had eaten a hasty breakfast, we left the Hill mansion and walked briskly toward St. Paul's business quarter. Arrangements had already been made to bring our luggage to the depot, and since our train for Hinckley did not depart until one o'clock, we had the entire morning to explore St. Paul.

The morning was bright and warm, though a faint blue haze hung in the sky. Only later did we learn that this was the result of forest fires burning far to the north. After descending the steep hill below Summit Avenue, we passed through a rather decrepit neighborhood of small houses, poorly kept wooden sidewalks, and narrow dirt streets before entering the main business quarter. Here the buildings were mostly of brick. Yet even though many of these structures were substantial and pleasing in design, they seldom related to one another in that agreeable way so common to London's great squares. Instead, each building seemed to vie with its neighbors, exhibiting that free and wild individualism so characteristic of the American spirit.

Among these competing monuments to enterprise was a five-story building with large plate-glass windows and an air of tidy prosperity. Large signs identified it as the home of Schuneman's Dry Goods.[4]

"Here we are," Holmes said. "Let us hope that Mr. Pyle was correct."

Inside, we found a spacious sales floor stocked with apparel, shoes, linens, sundries of all sorts, and, at the rear of the store, perfume.

Holmes, who prided himself on his ability to elicit information from the working classes, was soon chatting amiably with the sales clerk at the perfume counter. She was a tall, fine-featured girl of twenty or so with long blond hair and blue eyes that suggested, as did her accent, Scandinavian origins. Holmes soon learned that the girl, whose name was Ilsa, had indeed come from Sweden with her family ten years previously and was to be married next month to another clerk at the store.

"Ilsa," he said after completing these preliminaries, "I do hope you can assist us. My friend, Mr. Smith, and I have been traveling for a month, and we are due back in Chicago tonight. It has occurred to me—rather late in the game, I must confess—that I would be terribly remiss if I failed to bring a present to my dear wife, Irene, who will meet us at the train station. I know how much she would love a bottle of perfume."

Holmes's choice of a name for his imaginary wife was quite suggestive, but I made no mention of it, knowing his sensitivity on the subject of Irene Adler.[5]

Ilsa, meanwhile, did her best to be helpful. "We have many fine perfumes, sir," she said, directing Holmes's attention to numerous bottles of scent arrayed in a large glass case behind her. "Is there a certain perfume that your wife prefers?"

Holmes made an elaborate show of looking disconsolate, letting out a mournful sigh as though disgusted by his own stupidity. "Ilsa, there lies the problem. I know there is one perfume my darling Irene loves above all others, but its name escapes me."

Ilsa smiled and confided that such memory lapses often occurred among her male customers. "But I have found, sir, that a gentleman will often remember a perfume's scent even if he has forgotten the name."

"What a capital idea!" Holmes said, as though the thought would never have occurred to him. "And if it will help, Ilsa, I believe I can say with some confidence that the perfume is French and has something of a lavender aroma."

"I will see what I can find," said Ilsa, turning to examine the contents of her perfume case. One by one, she selected bottles from the shelves and finally settled on six possibilities, which included the products of such celebrated French perfume makers as Houbigant, Mollinard and Guerlain.

Placing these bottles on the counter, she told Holmes: "All of these could be what you are looking for, sir."

"Ilsa, you are a marvel," said Holmes.

But his hopes were soon dashed, for after carefully removing the cap of each bottle and sniffing its contents, he shook his head in disappointment.

Ilsa's large blue eyes overflowed with sympathy. "I am so sorry, sir. Perhaps it is a rare perfume we do not carry."

"There is no need to apologize," said Holmes. "You have been most helpful. But tell me, is there another establishment here in St. Paul that might offer a larger selection of perfume?"

"Oh no, sir. Schuneman's is known throughout the Northwest for its perfume line. In fact, many of our items cannot even be found in the big Minneapolis stores."

Holmes thought for a moment. "One more question, Ilsa. Do you ever have occasion to order special perfumes for customers, perfumes that you would not otherwise keep in stock?"

"Certainly. We have a number of customers who order in that way. Usually, these orders are for very expensive perfumes, as I am sure you would understand, sir."

"Of course. I wonder, is it possible that any of these special perfumes might be the scent I am looking for?"

Ilsa considered this question for a moment, and then a bright smile flashed across her beautiful young face. "There is one, sir. Jicky, from Guerlain.[6] As it happens, a shipment has just arrived today from Paris."

Opening a cabinet to one side of the display case, Ilsa withdrew a small wooden box that bore the Guerlain label, pried open the lid and removed one of the dark green bottles—or, as she called them, flacons—within. The name "Jicky" was spelled out on the front of this simple but elegant bottle. Ilsa removed the seal, pulled out the stopper and handed the bottle to Holmes, who brought it slowly up to his nose.

"Eureka!" he exclaimed. "My dear Ilsa, we have found it!"

"Oh, that is wonderful, sir."

"But, tell me, are all of these bottles spoken for? Or would an extra perhaps be available? Price would be no object."

"I think you may be in luck, but let me check the order sheet."

Ilsa opened a drawer beneath the counter and removed a small stack of papers. "We have, let me see, one, two, three—yes, that is all, three orders. Since the shipments contain six bottles, I would be happy to sell you one of those left over."

"Splendid. And what is the price?"

"Jicky is twenty-five dollars for the one-ounce bottle."

"And a bargain at that, I am sure," said Holmes, smiling. "But I must say, I am surprised to find a perfume of this quality so readily available here. But then I have heard St. Paul is a city of great wealth. I would imagine most of these bottles go right up to that famous St. Paul street—I have forgotten its name—favored by the merchant classes."

"Do you mean Summit Avenue, sir?"

"Yes, that is it. Summit Avenue. I suppose that is where all of these bottles will eventually find a home."

"That is largely true, sir, although you might be surprised to know that I have one regular customer who lives in a small town far north of here."

"Really? How interesting. You know, Mr. Smith and I were only recently traveling north of St. Paul and were surprised to discover that even in the most remote communities one can sometimes find evidence of great wealth. Last week, for example, we had business to conduct in a village called Hinckley and—"

Ilsa let out a startled exclamation. "Why sir, what a coincidence! That is where the customer I mentioned lives."

Holmes feigned utter astonishment at this revelation. "What a small world this is," he finally said, shaking his head. "But I wonder, could by chance your customer in Hinckley be Mrs. Adelia Brown, with whom I have been acquainted for some years?"

"No, sir, the customer I am thinking of is Mrs. Mary Robinson. Perhaps you know her as well."

"Mary. Of course," Holmes said. "She is a good friend of the Browns. Isn't that amazing? I shall have to mention this little coincidence to Mrs. Robinson the next time I see her."

Holmes now drew out his pocket watch and looked at it with

evident alarm. "Oh dear, I fear we will miss our train if we do not hurry. If you would be so kind, Ilsa, as to wrap the perfume, we shall be on our way."

Ilsa accomplished this task quickly and Holmes handed her a pair of twenty-dollar gold pieces.

"It will take a moment to send for change," she said, noting that the store was equipped with an overhead cable delivery system that required payments to be sent to a central cashier.

"There will be no need for change," Holmes said, taking the perfume from Ilsa. "The remainder shall serve as a wedding present for you and your husband-to-be."

"Oh, but sir—"

"Good-bye, my dear Ilsa," Holmes said, ignoring her protests. "You have no idea what a great help you have been."

❊

"I say, Holmes, that was a bit of good fortune," I remarked as we left the store and emerged into the sunlight. Crowds of shoppers, among them many women in fine dresses, thronged the sidewalks but Holmes seemed oblivious to their presence.

"Luck, Watson, is a curious thing," he observed. "I have found that it comes most often to those who are prepared to receive it. Had the right questions not been asked of Ilsa, I do not doubt that the luck you speak of would have eluded us."

"Perhaps that is so. Still, how can we be sure that this Mary Robinson is the same woman who wrote the letters to Mr. Hill? Might not there be other women in Hinckley who use Jicky?"

"It is possible, but I do not think it likely. The village of Hinckley, according to Mr. Pyle, contains no more than a thousand souls. Of this number, the vast majority are no doubt men, since frontier communities typically are dominated by the male of the species. We can safely assume that the lumberjacks, sawyers and mill hands who inhabit Hinckley do not wear perfume. And we can also assume that, in the case of married men, their incomes are insufficient to allow them to buy for their wives perfume that costs twenty-five dollars an ounce. No, Watson, I should be rather surprised if there is anyone in Hinckley besides our Mary Robinson who buys this particular and expensive scent."

After leaving Schuneman's, we walked several blocks until we came upon the Ryan Hotel, an imposing edifice of red brick and white stone that bore some resemblance to the St. Pancras Hotel in London.[7] The Ryan's dining room had been recommended to us by Pyle, and since our train was still two hours from departure, we went inside for tea and sandwiches.

Pyle's culinary advice proved to be excellent, for the Ryan's surprisingly elegant dining room offered admirable sandwiches of sliced ham and thick cheddar cheese, along with the best tea we had thus far found in America. Holmes ate this hearty fare with unusual gusto, then took out his favorite black clay pipe and smoked a bowl of tobacco. Normally, he would have smoked with an air of contentment, but instead he betrayed signs of restlessness, drumming one finger incessantly upon the table and showing no interest in the pleasantries of idle conversation.

And certainly I was not prepared for the question which he abruptly put to me. "Watson, did you bring along your revolver?"

"It is in my bag," I said. "But why do you ask?"

In response, Holmes pulled his chair closer to the table, clenched his jaws, and said: "There are sinister features to this case, Watson, and we must be prepared to face a foe who will resort to the most extreme forms of violence to gain his ends."

Holmes's concern struck me as premature, since we had not yet even reached Hinckley, where our inquiries were to take place. But I could not discount his fears, for Holmes had always displayed the utmost prescience in his investigations. His mind was uniquely attuned to the dark shape of criminality, and he could see forms where others saw only shadows.

"What is it about this case that worries you so?"

"Everything, Watson, everything. The disappearance of Mr. Mortimer is particularly troubling. It suggests that the Red Demon is alert to the possibility of discovery and will take whatever steps are necessary to prevent that from happening."

"Then you believe Mr. Mortimer has been murdered?"

"Is there really any doubt? People do not simply disappear, even in the far-off pineries. Mr. Mortimer was by all accounts a skilled and reliable investigator. And yet, after only a few days in Hinckley, just as he had begun to develop certain suspicions, he vanishes. That cannot be a coincidence."

Holmes tapped the tobacco from his pipe and stared up at the skylit ceiling of the dining room. He said: "The letters are also disturbing. Their bitter, mocking tone suggests the darkest sort of motivation. The man who composed these letters is propelled by fierce anger, directed not only at Mr. Hill but at the entire human race. We are dealing, I suspect, with a wounded animal, and such animals are at their most dangerous when cornered. That is why we must be very careful, Watson, very careful. Our lives could depend on it."

❋

We left the Ryan before noon and proceeded to the Union Depot, which was only a few blocks away. We walked at a leisurely pace, since our train—the Daily No. 3 of the Eastern Minnesota—was not scheduled to depart until one o'clock.

As we approached the depot, which stood next to the Mississippi River at the bottom of a steep hill, we saw a commotion along the railroad tracks paralleling the river. A crowd had gathered around a locomotive, and from somewhere inside this multitude came terrible cries of agony.

"I wonder if there has been an accident," I said.

"By all means, see if you can help," said Holmes.

I made my way through the crowd and saw immediately a most horrible sight. A young girl of perhaps three lay beside the tracks, screaming in a way that could not fail to wrench the heart of anyone who heard her. It was apparent that she had fallen beneath the train, for one of her legs had been severed above the ankle and the other was mangled so cruelly that little of the foot remained. A woman, whom I took to be the child's mother, knelt beside her, holding her head, while two men worked—none too skillfully—to wrap her wounded extremities and stop the bleeding.

I had, of course, seen all too many amputated limbs during my service in Afghanistan, but the sight of this poor child so grievously wounded was almost beyond my ability to endure. I immediately went to her aid, showing the men how to make a proper tourniquet and doing my best to console the child and her mother. But since I did not have my medical bag with me, I could do nothing to relieve the girl's agony. Fortunately, another doctor soon arrived on the scene. He administered morphine to the child and together we managed to wrap her legs in cotton towels someone had brought from the depot. Moments later, a carriage arrived to take the child and her mother to the hospital.

I now noticed that Pyle, who was to accompany us to Hinckley, had joined Holmes in the crowd of onlookers.

"You were magnificent, my dear friend," said Holmes, helping me on with my coat, which I had removed before tending to the girl. "You have saved a life."

"It is nothing. I did only what I have been trained to do."

"Will the child live?" Pyle asked.

"Probably, if infection does not set in, though I do not know how much of a life she will have without feet."

Pyle shook his head in sympathy. "It is indeed a terrible thing, but I fear hardly a day goes by in this city without someone being mutilated by a train. It has become so common that the *Globe* no longer reports such cases unless they are fatal."

"Is there nothing that can be done to stop the carnage?" I asked, the little girl's awful agony still fresh in my mind.

"Of course there is, but the railroads will not hear of it. They will not slow their trains because they insist that their schedules must be maintained above all else. Nor do they wish to spend money for the bridges and underpasses that could reduce the number of accidents. I have broached the subject with Mr. Hill himself on more than one occasion, but his response is always the same. People, he says, must be more careful around trains."[8]

"That is no doubt good advice," said Holmes, "and we shall be most mindful of danger as we board our train, which, if my watch is correct, will be leaving in five minutes."

✳

We raced through the crowded depot and into the long iron train shed behind, where Eastern Minnesota No. 3 was waiting. Within moments of our boarding, the train was on its way, and so began the final leg of our transatlantic journey. The cruel ordeal of the little girl still occupied my mind, but Holmes, for whom life was essentially an intellectual problem, showed no effect from the episode. Instead, he stared out the window of our parlor car, his great long face a study in concentration.

When I mentioned that this was the first time during our travels that he had taken an interest in the scenery, he said with some asperity: "We will soon enter a world entirely strange to us, Watson, and we must get into the habit of observing everything around us with the closest attention. Everything! The success of our endeavor, I assure you, will depend on it."

It occurred to me that Holmes was, in effect, "practicing," sharpening his senses for the days ahead. This was later confirmed when, as we approached Hinckley, Holmes casually remarked on the "amazing similarity" between a house he had just seen and another that we had passed hours before in St. Paul. He then went on to describe both houses in the most minute detail, observing finally that the house near Hinckley displayed Doric columns while those of the St. Paul house were "modified Tuscan." Had I asked, I suppose he might also have given me a complete description of every person we saw on the train, for such were his phenomenal powers of observation in the midst of a case.

Less than half an hour out of St. Paul, we reached its sister city of Minneapolis, where we crossed the Mississippi on a magnificent stone bridge directly below the famous Falls of St. Anthony.[9] To either side of the cataract, massive stone mills formed a mighty fortress of industry, producing enough flour in one day, Pyle informed us, to feed half a continent.

"Not even Budapest can match Minneapolis, which is now the world's center of flour production," Pyle said with obvious pride in the accomplishments of a city that, we were surprised to learn, had been founded less than forty years before.[10]

"I am impressed," Holmes remarked, "though I think it shall take at least another forty years before your Minneapolis is as beautiful as Budapest."

After a brief stop at the Minneapolis Union Depot, we continued to the north. Soon, the land opened up into a mixture of farms and woods, though without the gentle hills or handsome villages that so enliven the English countryside. Just after two o'clock we reached the town of Anoka, where we crossed the Rum River, which Pyle informed us had been one of the first major arteries of the logging industry in Minnesota.

"A timber cruiser who scouted out the Rum forty years ago said that seventy mills in seventy years could not exhaust its pineries," Pyle noted. "But the trees have already been cut and the Rum has died as a logging stream. In fact, I should not be surprised to find in twenty years that all of northern Minnesota has been cut over and made into productive farmland."[11]

"A pity," Holmes said, the first words he had spoken in nearly an hour. "A forest always holds out the promise of mystery, don't you think? But what mystery is there in the great vacancy of the prairie, where all is open and visible?"

There was no answer to this question, and we sat in silence for a time, watching the flat, empty landscape roll by our window. But when, at half past three, we reached the community of Milaca, the scenery underwent a sudden change. Here, forty miles from Hinckley, the loggers had been at work only recently, and as we approached our destination the evidence of destruction became increasingly evident with each mile.

The landscape was desolation itself, and I doubt that even the moors of Devonshire could present a more bleak and melancholy appearance than these ravaged pineries. In every direction could be seen the work of the ax and the saw, and for mile after dreary mile we passed through the remains of a great dead forest. Indeed, I could not help but feel as though we had ventured into some vast burying ground, its memorials formed by huge stumps that, for as far as the eye could see, rose out of the withered earth like tombstones. Littering this arboreal cemetery were low piles of refuse—discarded branches and crowns, tangled undergrowth, bits and pieces of waste wood—which Pyle referred to as "slash." Here and there, a magnificent solitary pine, rising above its environs like the miraculously preserved tower of a ruined cathedral, held out against the general devastation.

Heightening the sense of gloom was a pall of smoke which thickened as we approached Hinckley. This persistent haze invested the atmosphere with a sickly blue hue and produced a pungent odor of burned wood.

"Small fires have been burning throughout the pineries since mid-July," Pyle told us, "and there has hardly been a drop of rain in all that time. You can see for yourself how brown everything has become."

In fact, not a blade of green grass was to be seen anywhere, and the few small streams we passed were so low and sluggish that they resembled fetid swamps more than flowing watercourses.

"It is a cruel, empty landscape," said Holmes, caught up in the grimness of the spectacle, "a place where the darker impulses of the human heart might easily take root and flourish. Do you not think so, Watson?"

"Perhaps, though I think you take too dim a view of the human condition, Holmes, for even in this forsaken corner of the world I am sure we will find many good and kindly people."

"Ah, Watson, the perpetual optimist! Let us pray those 'good and kindly people' materialize because we shall undoubtedly need their help. And now, if I am not mistaken, there is a sign up ahead for Hinckley."

And so it was that we at last arrived in the village of Hinckley to begin our search for the Red Demon.

Chapter Four

"We Have a Shadow"

✳

Our first order of business in Hinckley was to bid farewell to Pyle, who was continuing to Duluth on an errand for Hill.

"Good luck," he shouted as we stepped out onto the platform, "and be careful!"

We had learned from Pyle that the No. 3 would stop in Hinckley for fifteen minutes or more to take on water, and Holmes—leaving our luggage in the care of a porter—immediately strode up the tracks toward the front of the train.

"Where are we going?" I asked, for there had hardly been time to say good-bye to Pyle.

"I should like to talk to Mr. William Best," said Holmes.

We found him by the locomotive, oiling wheel fittings with a long-spouted can. Holmes immediately struck up a conversation.

"Your No. 125"—for that was the designation on the locomotive's tender—"is a fine-looking engine. She is, I see, of the American type and a product of the excellent Baldwin Works.[1] Tell me, sir, what is her tractive force? I should guess twelve thousand pounds, with an adhesion ratio approaching four, though I am hardly an expert in such matters."[2]

"You are close enough, sir," replied Best, turning around to look up at Holmes. "Her ratio's 3.8 and she's rated at twelve thousand two hundred pounds but she can pull harder if you know how to ask her real nice."

I had no idea what these terms and figures meant, but Holmes—who had apparently turned himself into an authority on the railroad locomotive during our week of travel—was soon engaged in an animated conversation with Best. They discussed "firebox heating surface," "weight on drivers," "feed injectors" and other arcane aspects of locomotive lore until Holmes finally said:

"Pardon me, sir, for not asking earlier, but may I take it that you are the engineer of No. 125?"

"I am," replied Best, who had the stalwart appearance so common to the better members of his class. He was about forty years old, with short-cropped brown hair, a broad firm face punctuated by a well-tended handlebar mustache, and wide dark eyes that suggested both native intelligence and great resolve.

"Well, it is a pleasure to meet you, sir," Holmes said, donning his best smile. "My friend Mr. Smith and I have only recently come from England, where we seldom see locomotives of this sort. But I should introduce myself. I am John Baker and this is my associate, Peter Smith."

"Bill Best," the engineer replied, shaking our hands after first removing one of his heavy gloves. "Pleased to make your acquaintance. You gents are a long way from home."

"Indeed we are," said Holmes. "I should explain that I was once in the railroad business myself, in England. But that was long ago. I am now a member of that lowly tribe of journalists who inhabit Fleet Street. In fact, my associate and I have come here to acquaint our English readers with certain aspects of life in the great American pineries. The railroad industry must naturally be part of our story, since it is so important to the well-being of communities such as Hinckley."

"Well, I can't say as how you'll find much here to make headlines," said Best. "Is there something you gents are particularly interested in?"

"There is little we are not interested in, Mr. Best. Our assignment is to paint a picture of life on the rugged northern frontier of America. Naturally, we will also devote much attention to the logging industry, which like railroading is so vital to this region. But with the air so dry of late, I imagine there is much fear of forest fires."

"There's always fires in the woods. Happens every year."

"No doubt," replied Holmes amicably. "The loggers must be quite worried, however, since the fire danger this year seems to be much worse than usual."

"Wouldn't know," said Best, bending down to inspect a pair of rods beneath the locomotive's huge drive wheels. "Lumbering ain't my business."

"True enough, sir. But even so, I suppose you have had to take unusual precautions to prevent sparks from your locomotive starting a conflagration somewhere along the tracks. In fact, I recall hearing that there have been fires this summer right here in Hinckley. An arsonist has been at work, or so I have been told. Hard to believe, is it not, that someone would actually try to start a fire in the middle of a drought?"

Best put down his oilcan and swung around to face Holmes once again. Suspicion glimmered in his dark eyes. He said: "Many things are hard to believe in this day and age, Mr. Baker. Is there something you're driving at?"

"No, I was merely curious about these fires. Who do you imagine might be setting them?"

"Maybe you should go ask some of the loggers hereabouts. I wouldn't put anything past them, even setting the woods on fire. They're all a bunch of thieves, anyway. Everybody knows that. Now, if you gents'll excuse me, I got work to do."

"Of course. Well, Mr. Best, I have enjoyed talking with you," Holmes said, turning away but then stopping suddenly as though he had just remembered something. "Oh, by the way, the Eastern Minnesota is one of James J. Hill's roads, is it not? The Empire Builder—I believe that is what he is called—has a reputation even in England."

"I suppose," said Best with a noticeable lack of enthusiasm. "If a man's got enough money—and Jim Hill's got plenty—then I guess everybody knows all about him."

"Indeed. But tell me, what sort of man is he to work for? I seem to have heard there was a bit of trouble along this line recently—a strike or something of that nature. There was even some vandalism, as I recall."

Best cast a shrewd look at Holmes. "You seem awful interested in this old railroad, Mr. Baker, considering that you're just here to write about the lumbering business."

Returning Best's stare, Holmes said in an even voice: "I certainly did not mean to intrude, sir. It was merely idle curiosity on my part."

"Well, too much curiosity can get a man in trouble. That's what I was taught," said Best, still looking Holmes straight in the eye. Then he added: "Hill sent you, didn't he? You one of his Pinkertons?"

"I'm afraid I have no idea what you mean."

"Sure," Best said, "and cows fly."

Holmes reacted to this skeptical utterance with a look of bafflement. "I am positive, Mr. Best, that there has been some misunderstanding, and we will trouble you no further," he said as we turned to go. "Have a pleasant day!"

But Best, whose face had grown quite red, was not to be put off so easily. Grabbing Holmes by the shoulder, he spun him around, poked a finger in his chest and said vehemently: "You tell Jim Hill this. Tell him that me and the other boys up here'll keep on doing our work just like we always have but we won't work for slave wages. And tell him if we have to fight to feed our families, then by God we will. You tell Jim Hill that!"

With those parting words, Best climbed up into the locomotive cab and began preparing for departure.

"Well," I said as we walked back toward the depot, "what did you think of Mr. Best?"

"He is an interesting character," Holmes replied, "and very much in the American grain, which is to say he is blunt, intelligent in an uneducated sort of way and quite obviously fearless. His chief defect, I suspect, is that he is perhaps overly excitable by nature."

"Did anything else strike you?"

"Only that Mr. Best has several scars upon his right hand which indicate that he was once badly burned."

"And what is the significance of that?"

"It may mean a great deal or it may mean nothing," Holmes said, after which we returned to the depot in silence.

※

Best's train soon resumed its way, and as it disappeared down the tracks I felt as though our last link with civilization had gone with it. No such melancholy thoughts seemed to perturb Holmes, who occupied himself with more prosaic concerns. He found a man to deliver our baggage to the Morrison House, which Pyle had informed us was Hinckley's best hotel. This establishment, as it turned out, was three blocks from the Eastern Minnesota depot, and Holmes suggested we walk so as to gain a better impression of the town.

It was not the most pleasant of days for a stroll, for even though evening was at hand, the heat—the temperature easily exceeded ninety degrees—remained stifling. The smoke in the air contributed further to the discomfort of our situation, causing my eyes to sting and burn.

Hinckley was a true frontier community, rough and tumble in appearance, with none of those pretensions found in places which aspire to a more advanced stage of development. Lacking the cozy confines and winding lanes of a typical English village, Hinckley instead resembled a great checkerboard carved out of the measureless forests around it. The grid of streets that formed the village was dotted with small, widely spaced buildings. These structures — simple frame houses, small churches, crudely built saloons, false-fronted stores and a surprising number of hotels — were scattered about with no apparent regard for system or logic. The streets themselves, all of dirt, were exceptionally wide, as though the founders of the town fully expected that it would one day blossom into a vast metropolis.

Most remarkably, almost all of the town's architectural elements — buildings, sidewalks, fences, utility poles — were of wooden construction, so that the entire village, which did not appear to extend more than a few thousand feet in any direction, was the most perfect firetrap imaginable. Curiously, this town made of trees was itself almost treeless, though here and there a maple or oak sapling grew beside the dusty streets, perhaps in expectation of the greater community to come.

Holmes, of course, was a man of the city, used to the crowded pleasures of London, and he was inclined to view the countryside as an unfortunate mistake of nature. Villages of all sorts he found equally wanting, and under normal circumstances he would never have deigned to set foot in so rude a hamlet as Hinckley. But when he was engrossed in an investigation, all such prejudices vanished. In such a situation, the place where he happened to be was always the most interesting place in the world, and so he took in the sights of Hinckley, however uninspiring they might be, with a keen and probing eye.

"I suppose that London was once like this," he remarked as we approached a plain two-story building that, by Hinckley's standards, was quite large. A sign proclaimed this establishment to be: "The Morrison House, Largest and Finest Hotel between Duluth and the Twin Cities."

"The Morrison, I see, has a high opinion of itself," said Holmes as we stepped into the lobby, a dim room decorated with green floral wallpaper and fitted out with wicker chairs, brass spittoons, and a large oil painting which depicted a forest hunting scene.

We engaged two rooms from the clerk, a short nervous man with shrewish eyes, and Holmes made a point of announcing that we were representatives of "England's greatest newspaper."

"That so?" the clerk said, his beady eyes registering no hint of surprise. "Had a fella here last year, lord something or other he called himself, said he was from England."

"How interesting. Do your recall the gentleman's name?"

"Afraid not. Do remember one thing, though. He stiffed me for the bill." An insufferable grin now appeared on the clerk's face. "That'll be four dollars for the rooms—in advance."

Holmes reacted to this insult with a disdainful smile of his own, after which he withdrew a twenty-dollar gold piece from his pocket and put it on the counter. "We shall be staying for several days," he told the clerk, "and I assure you that our money is far better than your manners. Now, would you be so kind as to show us to our rooms, or is that too much trouble?"

"Up the steps and to your left," came the curt reply. "The rooms are numbered."

"Numbered rooms! What a thoughtful touch!" said Holmes, picking up his large bag, which the clerk had made no effort to assist him with. "Come along, Mr. Smith, I am sure the lap of luxury awaits us."

I shouldered my bag as well, and we climbed a set of creaking steps to a narrow, airless hallway lit by kerosene lamps. We soon found our adjoining rooms. Mine was small, poorly furnished and extremely hot, since the only window faced toward the setting sun. After inspecting his quarters, which were identical in their meagerness to mine, Holmes returned to my room and directed my attention to the view out the window.

"Take a look, Watson, and tell me what you see," he said. He then lay down on my bed, put his hands behind his head and stared up at the tin ceiling with a look of studied indifference.

I pulled aside the heavy red drapes and peered out the window. Across the street was a train depot, with tracks behind it. Signs identified this as the station of the St. Paul & Duluth Railroad, the other line which passed through Hinckley. No trains were in sight and there appeared to be little activity at the depot. The street itself was equally sedate. Two women in white bonnets walked along the sidewalk, a pair of men idled about on a bench near the depot and several children busied themselves playing in a gravel pile across the tracks.

"I see nothing out of the ordinary," I told Holmes, "though I have no idea what it is I am supposed to be looking for."

"Look at the two men seated on the bench in front of the depot. Note especially the man on the left, the one with the long gray beard who, as I recall, is wearing a buckskin cap, a red checkered shirt and black pants."

"What about him?"

"Oh, nothing really, except that we have a shadow. That gentleman has been following us since we got off the train."

✳

"Following us?" I said, astonished. "I did not notice him."

"You were not meant to. Our bearded friend did much to make himself inconspicuous. At one point, he even went to the extreme of leaving the street behind us and following our progress from a parallel alley. In any event, it is not a matter to concern us at present. What we need is something to eat."

"But Holmes," I protested, "should we not find out who this man is and why he is following us?"

"In good time, Watson. But now, let us see if there is a meal to be found anywhere in Hinckley. I am famished."

This statement was truly curious, for Holmes normally was a most delicate and irregular eater, and I had seen him survive for days at a time on little more than tobacco and tonic water.[3] But for some reason—perhaps it was the unfamiliar surroundings or the effects of our prolonged travels—Holmes's appetite was to prove ferocious during our stay in Hinckley, to the point that he would sometimes devour five large meals a day. Surprisingly, these prodigious bouts of eating appeared to have no effect on my friend, who remained as thin and wiry as ever.

After consulting with several drummers in the hotel lobby, we were informed that Hinckley's most popular restaurant was an establishment called, in typically direct American fashion, the Eating House. Here, a block from the hotel, in a tidy but crowded dining room, we found breaded pork cutlets, mashed potatoes, larded peas, thick slabs of apple pie and strong coffee—all of which Holmes downed with uncommon gusto.

While Holmes tore through his food, I noted that the bearded man who had followed us from the train station was seated just two tables away, talking loudly with a group of burly, red-shirted men whom I took to be lumberjacks.

Holmes saw me glance in that direction and put one finger to his lips as a warning.

"You are being far too obvious, Watson," he said softly, in a tone that suggested he was admonishing a small child. "Concentrate on your food and pay no attention to our bearded companion. After all, he knows perfectly well that we are here, but what he does not know is that we know he is watching us. Let us keep matters that way."

"Very well. But how can this man have come to follow us when our mission here is supposedly a secret?"

"At present, I can think of only one possibility."

"What is that?"

"The obvious one," said Holmes, offering no further explanation.

"Well, I think we should confront this person and find out who he is and why he is following us."

"No, it is too early. We will learn his identity and purpose soon enough. In the meantime, if you are through with those potatoes"— he pointed with his fork to a small pile remaining on my plate—"I will gladly finish them for you."

It was close to eight o'clock when we left the Eating House, and the light of day was fading as we walked back toward the hotel. There were few people about and the wind had died down almost completely, so that the town was deathly still except for the tinkling sounds of a piano from a saloon somewhere nearby. Habituated as I was to the remorseless din of London, this silence was disconcerting, and for a moment I felt myself back in the camps of Afghanistan, waiting for darkness to fall and wondering what dangers it might bring. Now, with night coming on in this remote village encircled by a vast smoldering forest, I felt a similar sense of nameless apprehension.

I mentioned this to Holmes, who noted that he, too, had a foreboding of something sinister lying in wait. "The fact that we are being followed only underscores the peril of our situation. We must proceed with great caution."

As he spoke, we reached our hotel, but to my surprise Holmes walked straight past the front door.

"Are we not returning to our rooms?" I asked.

"Soon," Holmes responded, "but first I should like to have a talk with Mr. Benjamin Cain."

✳

Cain, we had been told, maintained his residence above the Eastern Minnesota depot, and so we walked in that direction. Along the way, I kept an uneasy eye out for the mysterious bearded man but detected no sign of his presence. Nonetheless, I had the distinct impression that he was somewhere behind us in the deepening darkness. Holmes, whose uncanny powers of observation never failed him, soon confirmed this.

"Our shadow is in the alley to our right, behind the little church we just passed," he remarked as we approached the depot. "But, pray, Watson, do not turn around. I am not of a mind to frighten him away just yet."

The depot, our point of arrival in Hinckley only hours before, was now deserted, the last train of the day having departed. However, a light in one of the second-floor windows suggested that Cain was at home. I expected Holmes to approach the depot and knock upon the stationmaster's door, but instead he turned off on a rutted lane parallel to the Eastern Minnesota tracks. When we had gone a block in this direction, Holmes made another abrupt turn. Then, grabbing the sleeves of my coat, he pulled me into the yard of a small house.

"Quick, Watson," he said, "follow me and ask no questions."

We ran down an alley, climbed over a picket fence and passed through another yard before arriving at the door of a tumbledown structure that identified itself as Swede's Saloon.

To my consternation, Holmes immediately entered this foul establishment, which consisted of a single dark room fitted out with wooden tables, plank floors and a cutaway log serving as the bar. Animal heads decorated the unpainted walls, while at the tables sat as rough-looking a crew as could be found in any West End groggery. A blue haze of tobacco smoke, its aroma mixed with those of beer and cheap whiskey, added to the singularly unpleasant atmosphere of the place, whose clientele obviously came from the poorest classes. Fortunately, the saloon's occupants seemed more startled by our appearance than we were by theirs.

Holmes, as usual, was complete master of the situation. "Good evening, gentlemen," he announced as we made our unexpected entrance. "Please, there is no need to stand, as we shall be staying only long enough to say good-bye."

Hardly had Holmes spoken these words, which produced a unanimously mystified look from the tavern's patrons, than we were out the back door. This in turn led to an odoriferous privy, behind which we reached yet another alley. Without hesitation, Holmes led the way to a small shed a few paces distant and motioned me to follow him inside through a door that was slightly ajar. He closed the door behind us, after which we sat silently, in absolute darkness, for what seemed like many minutes.

I was about to question Holmes about this curious escapade

when I heard, coming down the alley, the soft but unmistakable sound of footsteps.

"Be utterly quiet," Holmes whispered into my ear. I became conscious of my heart pounding in my chest as the footsteps approached. I reached for my revolver, not knowing who might be approaching, and I expected the door of the shed to be flung open at any moment, with results impossible to predict.

But the footsteps, to my relief, gradually began to fade away. Soon, all was silent. Holmes went to the door, opened it slightly, peered out into the pitch-black night, and said: "We have lost him, Watson."

"The bearded man, you mean?"

"Yes, but it was a near thing. Whoever this shadow of ours is, he is most skilled at his occupation. It was only by detouring through that delightful tavern that we were able to throw him off our trail."

"I don't understand. Did you not say earlier that this man following us was of no great concern?"

"That is true," Holmes acknowledged. "But it is also true that our unwanted companion, if he is to be at all useful to us, must know only what we want him to know. And at the moment, Watson, I think it best that he know nothing of our contact with Mr. Cain. Therefore, it was necessary to shake free of our shadow for a short time. But he will find us again soon enough. Meanwhile, let us see what Mr. Cain can tell us."

Chapter Five

"I Was Awakened by the Smell of Smoke"

❋

After leaving our dreary hideaway, we passed through several alleys until the Eastern Minnesota depot was again before us. Since the town of Hinckley had yet to lavish any expenditure on streetlighting, our walk was accomplished in almost complete darkness, the lights from houses providing our only illumination. Holmes's ability to find his way in this Stygian atmosphere was quite amazing, and I could only conclude that during our earlier stroll through town he had memorized certain landmarks which now served as guideposts.

The light on the depot's upper floor was still burning as we approached, and Holmes—taking a last quick look around—motioned me to follow. He delivered three sharp knocks to the door, and moments later Benjamin Cain appeared.

He was a handsome man of thirty-five or so, well over six feet in height, lean and sinewy, with wavy black hair, a thick mustache, a firm chin that bespoke an equal firmness of character, and close-set brown eyes that peered out at us from behind round wire-rim glasses. Despite the lateness of the hour, he was still dressed in his station agent's uniform, which consisted of dark gray pants and a blue coat emblazoned with brass buttons and various insignia of the Eastern Minnesota.

"Can I help you?" he asked.

"I hope so," said Holmes with a smile. "I am John Baker of London and this is my associate, Peter Smith. Mr. Hill, I believe, mentioned to you that we might stop in for a visit."

"The English newsmen!" Cain said, extending his hand. "By all means, please come in."

"I must apologize for the lateness of the hour," Holmes said as we followed Cain, lamp in hand, up the narrow staircase to his quarters. "But as we had some time this evening, I thought it might be convenient to have a talk."

"Of course, of course. You are always welcome here," said Cain. "Please, make yourself at home."

His quarters were plain but comfortable and included a cozy parlor, where we now found ourselves. Although Cain was evidently a bachelor, the room was tidily kept, with a vase of cut flowers on a large round table, pictures of railroad scenes adorning the papered walls, and a sizable collection of books arrayed in tall cases to either side of a pair of large windows. Holmes, as was his wont, made a rapid inspection of the room, paying particular attention to the library.

"Ah, Mr. Cain, I see that you are a great reader," he observed, holding up a leather-bound volume. "Why, look at this, Mr. Smith. Here is a copy of *The Sign of the Four*, by one of my favorite authors, John H. Watson, M.D."[1]

"He is one of my favorites, too," said Cain. "I look forward to each of his new adventures. That Holmes fellow he writes about is quite the genius, don't you think?"

"Without a doubt," replied Holmes, who had never been burdened with an overly strong sense of modesty, "though I sometimes think Dr. Watson writes rather too sensationally."

"Well," said I, "I am of the opinion that he writes extremely well and does not receive the credit he deserves for his literary skills."

Holmes favored me with a deferential smile, then took a seat at the round table, where I had already joined Cain. "Perhaps Mr. Smith is correct," he said, addressing his comments to Cain, "but in any event we did not come here to argue over popular literature. As Mr. Hill may have mentioned to you, my associate and I are here to write a series of reports for *The Times* of London on life along the American frontier. Naturally, we would like to learn all that we can about Hinckley and its prospects. I am hoping that you can be of assistance to us in this regard."

"I will do my best, Mr. Baker."

Holmes then asked Cain a series of perfunctory questions about the lumbering business in Hinckley. He soon got through these preliminaries, which I knew were of only minimal interest to him, and turned to more pressing issues.

Taking out his black clay pipe and filling it with tobacco, he said: "I am also interested, Mr. Cain, in the drought here and the fire danger it poses. When I interviewed Mr. Hill, he told me that the situation is particularly worrisome because of a series of fires that have occurred in town this summer. He says arson is suspected. I find that hard to believe, for what kind of a man would set fires in the midst of a drought? In any case, I should very much like to hear more about these fires and what has been done to find the culprit. It is a dramatic element my readers, I am sure, will find fascinating."

"I will tell you all I know," said Cain, "though I would ask that you not spread the story around town. Mr. Hill does not wish to start a panic, nor do I."

"You may count upon our discretion, Mr. Cain. Besides, by the time my account appears, I do not doubt that the arsonist will have been captured."

"I pray you are right, Mr. Baker. Well, here is what I know. The first fire, on July 19, occurred right here at the depot in the wee hours of the morning."

"My God," said Holmes, "were you in any danger?"

"No, but I must tell you truthfully that it was a narrow thing. I had gone to bed quite early that night, for the day had been a trying one, and it was around four o'clock in the morning when I was awakened by the smell of smoke."

"That must have been a disconcerting experience. I take it the odor was quite strong?"

"It was. I immediately jumped out of bed and, as it were, followed my nose to the source. Once I got outside, I could smell smoke coming from the north end of the depot, where several barrels are used for trash. When I reached the barrels, they were burning quite nicely. It was plain as day that someone had set them on fire, for pieces of wood and sheets of paper were piled up all around."

"Had the fire by this time spread to the depot itself?"

"The flames were just starting to attack the walls. I immediately ran around to the back of the depot, where we keep barrels of water and buckets on hand, and I was able to douse the fire pretty quick. But, as I said, sir, it was a close thing."

"That is obvious by the burn I see you received," Holmes said, pointing to a scarred patch of skin on Cain's right hand.

"Oh, that is nothing. I'm just happy I was able to save the depot."

"Not to mention your own life," Holmes said, "for had you been inside once the fire spread, you might have perished."

"I have thought of that, and I will tell you, Mr. Baker, it makes me mad as Hades, if you'll pardon my language. I would like to get my hands on the fellow who set the fire. I would make short work of him, you can be sure of that!"

Holmes smiled. "Well, Mr. Cain, I do not blame you for that sentiment. But tell me, did you see anything at all that night which might have helped authorities identify the arsonist?"

"No, sir. I saw or heard nothing until I was awakened by the smoke, and by the time I got outside, whoever had done the dirty deed was long gone. There was not a soul to be seen."

"What about the charred barrels? Do you suppose there was any evidence to be found there?"

Cain frowned. "I never thought of that, sir, though I guess I should have. Fact is, everything was hauled away a month ago. It stank up the place and I saw no point in leaving it there."

"Quite right," Holmes said, dismissing the issue with a wave of the hand. "One can't keep trash lying about forever. Now, there was another fire, was there not? As I recall, Mr. Hill mentioned one that occurred on July 29."

Cain then offered a similarly concise account of the second blaze, which had destroyed the Eastern Minnesota roundhouse. The resident of a nearby house, Cain informed us, had sounded an alarm and the fire was contained before it could spread to nearby houses or the woods. Unfortunately, this person did not see the arsonist at work, nor did anyone else.

"And there is no doubt the fire was set?" Holmes asked.

"No doubt whatsoever," said Cain grimly. "Cans of kerosene were found at the scene." He went on to say that the roundhouse had already been substantially rebuilt and that no evidence from the fire, to his knowledge, had been preserved.

Holmes was disappointed to hear this news, since he had hoped to examine the burned-out roundhouse. He then inquired whether there were any theories in town as to the arsonist's identity or motive.

Cain scratched his head. "To tell you the truth, Mr. Baker, I haven't heard any. And as I said, we have tried to keep the matter quiet. But firebugs are strange birds, or so I've heard."

"Indeed. Yet there is another mystery of sorts associated with this terrible business, for Mr. Hill told us that he sent an agent of his own to investigate and that this poor fellow then disappeared. His name, I believe, was—"

"Mortimer," Cain said, bowing his head slightly as though

speaking of the dead. "Thomas Mortimer. You are correct, Mr. Baker, it is a very disturbing thing."

"Did you know this Mortimer?"

"Not well, though he seemed like a fine fellow. In fact, I saw him on the morning he disappeared. He told me he was going out to the 'wilderness'—that, you understand, was his way of referring to the woods—and that he was on a 'hot trail.' And that was the last I saw of him."

"How intriguing. Where do you suppose he was going?"

Cain shrugged. "He didn't say. Mr. Mortimer, being in the business he was, was pretty tight-lipped about such things. But there are a number of logging camps out in that direction."

"So I have heard. But the camps are ten miles or more away, as I understand it, and Mr. Mortimer was on foot. Does it not seem odd to you that he would have wanted to walk so far, especially in the heat of summer?"

"Now that you mention it, that is an odd thing, Mr. Baker. Usually, anybody going out to the camps hitches a ride with one of the teamsters."

Holmes considered this conundrum for a moment and said: "There is one other possibility, I suppose. Perhaps Mr. Mortimer was not going to the camps. Perhaps he was going somewhere else, much closer to town. Tell me, Mr. Cain, are there any houses along this particular road?"

Cain's face instantly flushed. "Well, sir, there is a house out there, about a mile from town, but it is not the sort of place Mr. Mortimer would have gone to visit, I'm sure."

I could not fathom the reason for Cain's sudden embarrassment, but Holmes grasped the situation at once. "I take it the house you are referring to is a brothel," he said.

"It is, sir, and a particularly vile one, if I may say so."

"I see. Then you are no doubt correct that it cannot have been Mr. Mortimer's destination," said Holmes, leaning back in his chair and tapping a finger upon his knee. "Now, what of the lumber camps along this road? What can you tell me about them?"

"Not much, sir. Railroading is my business, not lumbering, and as I have been in Hinckley for only a year or so, I know very little about the camps. But they are rough places, that I can tell you, and full of rough men."

"So I have been told. Yet I wonder why Mr. Mortimer would have bothered to walk all the way out to the camps when his purpose here was to investigate fires along the railroad tracks."

"I have wondered the same thing," Cain said, "though I recently heard a rumor—I cannot remember where—that might shed some light on the matter."

Holmes snapped forward in his chair. "Really? And what is this rumor, if I may ask?"

Cain lowered his voice, as though anxious that what he was about to say should not be overheard despite the fact that only the three of us were in the room.

"The rumor, sir, is that the proprietor of one of the camps, the Big Pine, bears a grudge of some kind against Mr. Hill. I do not know the nature of this supposed grudge, but it has occurred to me that Mr. Mortimer may have been going out to the Big Pine Camp to investigate the matter on the day he disappeared."

"And who is the camp proprietor in question?"

"A man by the name of Jean Baptiste LeGrande. I have never met him but I have heard he is a fearsome character known throughout the woods for his cruelty."

Holmes grinned. "This LeGrande sounds like just the sort of man I would like to interview for one of my articles, since our English readers are always fascinated with the more primitive type of American. Is there someone in town who could tell me more about him?"

"I believe Mr. Hay, who edits our local newspaper, the *Hinckley Enterprise*, could help you. Angus Hay knows as much about the logging business hereabouts as anyone."

"Then I shall speak to him in the morning without fail," said Holmes, who rose from his chair, went to the nearest window, pulled the curtain aside and stared out into the night.

Apparently finding nothing of interest in the darkness, he turned back toward Cain and said: "There is one other matter I wish to discuss. What can you tell Mr. Smith and me about the recent strike along the Eastern Minnesota line? As I am sure you can appreciate, labor problems in America are of considerable interest to our readers."

Cain shook his head and sighed. "The strike was a bad business, Mr. Baker, a bad business all the way around. Many engineers abandoned their trains in midrun, as did conductors and firemen, and the traffic all but stopped for a week. There was vandalism, too—lubricating oil removed from locomotives, holes chopped in water tanks, coal emptied from tenders—and the like. Mr. Hill himself came up in May to meet with some of the strikers, and I have never seen him so mad. I do not know how well you are acquainted with Mr. Hill, but it would take a braver man than I to cross him when he is in one of his furies."

"I can imagine," Holmes remarked drily. "And what was the effect of his meeting with the workers here?"

"They agreed to return to work after Mr. Hill told them the issues would be arbitrated. But there were a few hard cases like Bill Best who wanted to hold out, and Mr. Hill got into an awful row with them."

Holmes's attention perked up at the mention of Best's name. "How odd that you should mention Mr. Best, for we by chance had a conversation with him earlier today. He seemed like a very strong-minded man."

"Stubborn, others would say. Best was certainly the leader of the malcontents during the strike. He's a tough one, he is. Why, he and Mr. Hill almost came to blows right out there on the tracks back in May. Bill Best is not a man who knows the meaning of fear."

"Do you think he is a dangerous radical of the sort who might provoke another work stoppage?"

"I couldn't say, Mr. Baker. I make it a point not to get mixed up in union business."

"A wise policy, I am sure. But there must be suspicions that the union is somehow involved in these recent fires."

"I would not like to think that any union man would stoop so low as that, Mr. Baker. But there has been gossip to that effect. It is just gossip, however, and I have seen no proof. Still, I must admit that Bill Best in particular is a hothead of the worst kind and I would put nothing past him."

"He does indeed seem to be a hot-tempered man," Holmes acknowledged. "Yet I am curious about one thing. How is it that this Best remains employed when, as you told us, he nearly came to blows with Mr. Hill? I should think Mr. Hill would have fired him on the spot."

"Well, if it had been anybody else, that's what the old man would have done for sure. But he and Bill Best go back a long way together, or so I've heard. Besides, there's one thing you ought to know about Best, which is that there's no better engineer to be found between here and Chicago."

After providing additional details regarding the strike and Best's role in it, Cain offered us lemonade (he was apparently a teetotaler) and sandwiches. I accepted the lemonade but declined the sandwiches, since the extreme heat had lessened my appetite. Holmes, however, gratefully accepted our host's offer and was soon working enthusiastically on a thick sandwich of hard cheese and salted beef.

"Thank you for the excellent information, Mr. Cain, and also for the excellent meal," Holmes said when he had finished his sandwich by picking up the last crumbs with his fingers. "Incidentally, do you know of anything that might explain why we have been followed since our arrival in Hinckley?"

"Followed? By whom, sir?"

"Perhaps you can assist us in that regard," Holmes said, providing Cain with a detailed description of the bearded man.

Cain listened intently, nodding as each new detail came forth. After a moment's thought, he said: "I would say almost certainly that your man is a jack, though I cannot recall seeing one of that breed who fits your description. But I could ask around town."

"Do not trouble yourself with the matter, for I am sure our shadow is only some curious soul with nothing better to do," Holmes replied. "Now, Mr. Cain, I need trouble you with only one more small question. Where in this lovely community of yours might I find a woman by the name of Mary Robinson?"

A swift, surprising change came over Cain's normally placid features. His eyes narrowed and he stared for several moments at Holmes, as though the question was not merely unexpected but highly improper as well.

"Mary Robinson," he said, in a contemptuous tone which suggested that the very name was painful for him to pronounce. "Why ever do you ask, sir?"

"Only because the name was mentioned to me by an acquaintance in St. Paul," Holmes replied coolly. "I take it by your demeanor that you know the woman?"

Cain responded with a vehement shake of his head and said: "Oh no, Mr. Baker. I am a Christian man. And I hope, sir, that you are the same."

This rejoinder clearly was not what Holmes had expected, for he looked at Cain with a mixture of curiosity and bafflement. "Mr. Cain, I fear the meaning of your answer eludes me for the moment. Please explain yourself."

"Very well, sir," he said, in complete command of himself now. "Let me first apologize if I have given offense. But you see, Mr. Baker, I am a member of the Hinckley Christian Committee, which has for many months now waged a campaign against this Robinson woman and her kind."

I could not imagine what Cain was getting at, but Holmes—one look at his face told me—had seen the light.

"Go on, Mr. Cain," he said, a slight smile creasing the corners of his mouth.

"Well, sir, I must tell you that the woman you seek owns the 'sporting house' of which we spoke before. It is the largest such establishment for fifty miles around, and it is generally agreed upon by good Christian people that no darker den of vice and iniquity exists in all of the Northwest."

❈

It was almost midnight by the time we left Cain and began the short walk back to our hotel. Despite the lateness of the hour, the day's heat had hardly dissipated, and the atmosphere—still heavy with smoke—was suffocating. But as we made our way along Hinckley's drab, deserted streets, Holmes was in an inexplicably jovial mood, and even took to whistling a lighthearted Italian tune he sometimes played on the violin.

"You seem quite content," I observed.

"I am always content when I have learned something useful, Watson, and I have learned much in the last few hours."

"I presume you are referring to the fact that we now have a clue as to Mr. Mortimer's destination on the day he disappeared."

"That is certainly significant," Holmes agreed, "but our visit with Mr. Cain produced at least one other intriguing piece of information, don't you think?"

I thought back on our long conversation with the station agent but could not discern what this "intriguing" clue might be. While we had indeed learned more about the two fires, Cain's account of these incidents did not seem to point toward any particular suspect. Nor, I thought, did the revelation regarding Mary Robinson's unsavory occupation significantly advance our prospects in the case, though the fact that Mortimer may have walked by her establishment on his way to the camps was an undeniably interesting coincidence. However, when I mentioned these conclusions to Holmes, he took strong issue with them.

"I think, my dear friend, that you underestimate the value of what the estimable Mr. Cain told us. He made one point in particular which I found to be quite suggestive."

"Indeed, and what might that be?"

"The answer, I think, will become apparent soon enough. In any event, tomorrow we shall look more closely at the scene of the fire. Ah, here is the Morrison House, whose comforts await us. I should think a good night's sleep will do wonders for you, Watson."

"And what of you?" I said. "Will you rest as well?"

Holmes smiled and put his hand upon my shoulder. "My dear Watson, sleep is a luxury I cannot afford at the moment, and so Hypnos and Morpheus shall have to be content with you this evening.[2] I prefer a state of wakefulness at times like these. I only regret that I did not bring along my violin, which I have often found to be a wonderful aid to thought."

"I suspect that other occupants of the Morrison House might be thankful for this oversight on your part," I remarked, since I could recall more than one occasion when Holmes's penchant for nocturnal music making had brought angry neighbors to our door.

As we reached the hotel's front porch, Holmes swung around to survey the wide and empty street that served as Hinckley's major artery of commerce. A few idlers stationed in front of a saloon down the block were the only persons in evidence, and I was reminded anew of how far we had come from London.

"There is not much to see," I noted. "The street is all but deserted."

Holmes, however, thought otherwise. "I beg to differ, Watson. There is nothing more instructive than that which cannot be seen. Take, for example, the man who has been following us. He has disappeared from view, but you may rest assured that he is watching from somewhere. Except that he now knows we are aware of his presence, which means that he must of necessity become more subtle and elusive. The very emptiness of the scene before us is proof of that fact. But now, Watson, let us retire to our rooms, for there is nothing more to be done tonight, and tomorrow promises intriguing revelations."

Chapter Six

"He Is a Giant of a Man"

✳

I did not sleep well that night. Perhaps it was the heat and smoke, against which my room offered little protection. Or perhaps it was the fact that I could hear Holmes in the adjoining room, his footsteps moving back and forth on the creaking floor, with hardly a break in their regular rhythm. Holmes often became extremely restless during the course of an investigation, for the pace of events could never match the rapid movement of his thoughts. At such times, the world did not seem large enough to contain his soaring imagination, and so he paced incessantly with a kind of anxious boredom, impatient for reality to catch up with the events unfolding in his mind's eye.

How many hours I lay awake I do not know, but at length the day's exhausting activities had their effect, and my next memory is of seeing Holmes's long, pointed face peering down at me.

"Come, Watson, it is time for breakfast. I am told the Morrison House serves a decent morning plate."

The dining room was crowded, and we had to settle for a table near the kitchen. Holmes's ravenous appetite showed no sign of abating. He ordered bacon and eggs, hashed brown potatoes, four slices of toast, a half dozen flapjacks, stewed fruit and tea. I confined myself to eggs, toast and coffee.

"You have not yet begun to dress like a lumberjack," I told Holmes, "but you certainly are eating like one."

"And you, my dear Watson, have acquired the eating habits of a small and picky bird. Besides, our fellow diners do not seem content with small portions, and when in Rome—"

"Very well," I said, and instructed our waiter to add a rasher of bacon to my order.

Holmes, I must admit, had not been off the mark in assessing the gustatory behavior of the dining room's patrons. Heaping piles of food were the order of the day, and most of the diners ate rapidly and in silence, as though fearing their food might disappear if they lingered too long over it.

These trenchermen were a mixed lot—drummers in dark suits and bowler hats fortifying themselves for another day on the road, a pair of railroad conductors in full uniform, a young doctor whose medical bag sat beside him, and a number of other men whose occupations I could not readily determine.

Holmes, however, soon made a surprising observation. After briefly inspecting the room, he announced that he could identify the trade or profession of everyone present. Skipping over those whose line of work was obvious, he pointed out four sawyers, two men whom he called "swampers," and a mechanic, among others.[1]

"I probably should not ask," I said, "but however did you come to these conclusions?"

Holmes, who appeared to be in an ebullient mood, explained that the answer was in the men's hands, and he went on to describe in minute detail how he had determined the occupation of each.[2] I will not trouble the reader with a full account of Holmes's deductions, which were in truth based on very simple yet irrefutable observations. In the case of the sawyers, for example, Holmes noted that cuts evident on the left thumbs of these men, combined with calluses located on the lower edges of their right palms, led to an inevitable conclusion regarding their use of large saws and therefore their occupation.

He continued: "The hands, Watson, are the Rosetta Stone to the human character. Once you have looked at a man's hands, you can discern almost everything important about him—if he is well- or ill-educated, how old he is, what kind of work he does, whether he is rich or poor, even his religious affiliation."

"Really, Holmes, this is too much. Surely you do not expect me to believe that one look at a man will tell you whether he is, say, Catholic or Protestant?"

"And why not?" he replied with a smile. "It is simple enough, as I shall prove to you. Do you see the two railroad conductors at the table next to us? Well, they are Catholic. That is evident from their right hands, which show small depressions on the thumb and forefinger caused by holding the beads of a rosary, an artifact unique to the Roman Catholic religion. The three gentlemen seated by the window"—he pointed to a group of drummers I had noticed when we came in—"are of a similar religious persuasion, since small depressions can also be seen on their fingers and thumbs."

"This is preposterous. You are toying with me."

"Well, there is only one way to find out."

Holmes turned around and struck up a conversation with the conductors. He explained that he was visiting Hinckley for the first time and wished to know whether there was a Catholic church in town. With a few more skillfully put questions, Holmes soon learned not only that there was a Catholic church but that the conductors were among its members. And then, to my astonishment, Holmes—again by clever use of leading questions—established that the three drummers, who apparently were regular visitors to Hinckley, attended the same church on occasion.

There was nothing I could do now but apologize. "I have done you a grave disservice, Holmes. I should have known better than to question you."

Holmes's next comment was quite unexpected. In a quiet,

forceful voice, he said: "You should never apologize for being right, Watson."

"I don't understand what you mean."

"What I mean, my dear friend, is that all this business about rosaries and small depressions on the thumbs and forefingers was nothing but a perfect cock-and-bull story."

"But how then did you know these men were all Catholics?"

"By the simplest means imaginable, Watson. I went for an early walk while you were sleeping and happened to pass by the local Catholic church as the morning service ended. Among those I saw leaving the church were the five men in question."

"Then you were toying with me after all," I protested, angry that Holmes had gone to so much trouble to play me for the fool.

"No," Holmes said with the utmost seriousness, "my purpose was not to embarrass. My purpose was to demonstrate a simple lesson, which is this: If the best evidence of your senses leads you to believe that a thing is impossible, then it probably is."

It was a lesson that Holmes was to demonstrate even more brilliantly in the days ahead.

❅

The offices of the *Hinckley Enterprise* occupied a small false-fronted building a block from the Morrison House. And there, after breakfast, we found Angus Hay in a chaos of paper, which was piled all around him in promiscuous heaps. In its utter and apparently quite comfortable disarray, the office reminded me of nothing so much as our own Baker Street flats when Holmes was in the midst of a case.

The ruler of this untidy empire sat at a rolltop desk, a visor shading his eyes and a fountain pen in his hand. He was a broad-shouldered man of perhaps thirty years, with neatly combed blond hair, regular features and, as we were soon to discover, a rather curt manner. He glanced up as we entered and said without preamble: "I'm on deadline, gentlemen. Come back later."

"Allow me to introduce myself," said Holmes, ignoring this brusque dismissal. "I am John Baker of London and this is my associate, Mr. Peter Smith. We would be most interested in talking with you about the community of Hinckley."

Holmes then handed Hay his card, which bore the insignia of *The Times*. In an instant, Hay's attitude was transformed.

"*The Times* of London," he said, staring down at the card. "Well, I'll be d--ned. What in God's name are you doing here?"

Holmes, with a charming smile, quickly explained our journalistic mission, making sure to insert a few soothing words about the *Enterprise* and its excellent brand of journalism.

"Well, that is very kind of you to say so," Hay remarked, clearing several chairs of their piles of documents so that we could be seated. "Now, how can I help you gentlemen?"

After the usual harmless questions, Holmes discreetly moved to his real topic of interest—Mortimer's disappearance. Hay seemed surprised by this line of inquiry but provided what answers he could. He added little to our fund of knowledge, however, until the name of Jean Baptiste LeGrande was introduced.

"Now, there would be a profile for your English readers," Hay said enthusiastically. "LeGrande is as fine an all-around scoundrel as you're likely to find anywhere in the North Woods."

"How interesting," said Holmes. "Pray, tell us more."

"Well, sir, the rumor is that LeGrande and his cutthroat band have been stealing timber for years in the Big Pine area, which contains the finest timber left in the county. Why, last year, I saw logs here from the Big Pine section that were six feet in diameter. A scaler I talked to said he had never seen their like.[3] Several major concerns—Laird & Norton out of Winona, the Isaac Staples firm from Stillwater, and even the almighty Weyerhaeusers—have holdings in the area.[4] But this LeGrande, it is said, has lifted timber from all of them."

"Has he been prosecuted for these thefts?"

"Oh, attempts have been made but proof is hard to come by.

And it's even harder to find anybody willing to take LeGrande to court, though Jim Hill tried it once some years ago."

"Really? And did Mr. Hill prevail?"

"No. All he got for his efforts was a hung jury."

"I must say, Mr. LeGrande appears to be a force unto himself. How do you account for that, Mr. Hay? Does not the rule of law hold sway here?"

Hay hesitated, then said: "The only explanation I can offer is that LeGrande is a man of daunting presence. I have only seen him once, but I shall never forget him. He is a giant of a man, three hundred pounds easily, with a wild red beard and the kind of look in his eye that makes you want to stay clear of him at any cost. I have been told that he rules his camp with an iron hand, and I know for a fact that the jacks hereabouts, who are as sturdy and fearless a collection of ruffians as you are likely to find anywhere, speak of him in hushed tones. It is well known, for instance, that he has killed several men, the most recent being over in Kanabec County. In that case, as I recall, he bit off the man's ear before slitting his throat."

"And was he tried for this singularly brutal crime?"

"He was, but the jury acquitted him on grounds of self-defense. The jurors, Mr. Baker, apparently valued their personal safety more than the interests of justice."

"I see. This LeGrande does indeed sound like a most fascinating character. But I wonder: Is it possible he might have been involved in Mr. Mortimer's disappearance?"

"It's possible," Hay acknowledged, "but I don't suppose we'll ever know."

"Why is that?"

"Well, sir, you didn't hear it from me, but the fact of the matter is that LeGrande's got friends in high places, if you know what I mean."

"I am afraid you will have to be a bit more specific, Mr. Hay. You mean, political friends?"

"Could be, I suppose. But his chief ally is the town marshal,

William Thompson, or Big Billy as he's known hereabouts. It's common knowledge those two are thick as thieves."

"And yet this Thompson remains in office despite such an unsavory connection?" I protested. "How can that be?"

Hay grinned. "You must understand, Mr. Smith, that this is the frontier and that all manner of—how shall I put it?—'irregularities' are tolerated. Big Billy has done a lot of favors for folks here and they remember them come election time. Besides, half the men in town are afraid that if they don't support him, he won't let them into Mother Robinson's place."

Holmes, who had been sitting rather idly with his legs crossed, instantly straightened up in his chair. "Did you say Mother Robinson, Mr. Hay? Would that be Mrs. Mary Robinson?"

Hay's sharp blue eyes registered surprise. "You have heard the name, I see. Her sporting house is famous in these parts. Been there a few times myself," he added, with a salacious wink.

"And Mr. Thompson works there?"

"Every night. Jacks can get a trifle ornery when they're in a randy mood, and Big Billy's job is to keep order."

Holmes rose from his chair. "Well, Mr. Hay, I thank you for your time. You have been most helpful."

"Don't mention it," said Hay, escorting us to the door. "By the way, how long are you gents going to be in town?"

"I am not sure," Holmes replied, "but I am beginning to think that we may be here for quite some time."

❈

After leaving Hay's office, Holmes suggested a stroll to the Eastern Minnesota depot, where he wished to examine the scene of the first fire. Although the sun was still low in the sky, the morning offered no respite from the heat to which we had become all too accustomed since arriving in the pineries. Indeed, the air was so hot and dry that it seemed as though we had stepped out into a giant oven. This hellish heat was accompanied by strong winds, which pushed along so much smoke and dust that the sky took on the sooty brown look of an old kitchen ceiling.

"What I wouldn't give for a good, bone-chilling London rain!" I told Holmes as we neared the depot.

When we reached our destination, Holmes went at once around to the north side of the depot and studied the two trash barrels there. He then used his magnifying glass to examine the clapboard wall behind the barrels. This wall, like all those of the depot, was painted a dark green and showed no evidence of damage from the fire. Apparently satisfied by what he had found, Holmes walked back around to the front of the depot in measured steps. Finally, he peered through the front window into the small waiting room, which was unoccupied.

These activities aroused the curiosity of one of the loungers sitting nearby. This worthy—a huge bear of a man with dull blue eyes, a pink jowly face, and a homburg hat tilted precariously atop his large round head—stood over Holmes's shoulder and watched as Holmes went about his business.

"Somethin' wrong?" the man asked in a low, hoarse voice, a massive gold tooth glinting from his cavernous mouth.

Turning around to look at his questioner, Holmes said: "Remarkable, is it not, to find such excellent construction in so simple a building. We have nothing to compare with it in England, I assure you. And now, sir, if you will excuse—"

"You must be that English newspaper fella," the man said, interrupting Holmes. "I kin tell by the way you talk."

"You are most perceptive, sir. I am indeed John Baker and this"—Holmes swept a hand in my direction—"is my associate, Mr. Peter Smith. And you, sir, would be . . . ?"

"William Thompson, but you kin call me Big Billy. I'm the marshal here," he said, opening his coat to reveal a badge pinned to his vest and a pearl-handled revolver holstered at his hip.

"Well, Big Billy, I am pleased to make your acquaintance, and I have no doubt that fate brought us together, for you are just the man I would like to talk to."

"Why's that?" Thompson inquired, cocking his massive head to one side and looking at Holmes with undisguised suspicion.

Holmes responded with a suave smile and then paraded out his usual tale of being a news correspondent in search of a story. "It is a big story," he told Thompson, "as big as these forests of pine. How a new land is being conquered. How brave men in flannel shirts, with heavy boots on their feet and axes in their hands, are felling lumber for a growing nation. And, of course, it is also the story of how law and order is being brought to a wild land. And that is why I am glad we met, Big Billy, because I am sure you can tell me many wonderful stories about the steady march of order and civilization in this as yet untamed frontier."

"Well—"

"In fact," Holmes continued, giving Thompson no chance to reply, "I am particularly interested in the saga of this wild man of the woods who goes by the name of LeGrande. I have heard he is a timber thief, a brawler, and even"—here Holmes lowered his voice to a conspiratorial whisper—"a murderer. Why, 'tis common knowledge, or so I am led to believe, that he can even make a man disappear. Now, Big Billy, what can you tell me about this fellow? Will he be brought before the bar of justice soon?"

"I wouldn't know nothin' about that," Thompson replied, resting one hand on the butt of his revolver. "Mr. LeGrande is a law-abidin' citizen as far as I'm concerned."

"Well, then, perhaps I have received erroneous information," said Holmes. "So I take it he is not a suspect in the recent and mysterious disappearance of Mr. Mortimer, despite all of the evidence which points in that direction."

The mention of Mortimer's name caused a small muscle to begin twitching in the marshal's right cheek. "What . . . ," he began and then stopped himself, as though responding to some invisible internal governor. "I . . . I don't discuss the status of . . . of criminal investigations except with the proper authorities," he finally said, the words being delivered in a halting manner which left the unmistakable impression that they had been memorized.

"I see," said Holmes, whose penetrating gaze never left Thompson's florid face. "Still, I would imagine that you are doing your utmost to solve the case, especially in view of the huge reward being offered for any conclusive information as to Mr. Mortimer's whereabouts."

Thompson's face took on a blank, quizzical look in response to this revelation, which I also greeted with surprise, since I knew of no reward connected with Mortimer's disappearance.

"Don't tell me you haven't heard about the reward?" said Holmes, his face a perfect picture of astonishment. "Dear me. That is odd. You see, Mr. Smith and I were in St. Paul earlier this week and had occasion to interview the fabled Empire Builder himself, James J. Hill. Now, I am certain Mr. Hill, in discussing the general situation in the pineries, mentioned his outrage over the disappearance of one his agents here in Hinckley and his intention to post a large reward for information. Am I not correct, Mr. Smith?"

Though I had no idea what Holmes was talking about, I nodded vigorously.

"I thought as much," said Holmes, turning his attention back to Thompson. "Now, let me see, what was the amount Mr. Hill mentioned? It was sizable, Big Billy, very sizable. Wait, I remember. Ten thousand dollars. That was it. Can you imagine? Ten thousand dollars, enough to set up a man for the rest of his life, simply for information regarding the whereabouts of one person, dead or alive, and no questions asked. I don't mind saying that I could use a windfall like that, Big Billy. Well, in any event, I am sure the reward will be posted here in Hinckley soon enough. And somebody will talk, don't you think?"

Thompson made no immediate reply, though it was obvious, from the strained look on his face, that he was deep in thought. Finally, he said to Holmes: "An' you say this reward comes with no questions asked?"

"Yes, Mr. Hill was quite insistent on that point, as I recall. He said that the only way a reward will elicit useful information is if it has no strings attached and if it is large enough to make men covet it. And ten thousand dollars is certainly an amount worth coveting, at least in my book."

At the renewed mention of this figure, Thompson rubbed his chin as though weighing a crucial decision. "'Tis a heap of money," he finally acknowledged. "But just how would a fella go about collectin' such a reward if he had that kinda information?"

"Oh, I imagine an anonymous letter to Mr. Hill would do, with some sort of identifying device—say, a six-digit code number—written on the letter. The sender then tears a corner from the letter and writes the same number on it. This will serve as proof when the time comes to claim the reward. Isn't that the way it's usually done, Mr. Smith?"

"I believe so."

Thompson, who had listened intently to these directions, now said: "Well, that's very interestin', Mr. Baker. I've got to be moving along but I'll be lookin' for notice of that reward. Maybe it'll help us find that poor fella Mortimer."

"I'm sure it will," Holmes agreed. "In fact, I suspect there will be plenty of competition for that ten thousand dollars once the word is spread. Have a pleasant day, marshal."

"Oh, I will," Thompson replied, smiling for the first time.

❋

As the marshal sauntered away, Cain emerged from the depot with a telegram, which I later learned was from Hill. Holmes scanned it with his usual rapidity. He then took a small pad from his coat pocket, made a few quick scribbles in his distinctive and precise hand, and handed a reply to Cain with instructions to send it at once.

"How were you able to read the telegraph and respond to it without consulting the code book?" I asked after Cain had gone back into the depot.

"I have already memorized the book," Holmes said casually. "There are but a few hundred terms in it."

That Holmes could commit so many terms to memory so quickly came as no surprise. When it served his purpose, he was capable of prodigious feats of memorization. I shall never forget how in the bizarre case of Huddleston, the Australian financier, Holmes was able to retain the numerical contents of an entire ledger sheet in his mind after a single glance at it.[5] Yet on other occasions, Holmes seemed incapable of remembering the simplest things, and in all the years of our friendship he has never been able to recall the date of my birthday.

"What does it say?" I asked as Holmes folded the telegram and put it in his pocket.

"Mr. Hill says he wishes to know how our investigation is progressing and is most anxious for details. The answer I left with Mr. Cain, I fear, will not prove entirely satisfactory, since there is little to report at this point. But I have a feeling, Watson, that we shall know much more once this day is done. By the way, have you seen our bearded friend today?"

I admitted I had not, adding: "Perhaps he has given up."

"Perhaps," Holmes replied, "though I am inclined to think that he remains very much with us."

❅

We spent the remainder of the morning on the Morrison House's front porch, where Holmes sat in a large wooden chair and propped his legs on the railing. He was, for the moment at least, in an expansive mood and the talk quickly turned to his extraordinary conversation with the marshal.

"You are probably wondering, Watson, why I fabricated that fabulous tale of a ten-thousand-dollar reward," he began.

"The thought has crossed my mind."

"Then I shall explain with an analogy to the art of medieval warfare. A criminal investigation, especially one such as this in which so many possibilities present themselves, is rather like an assault on a fortified castle. You must scout out the terrain, circle around the entire perimeter and look for the weak point in the castle's defenses. The marshal, I suspect, is that point, and now, like good sappers, we must seek to undermine it."

"And what leads you to believe the marshal is the weak point?"

"Everything about him. And, as you know, I am not without a certain skill when it comes to assessing my fellow man."

This was undeniably true, for if Holmes had one trait that stood out above all others, it was his ability to judge men (he was, I must confess, not always so astute regarding the female of the species). Just as a virtuoso can glance at a piece of music and instantly play it to perfection, so Holmes could size up a man almost instantly and then "play" him accordingly. A man's intelligence ("It is all in the eyes, Watson"); his state of mind ("Watch how he carries himself and pay special attention to the cleanliness of his ears"); and particularly the force of his will ("The weak man will invariably reveal himself by his pronunciation of the vowels")—all of these and many other qualities Holmes was able to deduce at a glance. Nonetheless, it must be said that Holmes's quick judgments were not always on their mark, as the Red Demon was subsequently to demonstrate.

In Thompson's case, however, Holmes harbored no doubts. "I am certain that the marshal is involved in this business," he said. "I am equally sure that like most weak men—did you see the peculiar vacancy in his eyes?—he cannot resist the lure of gold. Why, he positively licked his lips when I threw out the possibility of a ten-thousand-dollar reward! Greed will make him talk, Watson. Mark my words, we will soon have the truth out of the good marshal!"

"And what will he tell us?"

"We shall have to see," Holmes replied.

I did not press the point further, for I could tell that a change had come over Holmes, whose mood could shift as quickly as an ocean breeze. He had a distant, dreamy look, and soon his eyes closed. I knew from experience that he had now settled in for a bout of "thinking time." This was a trancelike state in which he periodically put himself in order to let his mind roam, as he described it, "like a child let loose in a fun house."

Although Holmes could be extremely systematic when the occasion demanded, his normal method of ratiocination was seldom straightforward. His mind, rather, was a wide and promiscuous net that gathered all before it, selecting the facts it wanted only after examining and rejecting a hundred others. Solely in this fashion, Holmes believed, could the truth—however improbable it might appear—emerge. I recall how, at the conclusion of the fantastic affair of the one-legged Peruvian goldsmith, he told me that only a "courageous indifference to the obvious" had enabled him to solve the case.[6] This remark, I believe, was Holmes's way of saying that all inquiry, if it is to be successful, must proceed with an open, or as he once called it, "freely wandering" mind.

As I sat on the porch of the Morrison House in the almost unbearable heat, Holmes's immobile form beside me, I now wondered where his mind was taking him and where it would lead us in the hours and days ahead.

❋

The answer came soon enough, for just after noon Holmes emerged from his trance and announced that he had struck upon several "peculiar and suggestive ideas."

"I should be most interested to hear them," I said.

"You shall have that opportunity in due time, Watson. But first let us have some lunch. And then, I think, it will be time for a visit to Mrs. Robinson."

At the hotel's dining room, to which we immediately repaired, Holmes again proved himself to be a trencherman of the first order. A whole fried chicken, roasted potatoes, mounds of syrupy baked beans and a side plate of biscuits with gravy all disappeared before his insatiable appetite, and it was only after he had finished a large slice of apple pie that he turned his attention to our impending interview with Mary Robinson.

"It will be a delicate matter," he observed, forking up his last bite of pie, "since this woman is unlikely to admit to writing letters on behalf of the Red Demon."

"Should we not confront her?" I asked. "Surely she could not withstand strong questioning in light of what we know of her connection to the letters sent to Mr. Hill."

"You underestimate the fair sex, Watson. A woman who would write such letters would do so only because she is in the grip of some powerful passion. Men murder, rob, cheat and steal for reasons that often involve the coldest sort of calculation. But the woman who turns to crime almost always does so out of love. Her motive may be the love of a man—in this case the Red Demon—for whom she will do anything. Or, it may be a matter of some unrequited love. Or, she may desire to gain revenge for a wrong done to her or a loved one. But whatever the motivation, it will rise out of an overriding passion. Of that you may be sure!"

"But what of Constance Kent?" I protested, recalling that cruel and calculating murderess who had brilliantly outwitted the best minds of Scotland Yard. "Or Catherine Wilson, who poisoned seven times? I fail to see anything in her case but the desire to enrich herself."[7]

"Bah, there are exceptions to every rule," Holmes said irritably. "My point is this, Watson: If, as I suspect, some deep current of feeling has driven Mrs. Robinson toward her desperate action, then she will not easily yield to our inquiries. Only if we understand her guiding passion will we discover the truth."

"But how shall we approach her? She will be suspicious if we simply come to her establishment and begin asking questions."

"Ah, my dear Watson, you have hit upon the central point. You are correct in assuming that Mrs. Robinson is likely to be suspicious of us if we approach her too directly. Therefore, we must be extremely subtle. At the same time, we must not forget the fact that men call upon Mrs. Robinson and her employees for one reason and one reason only. We must be prepared to do likewise if we hope to gain useful information."

"What are you suggesting, Holmes?" I said, for I did not like the tenor of his remarks.

"I am suggesting, Watson, that we must not seem utterly uninterested in the services which Mrs. Robinson provides."

"This is too much, Holmes!"

"Oh come, Watson, you are a well-traveled man of the world. Do you mean to tell me that during your medical services in Afghanistan and elsewhere you never set foot in a bordello or treated the illnesses which invariably afflict men who frequent such places?"

"That is a completely different matter," I said with some asperity.

"Well, then, what do you suggest?"

I thought for a while but finally had to acknowledge that a better idea did not immediately come to mind. Nonetheless, I informed Holmes in the strongest manner possible that I did not intend to put myself in a compromising position merely to satisfy his lust for information.

Holmes laughed, rather impolitely in my view. "Ah, Watson, you are ever an inspiration to me. Very well, you have my assurance that your precious virtue shall not be sullied."

Chapter Seven

"I Am Always Pleased to Speak with a Gentleman"

✳

L ate that afternoon, Sherlock Holmes and I found ourselves seated in a rude wagon, bouncing along a narrow road on the outskirts of Hinckley. Our destination—Mother Mary's, as it was known locally—was a mile west of town, its remote location having been selected, our driver told us, so as to avoid any costly entanglement with municipal authorities.

Once we had passed the last scattering of houses at the edge of town, the road ascended a long hill before dipping into a shallow valley heavily wooded with tamarack, spruce and other lesser species ignored by the pine-hungry loggers. Although the sun was high in the sky, a cloud of bluish smoke had drifted into this little valley, floating among the trees like a luminous shroud. The effect was eerie and unsettling.

"I do not like the look of this place," I confessed to Holmes. "It would be perfect for an ambush."

"Indeed it would," said Holmes, whose eyes displayed a high state of alertness. "Perhaps our friend has similar thoughts."

"Our friend?"

"Observe," replied Holmes, pointing off into the woods, where I caught a glimpse of a solitary horseman. "We are being followed. No doubt it is the same man I first saw in Hinckley."

"What shall we do?"

"We shall be prepared for whatever may happen."

The road soon began to climb a low ridge into an area of cut-over pine, and as we emerged from the murk of the valley, I glanced anxiously for some sign of the horseman. But he had vanished— how and where I could not say. As I was about to mention this fact to Holmes, I received my first view of Mother Mary's bordello. It stood in the midst of a grassy clearing and formed an altogether unforgettable picture.

I had expected a tawdry establishment not unlike those to be found in the most vile precincts of London. Instead, Mother Mary's occupied a large, handsome and elaborately ornamented wooden house that would have done justice to the finest street in St. Paul or the most pleasant lane in suburban London. But the house's most astonishing feature was its color—a deep and provocative shade of red, which gave it the look of some vast hothouse blossom that had somehow bloomed amid the withered brown forests that surrounded it. Were it not for this intense and bizarre coloration, the house might have been mistaken for the country estate of some well-to-do gentleman rather than the den of unrestrained carnality I knew it to be.

Even Holmes was impressed. "It would appear, Watson, that logging is not the only lucrative business in Hinckley," he remarked as we followed a winding driveway that led to the house.

Our driver—a gaunt and taciturn man of indeterminate age— brought the wagon to a stop beneath a porte cochere. Holmes gave the man one dollar and promised to double that amount if he would wait for our return. The driver readily agreed and went off with his team to seek shade beneath a nearby oak.

We now approached the front door, which was set between two low walls, each of which held small lanterns mounted on curiously tapered wooden shafts.

"A case of architectural form following function, I should think," said Holmes, examining these peculiar and evocative shafts. "Ah, and look here, Watson, Mrs. Robinson even maintains regularly posted business hours."

This was a reference to a handwritten sign on the heavy wooden door announcing that the establishment would open at five o'clock. Ignoring this announcement, Holmes rapped the handle of his cane upon the door. There was no answer. Holmes pounded at the door again, creating a commotion such as might have awakened the dead. At length, a man's voice could be heard inside.

"All right, all right," the voice said with evident annoyance. "Hold your horses, for God's sake! I'm coming."

When the door finally swung open, it was with no small surprise that I saw, dressed in a red robe and slippers, the massive figure of William Thompson. His astonishment was as great as ours, for he stared at us, mouth agape, as though he had just encountered some specter from the beyond.

"I'll be damned," he finally said, "if it ain't a couple of English gents out whorin' in the woods. Well, like the sign says, business commences at five o'clock."

Holmes merely smiled at this gross characterization of our motives. "Big Billy, what a delight to see you again," he said. "Now, if you would be so kind as to inform Mrs. Robinson that she has visitors, we will let you return to the duties, no doubt official in nature, which occupy you here."

Thompson shook his head, and his face hardened into a scowl. "The lady, she don't entertain visitors at this hour. So you best be movin' along."

"How unfortunate," Holmes replied, "for I have bought the lady a present that I would very much like to deliver in person."

Then, with a suddenness that startled me, Holmes pushed the marshal aside with his cane and entered the house. Thompson swung around to confront Holmes, and I instinctively reached for the revolver in my coat pocket. But my precautions were unnecessary, for Thompson came to an abrupt halt when he found his throat being tickled by a razor-sharp blade which had emerged from the bottom of Holmes's cane by means of some hidden spring mechanism. Where my friend had acquired this deadly device was beyond me, but I had no doubt he was skilled in its use.

"I should be careful, Big Billy," Holmes said as he pushed the marshal back against the open door. "If it is trouble you seek, you shall find it from me."

"I don't want no trouble," Thompson rasped, feeling the cold steel against his throat and looking none too happy about it.

"Good," said Holmes, pulling back the blade. "And remember, it behooves you to be polite. After all, I am the man who can make you ten thousand dollars richer if you mind your manners. Do you understand?"

Thompson nodded, his eyes still fixed on the blade.

We were now in a small foyer decorated with red floral wallpaper and heavy, electric-blue drapes. Leading up from this entryway was a wide staircase, its thick newel posts serving as pedestals for a pair of small plaster statues depicting activities too lewd to describe. A cloying aroma, not unlike that of magnolia, saturated the air.

"Truly, this must be a lumberjack's paradise," said Holmes, though I did not see how an enterprise devoted to satisfying the basest appetites could qualify as heavenly. "I am sure it is a pleasure to work here, Big Billy, but it is rather unorthodox, is it not, for a marshal to be employed at a brothel?"

Thompson managed a wan smile. "It's a job, that's all."

"And part of that job is to satisfy your customers," Holmes responded, jabbing the blade back toward the marshal's neck. "And that is why I shall now ask you for the last time to notify Mrs. Robinson that we wish to speak with her at once."

❈

"There is no need to frighten the poor man out of his wits," a mellifluous voice announced. "I am here, and I am always pleased to speak with a gentleman, especially one armed with such an interesting cane."

With these words, we received our first glimpse of Mary Robinson, who stood at the top of the steps and gazed at us with a look that can only be described as a mixture of fascination and scorn. I would be dishonest if I failed to report that her appearance was quite contrary to my expectations. Having accompanied Holmes on numerous excursions into the vice-ridden depths of the London underworld, I had naturally come in contact with many women of ill repute. Most of these pitiful creatures could only be described as hellish crones devoid of feminine beauty. But Mrs. Robinson was an entirely different matter.

She was, I would judge, near her fortieth year, tall, finely proportioned, and elegant in posture. She wore a flowing dress of pink silk, with delicate white lace at the sleeves and around the bodice, which was cut sufficiently low to reveal her ample bosom. Her long, rather haughty face was at once strong and sensuous, with high cheekbones, a Roman nose, a small mouth delineated by thick ruby lips, and most remarkable of all, intense violet eyes. A luxuriant cascade of auburn hair fell past her shoulders, and on her thin wrists she wore two gold bracelets studded with stones of the greatest brilliance. In every respect, I thought, she was the perfect incarnation of some royal concubine, and her presence in this far-off and uncivilized corner of the world seemed to me as inexplicable as the discovery of a gorgeous rose in a field of noxious weeds.

"Ah, Mrs. Robinson," Holmes said, lifting his cane from Thompson's throat and making a slight bow, "how good of you to see us. If it is not too much trouble, my friend Mr. Smith and I"— he pointed at me with the cane, its blade now mysteriously gone— "would like to have a brief conversation with you."

The lady smiled demurely, though there was something in her way of doing so that suggested a tigress on the hunt. "You must be

Mr. Baker of *The Times*," she said, descending the staircase and approaching Holmes. "I have already heard much about you."

A familiar fragrance now wafted into my nostrils. The aroma instantly brought me back to that moment at Hill's mansion in St. Paul just two days earlier when I had first smelled the scent of lavender perfume on the Red Demon's letter.

❋

Holmes, I presumed, had also picked up the scent, but his face remained an impassive mask. "I trust that all you have heard about me is favorable," he told Mrs. Robinson, meeting her eyes with his usual unblinking gaze.

"How could it be otherwise in the case of an English gentleman such as yourself," she said, undaunted by Holmes's cool stare. "But come, let us have tea. Billy"—she now turned to the unfortunate marshal, who seemed to have lost his voice after encountering Holmes's steel—"why don't you run along and fetch some tea while I entertain my visitors."

With a sullen nod, Thompson did as he was instructed, leaving by a side door.

"It must be convenient to have law enforcement so readily available on the premises," said Holmes.

"Unfortunately, our clientele can become rambunctious at times. It was necessary to hire the marshal to provide security. He is here almost every evening."

"But is your business not illegal?" I asked.

"Perhaps. But then, so are many things which people desire. Now, gentlemen, come along and we will have that tea."

We followed Mrs. Robinson up the staircase and into a spacious parlor furnished with richly upholstered divans and ornate French side chairs. Large oil paintings, many of them depicting undraped females from classical antiquity, adorned the papered walls, while a plum-colored carpet of excellent weave covered the floor.

An upright piano stood in one corner, a fine glass étagère in another. It might have been a room from some handsome London townhouse, except for a hand-lettered sign over a curtained doorway which read: "No Boots Beyond This Point."

"Our reception area," Mrs. Robinson said. "On a good night in winter there might be fifty customers waiting here."

We passed through the doorway and down a narrow hall, thereby gaining access to a small suite of rooms which I took to be Mrs. Robinson's personal quarters. Here, in a cheerful room fitted out with a sofa, several high-backed chairs and a small library table on which rested a beautiful vase of flowers, our hostess invited us to sit. I chose one of the chairs while Mrs. Robinson sat at the end of the sofa. Sunlight streamed through a large window which looked out over the forest, and the scene could have passed for one of the utmost domestic tranquillity.

Holmes, meanwhile, paced the room, taking in every detail with his unfailing eye. "The flowers are lovely," he remarked, examining the floral arrangement on the table. One flower in particular—a black rose—caught his attention, and he bent over to inspect it more closely.

"I am surprised to find such a rare bloom flourishing here," he said to Mrs. Robinson. "Did you cultivate it yourself?"

"Yes. Roses are most interesting, don't you think, Mr. Baker? So beautiful, and yet with such large pricks. One must always be careful when handling them."

"Indeed," said Holmes, arching his eyebrows in a way that suggested he had found Mrs. Robinson's remarks amusing, though I failed to see the humor in them.

Holmes went to a small bookcase and scanned its contents, which included a large collection of bound volumes as well as several distinctive curios. He picked up one of these objects—a large wooden disk that appeared to be a thin section cut from a log.

"How interesting," he said, turning the piece over in his hand before giving it to me. "Note the letters so neatly stamped within—

BPC. I wonder what they stand for? Would you happen to know, Mrs. Robinson?"

The madam, for the first time, showed some hint of discomfort, as evidenced by a slight quavering in her voice as she told Holmes: "I would not know. It is merely a trifle brought in by one of the jacks. We have acquired many such meaningless souvenirs over the years."

"No doubt," said Holmes amicably. "I asked only because the stamped letters suggest a log mark, perhaps from the Big Pine Camp, which I am told is not far down the road.[1] In fact, Mr. Smith and I have been thinking of paying a visit to the camp to interview Mr. LeGrande, who is apparently quite an infamous figure in this area. Do you happen to know him?"

"I know many people," Mrs. Robinson replied in a tone that suggested she had no interest in discussing the matter further.

Holmes did not force the issue. Instead, he continued browsing at the bookshelf and soon removed a slim volume whose title I could not decipher. "I see you are a great reader, madam, though of a rather incendiary brand of literature."

"You do not approve of Marx and Engels, I take it," said Mrs. Robinson, who obviously recognized the book.[2] "But then, being a wealthy Englishman, I suppose the status quo suits you perfectly."

"Not always. I find it disturbing, for example, that we live in a world in which young women can be turned toward a life of debauchery by the unscrupulous operators of brothels."

These words, spoken with great force, were clearly meant as a challenge to Mrs. Robinson. I had often seen Holmes confront opponents in this way, lunging at them with a swift surprise attack in hopes of destroying their will to resist him. How, I wondered, would Mrs. Robinson respond?

The answer came quickly enough, and it showed Mrs. Robinson to be a worthy adversary, for Holmes's biting remarks did not seem to disconcert her in the least.

"I find it hard to believe that the idea of brothels could offend a gentleman such as yourself, since I am told the English upper classes are quite fond of such establishments. As for the young women I employ, whom I prefer to think of as sales associates, you may be assured that none works against her will. Surely, you of all people, Mr. Baker, being a journalist and therefore a tool of the capitalist interests, must realize that I am merely selling a product, one which customers are ever anxious to purchase. After all, men are always in rut, and since their itch requires constant attention, I see no reason why I should not be the one to scratch it—for a profit, of course."

The frankness and amorality of her comments, not to mention the unladylike way in which she uttered them, left me quite appalled, and I felt compelled to raise my voice in protest. "You are defiling young women in this sinkhole of depravity," I said heatedly. "Where is the morality in that?"

She turned those violet eyes upon me, and there was something in them like cold fire. "Morality, Mr. Smith, is a matter of power, nothing more and nothing less. The rich impose it upon the poor, men impose it upon women, and the forces of reaction impose it upon those who seek a better world. Thus, it hardly surprises me that while no opprobrium attaches itself to the men who visit my establishment, the women who work here are universally scorned. Where, Mr. Smith, is the morality in that?"

I began to respond, but Holmes, with an irritated wave of his hand, indicated that he wished to hear no more of the matter.

At this point, Thompson—who had exchanged his robe for a suit and had also donned his holster and pistol—arrived with our tea. Fearing he might seek revenge against Holmes, I kept my revolver at the ready. But Mrs. Robinson quickly dismissed the marshal, who seemed to be completely in her thrall, and we drank in silence for a moment before Holmes resumed the conversation.

"Since we cannot solve the world's problems, Mrs. Robinson, perhaps we can help each other," Holmes began. "Quite frankly, I am looking for what you Americans call an 'angle.' As you apparently have heard, I have come here to paint a picture of life in the pineries for our English readers. And as it appears that your establishment is one of the major—how shall I put it?—'institutions' in this region, I naturally would like to know as much about it as possible. I would be interested, for example, to know how you became involved in this particular line of work and to learn more about your customers and their habits."

"I am afraid I cannot be of help to you," Mrs. Robinson said. "I do not seek publicity for myself or my clientele. In my business, as I am sure a worldly gentleman such as yourself must understand, discretion is everything."

"Of course. A brothel, after all, is a place where even the most secretive man, caught up in the passions of the moment, may let down his guard and reveal information of extreme value."

"And you hope I might share such information with you?"

"The thought has occurred to me," Holmes acknowledged.

"But why should I do so, Mr. Baker? What would I gain?"

Holmes smiled. "Those are fair questions, madam. Let us just say that it could be worth your while to talk, for reasons which may become obvious to you momentarily."

Following this cryptic comment, Holmes reached into his coat pocket and removed a small package. "This may enlighten you," he said, handing the package to Mrs. Robinson. "Think of it as a small gift that is also a gesture of our good intentions."

"How thoughtful of you," she said, a tinge of nervousness once again apparent in her voice. "Shall I open it now?"

"Please do, madam."

I watched with the closest interest as Mrs. Robinson slowly unwrapped the package and removed the small bottle of perfume inside. There was, I thought, a flash of alarm in her eyes as she recognized the Jicky bottle, but her usual poise returned almost instantly.

"Fine perfume is always a most welcome gift," she said. "Thank you very much, Mr. Baker."

"It is nothing really," said Holmes, scrutinizing her face for signs of distress. "Naturally, I did not know which perfume a woman of your accomplishments would prefer, and so I was compelled to make an educated guess. But it seems my surmise was a good one, for if I am not mistaken, you are wearing Jicky at this very moment. What a marvelous coincidence!"

Holmes had laid down the gauntlet once again, for the mocking tone in his voice made it clear that his selection of Jicky was no accident. But as had been the case earlier, Mrs. Robinson displayed perfect aplomb. Her beautiful face showed not the least hint of alarm, though I had the distinct impression that her mind was moving at lightning speed. There was, in fact, something about the dense and concentrated nature of her gaze which suggested a chess master at work, analyzing all of the possibilities on the board.

"You are unusually observant, Mr. Baker," she said at last. "Jicky is a perfume I wear on occasion, as do many of my sales associates. Our customers, it seems, find the scent especially intoxicating, and I suspect that not a few samples have gone out our doors. In any event, it is indeed a happy coincidence that you have chosen this perfume. I shall certainly think of you from now on whenever I wear it."

It was a brilliant rejoinder, for Mrs. Robinson had neatly parried any attempt to link her, and her alone, to the perfume. Holmes, judging by the crooked smile on his face, was equally impressed.

He said: "You flatter me, madam, and I am happy that you have found this gift to your liking. As I suggested earlier, gifts of a far more substantial nature could accrue to you if you could help us in our quest for useful information. After all, information is simply another commodity that can be bought and sold. And if the information is valuable, the price must naturally reflect that value."

"Naturally. But the fact of the matter, Mr. Baker, is that I know nothing about you. You claim to be from London, you claim to be a journalist, you claim to be writing a story. What proof do I have that any of this is true? How do I know, for example, that you and Mr. Smith are not simply agents of the police?"

"What sort of proof do you seek?" Holmes asked.

"The proof of the flesh," Mrs. Robinson said as she pulled a cord that hung down beside the couch.

Had I known at that moment what Mrs. Robinson intended, I should have fled at once from that evil woman's chambers, for the episode that followed was the most unpleasant duty I have ever performed on behalf of my friend Sherlock Holmes.

❀

"What exactly is this 'proof of the flesh'?" Holmes asked.

"A simple test. If you are indeed who you claim to be, then the test will not be unpleasant."

I had no idea what she meant, and even Holmes seemed baffled by her comments. Our puzzlement only increased when there suddenly appeared at a door to our left two tall, thin and scantily attired girls whose occupation could not be doubted.

"Ah, here you are," Mrs. Robinson said. "Come right in."

The women, who were identical twins and no more than twenty years old, entered the room and stood beside their mistress. Their faces were long and sallow, and their large blue eyes lacked the shimmering hope of youth, displaying instead the sorrowful wisdom which comes only with hard experience. Both had short blond hair parted down the middle and both wore pearl earrings, bracelets and an abundance of other jewelry. Their attire, such as it was, consisted of long, sheer gowns of scandalously diaphanous material. Yet they seemed to have lost all traces of that modesty which naturally becomes the fair sex, for they stared at us in a most frank and impudent manner.

This display of depravity was more than I could tolerate, and I lost my composure. "Really, Ho—," I blurted out, but before I could utter his name, Holmes coolly interrupted:

"What my friend is trying to say in his somewhat excitable way is how nice it is to meet these young ladies. I take it, Mrs. Robinson, that they are, as you put it earlier, sales associates?"

"That is correct, Mr. Baker. This is Laura"—she pointed to the girl at her far left—"and next to her is Dora. Our customers know them better as the jack pine twins."

"Pleased to meet you," said Laura, smiling.

"Me too," said Dora.

"The pleasure is all ours, I'm sure," said Holmes, who did not seem in the least embarrassed by the presence of these all but naked females. "And now, Mrs. Robinson, let me guess. Is it possible the test you spoke of earlier might involve our willingness to spend some, ah, time with these beautiful young ladies? If so, it is a rather strange sort of test."

"Perhaps. But if you are what you claim to be, then I would imagine your travels have been long and exhausting and that a little companionship at this moment would be most inviting."

"Indeed it would," said Holmes, "but I have long maintained an ironclad rule, which is that I never put pleasure before business. And since there are several other matters I should like to discuss with you, in private, I must decline your kind offer. On the other hand, I am sure my associate"—Holmes nodded in my direction—"would be pleased to entertain Laura and Dora while you and I, Mrs. Robinson, conduct our business."

I need not say how angry I was at Holmes, and it took every ounce of self-restraint I possessed to keep me from fleeing the room immediately.

"I am a married man," I said, hoping that this might deter Mrs. Robinson's plans. This was not true, of course, for I was then a widower, my beloved Mary having passed on only recently.[5] I could not help but wonder what that pure and kind woman would have thought of me in these circumstances, and I made a silent vow that I would do nothing to shame her memory.

Mrs. Robinson, however, greeted my protestations with a derisive laugh. "Why, Mr. Smith, if it were not for married men, I should be out of business in a fortnight. Besides, the jack pine twins will treat you well. Isn't that right, girls?"

The two vixens beside her nodded, and one of them—I cannot

say which—came over to me and began running her fingers through my hair. "Don't worry," she said as I pulled her hand away. "We'll treat the gentleman real nice."

"Splendid," said Holmes, ignoring the venomous glance I cast in his direction. "And now, Mrs. Robinson, perhaps we could retire to a more secluded place to discuss business."

"As you wish. I am sure you will find my boudoir a most intimate and satisfying place for conversation. Come this way."

Before I could protest, Holmes and Mrs. Robinson were gone, leaving me alone to face the jack pine twins.

Chapter Eight

"Have the Twins Been Too Much for You?"

✳

"I suppose you'll be wanting to bake a batch of rolls," one of the girls said.[1]

"I do not know what baking has to do with anything," I replied, moving across the room in hopes of escaping the clutches of these two brazen harlots. "Besides, I am not hungry."

"Not hungry, sir?" said the other girl, putting her hand upon my chest in a most licentious manner. "Why, most men who come here are starving. They want feeding in the worst way. Ain't that right, Dora?"

"That's right," agreed Dora, who grabbed my right hand and brought it to her bosom. "But maybe this gentleman is hungry and don't know it. Maybe his appetite needs stimulating."

Such repulsive talk continued for several minutes, for it seemed that nothing could embarrass these trollops. We were soon circling the room, the girls constantly reaching for me while I did my manly best to fend off their advances. Nonetheless, one of them finally got her hands around mine. I attempted to pull away, but the other twin — Dora, I believe — suddenly shoved me with such force that I fell backward on the sofa. Before I could arise, the two of them were upon me, whispering into my ear suggestions so shocking that they might have caused even the most promiscuous London roué to blush.

My immediate impulse, quite naturally, was to push these vile girls away, by brute force if necessary, and so make my escape. But my loyalty to Holmes was such that I could not justify this course of action. I knew that Holmes, now occupied with Mrs. Robinson, wished to learn all that he could about that infamous woman in hopes she could lead us to the Red Demon. I therefore determined that, despite the unpleasantness of my situation, I would attempt by means of clever questioning to elicit whatever facts I could regarding Mrs. Robinson. Before I could launch my inquiries, however, the two girls assailed me with questions of their own.

"Are you really from England, sir?" asked Dora.

"Yes."

"I hear it's very pretty there," said Laura, rubbing my neck.

"Very pretty," I agreed, feeling another hand — Dora's presumably — sliding down my back and inside my shirt.

"And you're from London, aren't you, sir?" said Dora as I twisted around in an attempt to remove the hand at my back.

"Yes."

The manual activity about my person was now at such a lewd and alarming level that I saw no choice but to take the offensive, as it were. I grabbed one wrist from each of the twins, using sufficient force to cause them to cry out.

"You're hurting us, sir," cried Dora, or perhaps it was Laura.

"I'm sorry, but I must have your attention, ladies. I am tired of answering questions about myself. Instead, I should like to know a thing or two about you and your life here."

"Why is that, sir?" asked Laura, nibbling at my ear in a way I found quite annoying.

"It is merely a matter of idle curiosity. I am new to America and anxious to learn more of the country. For example, I wonder about Mrs. Robinson. How is it that a woman of her attainments should end up operating a business such as this?"

"You'd have to ask her that yourself, sir," said Dora, whose hands had already resumed their wandering and were now reaching areas where those of no respectable woman would ever think to venture. "Mrs. Robinson is a woman who likes her privacy."

"No," giggled Laura. "It's privates that she likes."

Both slatterns laughed at this crude joke and continued their relentless pawing. "Stop it!" I commanded. "Please, be serious. I must know more about Mrs. Robinson. Can you at least tell me if she is from this area?"

"I wouldn't know," said Dora. "It don't pay to ask too many questions around here. Mrs. Robinson, she don't like that. Just do your work and shut your mouths, that's what she always says."

"She pays you well, I trust."

Dora laughed. "Not as well as she pays herself and that hypocritical pimp of hers."

Laura's face flushed with alarm. "You be quiet, sister, or you'll get us both in trouble."

"Tell me more about this pimp," I said, sensing that I had opened a potentially significant line of inquiry.

"It's of no concern to you, sir," said Laura, who appeared to be the more clever of the twins. "Have you noticed, sir, that it's getting hot in here? Why don't you let me take off that heavy suit coat of yours? I'm sure you'd be more comfortable."

"All right," I said, hoping that by agreeing to this modest step I might eventually be able to solicit more information from the women. It was also true that the room had grown stiflingly hot, or so it seemed to me.

"That's better," said Laura as I removed my coat and set it on the sofa, somehow forgetting that my revolver was in one of the pockets.

Dora now began to pull at the knot of my tie, while Laura

started to loosen the buttons of my shirt. It soon became apparent that no amount of protest on my part could hope to deter their lascivious intent. As a result, I had no choice but to resort to stronger forms of resistance. Catching my tormentors by surprise, I thrust myself up and off the couch. As I did so, however, a part of my shirt was torn.

Alas, this was the moment that Holmes and Mrs. Robinson chose to reenter the room.

"My dear Mr. Smith," Holmes said with an insolent grin, "you look a trifle disheveled. Have the twins been too much for you?"

"Hardly," I said, aware that my appearance was somewhat irregular. "Our discussions were most interesting. We were, in fact, just finishing some stimulating social intercourse as you arrived."[2]

"Well, then," said Holmes, still grinning, "I think it best that we be on our way. Oh, and don't forget your jacket."

I went to retrieve this item, but was astonished to find that my revolver—the weight of which normally made its presence obvious—had vanished.

"I'm afraid I have lost something," I said.

"Your revolver?" Holmes asked as though reading my mind. "Perhaps it fell under the sofa. Why don't you look there?"

I did not see how the gun could have slipped out of my coat pocket, since I surely would have noticed such an accident. Nonetheless, I did as Holmes asked. To my surprise, the revolver was indeed wedged beneath the couch, though so far back from the edge that it hardly could have fallen into that position.

I was about to remark on this fact when Holmes interrupted: "Perhaps you should make sure that you have your wallet as well, Mr. Smith. It is so easy, after all, to lose things when one is preoccupied with other activities."

A quick examination of my pants pocket revealed that Holmes was again correct. My wallet was gone. No sooner had I made this discovery than Holmes, with a triumphant cry, retrieved the missing object from beneath the cushions of the sofa.

"It is amazing how far down the wallet had lodged itself," he said to Mrs. Robinson. "Who knows how long it might have gone undiscovered had we not thought to look for it."

"Your friend is most fortunate," she agreed, "though I am sure the wallet would have been found and, of course, returned."

"Of course. Well, Mrs. Robinson, I wish you, Laura and Dora a good day. It has been a most enjoyable and productive afternoon, as I'm sure Mr. Smith will agree."

❁

As might be imagined, I was extremely relieved to depart from Mrs. Robinson's house and to be rid of the jack pine twins, though I was inclined to think that our visit had hardly been worth the trouble. Holmes, however, thought otherwise.

"We have learned much today," he said as we stepped out beneath the porte cochere. "Of course, the young women with whom you were so vigorously engaged also hoped to learn something, which is why they attempted to steal your wallet. Mrs. Robinson, I am sure, would have found its contents quite revealing."

"Then the loss of my wallet was no accident?"

Holmes laughed. "An accident? Come, Watson, why do you think Mrs. Robinson suggested her little 'test' and introduced us to the jack pine twins? Obviously, the twins are skilled pickpockets. They first took your revolver as a precaution, then went after your wallet, secreting it in the couch in hopes you would leave without noticing that it was gone."

"But what made you suspect their intentions?"

"Women who ply their trade are always to be suspected. I was simply exercising a normal degree of caution. Besides, was it not obvious to you from the beginning of our interview that Mrs. Robinson knows that we are not who we claim to be?"

"Why are you so certain of that?"

"I will explain at another time, Watson. For now, it is enough to know that Mrs. Robinson is all too aware of our true purpose here."

"Very well, Holmes, but I must tell you that this afternoon was the most unpleasant of my life!"

"Ah, Watson, how can you say an afternoon spent in the company of two lovely young ladies was disagreeable? But come, you can tell me all about your 'unpleasant' experiences on our way back to Hinckley."

It was now almost five o'clock, the hour at which Mrs. Robinson's establishment opened for the night, and a motley crew of customers had already gathered outside the door.

"You're going the wrong way, gents," one of these rustics said with a crooked smile as we walked toward our wagon.

"You may be right, sir," Holmes replied with a tip of his hat. Not until much later did I appreciate the full significance of this curious remark.

❋

Our driver, as it turned out, was not the man with whom we had come. In his place atop the wagon sat a figure of such odd and startling appearance that he might have come from the perfervid imagination of Doré.[3]

"Evenin' gents," said this strange creature as he ignited a small cigar with an unusual silver lighter. "Bob had to leave on account of his wife took sick, but since you gents already paid for your ride back, he asked me to help out. The name's One-eye Johnson and I'm pleased to be at your service."

It was not difficult to see how Johnson had acquired his sobriquet. A small, wiry man like most teamsters, his appearance might have gone unremarked except for one fantastic accident of nature—a grotesquely deformed left eye. Set crookedly in its socket and streaked with blood vessels, this sightless orb had the hue and texture of an old marble. Its most remarkable feature, which conveyed a decidedly sinister impression, was a thin white ring surrounding the pupil. In all my years as a practicing physician, I had never seen an eye like it, and I wondered why Johnson had not taken the obvious course of wearing a patch to mask his terrible deformity.

The answer came soon enough, for as we stepped up into the wagon, Johnson caught my stare with his good eye and began to cackle in a most unpleasant way.

"Scary, ain't it, gents," he said. "You're thinkin', why don't he put a patch on the d--ned thing? Well, gents, I choose not to, so stare all you want. Stare 'til your eyeballs pop right out of your heads, if that's your taste. It don't matter none to me. But just remember: I see better with one eye than most men do with two, and I dare anyone to say different!"

I had no idea how to respond to this remarkable utterance, but Holmes seemed to find it quite amusing. "It is a pleasure to meet you, Mr. Johnson," he said, shaking the teamster's hand as he slid up next to him on the seat. "I am John Baker and this is my associate, Mr. Smith. And while your eye is indeed an unusual phenomenon, we are more interested in your skills as a driver. We would like to return to Hinckley as quickly as possible."

"That's what I'm here for," said Johnson. "I'll have you back in town in no time." With a crack of the whip, he put his team of matched geldings in motion, and we were soon on the road to Hinckley once again. Johnson, meanwhile, proved to be far more talkative than the man he had replaced.

"Pardon me for sayin' it, but you gents talk funny. Are you them English fellas folks been talkin' about?"

"We are," said Holmes, who then provided the usual introductions. Before long, he and Johnson were engaged in a far-ranging conversation about Hinckley, the art of driving a team, railroads, James J. Hill ("a real fine gent," according to the teamster) and the logging industry.

As we descended again into the smoky valley separating Hinckley from Mrs. Robinson's house, Holmes brought up the subject of LeGrande. "I have heard intriguing stories about one of these rough-hewn woodsmen in particular," he said to Johnson. "Ah, if only I could remember his name. I believe it is Legree, Leggard, something like that."

"You must mean Mr. LeGrande—Jean Baptiste LeGrande."

"Yes, that is it!" Holmes replied excitedly. "LeGrande. I should very much like to meet the fellow, for he sounds like just the sort of rugged character our readers would find fascinating. Do you know him?"

"Know him?" said Johnson. "I sure do. I've hauled logs on his skid roads for three years now."

"Really? How interesting! But tell me"—here Holmes dropped his voice to a whisper as though the woods might have ears—"is he the timber thief and outlaw he's made out to be?"

Johnson, who seemed to find Holmes's rapt attention quite flattering, responded by expectorating a great wad of tobacco over the side of the wagon. "Let's just say, Mr. Baker, that the Cat—that's what we call LeGrande—ain't a man to let much of anything stand in his way. As for him bein' a timber thief, well, that's a matter of opinion. The way I sees it, just about everyone in these woods is a thief of one kind or other. It's just that some does their thievin' legal-like and some don't, if you get my drift. But if I was you, I'd judge for myself."

"But how would I do that?" Holmes asked.

Johnson shrugged. "Just go out to the Big Pine Camp. You'll find him there easy enough. It's only ten miles from town. I could take you out there myself. I go 'most every day as it is."

"But would Mr. LeGrande welcome visitors?"

"Don't see why not. The Cat, he loves to talk, and he'd be happy to entertain a couple of English gents such as yourselves."

"Well, Mr. Johnson, we may just take you up on your offer. Besides, Mr. Smith and I have not yet had the opportunity to visit a logging camp. I am sure there is much we could learn."

"You just let me know when you want to go. I'm down at the St. Paul & Duluth depot every mornin' 'cept Sundays. You can find me there."

We were now nearing the outskirts of Hinckley, and as the

road took a sharp turn, Holmes suddenly pointed into the woods to our left. "Look! Do you see him!"

"See what?" Johnson said, swiveling his head to peer out in the direction indicated by Holmes.

"A man on horseback. I am sure I saw him."

"I don't see nothin'," Johnson said.

"There, right over there," Holmes insisted, pointing a bit farther to the left.

"I still don't see nothin'," came the exasperated reply.

I saw no sign of a rider either, and Holmes—somewhat uncharacteristically, I thought—admitted that he might have been mistaken. "Perhaps it was just a deer. In any event, it doesn't matter, for I see we are almost back in Hinckley."

Johnson let us off in front of the Morrison House and received a handsome tip from Holmes for his services.

"Thank you kindly," said the one-eyed teamster, "and if you gents need that ride out to the Big Pine, you just let me know."

"We shall," said Holmes.

As we went into the hotel, I asked Holmes about the horseman he thought he had seen in the woods.

"Do you suppose it was the same man whom you saw on our way to Mrs. Robinson's?"

"My dear Watson, I saw nothing in the woods, though I have no doubt our shadow was still with us."

"Then why did you pretend to see something?"

"For the simple reason that it provided a diversion while I took the liberty of picking Mr. Johnson's pocket."

"What? Really, Holmes, why should you want to pick the poor man's pocket?"

My friend seemed stunned by the question. "Why do you think, Watson? I picked his pocket to find out what was in it."

"And what did you find?"

"Only this," said Holmes, removing from his coat pocket the silver lighter Johnson had used earlier. "Unless I am mistaken, it may one day lead us to the remains of Mr. Thomas Mortimer."

❋

After a hearty dinner—my friend's appetite remained gargantuan—we walked to the Eastern Minnesota depot, where Holmes sent a long coded telegram to Hill. He was silent as to its contents, but I presumed the message to be a report on our activities in Hinckley. We then returned to the hotel and took seats on the front porch to smoke. I hoped Holmes would now explain his statement regarding the silver lighter—he had not broached the subject during dinner—but he deflected my inquiries while counseling patience.

"The significance of the lighter, I believe, will become apparent soon enough, Watson. But for the moment, let us enjoy the evening breeze, which I fear is the only respite we are likely to have from this awful heat."

It was now dusk, and the wide street in front of the hotel grew extremely active as lumberjacks poured into town for a Friday night's entertainment. Several disreputable-looking saloons to either side of the hotel appeared to be among the more popular destinations. Across from us, in front of the St. Paul & Duluth depot, an especially boisterous group of men—perhaps a dozen in all—sat in two large wagons, evidently awaiting a trip of some kind. Near these wagons, I was surprised to see—dressed all in black—our friend William Thompson. He accosted every man who passed his way, and as often as not found one willing to join the others in the wagons.

"What do suppose that is all about?" I asked Holmes.

Holmes, already working on his second pipe of the evening, smiled and said: "Is it not apparent, Watson? Big Billy is lining up customers for Mrs. Robinson. Undoubtedly, that is one of the marshal's duties in addition to providing security."

It now dawned on me what Dora—or was it Laura?—had meant when she referred to Mrs. Robinson's "hypocritical pimp," and I mentioned this to Holmes. But Holmes, who during our supper had solicited and received a complete account of my conversation with the jack pine twins, gave a surprising reply.

"Your deduction is the obvious one, Watson, and perhaps even correct. But I should not be surprised if Big Billy is not Mrs. Robinson's only agent in town."

"Who might this other agent be?"

"I have several ideas in that regard, but they are too ill-formed at this point to bear repeating."

"And what of Mrs. Robinson herself?" I asked, for I was anxious to hear what she and Holmes had discussed while I was in the clutches of the depraved twins. Holmes had said nothing on the topic over dinner, and my curiosity was naturally aroused. "Did your conversation with her produce any clues?"

"Mrs. Robinson," Holmes said, striking a match to his pipe, "is not the sort of woman who readily provides clues about anything. She is at once very clever and very cautious—two traits that are not often found together. Our conversation was therefore something of a fencing match. I would thrust and she would parry, as it were. About LeGrande, for example, she would say nothing. She claimed, in fact, to hardly know the man. She also professed to have no strong feelings about the Eastern Minnesota Railway or James J. Hill. Still, her boudoir was not without points of interest."

"I can imagine that you made a thorough inspection of her private quarters," I said, by which I simply meant that Mrs. Robinson's boudoir undoubtedly provided a fertile opportunity for Holmes to exercise his tremendous deductive skills. Holmes, however, apparently took my innocent remark in another way, for he said sternly:

"What are you suggesting, Watson?"

"I am suggesting nothing," I said. "I merely observed that your examination of this lady's chambers must have exposed much about her character."

"Precisely," said Holmes, his face reddening slightly. "It would be inappropriate to suggest anything else."

"Absolutely. And what did your inspection reveal?"

"Several things, Watson. First, Mrs. Robinson knows that she is suspected of writing the Red Demon's letters."

"However did you deduce that?"

"It was Mrs. Robinson herself who gave the matter away. When we arrived at her chambers, she suddenly stopped outside the door and asked me to wait there, saying she wished to change into something more 'comfortable' before beginning our conversation. Naturally, I had no choice but to accede to her wishes. She then went inside her room and closed the door while I bided my time in the hallway. What does this suggest to you, Watson?"

I pondered this problem for a moment while Holmes, with a Buddha-like look of inscrutability, puffed at his pipe. However, no explanation occurred to me other than the obvious one, which was that Mrs. Robinson had indeed wanted to change her attire.

"I do not see anything especially suggestive about her behavior," I said at last. "Women, after all, often will put on new clothes before entertaining a gentleman."

"Ah, my dear Watson, I see I have not quite succeeded in making a detective out of you yet!" Holmes said. "There was, in fact, no good reason why Mrs. Robinson should feel compelled to change her clothes, since her attire was perfectly appropriate. Therefore, in order to determine her real motivations, I took the liberty of peeking through the keyhole."

"Holmes!" I said, shocked that he would resort to the unseemly behavior of a Peeping Tom. "That is not a thing a gentleman would do!"

Holmes reacted angrily to my protestation. "Oh come, Watson, do not stand forever on your precious morals. We are dealing here with matters of life and death. Besides, I had every reason to believe Mrs. Robinson's stated desire to change her clothes was only a pretext to cover some other course of action. This supposition on my part, you will be interested to know, proved entirely correct."

Not wishing to offend Holmes any further, I apologized for my outburst, though I remain of the opinion that gentlemen should not make a habit of looking through keyholes into ladies' boudoirs.

Even so, I must acknowledge that Holmes's bold action yielded fascinating results, as he now revealed to me:

"Once she had closed the door, Mrs. Robinson immediately went to a small desk in the corner of the room and removed several pieces of paper lying there. She put these documents in the top drawer of the desk and locked it. Next, she deposited the key in a place upon her person where—and you will be pleased to hear this, Watson—no gentleman would ever consider looking. Only after all of this did she begin to change her clothes, at which point I, of course, looked away."

"And then what happened?"

"Mrs. Robinson emerged from her room, invited me in, and we had our pleasant little conversation."

This was all most interesting and I pressed Holmes for additional details. "Do you suppose then, Holmes, that these documents Mrs. Robinson locked away in the drawer were in fact letters from the Red Demon?"

"That is possible, but I rather think they were simply routine pieces of correspondence. For all I know, they may have been nothing more significant than grocery lists."

"But why should she want to hide a grocery list?"

"For the simple reason, Watson, that it would provide a sample of her handwriting."

I now saw what Holmes was driving at. "And she did not wish you to see her handwriting for fear that it could connect her to the threatening letters! Then you are right, Holmes. She must know who we are, or at the least, that we are not mere journalists interested in a story."

"Exactly. This was confirmed to me when I asked her—on the pretext that I needed directions to a certain location in Hinckley—if she could write out the information for me. She politely but firmly declined, saying that she had injured her hand some time ago and found writing to be painful."

Holmes paused to empty the bowl of his pipe. When he resumed speaking, there was an unmistakable tone of concern in his voice. "Mrs. Robinson's behavior leaves no doubt that she knows our purpose here. The question which preoccupies me is how our mission came to be compromised so quickly. Once we know the answer to that, Watson, we shall have our hands on the Red Demon."

Chapter Nine

"His Only Crime Is That He Works Hard"

❋

The next morning, after a late breakfast, Holmes showed me a telegram he had received a few hours earlier from Hill.

"Tell me what you make of it, Watson," he said as we sat in my room, where we could already feel the discomfort of what promised to be yet another dry and insufferably hot day. "I should be interested to hear your thoughts."

As decoded by Holmes, the telegram read as follows: "Thomas Mortimer's middle name is John."

"I make nothing of it. Is there some reason why I should?"

A sly smile crept across Holmes's face. "Perhaps this will enlighten you," he said, handing me the lighter he had so skillfully purloined from One-eye Johnson. I found nothing remarkable about this object until, turning it over, I discerned three initials engraved into its ribbed silver finish. The initials were TJM.

"My God, Holmes. Do you believe the lighter belonged to Mr. Mortimer?"

"It is possible, perhaps even likely. The question, of course, is how the monocular Mr. Johnson came to possess it."

"We must talk to him again at once!"

"Ah, Watson, the directness with which you attack life is ever an inspiration to me. However, I think we would be wise to wait a bit before confronting our teamster friend. Besides, I have other plans today. I am of a mind to go to Pine City."

"Where is that?"

Glancing at a railroad schedule he had taken from his pocket, Holmes said: "It is fourteen miles to the south, on the St. Paul & Duluth Railroad. According to this schedule, there is a train, the No. 4 Limited, which will arrive here in twenty minutes and deliver me to Pine City half an hour later."

"But why on earth do you wish to go there?"

"Because it is the seat of Pine County, Watson, and therefore the site of the county offices, which hold certain records I should like to examine."[1]

"But today is Saturday. The offices will be closed."

"Then I shall have to have them opened. I cannot afford to wait until Monday to see the documents which interest me."

"I take it you wish to examine the lawsuit Mr. Hill brought against LeGrande."

"I do. But I am also interested in records of land ownership. If timber thievery is behind these fires and the threatening letters to Mr. Hill, then I should like to know more about who owns the pinelands in this area."

"But what does it matter who owns the land when it is the thieves who concern us?"

"An excellent question, Watson," said Holmes, trying on the deerstalker hat he usually favored. "Do you think it is too hot for a hat today?"

"It is too hot for just about any item of apparel," I responded.

"But you have not answered my question, Holmes. What will land records tell you?"

Holmes removed the hat, placed it in his coat pocket, and then offered a cryptic smile. Experience told me that I was about to receive a lecture. Holmes did not disappoint.

"Land, Watson, has always been one of the great motivating forces of human passion. What are most wars, after all, except squabbles over territory? Men will fight over land, try to steal it from their neighbors, covet it to their last breath. Why? Because it is a thing that endures. Men come and go, nations rise and fall, but always there is land."

Holmes paused to light his pipe before resuming: "But here, Watson, in this remote wilderness, land is a different sort of thing. It is not the ancestral property we are familiar with in England — the country field farmed by generations or the city plot passed down from father to son. No, the land here has only what might be called a commodity value."

"I am not sure what you mean."

"What I mean is that the land is worth little in its own right. Rather, its value lies in the treasure which it holds — white pine. Like any treasure, white pine is one that men will fight over to the bitter end. They will do so because they know they have but one chance at it, for when the pine is gone — as it surely will be in a decade or two — it will be gone forever."

It was quite a remarkable sermon, but I could not see the point of it, other than that it gave Holmes an opportunity to demonstrate his newfound mastery of arboreal economics.

"Really, Holmes, this is all very interesting," I protested, "but I am still waiting for an answer to my question."

"And you shall have it!" he said with a grin. "Why am I interested in land records? For this reason: Most timber thieves are themselves owners of timberland."

"You are not making any sense, Holmes," I said, rather severely I am afraid, for the heat and dust and stinging smoke of the morning, coupled with a poor night's sleep, had not done wonders for my disposition.

Holmes reacted to my brusque rejoinder with a raised eyebrow but otherwise displayed no sign of irritation. He said: "I am making complete sense, my dear friend. You see, the man who would be a timber thief of any consequence cannot simply wander into the pineries, assemble a large crew of lumberjacks and then go about cutting down whatever part of the forest he pleases. Such a brazen trespass would inevitably be discovered, since the woods hereabouts are full of loggers."

I was beginning to see Holmes's point. "So the thief must find some way to disguise his activities."

"Precisely. And the easiest way to do so is to steal timber from land that adjoins your own. This form of theft is virtually foolproof from the thief's point of view. For, if you are caught in the act, you simply claim a surveying error or the like and make restitution. But if you escape with the timber, and its true owner later accuses you of the crime, you simply deny it. In such an instance, the rightful owner will find it almost impossible to prove anything against you, since pine from one tract of land looks no different from that of another."

"And you are of the opinion that some of the large timber owners in this area may themselves be thieves?"

"It is possible. In any case, I shall be especially interested to learn who owns the land on which LeGrande operates with such apparent impunity."

To this point, Holmes had said nothing about my accompanying him, and I assumed he intended to travel alone to Pine City. This was confirmed, albeit indirectly, when Holmes mentioned that he expected I would learn much during his absence. Though I had no idea why this should be the case, I said nothing so as not to appear ignorant. Instead, I greeted Holmes's comment with a nod and a look of studied sagacity. This stratagem proved effective, for Holmes now outlined my day's work.

"Saturday is a day on which many men come into Hinckley

from the surrounding woods for business or pleasure, and I want you to engage as many of them as you can in conversation. I should imagine the hotel's dining room would be a good place to start, since it always seems crowded."

"I will make it a point to be there at lunch," I said, pleased that I was now being entrusted with an important role in the investigation. "Are there particular topics on which I should sound these men out?"

"It would be especially useful to know what they think of LeGrande and his operation. But be very cautious, Watson. You must not arouse suspicions."

"Rest assured I will do my best."

Holmes smiled and touched my knee. "Of course you will," he said. A train whistle now sounded in the distance. "Ah, the No. 4 is right on time. I shall be on my way."

"When will you return?"

"There is a late afternoon train that will bring me back to Hinckley at five o'clock. We shall have supper at the hotel."

After Holmes left, I watched from my window as he crossed the street and entered the St. Paul & Duluth depot. Shortly thereafter, the No. 4 train, with two blasts of its whistle, departed for Pine City and points south. And so I found myself, for the first time since we had come to Hinckley, alone.

❋

I appeared in the Morrison House's dining room promptly at noon and found it crowded as usual. Since Holmes had provided no specific instructions as to whom I should approach, I decided to sit for a while and try to formulate a plan.

How, I wondered, as I sipped on a bowl of bean soup, would Holmes have handled the matter? Would he have noted some quirk of appearance suggesting that a certain man was likely to be a fertile source of information? Would he have listened to the babel of conversation and extracted from it something that would point him to the right group? Or would he, perhaps, have staged some elaborate scene designed to draw out a particular type of individual? At length, it occurred to me that Holmes would have done the obvious thing, which was to ask one of the waiters about the other diners. I was about to do so when a man who had been sitting at a nearby table stood up and approached me.

"Excuse me," he said in a sonorous voice that displayed a slight Scottish burr, "but I am wondering whether you might perhaps be Mr. Baker, the English journalist?"

He was a tall man of unhealthy corpulence, perhaps fifty years in age, with a large round face of the kind Holmes liked to call "geological." That is to say, it was a face so furrowed and irregular, with lines cutting through it like old dry riverbeds, that it seemed to have been eroded over time by the forces of nature. Perspiration bathed the man's high forehead, which ended in a tangled forest of curly gray hair. His small brown eyes, set close together in creased slits of a decidedly reptilian appearance, were sharp and shrewd, while his attire—dark wool suit, red silk vest with matching pocket handkerchief, and perfectly polished oxfords— suggested a man of considerable means. He also wore a pair of immaculate white gloves, an extreme affectation given the suffocating heat of the room.

"I am Mr. Baker's associate, Peter Smith," I replied, mustering my warmest smile as I did so. "Mr. Baker is attending to business elsewhere at present."

"Ah, I am sorry to hear that as I had hoped to meet him. But permit me to introduce myself. I am Bartlett Chalmers, president of the C & L Timber Co., and I should very much like to have a talk with you, if, of course, the time is convenient."

"By all means, Mr. Chalmers. Please, join me if you would."

"Thank you, sir," he said and slowly squeezed himself into one of the armchairs at my table, much as a big ship might slide into a narrow berth. His massive thighs bulged out beneath the armrests, and new beads of sweat appeared under his dark lizard eyes, which never left mine.

A waiter now appeared and I ordered a ham sandwich to go with my soup. Chalmers, whose pendulous belly betrayed him as a trencherman of the first rank, ordered nothing for himself, noting that he had already finished his meal.

"Let me begin, Mr. Smith, by asking what you think of Hinckley and whether your stay has been a pleasant one, despite the abominable heat."

Adhering to Holmes's directive that I should be as discreet as possible, I chose the words of my reply carefully.

"Mr. Baker and I have found Hinckley to be most interesting. As for the heat, it has indeed been trying, though it is the smoke I find most bothersome. In fact, I am beginning to fear the pineries will burn up before they can be cut down."

Chalmers greeted this remark with a small chuckle. "You need have no fears in that regard, Mr. Smith. There are always fires in the autumn, and while this season has been drier than most, the rains will come soon enough and take the heat and smoke with them. Of that you may be certain."

We continued a desultory conversation on the weather and other insignificant topics until I finished my meal. Once our table was cleared, Chalmers lit a large cigar and leaned over toward me, an indication that the time had come to turn to more important matters.

"Let us get down to brass tacks, Mr. Smith," he said. "I have been told that you and Mr. Baker are English journalists here to gather information for a story about the logging industry in Hinckley, among other things. At the risk of sounding overly inquisitive, may I ask if that is correct?"

"It is."

"Now, sir, I have also been informed that one of your lines of inquiry concerns Mr. Jean LeGrande. Is that true as well?"

I paused, trying to think how Holmes would have handled such a blunt question. I finally said: "And what if it were true?"

Chalmers's answer was quite unexpected: "Then I should be

happy to answer any question you might have, for it so happens that I am Mr. LeGrande's business partner."

This revelation came as such a welcome surprise that I could scarcely conceal my excitement. Yet I knew that I must now proceed with the utmost caution so as not to raise any suspicions on Chalmers's part.

"Then you are in the timber business together, I take it. Is your firm a large one?"

Chalmers let out a guttural laugh. "It depends on what you mean by 'large,' Mr. Smith. Compared to Mr. Weyerhaeuser, for example, we are small-time operators indeed. But we own some excellent stands of pine and have cut upwards of thirty million board feet in a season."

"I see. Does most of that come from the Big Pine Camp?"

"It does. But we maintain several smaller camps as well. Mr. LeGrande, who is a highly experienced woodsman, supervises all of our logging operations while I handle the financial end of the business. It has been a very successful partnership."

"I am pleased to hear that," I said. Since LeGrande's name had been mentioned for a second time, I thought it an opportune moment to broach the subject of his character. "I must confess, Mr. Chalmers, that I have already heard a great deal about your partner. His reputation, as you surely must be aware, is not a savory one in certain quarters."

"Lies," Chalmers declared, smashing his fist down upon the table with such force that all conversation in the dining room came to a halt and all eyes turned toward us. "D—nable lies, and I am tired of hearing them!"

"I am sorry—"

But as quickly as the tempest had arisen in Chalmers, it subsided, and he apologized at once. "Forgive me, Mr. Smith, forgive me. But I have had to abide so many monstrous lies about my friend and partner that it has driven me to distraction. As a matter of fact, that is why I sought you out today—to set the record straight. Mr.

LeGrande has been accused of being a timber thief, a ruffian, an arsonist, and even a murderer. And I am sure that if the sky were to fall in tomorrow, that catastrophe too would be blamed on him. But the truth is that he has done none of the things of which he has been so unfairly accused. His only crime is that he works hard and takes guff from no man. I would swear to that on a stack of Bibles!"

I was unsure how to respond to this impassioned defense of LeGrande but thought it important to keep Chalmers talking. "But why do you suppose Mr. LeGrande has been the subject of such vilification if he is innocent?"

"Because he is a strong yet reticent man, Mr. Smith, and therefore a target for all manner of gossip and innuendo. Take this recent case involving the fellow who disappeared —"

"Do you mean Mr. Mortimer?"

"Yes, Mortimer. Now, from what I have read of the matter in the *Enterprise*, this Mortimer just walked off into the woods and vanished. But because Mortimer happened to work for James Hill, with whom Mr. LeGrande has had some minor disagreements in the past, and because the road he was last seen on happens to pass by the Big Pine Camp (and many other places, I might add), people immediately leaped to the conclusion that Mr. LeGrande must somehow be involved in the disappearance. What nonsense! Why should Mr. LeGrande concern himself with the comings or goings of someone like this Mortimer fellow? It is absurd, simply absurd!"

As Chalmers seemed to be working himself up toward another outburst, I tried to think of a way to calm him. And then I had what seemed to be an inspiration.

"There is a way these issues could be laid to rest once and for all," I said soothingly. "Simply permit Mr. Baker and me to visit the Big Pine Camp and meet Mr. LeGrande. We could hear his side of the story and include it in any article that is written."

Chalmers removed a handkerchief from somewhere within the recesses of his coat and dabbed at the perspiration which now ran like rainwater down the sides of his face. He mopped up as best he could, staining his beautiful white gloves as he did so, and then responded to my offer with a shake of the head.

"No, Mr. Smith, I think not, though I know your suggestion is well-intentioned. Mr. LeGrande, I am afraid, has become so embittered by the whispering campaign against him that he no longer welcomes visitors. Besides, the camp has a large crew at work preparing for the winter season and he must attend full-time to his duties there. But I thank you for your concern."

"Well, perhaps we could talk with him during one of his visits to town," I suggested.

"He never visits town. Never."

"I see."

Chambers glanced at the clock in the dining room. "Ah, I am afraid I must be moving along, Mr. Smith. It is nearly one o'clock and I have another engagement. Please convey my regrets to Mr. Baker that I could not make his acquaintance."

"Mr. Baker will be back this evening. I am sure he would be happy to see you then."

"Unfortunately, I shall be gone by then. But perhaps Mr. Baker and I will have an opportunity to meet another time."

Chalmers stood and shook my hand. "It has been a pleasure, Mr. Smith. And remember: Do not believe every wild story you hear from the rumormongers who infest this community."

"I shall keep that in mind," I said and watched as Chalmers maneuvered his huge bulk through the crowded dining room and out the front door, like a big ship heading toward the open sea.

❋

Due to the wilting heat, I spent the remainder of the afternoon none too comfortably in my room awaiting Holmes's return. When I at last heard the whistle of the train from Pine City, I quickly made my way across the street to the Minnesota & Duluth depot. Holmes, springing down the steps of the rear car with his usual confidence, was the first person off the train.

"I see you have enjoyed a good meal in my absence," he said, "and have even managed to acquire some valuable knowledge regarding our investigation."

"How could you possibly know that?"

"The brown spot on your left lapel, which was not apparent this morning, suggests you have eaten a meal—soup perhaps, though I cannot be certain. As to the other matter, I trust you will not take offense, Watson, if I remark that your face has always been a most reliable guide to the state of your mind. Had you not enjoyed some success on your mission today, the distinctive smirk that now animates your features would not, I think, be evident. Am I wrong?"

I could only shake my head at this latest display of my friend's prowess, though I was inclined to believe that the alleged smirk was wholly a figment of Holmes's sometimes overactive imagination.

"I have had an interesting conversation with a local lumberman," I acknowledged. "You will find it quite revealing."

"Splendid! I knew I could count on you, Watson. Come, let us discuss it over dinner. I, too, have made some progress, though I shall be especially anxious to hear your account."

A half hour later, I once again found myself in the Morrison House's dining room, this time with Holmes as my companion. After we had ordered our meal, Holmes described his day:

"Pine City is a dreary little town much like this one, and the courthouse is hardly an imposing structure. Nonetheless, the records were in good order and the clerk whom I prevailed upon to open the office was most helpful. The lawsuit brought by Mr. Hill against LeGrande proved to be a disappointment, however. It involved a relatively small amount of timber, and the claims and counterclaims were extremely confusing. I am not surprised that a jury failed to decide the issue for either party."

"But could not even such a small dispute have been a continuing source of enmity between LeGrande and Mr. Hill?"

"Perhaps," said Holmes, with a shrug. "In any event, my inspection of the land records proved far more rewarding. These documents revealed an interesting pattern to the land ownership around Hinckley."

"What sort of pattern?"

"It is this, Watson: There is one company which owns tracts of land adjoining virtually all of the big timber claims in the county. Its holdings are small—forty acres here, eighty there—but they are strategically placed. One tract, for example, lies adjacent to five thousand acres of prime timberland owned by the Weyerhaeusers. Timber theft could easily flourish in such an environment, since the small landowner would be in a perfect position to steal from his larger neighbor. What makes this arrangement even more intriguing is that the company in question also owns the land around Big Pine Lake, where Mr. LeGrande is said to be based."

I have not often been able to spring a surprise on Sherlock Holmes, but I did so now. "The firm you are referring to, of course, would be the C & L Timber Co., one of whose owners is Mr. Bartlett Chalmers," I said matter-of-factly.

My words had their desired effect, for Holmes snapped his head back and looked at me as though he had just seen the King of England in his underwear. "My dear Watson, you are a veritable font of unexpected information today. I am impressed!"

I now felt entitled to apply the smirk to my face that Holmes had claimed to detect at the depot. "Thank you, Holmes. It was elementary, if you must know."

Holmes smiled, but I also could see the bright glitter of curiosity in his eye. "I have been snookered, Watson, and you are the man who did it. Obviously, you have talked with Mr. Chalmers today."

"I have."

"Then we are doubly fortunate. Now, Watson, I want you to tell me everything that was said by Mr. Chalmers. Everything. Leave no detail out, no matter how insignificant it may seem."

And so I told my story, providing every detail which came to mind regarding my conversation with Chalmers. Holmes sat perfectly still and silent during this narration, his eyes closed and his hands drawn up to his chin in the manner of a supplicant.

When I had finished, he opened his eyes and said, in a quiet voice: "Is that everything?"

"I believe so."

"Belief is not good enough," he snapped. "You must be certain, Watson, absolutely certain."

I went back over the conversation in my mind, trying to recall every word and nuance. It was only then, as I formed a mental image of Chalmers, that I remembered the singular feature of his apparel. "Oh, did I mention that he was wearing gloves?"

"Gloves? What sort of gloves?"

"White gloves, like those a man might wear to the theater."

"How curious," said Holmes. "How very curious."

※

Sunday turned out to be our day of rest, at least in the physical sense, for though Holmes hardly stirred from his bed, I knew he was deeply engaged in thought.

"I do not wish to be disturbed," he had told me when I knocked upon his door in the morning. "I must think."

I have often been asked to describe the nature of Holmes's mind, though I doubt that anyone could ever hope to understand such a magnificent creation in its entirety. Nonetheless, I have always thought his mind must be rather like some vast yet eccentric reference library, its sturdy shelves stocked with innumerable volumes of esoterica. In this great library the antiquarian or specialist would find many wonders, while the general reader would merely be baffled by the overwhelming oddity of its collections. That is because many ordinary things were quite unknown to Holmes, whereas he knew a great many extraordinary things, especially as they related to crime.[2]

Yet what was most astonishing about the library within Holmes's head was the speed with which he could retrieve, connect and combine the information it contained. It was this ability, above all else, which enabled Holmes to detect cunning patterns of crime where others saw only the chaos of circumstance.

What was he seeing now, I wondered as I sat in the heat of my room, and what connections was he drawing to the Red Demon?

Chapter Ten

"Do You Suppose He Could Have Drowned Here?"

✳

The sun had barely risen on Monday morning when there was a frightful pounding at my door, followed by the familiar voice of Sherlock Holmes.

"Come along, Watson, the hour is late and we are off to the woods. I think it high time we pay Mr. LeGrande a visit."

"I shall be with you in a minute," I replied, rubbing the sleep from my eyes. Although Holmes's loud announcement had startled me, it hardly came as a surprise. I knew from the moment Chalmers advised against a visit to the Big Pine Camp that Holmes would go there, if for no other reason than that he never allowed anyone to dictate his conduct during an investigation.

Still in my nightgown, I stumbled to the door and flung it open, and was thereupon greeted with an astonishing sight. Instead of Sherlock Holmes the English gentleman and consulting detective, I found Sherlock Holmes the lumberjack. His peculiar raiment included leather boots, dark brown trousers (or "stag pants," as he insisted on calling them), suspenders, a red plaid shirt and wide-brimmed black hat of the fedora type.[1] He also held a large bag in one hand.

"Well, Watson, what do you think?" he asked, doffing his cap and bowing as though expecting the plaudits of an audience.

Holmes, of course, had long been fond of disguises, and I had seen him in so many different manifestations over the years that this latest sartorial detour was not entirely shocking.[2] Even so, I did not know quite what to think, since I could see no reason why a visit to the woods should require him to don the guise of a lumberjack.

"You look quite woodsy," I finally said, "though I am not sure I understand the point of your disguise."

"Disguise? What makes you think this is a disguise?" There was a distinct note of petulance in Holmes's voice.

"Well, why else would you dress up in such a fashion?" I said, retreating back into my room. Holmes followed and dropped the bag he was carrying on my bed.

"My dear Watson, have you never heard the old saying, 'When in Rome, do as the Romans do'? Well, we are about to venture off into the pineries and I do not think a broadcloth coat and a silk tie would be appropriate in such circumstances."

"I cannot see that a suit coat would be an impediment to our endeavors," I said, thinking that Holmes looked ever so slightly ridiculous in his woodland garb. "After all, I presume it is not our intent to scale trees in lumberjack fashion or roll logs down a river."

"Watson, you are hopeless! Very well, dress as you like, but do not blame me if you return with your clothes in tatters."

"I shall not," I said. "By the way, what is in the bag?"

"Take a look, though I doubt you will be interested."

I opened the bag and discovered to my chagrin that it contained a set of clothes identical to those worn by Holmes.

"I simply thought you would find these clothes more comfortable for our journey," said Holmes, "but as you are not inclined—"

"All right, all right, I shall wear them," I agreed, sensing that

Holmes had gone to some length to acquire the clothes and would be deeply offended if I failed to wear them. "I am sure it is the practical thing to do."

Holmes smiled. "That's the spirit, Watson. Besides, I think you shall cut quite a dashing figure as a lumberjack."

I did not share that sentiment but kept my thoughts to myself. "I am curious, Holmes. Wherever did you find these clothes? Did you buy them here?"

"No, I had Mr. Hill obtain them in St. Paul. It is always wise, I believe, to plan ahead in matters of wardrobe. Now, if you will put your clothes on, Watson, we shall be on our way."

"We are leaving immediately?"

"After breakfast. I have made arrangements for our one-eyed friend, Mr. Johnson, to pick us up in his wagon at seven o'clock sharp. He will take us to the camp."

"And you are certain this is a wise thing to do in view of LeGrande's fearsome reputation?" I asked.

"I am certain of only one thing, which is that Mr. Chalmers does not wish us to visit the Big Pine Camp, despite all of his protestations as to LeGrande's innocence. I am of the opinion that Mr. Chalmers—who, I might add, seems to have no personal acquaintances in Hinckley and no known forwarding address—was not entirely honest with you. In fact, I suspect that he knows far more than he told you and that his partner, the shy and retiring Mr. LeGrande, was involved in Mortimer's disappearance. I see no other course but to meet this LeGrande for myself. Now, hurry along, Watson. The Morrison House's excellent flapjacks await us! Oh, and do not on any account forget your revolver."

❊

Holmes's casual demeanor, which continued over breakfast, seemed to suggest that we were about to embark on a country holiday. I knew otherwise. The fact that he had made a point of mentioning my revolver underscored the true nature of our trip. We would be leaving the last traces of civilization to journey deep into the pineries, there to confront a man suspected of numerous cruel and desperate acts. I did not like our prospects and told Holmes so after breakfast as we walked to the St. Paul & Duluth depot, where One-eye Johnson was to meet us.

"I must ask again, Holmes: Is this wise? Once we are alone in the woods, anything could happen. Think of poor Mortimer."

"Do not worry, Watson. If there is trouble, I am sure we shall be able to handle it. You have your revolver in your knapsack and, as you see, I have brought along my lovely little cane"—he lifted it off the ground so that its wicked blade sprang into view—"which I will not hesitate to use. Ah, Mr. Johnson is right on time."

Johnson was indeed waiting for us behind the depot, and the redoubtable teamster greeted us warmly.

"Climb aboard, gents. If the axles don't break or Jim and George here"—a reference to his team—"don't go lame, I'll have you at Big Pine before noon."

"Splendid," said Holmes. "We are in your capable hands."

The morning was hot, dry and windy, and as we moved out from the station I could see a faint orange glow to the southwest, evidence of yet another fire burning in the parched woodlands. The first mile of the road, which led to Mrs. Robinson's, was familiar to us, and as we passed that incarnadine establishment, I could not help but wonder what new evils its mistress, not to mention the jack pine twins, might be perpetrating on the souls of men. I mentioned these thoughts to Holmes, whose only comment was: "The sins of the flesh, Watson, have never been of great interest to me. It is the devious methods of the human mind which cause all of the troubles in this world."

Within minutes, the red house and all other signs of civilization had vanished behind us as we followed the rough, winding road. For the first hour or so of our journey, the countryside proved drearily similar to that around Hinckley, with patches of cutover land alternating with mixed stands of tamarack, spruce, jack pine and other trees ignored by the loggers. The road seemed to grow rockier and narrower the farther we penetrated into the woods, and our pace was little better than that of a man walking.

Holmes used the time to chat amiably with Johnson about a variety of topics, most notably the weather.

"It has been a particularly dry and hot summer, has it not?" he asked as we bounced along behind the geldings, which Johnson handled expertly.

"That's a fact. Been so dry my horses are p---in' stones," Johnson said, emitting a vulgar laugh. "Never seen nothin' to match it."

"Has there been any rain at all?"

"A little. Last I remember was on the Fourth of July. But it didn't amount to no more'n a glass of warm spit, if you know what I mean."

"Indeed, I do," said Holmes with a grin. For the most part, I paid little heed to this idle conversation. But I did notice that Holmes now and then glanced over his shoulders and into the woods, though he gave no clue as to the reason for his actions.

At length, after passing around a range of low denuded hills, the road descended into a broad valley and we suddenly entered a remarkable new world. Here at last, in all of their grandeur, were the pineries we had come halfway around the world to see. I cannot begin to describe the majesty of this ancient forest. The gigantic trees, some towering well over a hundred feet into the heavens, grew in great dense clumps, their huge trunks forming the columns of a natural cathedral more sublime in its way than Chartres or Amiens could ever hope to be. Overhead, the branches of these magnificent trees interlocked in a continuous canopy to form a green ceiling that blotted out the sky, and everywhere the scent of pine lingered in the air like sweet, clean perfume.

"What magnificence!" I remarked to Holmes, but his only response was to shrug his shoulders in a display of indifference to nature's wonders. Indeed, he had now, for some reason, become utterly absorbed in the rocky road beneath us, staring down at it as though looking for lost treasure.

Johnson told us that the largest pines in this grove could easily be three hundred years old, based on a count of their growth rings.

"Imagine," I remarked to Holmes, "one of these trees might have sprung from the earth the very year that the Spanish Armada sailed for England!"[3]

"Ah, Mr. Smith, your taste for the irrelevant historic detail is quite amusing," Holmes replied, his eyes still fixed on the road. "But while these trees are indeed beautiful, it is not their aesthetic value that has brought us here."

"Of course," I replied, reminded by Holmes's comment that I must not lose sight of our role as inquiring journalists.

Holmes turned his attention to Johnson. "Is this stand of pine typical of those owned by Mr. LeGrande and his partner, Mr. Chalmers?"

"Wouldn't know," Johnson replied. "Not my business. But Mr. LeGrande will fill you in soon enough. We're only a couple of miles from camp."

As the road swung around a pine-studded ridge, a superb vista appeared, for in the distance we could see a long, narrow lake fringed with tall trees. The water was a deep, glittering blue, and from our vantage point amid the heat and dust of the road this body of water had the marvelous appearance of a mirage.

"Big Pine Lake," Johnson announced.

"Ah," said Holmes, looking up from the road and showing an interest in the scenery for the first time. "I have heard that many logs are rafted at this lake and sent on their way down river to the mills."

"That they are," Johnson agreed. "'Tis an easy enough trip down the Big Pine River, into the Kettle and then the St. Croix."

"And Mr. LeGrande's camp, I take it, is near the lake?"

"Right up on the north end. We'll be there soon enough."

Half an hour later, we reached the south end of lake and came to a fork in the road. One fork veered toward the north and the other followed a steep hill down to the lake. Johnson turned his team to follow the north fork, but Holmes—to my bafflement and

Johnson's evident displeasure—reached over and pulled at the reins, bringing the team to a stop.

"My apologies, Mr. Johnson," he said, "but I should be most interested in taking a closer look at the lake. If I am to write a story about the logging industry here, I naturally must examine the means by which the logs are shipped. If you would be so kind, please drive us down to the lake."

"We should be gettin' to the camp," Johnson said, showing a trace of nervousness for the first time. "Mr. LeGrande, I'm sure, is waitin' for us."

"Then we shall not stay long at the lake," Holmes said, his tone leaving no doubt that he would not be denied.

"All right, you're the boss," Johnson said reluctantly and swung the wagon back around.

It took but a few minutes to reach the lake, where the road ended in a wide clearing around a white sand beach. There was evidence here of previous logging operations in the form of pieces of waste wood, rusted tools, empty cans of chewing tobacco and other items apparently thrown away by the local lumberjacks.

Holmes got down from the wagon at once and walked toward the water. I followed and watched with curiosity as Holmes bent down, scooped up a handful of water and splashed it over his face. I did so as well and found the water to be very cold.

"How invigorating," said Holmes, turning to Johnson. "Even in this terrible heat, the water feels exceedingly chilly. The lake must be quite deep."

"Wouldn't know," replied Johnson, who seemed anxious to avoid the water, even though he was sweating profusely in the heat.

"No doubt it is spring-fed," said Holmes, walking back toward Johnson. "I imagine many a poor jack has drowned in these frigid waters. And a lake such as this, being so cold and deep, would never give up its dead, would it?"

"Wouldn't know," Johnson repeated in what was becoming his standard reply. "Like I said before, we really should be gettin' to camp, Mr. Baker. I don't want to get Mr. LeGrande riled up if I can help it."

"By all means, let us be on our way," Holmes said amiably and started walking back toward the wagon. But an instant later, he spun around as though seized by an impulsive thought, and took a last look at the cold, dark waters of the lake.

"You know, Mr. Johnson, I was just thinking about something I heard in Hinckley," he said, his back turned to the teamster. "Do you recall the case of that poor fellow who disappeared in this area recently—ah, what was his name?—oh yes, I remember, Mortimer. Well, what if this Mortimer, who apparently became lost in the woods, found his way to this lake and went for a swim to cool himself off? And what if the brisk water proved too much for him? Do you suppose he could have drowned here?"

"Wouldn't know," came the familiar reply.

Holmes, the corners of his mouth now crinkled into the slightest of smiles, turned around to face Johnson once again. He spoke casually, as though his words were hardly of importance. "I only ask, Mr. Johnson, because there is something remote and haunted about this place, don't you think? In fact, I recall reading somewhere that the local Indians—the Ojibway, I think they are called—believe this lake to be inhabited by evil spirits.[4] What do you say to that?"

"I ain't got nothin' to say about that," Johnson replied contemptuously. "Now, are we goin' to the Big Pine Camp or are we goin' to sit here and jaw all day?"

Holmes's smile broadened. "By all means, Mr. Johnson, let us move on. And since the camp is so close, Mr. Smith and I will perhaps take a little exercise by walking the rest of the way, if you don't mind."

"Suit yourself," said Johnson, climbing back up on the wagon and setting his team into motion. "It's a free country."

❋

As we walked behind the wagon, I took the opportunity—since Johnson could not hear us—to ask Holmes why he had been so insistent upon stopping at the lake. "Do you really believe poor Mortimer drowned there?"

"It is a distinct possibility, Watson."

"Why? Was it something Johnson said or did?"

"No, it was something he—how shall I put it?—misplaced. This, to be specific." I now saw that Holmes had, cupped in his hand, Johnson's lighter.

"I do not understand, Holmes. What is the connection between the lighter and the lake?"

"It is quite simple, Watson. After relieving Mr. Johnson of his lighter, I naturally examined it with my magnifying glass. This showed the unmistakable presence of water stains upon the lighter. Now a good lighter is a thing a man does not normally get wet. In fact, he will take pains to keep it perfectly dry. Yet this particular lighter, it is clear, was at some point immersed in water. How do you suppose that happened?"

"Perhaps Mr. Mortimer, if it indeed was his, or Mr. Johnson dropped it into a puddle."

"Perhaps. Yet as Mr. Johnson himself told us earlier, there has been no rain here in some time, and hence no puddles. But there is another possibility. Perhaps the lighter fell from Mr. Mortimer's body, or was taken from it, as he was being dumped into the lake."

"Perhaps, but I must say that the mere fact that the lighter shows evidence of having been wet hardly proves your theory."

"You are correct, Watson. It is not proof. However, also consider this: Our one-eyed friend is rather more afraid of the water than he ought to be. You saw how nervous he appeared at the lake. There is one other item of evidence as well. It is based on something I noticed at the beach."

"I saw nothing," I said.

"That is because, my friend, you were too busy looking at the scenery," said Holmes, who was putting his walking stick to good use, stabbing into the ground at almost every step. "You take pleasure in the big picture, the grand view, the distant prospect. You are a tourist, Watson, whereas I am more interested in the small and particular, for the world is never more revealing than when it is studied in intimate detail."

I had learned long ago that Holmes enjoyed nothing better than hectoring me on my lack of acumen, but in this instance I could see no particular point to the discourse and told him so:

"This is all most instructive, Holmes, but I would be far more interested in learning what you saw at the beach."

"Ah, Watson, your devotion to brevity is, as always, admirable. Very well, then, here is what I saw"—and without another word Holmes pushed down on his cane with great force, leaving behind a small round impression in the soil. "I saw two such marks in the ground as we walked down to the beach, Watson. What does that suggest to you?"

Nothing came to mind and I could only shrug in response.

Holmes shook his head, more in sadness than disgust, much as a teacher might bemoan the failure of a prized student. "Do you not remember what Mr. Hill told us about Mortimer? As I recall, his exact words were: 'He had only one good leg, as I have but one eye.'"

"Of course. Now I remember. And from this fact you have deduced that Mr. Mortimer may have used a cane."

"A telegram to Mr. Hill, I am sure, will confirm the fact."

"And you therefore think the marks you saw at the beach were left by Mortimer's cane?"

"As I said, Watson, it is a possibility. Remember, Johnson himself told us that there has been no significant rain in this area for at least six weeks. That means it is entirely possible that any evidence left in the ground after Mortimer's disappearance in late July has yet to wash away."

"Still, you have no real proof that Mortimer's body lies somewhere at the bottom of the lake."

"No, and I may never have. Yet there can be no doubt that the lake is the most logical place for Mortimer's body to be."

"Why do you say that? If he did indeed meet with foul play, his body could easily have been buried anywhere in this vast wilderness with little chance of discovery."

"That is true, Watson, except for this: Why go to all the trouble of digging a deep hole in this hard, rocky soil"—Holmes pointed to the rough road at our feet—"when a deep lake is conveniently located nearby? A few chains around the body, an anchor or some other weight attached to it, and over it goes, never to be seen again."

Holmes had a point. Still, I wondered why he had not questioned Johnson more closely regarding Mortimer's fate, especially in view of the teamster's obvious reluctance to approach the lake. When I put this question to Holmes, he said:

"The time is not right, Watson. We must retain our disguise as journalists if we are to secure any useful information at the Big Pine Camp. Too many probing questions at this point would make Mr. Johnson unduly suspicious of our intentions. But rest assured, Watson, the day is not far away when I shall have a great many questions for One-eye Johnson."

As Holmes spoke, Johnson—who had remained for many minutes in a silent pose atop his wagon—looked back at us, and for a moment I thought he had overheard our conversation.

But my fears were quickly proved wrong by the teamster's words: "Look up ahead, gents. There she is—the Big Pine Camp in all her glory."

Chapter Eleven

"I Smell the Blood of an Englishman"

✳

The "glories" of the Big Pine Camp, we soon discovered, were not easy to discern. Set in a large clearing amid ragged stands of small trees, the camp offered little in the way of picturesque effects to redeem its essential bleakness, and it reminded me of nothing so much as a dreary little factory town.

The camp's dozen or so buildings, uniformly constructed of heavy logs, were arranged haphazardly along a central "avenue," and all were similar—long and low, with pitched roofs, few windows, and no sign of paint or any other adornment that might have improved their grimly functional appearance. Tall, scraggly weeds grew with abandon around these rough and forlorn structures, while the ground itself was littered with rusted chains, ax heads, saw blades and other discarded implements.

"This place does not bring to mind the finer neighborhoods of

London," Holmes remarked dryly as we followed Johnson to a small, square building near the center of the camp.

"Well, here's the wanigan," said Johnson, who jumped down from his wagon seat and went to the building's door.[1] "I'll tell Mr. LeGrande you're here." He pushed open the door, which required considerable effort on his part, and went inside.

"The camp appears quite deserted," I said to Holmes, for we had yet to see anyone other than ourselves and Johnson.

"So it would seem," agreed Holmes, whose face betrayed unmistakable signs of worry. His eyes—those great instruments of investigation—darted back and forth, as though searching the camp for its most minute secrets.

I was about to ask him whether anything was wrong when Johnson reappeared and climbed back onto the wagon. "Nobody here, I guess," he said. "Mr. LeGrande and the boys must be out workin'. If you gents'll wait here, I'll go fetch 'em."

Before we could reply, Johnson cracked his whip and went galloping off in the direction from which we had come.

We now had the camp to ourselves, a situation I found rather disconcerting. The day was deathly still, with the usual pall of wood smoke and not enough of a breeze to rustle even the tallest pine. It seemed as though the smoke had choked the very voices from the birds, for the silence was so pronounced that I could hear myself breathe. In this hushed atmosphere, I felt—more acutely than ever before—that peculiar sense of emptiness which must, from time to time, accost all travelers in the wilderness. London now seemed not merely half a world away but on some other planet, and I began to wish fervently that Mr. J. G. Pyle had never appeared at our flat in Baker Street. At the same time, I experienced a powerful sense of foreboding, occasioned not only by our distance from the usual intercourse of civilization but also by the eerie silence which enveloped us.

Nonetheless, I was surprised when Holmes suddenly grabbed my arm and said: "We are in grave danger, Watson. Ask no questions and follow me at once!"

He turned and, without another word, sprinted toward a line of trees to our right. I had learned long ago that Holmes could sense danger the way a good hound sniffed game, and I thus obeyed his command without hesitation. As I turned to follow him, I glimpsed several men—all dressed like lumberjacks—emerging from behind the "wanigan," as Johnson had called it.

"Get them," a voice said, and I began to run for my life.

✵

Holmes, whose long stride gave him the graceful speed of a gazelle, reached the woods well ahead of me, then stopped to urge me on. "Run, run as fast as you can," he shouted as I reached the trees and plunged into the forest.

I was aware of the sound of heavy boot steps behind me, but I dared not pause to look back. Instead, I put my energies into keeping up with Holmes, who had once again moved ahead. The forest in which we found ourselves was gloomy in the extreme, calling to mind the haunted woodlands of myth and legend. Blue smoke hung everywhere, floating among the treetops or settling like fog in the numerous swales, and as I followed Holmes I had the sensation of moving through a ghostly dreamland filled with the tangled skeletons of trees.

The rough terrain impeded our progress, as did the denseness of the forest itself. Although the pines had been logged away, smaller trees with sharp, low branches grew in abundance, often in such tight stands that it did not seem possible to find a way through them. Heavy underbrush also slowed our momentum, and it was not long before I felt myself growing faint from exertion.

"We must slow down, Holmes," I gasped, using my last ounce of energy to pull up beside him. "I cannot go much farther."

Holmes, with a glance to our rear, slowed to a walk and said: "All right, but we must keep moving. We have lost them for the moment but they cannot be far behind."

"Who are they?" I asked, trying to catch my breath.

"Killers, Watson. I should have listened to you. I have led us into a trap."

"But I do not—"

"Quiet," Holmes whispered, touching my shoulder and peering into the woods. "Do you hear them?"

I listened. Voices! Not far behind us.

"They are coming," said Holmes grimly. "Two men at least, possibly more. Quick, your revolver."

I grabbed my weapon from the knapsack and scanned the forest. But I still could see nothing.

"Come, we must take cover," said Holmes.

On a small hill in front of us stood a large pile of brush. We rushed toward it, but as I reached this line of defense my foot struck a gopher hole or some similar depression, and I fell to the ground, turning my ankle. The revolver slipped from my hand and tumbled into the brush pile. I let out an involuntary cry of pain and found myself momentarily unable to move. Even worse, I discovered that my revolver had dropped so far into the brush that I could no longer see it.

"My revolver! It is gone!"

"There is no time to look for it," said Holmes, helping me to my feet. "We must find shelter."

With one hand upon Holmes's shoulder, I limped around to the back of the brush pile. And there, like trapped animals, we awaited our fate.

"Are you all right?" Holmes whispered.

"It is at worst a sprain. But I am afraid I shall not be able to walk for a while."

"Then we shall have to stay here and fight," said Holmes, his sharp-bladed cane already prepared for action.

Crouched behind our fortress of brush, we waited for the inevitable attack to come. I do not know what Holmes was thinking, but I experienced in that desperate moment a peculiar sense of dread. It was not fear of death which gripped me, for I had been at the threshold of that dark door so many times in Afghanistan that it held no terror for me. What I felt rather was a gnawing sense of waste. Was the career of the world's greatest detective, a man who had foiled the most brilliant criminal minds of Europe, to end here, in this stunted woodland, at the hands of a few rustic thugs? It seemed a thing too absurd to contemplate, and yet the reality of it could not be denied.

And then I saw them—four men emerging out of the smoke. Spread out in line like military skirmishers, they walked slowly toward us, searching for their prey. They were dressed in plain cotton shirts, dark pants held up with suspenders, wide-brimmed black hats and heavy boots. All four were of tremendous size, but one was a giant who towered above the others.

This gargantuan figure might have been a biblical prophet were it not for his attire. He was easily six and a half feet tall, and I had never seen a more massive or menacing presence. Pausing for a moment, he removed his shirt and wrapped it around his waist, as though anxious to display his powerful physique. His bulging biceps were the size of an average man's thighs and an iron web of muscles rippled across his huge chest.

But it was his large, red face that inspired a kind of awe. All of its features—the broad nose, the long cruel mouth, the brutish eyes—were coarse and curiously flat, as if compressed by some terrible force. The result was a face that looked as blunt and blank as the business end of a club. A bushy red beard and long red hair unacquainted with the discipline of the comb added a final daunting touch to the man's feral demeanor.

"LeGrande," Holmes whispered. "I should have known."

The attire and physical prowess of all four men readily identified them as lumberjacks. Their appearance was made even more frightening by the long sticks they carried. These curious instruments were equipped at one end with a hook and a spike, either of which would undoubtedly be deadly in mortal combat.

"I heard 'em," one of the men now said. "They're here all right. I smell 'em."

"What do they smell like?" asked LeGrande, who was obviously the captain of this crew of cutthroats.

"English trash," came the response.

LeGrande laughed derisively. "Garbage does make an awful stink, don't it. All right, where are you, gents? You wouldn't be hiding, would you? We just want to have a little talk, so don't you be no jill-pokers.[2] Why, Jake, I believe our English friends are a trifle shy. They don't want to show themselves."

"Now, ain't that something," said the man named Jake, glancing in our direction. Suddenly, he stopped dead in his tracks. We had been discovered!

"Hey, Cat, look over there," he shouted, pointing toward us.

"I see 'em," said LeGrande, his face distorted by a malevolent grin. Then came a moment I shall never forget, for LeGrande began singing the words of the old nursery rhyme: "Fee, fie, foe, fum, I smell the blood of an Englishman."

Having no other weapon, I picked up a large rock at my feet, all the while cursing that I had lost my revolver. Holmes, meanwhile, maintained a look of the deadliest resolve, and I knew that the snarling men approaching us would soon find themselves in the fight of their lives.

"Holmes," I said, "if this is the end, I only want to say that you are the finest man I have ever known and the best friend any man ever had."

"My dear Watson," came the warm reply, "I will ever think the same of you. But the end is not here yet, I assure you."

And so we stood together, prepared to face what I could not help but think would be our final battle with the forces of evil. Brandishing their cruel sticks, the assassins let out bloodcurdling yells and rushed toward us.

What happened next was quite astounding. A loud report rang out from the woods behind us and LeGrande's hat flew from his head. An instant later, Jake lost his hat in a similar fashion. Both men froze, as did their companions. Two more gunshots—for that is what they were—followed almost at once, kicking up dust at the men's feet.

I could not tell where the shots were coming from, nor could LeGrande and his men, who seemed paralyzed with fear. For a moment, we all stood in a kind of frozen tableau, and then I saw, emerging from an opening in the woods, one of the most remarkable characters that Holmes and I were ever to meet.

❋

The man who came out of the woods, rifle in hand, was perhaps sixty years of age, of medium height, with a long gray beard, hair of similar color that fell almost to his shoulders, and small, coal-black eyes—set in deeply hollowed sockets— which looked upon us with the vigilant intensity of a hawk on the hunt. This startling figure was dressed from head to foot in buckskin, and not even Natty Bumppo himself could have formed a more perfect picture of the wild and primitive woodsman.[3] The rifle he used with such skill was not the only weapon he carried, for in his belt were a pistol and a long knife. As he neared us, his rifle aimed steadily at our assailants, I realized that the man was none other than our mysterious "shadow" from Hinckley.

I was about to remark on this fact when the man began speaking in a manner so strange and forceful that it commanded everyone's attention.

"Assassins, ye had best be moving on," he shouted at the lumberjacks in a high and clear soprano voice. "Ye are standing where Boston Corbett is about to shoot. And Boston Corbett is not a man to miss his mark!"

"This ain't your business, Tom!" growled LeGrande, who obviously knew Corbett. "Besides, there's four of us and only one of you. Those ain't good odds where I come from."

"Boston Corbett can count, but all he sees before him is a

corpse by the name of Jean Baptiste LeGrande with a hole the size of a silver dollar ventilating his miserable forehead."

Our savior then leveled his rifle at LeGrande and cocked the trigger. "What do ye say to that, assassin?"

LeGrande responded by raising his stick as though ready to attack. Instantly, a bullet cut the stick in two, driving splinters into LeGrande's palm.

"Jesus," he screamed, dropping to his knees as blood flowed from his hand, "you shot me, you son of a b----."

"No, ye have only received a final warning," said Corbett. "The next shot Boston Corbett fires shall give ye a new eye, right between the two peepholes ye have now. Boston Corbett will not say it again. Ye are standing where he is about to shoot and that is a dangerous place to be. Now, run, ye assassins, or face the wrath of God as John Wilkes Booth did! Run!"

"Don't shoot," the man called Jake said nervously, dropping his stick. "I'm going." The other two men did likewise, vanishing into the forest as fast as their legs could carry them.

LeGrande, still holding his injured hand, also turned to go but not before telling Corbett: "I won't forget this, Tom. I will kill you one day as sure as the sun rises."

"Ye will die trying if ye attempt it," Corbett replied and whistled a bullet past LeGrande's head. This was sufficient to persuade the giant to depart without further protestation.

After LeGrande had disappeared into the smoke, Holmes turned to Corbett and said: "A capital performance, sir. Mr. Hill will be pleased to know that you have done your job well."

"Thank ye, Mr. Holmes," said our rescuer, whose casual mention of my friend's name amazed me. "Boston Corbett is always pleased to be of service to good British gentlemen. And ye must be Dr. Watson," he added, nodding in my direction.

It was all I could do to nod back, for I must admit that I was somewhat at a loss for words. How, I wondered, had this man Corbett managed to arrive at such a critical moment, how did he know our identities and what had led Holmes to instantly conclude that he was an employee of Hill's? And for that matter, why had he been following us ever since our arrival in Hinckley?

I put these questions to Holmes at once, and his answers came as a revelation:

"As to your first question, Watson, the answer should be obvious. Mr. Corbett arrived at such an opportune moment for the simple reason that he has been following us ever since we left Hinckley. I saw him at least twice as we rode with Mr. Johnson."

"Ye saw Boston Corbett?" said our new-found friend with an incredulous stare. "Impossible, sir, impossible! Boston Corbett moves as swiftly and invisibly as the wind itself."

Holmes smiled. "Well, then, perhaps I have made a mistake. Perhaps it was one of LeGrande's men who caught my eye."

"Undoubtedly," said Corbett.

"Be that as it may, let us consider your other questions, Watson. As you know, I first noticed this gentleman"—Holmes bowed in Corbett's direction—"shortly after we left the Eastern Minnesota station in Hinckley last Thursday, and it soon became apparent that he was following us."

"The town, alas, does not provide the cover of the forest," Corbett explained ruefully. "That is why ye had the luck to get a glimpse of Boston Corbett, though it is obvious, Mr. Holmes, that ye are a man with an unusually sharp eye."

"Thank you," said Holmes. "In any event, it occurred to me, after I was fortunate enough to notice Mr. Corbett, to ask myself how it could be that someone was following us. Two possibilities presented themselves. One was that our mission had somehow been found out, by means unknown, and that our 'shadow' was in the employ of the Red Demon or his allies. The second possibility was that the man following us had been directed to do so by the one person who most assuredly knew our business in Hinckley."

"Mr. Hill," I said.

"Precisely. And so when Mr. Corbett came to our rescue a moment ago, I naturally concluded that he was an agent of Mr. Hill's and that he therefore knew our true identities."

"Ye have spoken the truth," Corbett acknowledged. "Mr. Hill's instructions were very specific. Watch those English gents like a hawk and let them come to no harm, said Mr. Hill, for he feared assassins would try to do their ugly work. And there is no one who knows the way of assassins better than Boston Corbett. Just ask John Wilkes Booth!"

❃

This was the second time Corbett had invoked the name of the man who shot Abraham Lincoln.

"You seem quite interested in Mr. Booth," I said, hardly anticipating the torrent of words my idle comment would provoke.

"Booth, sir, was the devil himself, the very Antichrist predicted in the Book of Revelation," replied Corbett, fixing me with the kind of stare one might have expected from an occupant of Bedlam. "Assassins deserve no quarter and Boston Corbett shot down John Wilkes Booth like the low, mangy dog he was. But did Boston Corbett receive the gratitude he deserved? Did the nation say 'Thank you' and shower its rewards upon him? No, sir! No, sir! Boston Corbett was thrown to the wolves and now ye see him, a poor old man with nary a roof over his head nor a dollar to his name. Where is the justice in that, sir?"[4]

I had no idea how to respond to this fantastic outburst, but Holmes—who took perverse pleasure in the more extreme examples of human character—seemed to enjoy the speech immensely.

"Justice, my friend, is indeed a rare and precious commodity," he said with a broad smile, "and at the proper time I should like to hear your story, which I am sure is not without many elements of interest. But first, sir, a question. How well do you know the men who accosted us?"

"Well enough," said Corbett as he picked up the pointed stick one of them had left behind and gave it to Holmes. "Jake O'Connell, Johnny Dokes and Matty Swenson are as fine as trio of scoundrels as ye could ever hope to find. Of course, they all work for LeGrande, who is the big man in this neck of the woods. Ye can also tell from that"—he pointed at the stick in Holmes's hand—"that they are all jacks, though of the lowest kind."

Holmes inspected the long stick, whose use I could only imagine, and said: "I believe this rather lethal-looking instrument is what is known as a peavey and is employed to move and sort logs during river drives."[5]

"That is so, Mr. Holmes. All the jacks hereabouts have one. As ye can see, it is a mean thing if used to ill purpose."

"Indeed," said Holmes, handing me the peavey, "though I think Watson may find it useful as a walking stick. In any case, I think it wise for us to be on our way as quickly as possible."

Corbett agreed, saying our assailants might work up the courage to return. "They are a bold bunch of ruffians," he said, "especially that blackguard LeGrande. Boston Corbett would not put it past them to make another attempt upon our persons."

"Let them try it!" I said, brandishing my revolver, which I had recovered from the brush pile. "I will be ready for them."

"Watson, you are quite the English bulldog," Holmes said with a laugh, "but Mr. Corbett is right. There is no point in staying here any longer. I am concerned about your ankle, however. Are you up to walking?"

"I think so," I replied, for my ankle, while slightly swollen, was not as seriously injured as I had first thought. With a little practice—and the help of the peavey—I was able to put weight upon it quite readily.

"Splendid," said Holmes. "Let us leave this dreary woodland before any additional misfortune befalls us."

And so, with Corbett in the vanguard, we began our long walk out of the woods. Since Corbett's eyesight seemed as keen as Holmes's, I had little fear that LeGrande and his men would be able to approach us unseen. Nonetheless, Corbett led us on a meandering course, stopping at regular intervals to survey the woods so as to avoid any possibility of ambush.

As we trudged along, I gradually learned more details of how

Corbett had come to rescue us. Secreting himself near our hotel, where he maintained a constant vigil, he watched as we met Johnson and then followed us on foot. It was a measure of his physical endurance that, despite a fast hike of several miles to reach the camp, he showed no sign of weariness. In fact, he moved so swiftly through the forest that even Holmes had difficulty staying with him, while I—sore of foot and as often as not breathless—could only do my best to keep pace.

More details of Corbett's own remarkable life also emerged. He described his service with a New York cavalry regiment in the War Between the States, his capture and subsequent imprisonment by the Confederates, his return to the Union army, and finally his role in shooting down the assassin Booth.

After this, however, his story grew confusing. He seemed to believe that all manner of plots had been directed against him after the killing of Booth, for reasons difficult to fathom. He mentioned an episode in Kansas—involving, as I recall, gunfire in the legislative chamber—and claimed to have been imprisoned by scheming enemies. Following what he described as a "miraculous escape," he came north to Minnesota, where he now made his living as a hunter for various logging companies.[6]

"And that is how Boston Corbett has come to see the evil that lurks in these woods," he concluded in that queer, high voice that made him sound almost like a child.[7]

Holmes, who had listened rather impatiently to Corbett's autobiographical narrative, seized upon the chance to change the subject. "I should be very interested to hear more about this 'evil' that you speak of, Mr. Corbett. What have you seen of the logging practices here that leads you to such a severe judgment?"

So began an animated conversation between Holmes and Corbett that was quite indecipherable. Strange terms—"Michigan jumper," "go-devil," and "robber's stick" are among the few I can recall—flew back and forth so rapidly that I might as well have been listening to a learned discussion in Swahili.[8]

Holmes, of course, had always been fascinated by the argot of the criminal classes, and on those many occasions when he donned a disguise to mix with the lower elements of London, his ability to speak the vulgar tongue proved most useful. But the language he used now, which I assumed to be a sort of lumberjack patois, was one never heard in London, and I could only suppose he had acquired command of this curious lexicon during his long days of study aboard the *Lucania*.

It was only when we finally reached the outskirts of Hinckley, after nearly four grueling hours in the woods, that Holmes reverted to more standard English.

"Well, Watson, we have made it," he said as the St. Paul & Duluth depot came into view, "and we have Mr. Corbett to thank for our good fortune."

Corbett's modest reply was typical of the man. "Boston Corbett was only doing his job and is pleased that he was able to assist ye gentlemen. But now he must be moving along, for it is best if he keeps to the woods. The assassins will not be bothering ye again today, but ye would be advised to keep a sharp eye out. God be with ye!"

And with this final salutation, Corbett—his rifle slung over his shoulder—turned back into the woods like a soldier marching off to battle.

"And God be with you," said Holmes.

Chapter Twelve

"I Cannot Discern the Dark Heart of the Matter"

※

Upon our return to the Morrison House, I secured a tub of the coldest water I could find and soaked my sore feet and ankle. Holmes, however, enjoyed no such rest. Instead, he fell into one of his dark reveries, smoking bowl after bowl of tobacco and all the while muttering to himself about his inexcusable stupidity.

"Really, Holmes," I said after this performance had gone on for some minutes, "you are too hard on yourself. You could not have guessed that LeGrande and his men would be so bold."

"Guessing is not my business," he replied sternly. "Knowing is my business, Watson, and today I failed miserably in that regard. The trap was set and I walked blithely into it."

"But that is not so. It was your quick action, after all, that permitted us to escape the camp. How did you know, by the way, that something was amiss?"

Holmes waved his hand as though the matter was hardly worth discussion. "The signs were obvious, or at least should have been to me. The camp, as you yourself noted, was deserted, with rusted equipment lying everywhere. Equally important, not a puff of smoke could be seen coming from any chimney. Had the camp been in operation, as Mr. Chalmers suggested to you, there would at the least have been a cooking stove at work. Remember, it was late in the morning when we arrived. But the surest sign of trouble came when One-eye Johnson took us to the wanigan."

"Why was that so suspicious?"

"First, because he had such difficulty opening the door, which should have served as warning sign to me but did not. Then, when he came out, I noticed a clump of cobwebs on his chest and neck. This could suggest but one thing: that the wanigan, with its balky door and its extensive population of spiders, had not been opened in a very long time. Ergo, the camp could not be in operation, as Mr. Johnson had represented to us. From this I immediately deduced that we had been lured to the camp for some sinister purpose, a fact which became even more obvious when Mr. Johnson departed with such unseemly speed. And that explains why I determined that we must make a run for it, since I had no doubt that we would be badly outnumbered."

"Are you certain that LeGrande and his thugs intended to murder us? Perhaps they simply wished to give us a fright."

Homes responded with a bitter laugh and said: "Mr. LeGrande does not strike me as the sort of man who would appreciate the subtleties of a good scare. No, Watson, I imagine that, if LeGrande had had his way, you and those painfully sore feet of yours would now be resting comfortably at the bottom of Big Pine Lake. And I would undoubtedly be right beside you!"

Though Holmes uttered these words matter-of-factly, I could not help but feel a chill as I thought about our narrow escape. "We owe much to Mr. Corbett. What an amazing character! Do you suppose he will continue to watch over us?"

"Mr. Corbett and I have come to an agreement in that regard.

If we need him, he will be available. Incidentally, Mr. Corbett's skill with a rifle is hardly his only virtue. For, despite his eccentricities, he is well posted on the logging industry here. During our hike this afternoon, he told me much about LeGrande's operation. It appears, Watson, that LeGrande is an even bolder villain than we had suspected. His activities, Mr. Corbett believes, encompass all manner of woodland larceny, from the alteration of bark marks—which are the means by which timber companies identify their logs—to outright trespass, not to mention deceptive scaling practices."

"What is scaling?" I asked, for the term—like so many Holmes and Corbett had used—was unfamiliar to me.

"It is a way of ascertaining the number of board feet of lumber in a log. As you might imagine, Watson, accurate scaling is vital to the logging industry, for it ultimately determines how much money the lumberman will receive for his work."

"And LeGrande has found a way to cheat?"

"So it would appear."

"What about Mr. Chalmers? Is he a party to this thievery as well?"

"Of course," said Holmes impatiently. "It was he, after all, who so skillfully lured us into LeGrande's trap."

"But he told us not to go to the camp," I protested.

"Yes, but he knew that such a warning would only whet my appetite to see the camp. It was all very cleverly done, Watson, and I proved to be an easy mark."

Holmes seemed so despondent over the matter that I tried to cheer him up. "Well, it is over and done with and there is no point in worrying about it now. Besides, I am more interested in what our next course of action should be. I assume you will report the attempt upon our lives to the proper authorities?"

Holmes, who had continued his relentless pacing during our entire conversation, came to a stop, his back to me. "Why do you assume that?" he asked, staring up at the ceiling as though looking to the heavens for inspiration.

"LeGrande and his men are murderers. We cannot simply let them go scot-free!"

"And what proof of their homicidal behavior do you have?"

"I should think their attack on us would be proof enough."

"Really?" said Holmes, turning around to face me, with the look of a barrister arguing his case to the court. "If I were Mr. LeGrande, I would simply deny it. Or, I would argue that it was all a mistake, that I assumed the two English gentlemen, dressed as they were in lumberjack garb, were prowlers out to loot the vacant camp. As for Mr. Chalmers, he will deny any knowledge of the events in the woods, and there will be precious little evidence to contradict him. Besides, if we present our complaint to the authorities, there will be many questions, even court proceedings perhaps, in the course of which our real identities would almost certainly become known. And that could only make it more difficult for us to find the Red Demon. Now, what do you say, Watson? Should we call in the authorities?"

I had no good retort and admitted so to Holmes. But there was one other matter that concerned me and I did not see how Holmes, for all of his logical powers, could refute it.

"Very well, Holmes, you have made your case so far. But I would now offer another point for your consideration. Our ambush at the camp suggests that the Red Demon suspects our true purpose here. If so, our failure to report the assault would, it seems to me, only confirm his suspicions. What do you say to that?"

Holmes's response took me by surprise, for he sat down beside me and softly clapped his hands. "Bravo, Watson, that is what I say, for you have hit upon an essential truth. The Red Demon, I am now certain, knows who we are. In fact, he has been leading us along on a leash, like a pair of dumb animals."

I thought this judgment rather harsh and told Holmes so, adding: "How can you be so sure that we have been manipulated?"

"I am certain for this reason: From the moment of our arrival here, our investigation has gone forward so smoothly that our discoveries seemed almost preordained."

"I am afraid I do not understand what you mean."

Holmes sighed. "Very well, Watson, let us recall the sequence of events which nearly led to our deaths today. Then, I think, you will understand. Consider: Our investigation here begins with Mr. Best, the engineer, who suggests that local loggers could be responsible for the acts of arson. The station agent, Mr. Cain, then introduces LeGrande's name while suggesting we talk to Mr. Hay, the newspaper editor, who paints a fuller picture of the feared woodsman. LeGrande is now a suspect in our minds. Next, Mr. Thompson, the marshal, accosts us and denies any wrongdoing on LeGrande's part, but in such a way that our suspicions are further aroused. Are you following me, Watson?"

"Of course."

"Good. Next, Mrs. Robinson enters the picture, and she too leaves a none-too-subtle clue—remember the stamped piece of wood from the Big Pine Camp?—that directs our attention to LeGrande. As we leave her establishment, we encounter—not by chance, I am now convinced—Mr. Johnson, who just happens to be in LeGrande's employ and even offers us a ride to his camp. Soon thereafter, while I am conveniently away, you are approached by Mr. Chalmers, who protests his partner's innocence with such vehemence that I have no choice but to conclude that he is deliberately hiding something. And so we go off to the Big Pine Camp to be ambushed. It was all brilliantly done, Watson."

Holmes was standing near a small night table by my bed as he spoke, and he suddenly wheeled around and pounded his fist on the table with such force that one leg broke off, sending the entire piece crashing to the floor. "I am supposed to be the violin player," he said in a fearsome voice, "but it is I who have been played. And I do not like it!"

Following this uncharacteristic outburst, Holmes quickly regained control of himself and apologized for his behavior.

"I am not myself," he said, picking up the broken table leg and then going over to the door. "I see that you are tired, and I will let you take your rest. We will talk again later."

It was now six o'clock in the evening, and I was indeed weary from our day's adventures. Once Holmes had gone, I lay back on my bed and fell asleep.

✳

Moments later, or so it seemed, I felt myself being rudely jostled and opened my eyes to see Sherlock Holmes standing over me in a state of high excitement. I glanced at my watch and was surprised to see that I had been asleep for an hour.

"Up, Watson, up!" he said. His eyes gleamed feverishly. "Our ship has come in."

"What did you say?" I inquired sleepily.

"Look at this."

With some effort, I sat up and peered at the piece of paper Holmes had thrust into my hand. It was a document in his distinctive handwriting, scribbled with obvious haste.

"What is it?"

"A telegram from Mr. Hill, which I have transcribed from the Great Northern's cipher. It is what I have been waiting for, Watson. It means we are at last moving in the right direction!"

The telegram read as follows: "Received following wire this p.m.: 'Rumors here that you intend to post $10,000 reward for information regarding disappearance of Thomas Mortimer. Please advise if true as reward would greatly assist investigation here. William Thompson, city marshal, Hinckley.' I assume you are behind this, Holmes. How shall I respond? J. J. Hill."

"It would appear the marshal is extremely interested in the supposed reward," I told Holmes.

"He is more than interested, Watson. Big Billy would send such a message for only one reason: He wants the money for himself. And that means he must know what happened to Mortimer, or at the least have strong suspicions. Now, we must convince him to reveal that information as soon as possible."

"How do we accomplish that?"

"By giving the avaricious marshal a take-it-or-leave-it proposition. We must also have the money in hand, for Big Billy will undoubtedly wish to see it and count it before he tells us anything. That is why I have asked Mr. Hill to inform Thompson that the reward is genuine. I have also asked our employer to provide us with ten thousand dollars in cash by tomorrow."

"That is a great deal of money, Holmes."

"It is nothing compared to the cost of the destruction which the Red Demon is planning," said Holmes, going to the door. I remained on my bed, for I assumed Holmes planned to retire for the night. Instead, he said: "For goodness' sake, come along, Watson. This is no time to dally."

"I was not aware we were going out," I responded, somewhat miffed by Holmes's cavalier assumption that I could read his mind—an impossible task if there ever was one.

"But of course we are going out," said Holmes, ignoring my look of reproach. "It is not yet eight in the evening and we must talk with the marshal tonight at all costs."

✳

Finding Thompson required no great feat of deduction, for he was busily at work across the street from the hotel procuring his night's quota of customers for Mrs. Robinson. Holmes immediately called him over. He was a menacing figure in his black garb, and yet all of his physical strength counted for little when matched against Holmes's powerful will and superior intellect.

"I trust you are having a profitable evening, Big Billy," Holmes said in a friendly way.

"I've had better an' I've had worse," replied Thompson, who pulled up a chair and joined us on the hotel's front porch. The odor of alcohol was strong upon his breath. "Business'll pick up once the snow flies and the jacks are back in camp."

"No doubt," said Holmes.

Thompson took out a cigar, lit it, and exhaled a large puff of smoke. The smell was disagreeable, suggesting that the cigar was not of vintage quality. The marshal appeared anxious, for he drummed his fingers incessantly on his knees and seemed to take no pleasure from his cheap cigar.

Holmes, whose ability to assess a man's state of mind was unequaled, said: "Big Billy, it is apparent that you wish to speak to us regarding a matter of some significance. Please feel free to do so."

"You're a regular mind reader, ain't you," Thompson replied, permitting himself a small chuckle. "Well, the fact is, I been thinkin' about that ten-thousand-dollar reward you talked about earlier. That would be cash money, would it not?"

"Cash money," Holmes agreed. "The telegram you will receive tonight from Mr. Hill will confirm that fact."

Holmes's statement, made in the most unassuming manner possible, startled the marshal.

"How did you know—"

Holmes interrupted: "I will be perfectly honest with you, Big Billy. Mr. Smith and I are not merely visiting journalists, as we told you. We are, in fact, in close alliance with Mr. Hill, who is determined to discover what happened to Thomas Mortimer. We are aware that you have been in contact with Mr. Hill regarding the reward."

"There's no crime in that," the marshal said.

"Of course not. But there could be ten thousand dollars in it for you, Big Billy, if you do as I tell you." Holmes's voice became stern and imperious. "Now, listen to me and listen well: The reward will be available here tomorrow, in cash. But be warned that Mr. Hill is not a patient man, nor will he be toyed with. If you have the information he is looking for, then this is the time to come forward. Have I made myself clear?"

Thompson took another puff of his cigar, which glowed like an ember before his face, and glanced around to make sure no one outside of our group could hear his words. Then, in a hoarse whisper, he said: "All right, I kin tell you what you want to know. But I want to see the money first."

"You'll see it," said Holmes, "when we meet tomorrow."

Thompson's brow furrowed, as though he were deep in thought. The look did not become him. "I was thinkin', Mr. Baker or whoever you may be, that ten thousand is a lot of money, but it'd only get a man so far. Considerin' what's at stake, and how hot Mr. Hill is to find out about Mortimer, it might be that fifteen thousand is what a man would need to start a new life somewheres, if you get my drift."

Holmes responded to this brazen display of cupidity with a sardonic laugh. "Greed does not become you, Big Billy. Ten thousand dollars is the amount being offered, no more."

"Well, it ain't enough. Fifteen thousand is what I need."

"Then, I am afraid you shall remain a poor man," Holmes said, abruptly rising from his chair. "Have a pleasant evening, Big Billy, and give my regards to Mrs. Robinson."

"Wait!" Thompson shouted as Holmes turned to enter the hotel. "You just wait a minute! All right. Ten thousand it is. When do I see the money?"

"You seem in a terrible hurry, Big Billy," Holmes remarked. "Are you afraid of something?"

Thompson glanced around again, as though suspecting the night had clandestine eyes, and pulled Holmes back to his chair. "I fear no man, Mr. Baker. But the sooner this is over an' done with, the better off it'll be for everybody."

"All right, let us do business as quickly as possible. But if you try to cross me, Big Billy, it will go hard on you."

"Don't you worry none. You just have the money, and you'll get what you want."

"Very well, it is settled. The money will be available by tomorrow evening. Where shall we meet?"

"There's a gravel pit in the woods near the Eastern Minnesota tracks just north of the Grindstone River at the edge of town. No one goes there after dark. Be there at midnight tomorrow, with the money, an' we kin do our business. An' don't bring along no one except your friend," he added, looking at me.

"Why such a late hour?" Holmes asked.

"I'm workin' at Mother Mary's tomorrow night an' I don't want to raise no suspicions by leavin' early."

"All right, Big Billy, we shall be there."

"Good enough," said Thompson, smiling broadly, for the thought of his newfound wealth clearly pleased him. He shook Holmes's hand and mine, and turned to leave. "Well, now, you two gents have yourselves a nice evenin'. Come tomorrow night, we'll all be happy as clams."

"Let us hope so," Holmes said, but unlike Thompson, he was not smiling.

"Do you really think this is wise?" I asked Holmes after Thompson had left. "We could be walking into another ambush."

"Your fears are well taken, my friend," Holmes said with an enigmatic smile, "but sometimes the only way to find a spider is to enter his web."

❋

Holmes wanted to send yet another telegram and prevailed upon me to accompany him to the Eastern Minnesota depot. We set out at once, along a route that had by now become as familiar as a stroll to Portman Square.[1]

There were few people about at this hour—it was now after nine o'clock—for all the town's life seemed confined to the clamorous saloons that could be found on almost every block. Still, it was not an unpleasant walk. The smoke and heat of the afternoon had subsided, and the dark dome of the sky was aglitter with stars. Never in the murky atmosphere of London had I seen such a display of nature's infinite majesty, but when I remarked upon this fact to Holmes, he was unmoved.

"Our business is not with the stars," he said brusquely as we approached the depot, where a light shone in Cain's second-floor apartment. Holmes was soon knocking on the door, but there was no immediate answer.

"Perhaps he has gone out for the evening," I suggested.

"Perhaps," Holmes said, pounding at the door again, "but that would be most inconvenient. We must send a telegram immediately. How much easier it would be if this cursed town had telephone service!"[2]

Holmes drew back his hand to knock yet a third time when a voice from within said: "Hold your horses, d--n it! I'm coming."

But when the door at last flung open, it was not Benjamin Cain who greeted us at the threshold.

"Gentlemen," said Angus Hay, "what a pleasant surprise, though I must say it's a bit late to be out pounding on doors. Is there something I can do for you?"

"Ah, Mr. Hay, what a delight to see you again," replied Holmes in his smoothest manner, giving no hint that he had been caught off guard by the newspaperman's unexpected appearance at the door. "In truth, we were looking for Mr. Cain. Is he in at the moment?"

"Afraid not, but he should be back shortly. He went out to deliver a telegram."

"I see. Well then, Mr. Hay, if you have no objections, we shall await his return, since I have a telegram myself that must be sent at once."

Hay grinned and said: "If that's all you need, I can help you right now, Mr. Baker. I'm what you might call Mr. Cain's evening stand-in when he's out on business. Learned telegraphy years ago. It's a useful skill in my line of business."

"Indeed it must be," said Holmes, returning Hay's smile. "Do you have occasion to practice your skill often?"

"Often enough. Mr. Cain and I like to play cards in the evening and I help him out whenever I can."

We now heard footsteps in the darkness, and Holmes spun around to see who was coming. A moment later Benjamin Cain emerged into view.

"Why, Mr. Baker, you're just the man I've been looking for," he said. "I have a telegram for you that's marked 'urgent.' "

"Ah, Mr. Cain, your timing is superb," said Holmes, greeting the station agent with a handshake. "As it so happens, I have an important telegram of my own to send. Your friend Mr. Hay was about to accommodate us but if you would be so kind . . . ?"

"Certainly," said Cain, who then turned to Hay and said: "I'll be up in a moment. And don't go looking at my cards the way you usually do."

Hay laughed. "Can you believe it? My friend here accuses me of cheating at cards. Why, the thought would never cross my mind. In any event, have a good evening, gentlemen."

"And you as well," said Holmes as Hay climbed back up the stairs to Cain's living quarters.

Cain now escorted us into the station office, lighted a pair of kerosene lamps, and handed the telegram to Holmes. "It came in about half an hour ago."

Holmes perused the wire without comment and later translated it for me. It read: "Funds you requested available tomorrow after 3 p.m. at First State Bank of Hinckley. Trust you will put them to good use. Latest reports indicate fire danger in pineries growing more grave by the hour. Please inform me of your progress and intentions at once. J. J. Hill."

Holmes stood by Cain's desk and stared out the office window into the darkness. His normally impassive face betrayed a hint of agitation, but he gave no clue of this when he spoke:

"Thank you for the telegram, Mr. Cain. Now, I should like to send a response. Do you have a pencil and pad handy?"

Cain took a seat at his desk and located the writing materials, which he handed to Holmes. With hardly a pause to think, Holmes rapidly penned a message. To the uninformed eye, it was complete gibberish, for it was written in the same code used for the message we had received from Hill.

"Send this at once," Holmes said.

"Yes, sir. Is that all?"

"That is all," said Holmes, after paying for the telegram. "And now, Mr. Cain, we shall not take any more of your valuable time. Thank you for your help. Good night."

"Good night, gentlemen."

As we walked back to the hotel, Holmes declined to reveal the contents of his message to Hill, other than to say he hoped the telegram might "help resolve one of the great mysteries of this case. But let us not talk of it anymore, for at the moment I find myself quite famished. The Morrison House's excellent kitchen is open until ten, I believe, and if we hurry, we shall have time for something to eat before bed."

❈

Although the Morrison House's larder proved less amply stocked than Holmes might have liked, we were able to obtain ham sandwiches and beer. After ordering a second glass of beer and lighting his pipe, Holmes sat back in his chair, gave out a deep sigh, and then began a most remarkable discussion of the strange business that had brought us to Hinckley.

As we were the only diners at this late hour, Holmes had no fear of being overheard, and so he spoke with unusual directness. It was a conversation I shall never forget. Holmes's gaunt face, caught in the flickering glow of the room's kerosene lamps, was a study in chiaroscuro, and the effect was almost diabolical. His words were equally eerie and ominous.

"This is a most singular case," he began, gazing out into the black tide of darkness that now held sway outside the room's two large windows. "It is all silhouettes seen through a gauzy screen, forms and shadows whose movements are at once visible and yet indistinct. I believe I know who the actors are and how the drama has played out thus far. I see them, Watson, these shadowy figures, strutting behind their accursed screen, moving in and out of view. I hear the awful clanking of the stage machinery all around. I perceive the filaments that bind them together in their evil conspiracy. And yet, for the life of me, Watson, I cannot discern the dark heart of the matter, the thing that has set all of these shadows in motion."

This was an extraordinary speech, and I felt a sudden chill despite the warmth of the room. Yet it was not clear to me what Holmes meant, though it almost sounded as if he were talking about ghosts. This made his comments seem especially provocative, for Holmes was among the least superstitious of men.

"I'm afraid I do not quite understand the point you are driving at," I said. "Are you suggesting there is some supernatural element to this affair?"

"Supernatural?" he replied with a great show of incredulity. "Bah! There is nothing otherworldly about this business, Watson. If anything, it is too much of this world, for at bottom, I fear, it is a case steeped in old and angry blood."

"You have lost me," I admitted.

"Perhaps that is because I am also lost, my dear Watson."

"What do you mean?"

Holmes sighed again, as though feeling the weight of some vast burden, and leaned his elbows upon the table, his chin resting in his hands. He said: "A crime, Watson, is a thing of nature. Like the trees that surround us, it is generated by a seed. That seed, or motive, may be avarice or revenge or lust or despair or one of a hundred other things. But no matter what the crime, no matter how minor or how terrible it may be, there is always this motive seed which generates all that follows. The form of the crime itself will often point back to the seed. If, for example, you discover a very rich man who has been murdered and whose safe has been broken into, then you may assume that greed was the motive, although you must not rule out other possibilities as the evidence unfolds. Do you follow me?"

"Certainly."

"But in this case, Watson, what is the seed? What is driving the Red Demon? Money? He has not asked for any. Revenge? No injury to him is stated or known. Power? Threats will not drive Mr. Hill from his position of command. Ideology? Despite your fondness for anarchistic plots, Watson, there is no concrete evidence to suggest that the Red Demon is driven by some social or political dogma. So you see my problem. This is a case with a large hole in the middle of it, and until we fill that vacancy, we shall not be able to stop the Red Demon."

"But what of Mr. Thompson's efforts to obtain the reward? Does that not indicate greed may be at the root of this matter?"

Holmes shook his head. "The good marshal is at best a minor player in this affair."

"Why are you so certain of that?"

"Because, my dear Watson, there is, behind all that is happening here, an intellect of tremendous subtlety, and I hardly think Mr. Thompson qualifies in that respect. Yet the Red Demon, whoever he may be, is also caught in the grip of some profound passion. That is a dangerous and unstable combination, Watson, and that is why I fear great peril awaits us. The Red Demon has struck at us once already, and I see no reason why he will not strike again if the opportunity presents itself."

"Do you have any clue as to who the Red Demon might be?"

"I have suspicions," Holmes acknowledged. "But I have no proof. The Demon has been extremely clever from the beginning."

"But it seems to me that we have him now, for the marshal must know the Demon's identity."

"Perhaps. Yet Big Billy is hardly a man to be relied on. He may, in fact, know much less than he claims to, and I should not put too much confidence in the value of his information. Still, we must find out all that we can from him."

"Well, let us hope all goes well tomorrow," I said, trying to stifle a yawn. "In the meantime, I am afraid I must go to bed. It has been a long and trying day."

"Ah, I envy you, Watson. You are a man of regular habits, and I have never known you to let the cares and troubles of the moment interfere with a good night's sleep. Very well, my friend, enjoy your rest," said Holmes, standing up and depositing two dollars upon the table for our meals. "I shall occupy myself with other matters while you dream your sweet dreams."

Chapter Thirteen

"I Have Been a Fool!"

✳

The next morning dawned as had all the others in Hinckley, with a pale red sun rising above the smoky horizon and a dry heat torturing the air. I made my toilette and knocked upon the door of Holmes's room. There was no answer, and I went downstairs to see if he was in the dining room. He was not. I then made inquiries at the front desk.

"Mr. Baker went out real early," the clerk replied sleepily. "Looked like he was in kind of a hurry. Haven't seen him since."

Assuming that Holmes would show up in good time, I retired to the dining room, ate a light breakfast, and went for a walk. I had gone barely a block down Hinckley's main thoroughfare when I saw Holmes approaching from the north end of town. He was walking at a leisurely pace and carrying his cane.

"Good morning, Watson," he said. "You are up early!"

"Not as early as you, I see. Have you been taking in the scenic wonders of the countryside?"

Smiling, Holmes said: "My, Watson, but you are in a cheeky

mood today. No, the countryside holds little appeal. It is vacant and formless. But I have found a place worth visiting."

"You have been on business, in other words."

"That is one way to put it. I went out to the gravel pit where we are to meet Mr. Thompson. Big Billy has chosen his rendezvous site well. Although the pit is but a quarter of a mile north of town, it is a remote and gloomy place. The pit itself is sunk well below ground, with steep banks on three sides, so that a person at the bottom would be all but invisible to passersby. We shall have to be very careful, for it will be black as Hades in that pit tonight."

"Do you think he intends an ambush?"

"If you are referring to Big Billy, he is not the man I am worried about. We have little to fear from him. But we will certainly have to be on our guard, and I have already arranged to take the necessary precautions."

We had been walking back toward the hotel, but Holmes now turned east down one of Hinckley's lesser streets.

"Where are we going?" I asked.

"To look at a house."

"A house?"

"Yes. And there it is," said Holmes, after we had walked several blocks. He pointed to a small dwelling with faded white paint over its wooden shingles. This cottage, for that is what it really was, sat rather forlornly at the edge of town, thick woods crowding up behind it.

"As you can see," Holmes continued, "it is a modest and none-too-well-kept domicile, but it has the decided advantage of being rather isolated, with only one other house within half a block. It also has—and this is one of its many charms, Watson—a large patch of woods to its rear."

"And why are you so interested in this house?" I inquired with some exasperation, for I did not understand why Holmes had taken me to see this undistinguished property.

"To tell you the truth, I had thought of burglarizing it," said

Holmes nonchalantly, "since—as you know—I have some experience along those lines.[1] But there will not be time."

"Burglary? Why should you want to do that?"

Holmes responded with a shrug.

"All right," I said, "I suppose I must ask the obvious question. Whose house is it?"

"You cannot guess?"

Trying to follow Holmes's line of reasoning has never been, I must confess, one of my strong suits, for his mind worked in a way entirely different from mine. I have always favored a direct approach to matters, as subterfuge does not come naturally to me. Holmes, however, was fond of moving more obliquely, preferring—as he once put it—to "enter by the back door" rather than to announce his presence at the front. In any case, I now tried to think as he would think, and after a time it occurred to me that the house in question must belong to William Thompson.

"Excellent!" said Holmes when I had made my conclusion known to him. "It is indeed the marshal's house, and we shall return this evening to keep watch on it."

"Why?"

"Because, Watson, I should be interested to know if the marshal entertains any visitors before he meets us at the pit."

"You mean the Red Demon, perhaps?"

"Perhaps," Holmes acknowledged, "though if the Demon is half as clever as he appears to be, I do not think it likely."

※

We had little to occupy us for the rest of the day. The heat, which even Holmes remarked upon, caused us to remain in the shade of the Morrison House's porch until late afternoon, when we went to the bank to retrieve the money sent by Hill.

Although the bank was only a short walk away, the heat had grown so intense that Holmes removed his broadcloth coat and loosened his collar, informalities he would never have considered in London. My experiences in the East had inured me somewhat to boiling temperatures, but even I found the parched, choking atmosphere to be oppressive, and the three blocks to the bank seemed like three long miles.[2]

The bank's chief cashier turned out to be a short, fat man of somewhat officious temperament, and it was only after Holmes had answered a number of sharply put questions that he received the cash. The money was in one-hundred-dollar bills, and Holmes carefully counted it, much to the cashier's displeasure, before placing it in a money belt he had brought along for that purpose.

As we left the bank, located directly across from the Eastern Minnesota depot, the afternoon train from Duluth arrived and began unloading passengers. I had just stepped out in the street to observe this scene when a fine carriage came around the corner at breakneck speed and nearly struck me.

"My God, did you see that?" I said angrily. "How can anyone drive so recklessly? I shall talk with the fellow at once."

"Save your talk for another time," replied Holmes, his eyes following the carriage until it stopped in front of the depot. "At the moment, I am more interested in the carriage's occupant than its careless driver. Observe."

I watched as a tall, elegantly dressed woman emerged from the carriage. Only when she turned her face slightly did I recognize the profile.

"Why, it is Mrs. Robinson," I said.

"Indeed. Do you suppose the lady is planning a trip?"

It soon became apparent, however, that this was not her intention, for instead of entering the depot she turned and began walking up the tracks toward the front of the train.

"Where could she be going?"

"A good question," said Holmes. "Let us find out."

We crossed the street and made our way to the station platform. Mrs. Robinson, meanwhile, had gone all the way forward to the train's locomotive, where she was engaging a man in conversation. An instant later, I recognized the man and let out a spontaneous ejaculation. "Holmes—"

"Yes, Watson, I see the little scene that has got your attention. It appears they have much to talk about."

Holmes was referring to Mrs. Robinson and William Best, the man with whom she was speaking. The conversation appeared quite animated, though we could not hear their words.

Mrs. Robinson, who wore a long white dress and carried a pink parasol as a shield against the sun, looked every inch the respectable woman. Best nodded as she talked, as though agreeing with her every word. Their conversation soon concluded, however, and Mrs. Robinson began walking back down the platform. When she saw us, she hesitated briefly before regaining her usual poise.

"Good afternoon, gentlemen. Are you leaving us so soon? The jack pine twins, I am sure, will be disappointed."

"Then you may tell those estimable ladies that they have no reason to mourn," said Holmes, "for Mr. Smith and I have grown rather fond of Hinckley and intend to stay for some time."

"Ah, well then perhaps we will see each other again."

"Perhaps. By the way, was that Mr. Best, the engineer, with whom you were speaking? We had an amusing chat with him the other day. He is a rather fascinating man, don't you think?"

I looked for any sign of alarm on Mrs. Robinson's part at the mention of Best's name. But her deep violet eyes, which seemed to me as alluring and treacherous as some poisonous tropical blossom, displayed no hint of consternation. "All men are fascinating, Mr. Baker, though some"—here she gave Holmes a look so provocative and impudent that I could scarcely believe it—"are far more fascinating than others. Don't you think?"

"Indeed I do. The same, of course, might be said of women."

Mrs. Robinson made no immediate response to this riposte other than to fix a pleasant smile upon her beautiful face. Then she said: "We really must talk again, Mr. Baker. But as I have a business to attend to, I am sure you will excuse me."

As Mrs. Robinson returned to her carriage, Best sounded his whistle and the train pulled out of the station.

"I wonder what those two were discussing," I said.

"No doubt they were remarking upon the uncomfortable warmth of the weather, Watson. Speaking of which, I think we should retire to the Morrison House for a drink, for we have a long night ahead of us."

❋

"It is time," said Sherlock Holmes, peering into my room. My watch showed quarter past nine and darkness had descended on Hinckley. "Do not forget your pocket Colt."[3]

"I have it," I said, feeling the pistol's reassuring heft in my coat. "Is there anything else I need bring?"

"Only yourself," said Holmes.

I put down the newspaper I had been reading, turned off the light in my room and went out into the hallway, where Holmes—an eager glow in his eyes—was waiting. He was darkly dressed from head to toe and carried his deadly cane in one hand.

"We shall use the rear exit, I think, on the chance that prying eyes may be watching," he said. "And be so kind as to pull down the shades in your room. I wish to leave the impression that we have retired for the night."

After complying with these instructions, I followed Holmes down the hall to the hotel's rear stairway. Once outside, we quickly made our way along backstreets to Thompson's cottage. Since a few pedestrians were still about, Holmes thought it best to approach the house from the rear, where the encroaching forest provided cover.

Once we plunged into this dim and tangled woodland, the blackness of the night became absolute, and had it not been for Holmes's uncanny vision—he was as sharp and sure as a cat in the dark—we might easily have become lost.[4] As it was, Holmes navigated so perfectly that we soon reached a point directly behind

Thompson's house, which was illuminated by the wan light of a newly risen moon. From our position, we could see anyone approaching the house from either end of the street.

"All is quiet and empty," Holmes whispered, leaning against a small tree. "Now, we must simply wait and watch."

The night was hot and breathless, and the famous mosquitos of the North Woods discovered us at once. I slapped at them as best I could, but Holmes stoically endured their attacks, as though the act of swatting them might somehow compromise his dignity. Aside from the incessant buzzing of these voracious insects, the night was perfectly still, though now and then a nocturnal bird cried after its prey in the darkness.

And so we waited, for what or whom I knew not. Soon, the wind began to pick up, providing relief from the mosquitos, and as ten o'clock approached I felt myself growing sleepy. I had nearly nodded off when Holmes jabbed at my shoulder.

"Wake up," he whispered. "Someone is coming."

Startled, I nearly fell off the low branch on which I had been resting.

"Quiet!" Holmes hissed.

I looked out at the street, which had grown brighter as the moon rose higher in the sky, and saw a figure approaching the marshal's house.

There was not enough light to identify this figure, who wore a long dark coat and a wide-brimmed hat that effectively shaded the face. Nonetheless, the person's modest size made it clear that this was not the marshal himself returning home. After pausing to look up and down the street, the figure turned into the walkway leading to the house's front door. Unfortunately, our vantage point was such that we could not see this part of the house, and I heard Holmes utter an expletive.

"We must get a better view," he said. "But let us first see what our visitor intends to do."

Hardly had Holmes spoken these words when a light came on in the back of the house.

"Ah, just as I thought," said Holmes. "It appears we have run across a burglar. Now, let us see if we can find a more convenient vantage point. Come along."

The only house near Thompson's was about twenty yards to the south. A long hedge, which ran all the way to the street, formed a protective barrier between the two properties. We made our way through the woods to a point near the end of this hedge, and used it as a screen as we crept along toward the street. When we could clearly see the front of the marshal's house, Holmes signaled a stop.

"This will do," he said.

"What do you make of it?" I whispered to Holmes, wondering all the while what the occupants of the house to our rear would think if they found us crouching beneath their hedge. "Why on earth would someone be burgling the marshal's house?"

"I can think of a number of reasons, Watson. After all, the idea occurred to me, so I do not see why it might not have occurred to others as well."

"Well, I —"

Holmes put his hand over my mouth. The light in the marshal's house had gone out!

A moment later, the front door opened and a figure emerged into the darkness of the front yard. It was obviously the same person we had seen enter the house. But despite our improved vantage point, identification remained impossible because of the hat brim bent down over the face.

Walking briskly from the house, the figure turned south and came toward us along the street. I dared not peer over the hedge for fear of being discovered, and so saw nothing as the figure went by us. But I did catch the whiff of a familiar scent.

"Jicky," said Holmes with a smile. "The aroma is quite unmistakable. And unless Mrs. Robinson has a twin in Hinckley, I have no doubt that it was she whom we just saw."

"What was she doing in Big Billy's house?"

Holmes stood up and dusted off his pants legs. "I imagine she was looking for something."

"Such as?"

"I am not sure, but I suspect we shall find out soon enough. Now, however, I think it is time we went to the gravel pit."

"The gravel pit?" I pulled out my watch and squinted in the dim light to read the time. "But it is not yet ten o'clock, and the marshal said he would not be at the pit until midnight."

"It would be to our advantage to arrive on the scene as early as possible," Holmes replied. "Besides, the marshal may not be the only person we shall meet there tonight."

❈

Holmes had not exaggerated the gloomy aspect of the pit, which we reached after a walk of fifteen minutes. It was a large, saucer-like depression, ringed by scraggly trees that rattled in the wind and sighed like old bones. The tracks of the Eastern Minnesota ran a few hundred feet to the east. To the south, the low and sluggish Grindstone River formed a moat separating us from Hinckley. A single main road bridged the river, and from this thoroughfare a smaller road led to the pit.

We had avoided this road, instead following a narrow path through the woods to the south rim of the pit. And there, crouched behind a row of bushes, we waited momentarily in silence as Holmes's anxious eyes scanned the scene before us. Apparently satisfied, Holmes cupped his hands around his mouth and emitted a strange warbling sound reminiscent of a songbird's call. Instantly, the sound was repeated from somewhere within the black wall of trees across the pit. Holmes made the sound again. This was followed by two echoes from across the pit.

"He is here," Holmes said, "and all is well. It is time to make our final plans."

The noble figure of Boston Corbett now emerged from the trees. He was dressed in buckskins and a rifle was slung over his shoulder.

"I trust ye are well," he said, greeting us.

"We are. And yourself?"

"Tolerable," said Corbett as we shook hands, "though the lumbago has been bothersome of late. But Boston Corbett's eye and his faithful Avenger"—this, I gathered, was a name he sometimes used for his rifle—"are as good and true as ever."

"I am pleased to hear that," Holmes said with a wide grin, "for we may have need of all of your talents tonight, Mr. Corbett. Now, are you clear as to our plans?"

"It could not be clearer. Boston Corbett will be watching, and should assassins make their foul presence known, ye may be assured that they will regret it! Have no fears, for ye are in good hands, gentlemen."

"I have no doubt of that," said Holmes. "Then if you will kindly take your position, Mr. Corbett, we shall see what manner of adventure the night brings."

Corbett nodded, gave a military salute, and went off into the forest behind us.

"And now, Watson, we shall wait," said Holmes as we returned to our position of cover. "Keep a steady eye out and be absolutely quiet. Unless I have misjudged, I suspect that our adventures this evening will begin well before midnight."

I glanced at my watch and noted that it was nearly half past ten. The wind, from the south, had become even stronger, a surging sirocco that bent the tops of the trees and turned the forest into a cacophony of cracking, creaking, crashing, whooshing and moaning sounds. This aboreal din drowned out all else and rendered almost useless Holmes's extraordinarily acute hearing, which in normal circumstances would have enabled him to detect a distant footstep or a suspicious movement in the brush. As it was, we could hear so little beyond the roar of the wind that we received quite a start when two deer came bounding out of the woods and nearly ran us down before veering off in panic.

After this incident, Holmes—by means of hand signals—instructed me to turn around toward the woods, while he watched the pit. At quarter to eleven, I noted a faint glow to the south and wondered whether something might be burning in town. But as Holmes had insisted upon silence, I made no mention of this phenomenon, since it seemed to have no bearing on our situation. We sat, back to back, for another twenty minutes, the distant glow in the night sky growing more pronounced. Yet the woods to my immediate front were so dense and dark that even the phosphorescent hound of the Baskervilles might have proved all but invisible in such an environment.[5]

During our long watch, I made no attempt to query Holmes about who or what we were looking for, though I naturally assumed that an ambush was his overriding fear. My suspicions in this regard were soon borne out, for as I was reaching down to look again at my watch, I felt Holmes nudge my back.

"Watson, over there," he said, gesturing across the pit, where two figures had emerged from the trees. They walked cautiously, one behind the other, and both carried rifles. One was extremely large, the other much smaller. We watched as these men, whose faces I could not discern, circled around toward us, though it was obvious that they had not detected our presence.

On they came, approaching closer with every step, until the two of them were so near I thought they would surely see us. I experienced now that intense and thrilling sense of apprehension that comes to every soldier on the brink of battle. Insensible to the roaring wind, the loud swaying trees, the gorgeous moon hanging in the heavens, I saw or heard nothing except the two men coming at us out of the gloom. And though my heart beat wildly in my chest, I felt supremely prepared for whatever the next moment would bring, for I was in the company of the most fearless man it had ever been my privilege to know.

I glanced over at Holmes as he crouched behind the bushes, his lethal cane at the ready, and what I saw was at once wonderful and frightening. His long, thin hair blew about wildly, while the moonlight cast crooked shadows across his sharply etched features. He looked, I thought, magnificently untamed, and I could appreciate now, more than ever before, his own frequent observation that had he not devoted his life to solving crimes he might well have busied himself committing them. All the fierce power of his being was now concentrated upon the task at hand, his every nerve and sinew taut with anticipation, like a tiger ready to spring remorselessly upon its prey.

And spring he did, for as the two figures passed in front of us, Holmes leaped out and with a single sharp blow to the back of the head knocked the larger man off his feet and sent him sprawling into the pit. His companion, with a startled grunt, endeavored to lift his rifle, but Holmes was instantly upon him. Again, the cane came down, striking the man's right arm with a terrible cracking noise. Stunned, he let out a cry and fell to his knees, his rifle clattering to the ground, and before he could rise he found my revolver at his temple. It was only then that I recognized him as One-eye Johnson, the very man who had tried to lure us to our doom at the Big Pine Camp.

What happened next occurred with startling suddenness, yet today—nearly two years after the fact—I can still see the entire incident as clearly as ever.[6] For, as I brought my pistol to Johnson's head, I noticed that the man in the pit, whom I now recognized as the killer LeGrande, had scrambled to his feet and had somehow managed to keep possession of his rifle.

"Watson, in the pit!" Holmes shouted.

I swung around to confront this new danger. LeGrande was leveling his rifle, and there could be no doubt as to his target— Sherlock Holmes! I got LeGrande in my sights but before I could fire off a round Johnson, with a terrific lunge, pulled my legs out from under me and we began to tumble into the pit. Then I heard another, louder report, and as Johnson and I plunged down the embankment, I caught a glimpse of Holmes on the rim above, a look of astonishment on his face as he dropped to his knees. And in that awful moment, I feared that the greatest detective the world has ever known had breathed his last.

❋

But I had other matters to occupy my mind, for as I reached the bottom of the pit, the revolver flew from my hand. Johnson, meanwhile, had rolled to a stop a few feet away. Badly bruised and somewhat dazed, I was nonetheless able to regain my feet, only to be confronted with a chilling sight. For Johnson, too, was on his feet, blood flowing like black syrup from a gash above his good eye, and my gun in his hand! A malevolent grin formed on his grotesque face. In that instant, I thought I would die.

Death, however, was not to claim me that night. Instead, there was a loud crack, the revolver flew from Johnson's hand and he dropped to the ground with an agonizing scream, blood dripping from one arm. And then, from somewhere up above, I heard the familiar, high-pitched voice of Boston Corbett.

"Do not move, One-eye," said our guardian angel, "or ye will join the other devils in hell!"

Johnson instantly raised his hands in surrender. "Please, don't shoot," he said pitifully. "He"—this apparently being a reference to LeGrande—"made me come along. I didn't want no part of it but he made me. Now, please, don't shoot."

"Shooting might be entirely too good a fate for you, Mr. Johnson," said another familiar voice. I looked up with a profound sense of relief to see Sherlock Holmes standing where I had left him a moment before.

"My God, Holmes, I thought you had been shot."

"That, I am afraid, was Mr. LeGrande's intent, and though I think I might have dodged the bullet, Mr. Corbett interceded with his usual proficiency. Unfortunately, it appears that in all the confusion Mr. LeGrande has made good his escape."

"A pity," said Corbett, who had come around the pit to join Holmes, all the while keeping his rifle trained on Johnson. "But as ye wanted Boston Corbett to merely wing the assassin LeGrande, that is what he did. But once the Cat felt the sting of lead, he skedaddled quick as could be. Yes, sir, the Cat moves fast for a big man. But Boston Corbett is ready and willing to track the dirty assassin down, if that is what ye want, Mr. Holmes."

"That won't be necessary," said Holmes. "I am sure we shall be able to find Mr. LeGrande again if we need him. But what of you, Watson? Are you all right? You took a terrible tumble."

"I shall survive," I replied, for a cut knee and minor abrasions were the extent of my injuries.

"Good," said Holmes. "Please examine Mr. Johnson to make sure he is not seriously injured and then send him up. I am certain he has much that he would like to tell us."

Johnson had been whimpering since his encounter with Corbett's bullet, and he let out a horrible moan when I examined his arm. But I quickly determined that neither the bullet wound nor the gash on Johnson's forehead posed a threat to his life.

"You'll survive," I told the teamster after dressing his arm with a handkerchief. "Now, up you go. There are a couple of gentlemen who would like to talk with you."

While Johnson walked warily up toward his captors, I collected my revolver and the rifle left behind by LeGrande. Then I began my own climb out of the pit. But by the time I reached the top, this strange and violent night had presented us with yet another surprise.

❊

Corbett was the first to see it. "Look yonder," he said, pointing south toward town. "That fire is getting out of hand!"

I turned and saw, above the treetops, a tremendous orange glow illuminating the night sky. It was the same fire I had noted earlier, only now it had grown to tremendous proportions.

"Looks like the woods east of town are burning," Corbett said, " 'Tis the devil's night, to be sure."

"I saw it earlier," I remarked, "but it hardly seemed anything to worry about."

The blood drained from Holmes's face. "When did you first see this fire, Watson?" he asked urgently.

"About quarter to eleven. But as I said, it did not strike me as anything of great importance. Is something the matter?"

Holmes stared off in the direction of the fire. His next words came with such vehemence that they startled me:

"Watson, I have been a fool! A fool! Come, there is not a moment to lose. Mr. Corbett, stay here with One-eye and do not leave until I return. If he tries to escape, shoot him dead! Watson, follow me."

Without another word, Holmes went sprinting back toward town. Wondering what had possessed him, I could do nothing except try my best to keep up. But when I reached the main thoroughfare leading back to Hinckley, Holmes was already so far in advance that I could barely make out his distant figure upon the bridge across the Grindstone River.

When I finally reached the bridge, Holmes had vanished, but I could see a great ball of angry fire in the sky to my left, and I ran toward it. A general alarm had evidently been sounded in Hinckley, for other people were racing along the street beside me, and off toward the center of town I could hear the clanging of fire bells. After turning left, I saw at once that the woods to the east of town were indeed on fire, the flames leaping and dancing through the tops of trees. I ran toward this terrible spectacle, and when I reached the last street at the edge of town, I finally understood why Holmes had reacted with such swiftness to news of the fire. For, directly ahead lay William Thompson's house, which was now a perfect inferno.

A small crowd had gathered in front of the house and several men busied themselves tossing buckets of water into the flames, with about as much effect as they might have had trying to dampen the fires of hell. The roof was already gone, and the house's clapboard siding had vaporized to ash. This exposed the framework of timbers that held up the structure, so that the house resembled nothing so much as a great burning cage.

"Where is the fire department?" I asked an old man who had come out in his pajamas to watch the excitement.

"They've come and gone," he replied. "The house was all burned up by the time they got here, so they went off to the woods to help out there. Good thing the wind is letting up or the whole d--n town might have burned down."

The old man was right. The strong winds of just half an hour earlier had subsided, and this benevolent turn of fate, along with quick action by fire crews, kept the fire from spreading more than a few hundred yards into the woods, as I learned the next day.

But this atmospheric change had come too late to save the marshal's house, which continued to burn fiercely.

"Was anyone in the house?" I asked the old man.

"Don't know. But if anybody was, they'll be lucky to find his bones."

So caught up was I in the drama of the fire that I entirely forgot about Holmes until the flames at last began to subside. But when I looked, he was not to be found. After a futile search of the immediate vicinity, I saw no choice but to return to the gravel pit in hopes that Holmes would be there. As I retraced my steps, an extreme fatigue came over me—no doubt as a result of my dash from the gravel pit—and I looked for a place to rest.

It was only then that I stumbled across Holmes, who was sitting on the stoop of a house some distance from Thompson's ruined dwelling. In his hands was the money belt containing the reward so coveted by the marshal. Holmes looked up when he saw me but said nothing, and his long face—normally so alive to all the possibilities of life—was a study in dejection.

"Holmes," I said, sitting down beside him, "what is the matter? Have you been hurt?"

"No, but I fear that Big Billy's ambitions to wealth have been dealt a severe blow. The marshal will find little use for this money now." Then, a deep sadness in his voice, Holmes said:

"If you ever set this adventure down on paper, Watson, make

sure to record that the night of August 28, 1894, was the nadir of Sherlock Holmes's career as a detective."

"I do not understand, Holmes. It seems to me that we have done well this night. The villain LeGrande has been foiled and there is a good chance that Big Billy, when he returns, will confirm the Red Demon's identity."

Holmes responded with a pallid smile. "Big Billy will not be returning this night, Watson, unless it is from the dead. He is in there"—Holmes nodded in the direction of the smoldering house—"and there will not be much of him to see when the firemen make their grisly discovery."

"But how do you know he is not at Mrs. Robinson's? After all," I said, consulting my watch, "he was not supposed to meet us until midnight and it is now only half past eleven."

"Watson, your faith is touching, but the simple fact of the matter is that I have failed. If I had not been so stupid, Big Billy would be alive at this moment."

"Well, I do not see how you failed. In fact, it appears to me as though our work here is nearly over."

"Really? And what leads you to that extraordinary conclusion, my friend?"

"It is all a matter of timing," I said, surprised that Holmes could have missed such an obvious point. "I know for a fact that the fire at Thompson's house had started by quarter to eleven, since that is when I first saw the glow in the sky. I also know that the gravel pit can easily be reached from Thompson's house in less than fifteen minutes. Finally, I know that LeGrande and One-eye arrived at the pit just after eleven. And so I conclude—"

Holmes broke in. "You conclude, Watson, that LeGrande set fire to Thompson's house. And this in turn leads you to believe that Mr. LeGrande and the Red Demon are one and the same."

"Exactly. Can you prove me wrong?"

Holmes, rising from his seat, smiled. "Watson, you are indeed balm for my troubled soul. Very well, I accept your challenge. Let us return to the gravel pit, where I shall put your theories to the test."

Chapter Fourteen

"Exactly How Was
Mr. Mortimer Killed?"

✳

We found Corbett waiting for us at the pit, his rifle still aimed at One-eye Johnson, who sat glumly atop a pile of debris.

"Mr. Johnson has been a model prisoner," Corbett reported, "though he continues to claim that he did not know what the assassin LeGrande intended this night. All in all, 'tis a pitiful story that he tells, and were he not such an obvious scoundrel, Boston Corbett might be inclined to believe him."

"He will soon tell another story," said Holmes, striding over to Johnson and roughly pulling him up from his seat.

"Do you know who I am?" he demanded.

"You are Mr. Baker," he said cautiously, and made a half-hearted attempt to push Holmes away.

Holmes, who suddenly seemed to be in a cold fury, responded by slapping Johnson so hard across the cheeks that tears came to his good eye. "Do not play games with me, One-eye. I am not in the mood. You know perfectly well who I am and why I have come here. I had hoped to have a pleasant chat with Mr. LeGrande this evening, but since he has chosen to depart rather abruptly, you will have to do. But be warned: If you fail to cooperate with me, I shall see to it that you do not leave here alive."

"Please, don't hurt me," Johnson whimpered, raising his hands to shield his face as Holmes again slapped him.

Holmes, however, showed no mercy. "I shall hurt you all I want, One-eye, until you are ready to speak the truth."

He then grabbed Johnson by the throat and throttled him so violently that the teamster began gasping for air. I could not countenance such cruel behavior, no matter what the motivation, and raised my voice in protest. "Holmes, for God's sake —"

"Keep out of this, Watson," said Holmes icily, tightening his viselike grip on Johnson's throat. "This is no time for your civilized niceties. Lives are at stake."

Displaying demonical strength, Holmes now lifted Johnson off his feet. The teamster's legs jerked spasmodically as he struggled to loosen Holmes's iron grip. His good eye bulged as though it were about to explode from its socket and his tongue hung out grotesquely. Soon, Johnson's spastic movements all but ceased and I could see that he was on the verge of fainting, or worse. I was about to intercede in the name of common decency when Holmes spoke again:

"Now, Mr. Johnson, what will it be? The truth or more lies? Talk, or Mr. Corbett here will have his way with you."

A broad grin appeared on Corbett's face. "Praise be the Lord!" he shouted, his eyes glittering like dark diamonds in the moonlight. He unsheathed a long knife from his belt and brandished it at Johnson.

"Just give Boston Corbett the word," he said to Holmes, who had at last loosed his grip upon Johnson's throat, "and he will see to it that this miserable creature tastes his own vile and polluted blood before he goes screaming to the gates of hell."

Corbett's demonstration of lethal intent was sufficient to un-
nerve Johnson, who fell to the ground and began gulping in air as
though it were as precious as gold.

"I'll tell you anythin' you want to know," he said after regaining
his voice. Getting up on his knees, he crawled over to Holmes and,
to my astonishment, bent over and kissed his shoe. I found this display of absolute abasement pathetic in the extreme, and even
Holmes, I think, was embarrassed by Johnson's unmanly gesture,
for he quickly pulled his foot away.

"All right, One-eye, that is sufficient," Holmes said, directing
Johnson to stand up. "Now, tell us exactly how you came here this
night and leave out no detail."

Johnson, his will to resist utterly crushed, responded with
a long and remarkable statement, which I must paraphrase due
to the teamster's irregular and often meandering manner of
speech:

The day before, LeGrande had come to Johnson at the Big
Pine Camp and told him he intended to teach "the famous Mr.
Sherlock Holmes a lesson." Johnson was told he could earn one
hundred dollars by accompanying LeGrande on this mission. The
two then agreed to meet at eleven o'clock the next night at
the gravel pit, where they would lie in wait for the "two Englishmen" and "show them who's boss," as LeGrande put it. Johnson
presumed this meant they were to "beat up" the Englishmen and
thereby scare them off. Had he known murder was on LeGrande's
mind—

Holmes, who had stood in a meditative pose throughout this
discourse, interrupted in a harsh voice: "You are lying to me, One-
eye, and you know the penalty for that."

"No, no, it's the truth, I swear," Johnson blurted out, cringing
as Holmes stepped toward him. "I didn't know the Cat aimed on
killin' nobody."

Holmes lunged at Johnson and grabbed him again by the
throat. But instead of throttling him, he brought his mouth up to

Johnson's left ear and said: "Then why did you and Mr. LeGrande bring your rifles along? To hunt squirrels?"

"That was the Cat's idea," Johnson insisted, his misshapen face a study in terror. "I figured it was just in case we needed to defend ourselves."

"I see," said Holmes, removing his hands from Johnson's neck. "Well, Mr. Johnson, I find that a bit hard to believe but I shall let it go—this time." There was an ominous tone in these last two words, and Johnson knew it. His nervousness increased when Holmes circled behind him and instructed him not to turn around. Though Johnson was a ruffian and, no doubt, a killer, I almost felt a measure of sympathy for him at this moment, so unsettling was his predicament.

Standing a good ten paces behind the teamster and addressing him like some unseen Grand Inquisitor, Holmes said: "Listen to me, One-eye, and listen well. I shall now put a series of simple questions to you regarding Mr. LeGrande. You will answer these questions with complete truthfulness. Is that clear?"

"Yes, sir. Whatever you say, sir."

The questions that followed were hardly what I expected, for Holmes asked nothing more about the events at the gravel pit, the fire at Thompson's house or anything else that had happened this day. But as peculiar as Holmes's questions seemed, the answers he received were to prove crucial in his hunt for the Red Demon.

"All right, One-eye," said Holmes, "here is the first question. Is Mr. LeGrande literate?"

This question was obviously as surprising to Johnson as it was to me, and the poor man reacted with a blank and desperate look. "Literate? I'm sorry, sir, but I don't know—"

Holmes let out an impatient sigh and said: "Can Mr. LeGrande read and write?"

"Oh, I get your drift. No, sir, I don't believe he has no book learnin'. Ain't much call for that out in the woods anyhow. Besides, the camp's got a pencil pusher who's handy enough with the swindle stick."[1]

I did not entirely understand this answer, but Holmes appeared satisfied with it. Pacing back and forth out of Johnson's view, he put forth his second question, which was quite different in character from the first:

"Has Mr. LeGrande ever mentioned the name James J. Hill?"

Johnson was perplexed. "You mean, the big railroad fella?"

"Yes."

"I heard him say somethin' once, after he'd been drinkin', about how this Hill fella had done him wrong, but I don't know what the deal was. Truth is, the Cat wasn't much for talkin'. But I know that partner of his, he sure hated Hill."

"You mean Bartlett Chalmers?"

"Sure, the big fat guy. He was out at the camp once—I guess it was last spring—and him and the Cat was talkin' and this Chalmers he was really hot. It was this d--n Hill did this and this d--n Hill did that. Went on and on, he did, but I didn't follow it all on account of I was busy doin' somethin'."

"All right," said Holmes. "You are doing well, One-eye. And I know you will keep it up, for I can see that Mr. Corbett is beginning to get unspeakable urges."

Johnson glanced over at Corbett, who smiled and slowly slid his knife across his throat in a malevolent pantomime. This caused the poor teamster to tremble uncontrollably. "I will do whatever you say, sir," he told Holmes. "You just say it and I will do it."

"I know you will," Holmes said soothingly. "Now, One-eye, tell me more about Mr. Chalmers. Was he at the camp often?"

"Nope, I only saw him that once. But he must have been the boss, 'cause before we'd start a job, the Cat'd go into town to meet with him. I guess he owned the land out at the camp."

"And did Mr. LeGrande ever say anything to you about his relationship with Mr. Chalmers?"

Johnson shook his head. "The Cat, he didn't discuss his business with nobody."

"Very well. Now, let me ask you this: How often does Mr. LeGrande visit Mother Mary's establishment?"

Johnson paused to consider this latest bolt from the blue, scratching his head as though the process of contemplation, with which he was obviously unfamiliar, caused a painful itch. He finally said: "Well, sir, he isn't much for that sort of thing. He has him a girl over in Milaca, and he goes there most every Saturday. I can't say as I ever saw him at Mother Mary's, though I'm not saying he never went there."

"I see," said Holmes, still pacing behind Johnson's back, while the teamster seemed to grow more unnerved by the moment. "And now we come to another question, which is perhaps a bit more complicated than its predecessors. So think carefully, One-eye, very carefully. Are you ready?"

"I will do my best, sir."

"Good. How often does Mr. LeGrande log on section thirty-seven?"[3]

This question baffled me, but Johnson appeared to know precisely what Holmes meant.

"I couldn't say, sir, as I got no idea as to who owns what out in the woods. Ain't my job. But some of the boys, they told me that trespassin's pretty much a regular thing with the Cat. But I guess he never got caught."

"Indeed," said Holmes, "that is one of the many curious things about Mr. LeGrande. And now, One-eye, the final question: Did you and Mr. LeGrande set fire to Big Billy's house tonight?"

The teamster reacted to the question with a look of utter astonishment. "Set a fire? I don't know what you mean, sir. Like I told you, we come here to this pit to do a job. I don't know nothin' about a fire."

Holmes received this answer without comment, then slowly

walked back toward the teamster until he stood directly in front of him. "Well, One-eye, you have been quite a help and I see no reason to detain you further."

"Holmes," I protested, "surely you do not intend to let this man go? He tried to kill us!"

Corbett weighed in with similar sentiments. "Assassins must be dealt with harshly, Mr. Holmes. Boston Corbett says this mangy, one-eyed cur should burn for all eternity in the fiery furnace of hell."

Johnson blanched and began to plead with Holmes, who silenced him with a single gesture of his hand, much as he might have directed an obedient dog. He then put his hands upon the teamster's shoulders, rubbing them in the manner of a masseur.

"Do not worry, One-eye. I will not let Mr. Corbett harm you, much as the prospect would please him. You are free to go."

Johnson, looking like a man who had just been released from his coffin after ringing the bell, smiled broadly and turned to leave, only to feel Holmes's hands clamp down on his shoulders.[3]

"Oh dear, I nearly forgot," Holmes said casually. "There is one more thing. Exactly how was Mr. Mortimer killed?"

❋

"Mr. Mortimer?" Johnson repeated in a fearful voice, as though uttering the name of something unspeakable. "I—"

Holmes returned instantly to his earlier state of unrestrained fury. "Spare me any protestations of innocence, One-eye. They do not interest me. I know you were present when Mr. Mortimer was murdered and I know who your accomplices were. Do not even think of lying to me or so help me God I will see to it that your bones are left here tonight for the buzzards."

Johnson, all resistance shattered, let out a long sigh and shook his head. "I got to sit down," he said, returning to his position atop the debris pile.

And then, in a flat and lifeless voice, he told us the tragic story of how Thomas John Mortimer had met his end. Acting on instructions from LeGrande, Johnson said he stopped Mortimer that day as he walked along the road and offered him a ride. As the heat was extreme, Mortimer gratefully accepted.

"And where was Mr. Mortimer going?" asked Holmes.

"Why, to Mother Mary's," said Johnson, as though the answer should have been obvious.

"I thought as much. You may proceed."

Johnson said that at a preordained place, just before reaching the clearing occupied by Mrs. Robinson's house, he stopped his wagon on the pretense that one of the horses had come up lame. Two of LeGrande's henchmen—the same pair who had tried to murder Holmes and me—then rushed from the woods and attacked Mortimer with clubs before he could defend himself. Knocked unconscious, Mortimer was placed in the back of the wagon, hidden beneath a canvas cover, and taken to the Big Pine Camp. Johnson told us in his own words what happened next:

"I didn't know nothin' about what they was up to, but when we got to camp, the Cat was there and he told me to go down to the lake. So—"

"And who was with Mr. LeGrande?" Holmes asked.

"With him?"

Holmes suddenly seemed to lose all patience. "Is there some problem with your hearing, Mr. Johnson?" he shouted. Johnson was nearly paralyzed with fear. "Mr. Corbett can fix that."

"A knife's a fine surgical instrument," Corbett agreed, coming over to Johnson and resting the sharp end of his blade atop the teamster's left ear. " 'Twill lop the ear off an assassin as neat as can be. Shall Boston Corbett have his trophy, Mr. Holmes?"

"No, wait, wait," cried Johnson in a piteous voice. "It was the marshal. Big Billy was there."

"Go on," said Holmes. "But do not forget that Mr. Corbett would very much like to have his trophy."

"Well, like I said, they was both there and they went with me down to the lake. I swear I didn't know what they was up to. When we got down to the beach, the Cat and Big Billy, they went to get Mortimer out of the back of the wagon. And that's when all of a sudden, he came to life."

"Mr. Mortimer?"

"That's right. He had a cane with him and swung it at Big Billy and knocked him flat to the ground and then he tried to get up out of the wagon. And that's when the Cat just stepped back and started shootin' with that big old Colt of his, and pretty soon blood was flyin' everywhere. Sprayed up right in my face. Anyway, Mortimer was shot all over and dead as dead could be, and the Cat pulled him out of the wagon and then Big Billy got up and kicked the body on account of he was still mad. And I said to the Cat, 'Jesus, what'd you do that for?' and he said, 'Never you mind. You just remember you didn't see nothin' here today.' "

We listened to this grim story in silence, and I could not help but think how fortunate we had been to avoid a similar fate.

"Finish your story," said Holmes.

Johnson complied. "Well, after that I got out of there, not wantin' no part of such a business, but then I got the story from one of the boys the next day. It was Jake O'Connell, and he said they took what was left of Mortimer out on a skiff and hooked him up to a couple of deadheads with a big chain and dropped him off in the middle of the lake where it's so deep nobody's got a rope long enough to reach bottom.[4] And the Cat, he said anybody who spoke a word about it would be the next one in the lake, and we all believed him. And that is a true and honest account, sir, of what happened, as best I know it."

There could be little doubt that Johnson was telling the truth. The longer he talked, the less fearful he seemed, and there gradually came over his features a kind of desperate serenity. It was a look I had seen only once before, among certain prisoners of war in Afghanistan — the look that comes to men when they have reached the end of hope.

Holmes listened to this story with rapt attention, and only lit his pipe after Johnson had finished. "Incidentally, One-eye, where did you acquire this?" he asked, handing Johnson the lighter engraved with Mortimer's initials.

"From the Cat," replied Johnson, who was obviously surprised to see the lighter again. "Where'd you find it?"

"On the person of a criminal," said Holmes, "and I'm sure you'll have no objection if I keep it. Now, One-eye, there is but one question that I have left for you. Precisely when were you notified that you were to pick up Mr. Mortimer?"

Of the many peculiar questions Holmes had asked thus far, this struck me as the strangest of all. I had expected Holmes to cross-examine Johnson regarding the circumstances of Mortimer's death, for there were—or so I thought—many questions raised by his singular story. But Holmes, for reasons I could not fathom, now appeared to be concentrating his attention upon an utterly insignificant aspect of the entire tragic affair.

Johnson, however, showed no surprise at the question, suggesting that he had by now grown accustomed to the peculiarities of Holmes's manner of interrogation. And so he answered without hesitation:

"Why, 'twas the evenin' before, sir. The Cat had just come back from town and he stopped me as I was leavin' camp and told me the plan. Said I was to look out for this Mortimer the next day and bring him to the spot near Mother Mary's place."

Holmes listened intently to the teamster's reply and then, to my surprise, helped him up from his seat on the debris pile.

"Up you go, One-eye. We have no further use for you, so you may be on your way. However, Mr. Corbett will keep your rifle for the time being, and if I were you, I should not make my face seen in Hinckley for a while, lest you tempt Mr. Corbett to take the law into his own hands."

Johnson glanced over at the grizzled woodsman, who glared back at him menacingly. "Don't you worry none," said Johnson, shaking Holmes's hand with great enthusiasm. "You won't be seein' me anywheres near this place for a long time. A long time."

And with that parting promise, the teamster ran off down the road toward town as fast as his short legs would carry him.

"Holmes, I really—"

"Not now, Watson," Holmes said with a dismissing wave of the hand. "You must trust me when I say there is a method in my apparent madness."

He then strode over to Corbett and put his hand upon that worthy's shoulder. "Mr. Corbett, once again it seems that we owe you our lives, and if there is ever anything you need of Sherlock Holmes, no matter where you are and no matter what it is, then you have but to say the word, and I shall move heaven and earth if necessary to be at your side."

Corbett appeared at once pleased and embarrassed by these effusive words. "Boston Corbett thanks ye for such kind sentiments, Mr. Holmes, and it has been his pleasure to serve ye. But are ye certain that this business of the Red Demon is truly finished in that the assassin LeGrande is still on the loose?"

"I am certain of nothing, Mr. Corbett, except that you have done noble work tonight. But if Dr. Watson and I should require your further assistance, be assured that we will let you know."

"Then Boston Corbett shall be on his way," Corbett said, shouldering his rifle and turning to leave. "God's work has been done this night, Mr. Holmes! Praise the Lord!"

As I watched Corbett slip silently into the woods, I could not help but wonder whether I would ever see him again, and if so, what the circumstances would be.

"Well," I said to Holmes, "it has been an extraordinary evening. Mr. Hill, I believe, will be most satisfied with what we report tomorrow."

"Perhaps," said Holmes, glancing out across the desolate pit, where the shadows of trees danced in the fragile moonlight. "But I fear that we are still a long way from being in possession of all the facts of this case."

※

Holmes's doubts came as a surprise to me, given all we had learned from Johnson, and I asked for an explanation as we walked back to town.

"It seems to me that we do have the facts," I said. "Now, it is simply a matter of finding LeGrande, who will not get far, I should think, with a bullet from Mr. Corbett's rifle in him."

Holmes, who showed no fatigue from our night's exertions and walked at his usual fast pace, looked at me and said: "So you continue to believe LeGrande is the Red Demon?"

"Of course," I said, rather exasperated by Holmes's behavior, for he was much too fond of playing the devil's advocate.

"Then let me hear the case for the prosecution, Watson. You may be sure that I shall hang upon your every word."

"I do not appreciate your sarcasm, Holmes, and I am not going to let you be entertained at my expense. Therefore, I shall not bother you with my insignificant opinions."

Holmes stopped and grabbed my arm. "You are right, Watson. I have spoken badly to you and I apologize. It is just that I have much on my mind. But I truly do want to hear you make your case. Your thoughts and opinions have always been as invaluable to me as your enduring friendship."

I felt sorry for having snapped at Holmes and told him I would be pleased to provide my assessment of the case. After marshaling my thoughts for a moment, I began thusly:

"I believe, Holmes, that all of the evidence points squarely to Mr. LeGrande as being the Red Demon. There is, to begin with, the information you yourself elicited when you questioned One-eye earlier this evening. First, LeGrande was illiterate, which explains why he had Mrs. Robinson write the letters. Second, he was a timber thief, and third, he hated Mr. Hill, undoubtedly because of the latter's effort to prosecute him for thievery.

"In addition, we know that he murdered Mr. Mortimer, that he tried on at least two occasions to murder us, and that the timing of tonight's events was such that he could easily have killed Big Billy and set fire to his house before accosting us in the pit, despite One-eye's claims to the contrary. In short, there is an overwhelming amount of evidence to support the conclusion that LeGrande is the Red Demon. Mrs. Robinson, I believe, will confirm this once we confront her with the evidence. Now, Holmes, if you can tear holes in my case, have at it!"

I expected him to try to demolish my analysis point by point, a form of destruction at which he excelled above all other men. But he steadfastly declined to do so, saying he could find "no real fault" with my reasoning.

"Your logic is impeccable, Watson," he acknowledged, and I must confess I took some pride in this admission on his part. "There is indeed some evidence which points toward Mr. Le-Grande. And yet—"

"What is it, Holmes? What is bothering you?"

He stopped in the middle of the road—we were now approaching the Grindstone River—and fixed on me a look of such painful intensity that I can still see it in my mind's eye as clearly as though it had all happened just a moment ago.

"What bothers me, Watson, is the sheer tidiness of the events tonight, the neatness with which every element of the case has been wrapped up and put before us. Life is many things, Watson, but one of the things it is not is tidy."

As Holmes spoke, we reached the bridge over the Grindstone, and I glanced east to see whether the conflagration was still raging in the woods. But the eastern horizon was now dark, and only the unusually thick smoke that drifted around us gave evidence of the fiery events of a few hours earlier.

We stopped at the river so I could dip my handkerchief in the sluggish water and mop my brow, for the combination of heat and smoke was stifling, even at such a late hour. As we sat on a rock near the stream, Holmes rather absentmindedly picked up an object he found at his feet. It was an old leather work glove, singed and torn, and probably lost long ago by one of the local mill hands.[5] Curiously, Holmes soon became preoccupied with this discarded item, turning it over again and again in his hands, studying it as though it might be as valuable as the Countess of Morcar's famous blue carbuncle.[6]

"Is something the matter?" I asked.

"What?"

"I asked whether something is wrong. You look, Holmes, as though you have just seen an apparition." This was hardly an exaggeration, since Holmes's austere face did indeed have a spectral look in the moonlight as he contemplated the old glove.

"Perhaps I have," came the reply.

"What do you mean?"

A sly smile lit Holmes's face, and he tossed the glove into the river. He said: "I have been thinking, Watson, about your analysis of the evidence. You have forgotten one major player in our little drama—Mr. Bartlett Chalmers. What role do you suppose he had in the affair?"

I confess that Chalmers had indeed slipped my mind. Nonetheless, I did not think the omission a significant one. "Mr. Chalmers undoubtedly was an ally of LeGrande, but I am not certain of the extent of his involvement in any illegalities. I am sure once we locate him we can press him for answers."

"Your confidence is inspiring, Watson," said Holmes, "and yet I wonder whether we shall ever see the mysterious Mr. Chalmers again."

※

A telegram, brought over some hours earlier by Benjamin Cain, was waiting for us at the Morrison House when we finally returned. Soon thereafter, Holmes sat in my room and read the decoded message out loud: "New letter from Red Demon. Contents as follows: 'Holmes the English pretender will not save you or your railroad. The end is near. The flames of hell shall purge you of your sins.' Handwriting is different. How were you detected? Do you wish to see letter? Please inform at once. J. J. Hill."

"LeGrande must have sent it yesterday or the day before, thinking we would be dead by now," I said.

Holmes slowly shook his head. "Mr. Jean Baptiste LeGrande, that illiterate woodsman of few words, did not send this letter, Watson. I only wish that he had."

Chapter Fifteen

"He Was a Very Clever Cat"

❈

I awoke the next morning to find daylight streaming into my room and the familiar figure of Sherlock Holmes hovering about like an annoying angel. He was sitting by the window, and when he turned to greet me I was struck by the fire in his eyes, which seemed to glow like hot embers in their deep sockets. I wondered—not for the first time—what strange and terrible furnace burned within Holmes and fueled his demonic energy.

"What is it?" I mumbled, reaching over to retrieve my watch from the nightstand. I was surprised to see that it was nearly eleven o'clock. "My God, you should have awakened me sooner. I had no idea of the hour."

"Do not worry, Watson. Your sweet repose has given me time to think. You see, early this morning I received a telegram from Mr. Hill which is quite revealing in its particulars."

"I should be interested to hear about it," I said, rising from bed and putting on my trousers.

"The gist of it, Watson, is that neither Mr. Hill nor any of his innumerable subalterns have ever heard of Bartlett Chalmers."

"And you find that peculiar, I take it."

"Most peculiar," said Holmes, moving to a seat beside my bed and lighting a cigarette, which he sometimes substituted for his pipe. "For it appears on one hand that Bartlett Chalmers is a man of substance and, on the other, that he is lighter than air."

"It is too early in the day for riddles. You will have to explain yourself."

"Very well. Consider this: Mr. Chalmers owns several strategic parcels of timber in Pine County, is the partner in a logging company operated by the renowned Mr. LeGrande, and appears in every respect to be, as I have said, a businessman of substantial means. And yet Mr. Hill, who has many interests of his own here, has never heard of him. Moreover, Mr. Chalmers appears to be equally unknown in the village of Hinckley."

"How can you know that?"

"Have you forgotten that I am a detective?" replied Holmes with a hint of asperity. "I make it my business to know things. Therefore, while you were resting in the lap of Morpheus this morning, I spent several hours talking with loggers, lumber dealers, store owners and other citizens of Hinckley. And though a few of these worthies acknowledged seeing Mr. Chalmers on occasion, and even talking with him once or twice, none could tell me anything about the man. Does he have a family? No one knows. Where does he live? No idea. Where is he from? Again, shoulders are shrugged. I tell you, Watson, it is extremely curious. I am hoping you might have some suggestions for me."

I thought for a moment. "Well, perhaps Mr. Chalmers is a naturally reticent man."

"Perhaps. Yet he was not so reticent that he failed to seek you out and argue on behalf of his supposedly misunderstood partner, Mr. LeGrande." Holmes put out his cigarette and rose to his feet. "In any event, Watson, it is time for us to go. Pack your bags at once. We must be prepared to move quickly."

"Move? Where are we going?"

"To a less vulnerable position," he said, opening the door into the hallway. "I no longer feel comfortable in Hinckley. Meet me in the dining room when you are ready."

❋

I dressed hurriedly, packed my bags and went down to the hotel's dining room. Although it was well before noon, the room was already crowded and a thick cloud of cigar smoke hung in the air. As I searched for Holmes amid the smoke and din, I heard a familiar name being uttered.

"They say LeGrande took a bullet last night. Serves the bas---d right," said a rugged-looking man at one table. His three companions—all woodsmen, judging by their attire—seemed equally pleased to hear of LeGrande's misfortune.

"Who do you suppose done it?" one asked.

"A jack, I'd bet," said another. "Why, there's road monkeys and swampers all over these woods that got a bad case of smallpox from that big frog."[1]

The table found these enigmatic remarks amusing, and there was hearty laughter all around. After taking in as much of this conversation as I could without appearing to eavesdrop, I continued my search for Holmes. I finally found him at a table near the kitchen, sitting with his back to the wall. A huge portion of fried chicken and dumplings was already on his plate.

"Now, what is this all about?" I asked after ordering my own more modest lunch of bread and cheese. "Where are we going?"

Holmes responded to my question with one of his own. "Have you ever noticed, Watson, how a cat hunts a mouse?"

"No, but I am sure you are about to inform me," I said, fearing that Holmes was now about to deliver one of those cryptic homilies on the art of investigation for which he was perhaps too famous. My fears were soon justified, for Holmes leaned back in his chair, rested his hands atop his head and began as follows:

"In my student days at Oxford, I had the misfortune to own a cat.[2] Or perhaps I should say, it owned me. This cat, whom I named Dupin, was a large black fellow of uncertain parentage.[3] Like most cats, he was lazy by nature and rather irascible by temperament, but he was undeniably a skilled mouser, and his technique was quite fascinating to observe."

"No doubt," I muttered, earning a sharp look of rebuke from Holmes for my trouble.

"As I was saying," he continued, "Dupin exhibited a distinctive method of hunting. Once he caught the scent of a mouse or some other rodent, he would become a model of patience and endurance, waiting hours on end as silently as could be for his prey to appear. Unlike a dog, which will react excitedly to a scent and move toward it unless trained to do otherwise, Dupin kept his distance, being careful to stay well back from the place where the mouse might be expected to emerge. In other words, he seemed to know instinctively that if he could smell the mouse, then the mouse could smell him as well. Yet he never moved so far away that he could not reach his target in a single, decisive leap. He was a very clever cat, that Dupin, and had he not been run over by a dray on High Street, I do not doubt that he would have had a long and successful career as a killer of rodents."[4]

"Very interesting," I said. "And what, pray tell, is the point?"

Holmes arched his eyebrows in the manner of a professor expressing displeasure with a particularly obtuse student. "The point, Watson, is that it time for us to leave Hinckley. We have been on the scent of the Red Demon for almost a week now, and yet we have little to show for our efforts because he has caught our scent as well. But if we back away a bit, as the admirable Dupin was wont to do, then perhaps the Demon will emerge one day from his lair and we shall be ready to pounce! Besides, there is something else to consider."

"What is that?"

"The last letter from the Demon," said Holmes. "It was most disturbing."

"You mean because his threats are growing more insistent?"

"That is part of it. But what worries me even more, Watson, is the fact that it did not come from the hand of Mrs. Robinson."

❊

Holmes would not explain his rather odd comment regarding the Red Demon's last missive, nor would he expand upon his reasons for wishing to leave Hinckley. I knew from previous cases that such mysteriousness on Holmes's part generally presaged a solution to the problem at hand, and I therefore took no umbrage at his behavior.

After lunch, Holmes insisted upon sending yet another telegram to Hill and so we walked once more to the Eastern Minnesota depot, where we found Cain working feverishly at his telegrapher's key.

"Good afternoon," said Holmes, catching Cain's eye. "I must say, it appears that a stationmaster's work is never done, for it looks as though you have hardly moved an inch since I stopped by earlier to pick up a telegram."

"You've hit the truth there, sir," Cain replied with a weary smile. "There's no end of messages coming down the line, especially with all the excitement over the marshal's death last night and the wounding of LeGrande. I have just now received a message that the sheriff will be coming up from Pine City on the morning train with several of his men to investigate."

"Do you suppose there was any connection between the two incidents?" Holmes asked.

"I don't know," said Cain. "But there are suspicions, from what I hear."

"Why is that?"

Cain glanced around to make sure no one else was in the office and then lowered his voice to a whisper. "Well, Mr. Baker, the theory here in town is that LeGrande and the marshal might have a had a falling out among thieves, as it were. You see, they found a bullet in Big Billy's brain when they recovered his body from the house."

"A bullet? You mean he was shot before his house burned?"

"It appears that way. In any case, a few hours later LeGrande shows up at Dr. Cowan's office with a bullet in his arm.[5] Could be a coincidence, but it set people to wondering."

"I can imagine that it did," said Holmes. "Is Mr. LeGrande's wound serious?"

Cain laughed. "From what I know, it would take more than a bullet in the arm to bring down a man like LeGrande. He'll recover. At least, that's what Mr. Hay over at the *Enterprise* tells me. He's putting out a special edition this afternoon with all the details. I'm sure it will make for interesting reading."

"Well, we shall have to take a look at it," said Holmes, handing Cain a scribbled note. "In the meantime, I should like to send this message to St. Paul. It is quite urgent."

"I shall send it at once."

"Good," said Holmes, "and thank you for all of your assistance during our stay in Hinckley. Mr. Hill told us that you were a man in whom he had the utmost confidence, and it is clear that his trust was not misplaced. I shall make sure that he is informed of your admirable efforts on our behalf."

"That is very kind of you, Mr. Baker, very kind indeed. But tell me, am I to take it that you and Mr. Smith are planning to leave town?"

"We are. Our business here is at an end, and we must move on. But it has been a pleasure to visit your fine community and I hope that one day we shall be able to return."

"I will look forward to that," said Cain, who rose to shake our hands before returning to his post beside the telegraph key.

"What did you tell Mr. Hill in your message?" I asked as we left the station and emerged into the hazy sunlight.

"I told him what he needs to know," Holmes replied with a peculiar smile, "though I fear he will find parts of my message rather confusing. Be that as it may, Watson, let us retire to a place in the shade and await further developments."

❉

We spent the next several hours on a bench near the Eastern Minnesota depot, shaded by a stately maple tree that had somehow eluded the busy sawyers of Hinckley. Holmes soon drifted off into a state of ruminative languor. He uttered not a word, sitting on the bench with his eyes closed and his body so still that not even the large black flies which buzzed around us could interrupt his intense concentration.

I had no doubt that he was now arranging into a coherent pattern the last pieces of the mystery of the Red Demon. It was common for Holmes to enter into a contemplative trance from which he could be aroused only with extraordinary effort. I especially remember the astonishing period of concentration, during which he fasted for forty-eight hours, that preceded his brilliant solution in the strange case of the Scafell Pike monster.[6]

While Holmes engaged in his deep and complicated thoughts, I did my best to remain comfortable, though this was not easy, for the day was rapidly becoming the hottest we had yet experienced in Hinckley. It was also the smokiest, with the aroma of burned wood so powerful and persistent that the air became disagreeable. My eyes teared, and a raw thirst assailed my throat no matter how many cups of water I obtained from the well next to the depot. I was beginning to fear that Holmes might spend all day on his mental journey when he abruptly turned to me and said:

"A cabin in the woods, Watson, that must be our next destination."

This statement, needless to say, left me baffled. "I have no idea what you are talking about, Holmes. A cabin in the woods? Whose cabin?"

"That hardly matters. What is important is that we find it this evening."

I now noticed a boy, with a stack of newspapers in his hand, walking toward us, presumably to make a delivery at the depot.

"Ah, this must be the special edition of the *Enterprise*," Holmes said, motioning the boy over toward us. "Let us see what the press had made of last evening's events."

The boy was at first reluctant to part with a copy, saying that all of the newspapers were intended for the depot. However, the offer of a shiny new silver dollar from Holmes changed the lad's mind in an instant, and we were soon in possession of the August 29, 1894, special edition of the *Hinckley Enterprise*.

I will not reproduce here the entire front page of the newspaper, which contained long stories on the death of Thompson and the shooting of LeGrande. But some suggestion of the tone and style of these articles may be gleaned from the headlines which erupted across the page in huge blocks of black type:

WAS IT MURDER? — MARSHAL WILLIAM THOMPSON INCINERATED IN HOME — BULLET IN HIS BRAIN — A MYSTERIOUS VISITOR SEEN AT HOUSE — FOUL PLAY SUSPECTED — CAUSE OF FIRE UNKNOWN — ARSON POSSIBLE — FIRE SPREADS TO WOODS AND ALARM SOUNDED — BLAZE NEARLY RAGES OUT OF CONTROL — BRAVE AND RESOURCEFUL FIREFIGHTERS PREVENT A GENERAL CONFLAGRATION — NEW WATEROUS ENGINE PROVES ITS WORTH.[7]

The wounding of LeGrande produced a lesser, but nonetheless interesting, array of headlines: J. B. LEGRANDE, FEARED TIMBER BOSS, SHOT — WHO GAVE THE GIANT LEAD POISONING? — A FIGHT WITH THE MARSHAL? — THE BIG MAN ISN'T TALKING — SHERIFF O'ROURKE COMING FROM PINE CITY TO INVESTIGATE — ALL OF HINCKLEY ABUZZ WITH RUMOR.

The articles themselves were less dramatic than the headlines and rather rambling in form, though Holmes — after reading every word at his usual breakneck pace — pronounced them to be "quite suggestive."

I then read the first of the articles, which dealt with the fire at Thompson's house. After noting that the marshal had been shot (a fact which did not surprise Holmes in the least), the story described how Thompson's charred remains had been found in the ruins of the house. Though no one had seen the fire ignite, the speed with which it spread raised suspicions that it might have been "incendiary in origin."

Next came a paragraph which Holmes specifically called to my attention. It read as follows: "Sources have told the *Enterprise* that only a few hours before the marshal's domicile went up in flames, a woman was seen entering the house in such a way as to suggest some clandestine purpose. Who was this mystery woman and what was she doing at the marshal's house at so unbecoming an hour? It is a question that Sheriff O'Rourke and his able deputies may well wish to answer."

This intelligence was indeed quite startling. "How do you suppose Mr. Hay found out about Mrs. Robinson's visit?" I asked.

"I intend to ask him that very question as soon as possible," said Holmes. "In the meantime, Watson, read on. There are several other items of interest in Mr. Hay's account."

The remainder of the story dealt with the marshal's character and background. Thompson was described as "a man with many enemies in the community owing to his forceful style of law enforcement. There were also allegations that he had allowed certain notorious criminal elements in the community to operate with impunity." These "elements," however, were not identified.

Holmes laughed with uncharacteristic gusto when I read this portion of the article aloud. "Notorious criminal elements! What a fine euphemism, Watson, for LeGrande and his gang."

I turned next to Mr. Hay's account of LeGrande's shooting. He reported that it had been just after two in the morning when LeGrande, bleeding from a bullet wound to his right forearm, sought treatment from Dr. Cowan in Hinckley. LeGrande had refused to say how he had been shot, but the story noted that in light of "Mr. LeGrande's crude and violent temperament, the number of men in the woods who might wish to perforate his person is quite large."

It was another paragraph in the story, however, that really

caught my eye: "The *Enterprise* has learned that both Mr. LeGrande and Marshal Thompson were seen earlier in the evening at Mother Mary's sporting establishment, and that a harsh exchange of words occurred between them. This must naturally lead to speculation that the two incidents—the death of Thompson and the wounding of LeGrande—are related in some manner, and it is certain that Sheriff O'Rourke will pursue the issue when he arrives in Hinckley this afternoon."

"Well, Watson, what do you think?" Holmes asked after I had finished my reading and folded up the paper.

I did not hesitate to reply, even though the conclusion I had reached was far from pleasing to me. "I think we must visit Mrs. Robinson again."

"And risk another assault at the hands of the jack pine twins? My, Watson, but you are in a brave mood this afternoon."

"I do not find the subject amusing, and I would rather not talk about it."

"As you wish," said Holmes with a smile as he rose from the bench. "But you are right. Though I am not anxious to stay in Hinckley any longer, there are certain questions which only Mrs. Robinson may now be in a position to answer. And we had best seek those answers before Sheriff O'Rourke begins his meddling work. First, however, I should like to have a little chat with Mr. Hay, who seems uncommonly well informed about last night's events."

❋

As it turned out, Angus Hay was close by, for as we prepared to leave our shady spot, the editor emerged from the depot and began walking toward the center of town at a brisk pace.

Holmes immediately called out after him. Hay turned around, waved, then—to our surprise—continued walking.

"Mr. Hay, I should very much like a word with you," Holmes shouted. "It is a matter of some importance."

Hay stopped and turned toward us once again. "I am very busy, Mr. Baker, very busy. My apologies, but I really must get back to the office. As you might imagine, I have a great deal of work to do."

"Then we will not detain you," said Holmes, leaping up from the bench and fairly sprinting toward the editor. I followed a few steps behind, and we were soon at Hay's side.

Hay appeared taken aback by this sudden movement and gave Holmes a peculiar look. Holmes, however, was the last man in the world to be put off by a look. Offering a suave smile, he said: "We shall be most pleased, Mr. Hay, to walk with you to your office, since our business will take but a moment."

"Very well," said Hay, though it was quite obvious that he was not anxious for our company.

"I had the pleasure of reading your stories just now," Holmes began as we made our way along the dusty street, "and I must say, as one journalist to another, that you have done a splendid job! Absolutely splendid!"

"Thank you," said Hay, who still showed no sign of warming to our presence.

Holmes, however, was undeterred. "No, Mr. Hay, it is you who deserve our thanks for providing such a full account of last night's most unfortunate events. But tell me, however did you learn of the woman who visited the marshal before his death? That is a most intriguing revelation. Was there, perchance, a witness to this tryst?"

Hay responded with a question of his own. "Why are you so interested in all of this, Mr. Baker? Surely, the great *Times* of London has more important things to occupy its attention than the murder of a man in Hinckley."

"Perhaps. But since *The Times* has seen fit to send me here, I would be remiss in my duties if I failed to learn all that I could about such a murder. But I can see that you are reluctant to discuss this tragic affair, especially when it comes to the matter of the 'mysterious woman' described in your story. I wonder why that is. I must also confess, Mr. Hay, that I find your reticence rather curious, since in my experience journalists usually love nothing better than to describe how they have ferreted out some crucial piece of information."

If Holmes intended his comments to provoke an angry response, he succeeded all too well, for Hay—fire flashing in his deep blue eyes—now turned to confront my friend. "Mr. Baker, how I go about getting stories is my business and no one else's. Do you understand that, sir? It is none of your d--ned business. Now, as my office is just up ahead, I would be most pleased if you and your friend would bother me no further!"

Holmes's reaction to this tongue-lashing was so strange and unexpected that it caught both Hay and me by complete surprise. For, without a word, Holmes suddenly reached out and grabbed Hay's hands, on one of which he wore a large gold ring inlaid with precious stones. Startled, Hay pulled his hands back but not before Holmes had twisted them around to reveal the palms.

"Good God, sir, what do you think you're doing?" Hay blurted out.

"I was merely admiring your excellent ring," Holmes said, as calmly as though seizing a man's hands in this manner were a normal mode of social intercourse. "It is twenty-four-carat gold, if I am not mistaken, and of very fine workmanship."

Shaking his head in disbelief, Hay slowly backed away from us until he had reached the front door of his office. There, he offered a parting comment: "I believe you are mad, Mr. Baker, absolutely mad!" An instant later, the door slammed behind him.

"Well, Holmes," I said, "I am sure you have an explanation and I would be most interested to hear it."

"What is there to explain, Watson? I am a detective and I have been detecting. But if you are seeking some explanation for Mr. Hay's choleric outburst, I am afraid I do not have one."

"Come now, you know what I mean. It is the business with Mr. Hay's ring that I should like to have explained."

"Oh that," Holmes said with a dismissive wave. "That shall

become clear enough in due time. Meanwhile, I think a quick visit to the Morrison House for some liquid refreshment would be in order."

As we walked toward our destination in the wilting heat, Holmes posed a surprising question. "Tell me, Watson," he said with a most serious expression, "do you think I am mad?"

"Not entirely," I said, a response which Holmes found so satisfactory that he smiled all the way back to the hotel.

❈

Later that afternoon, we found a driver with a fast team near the station, and for the sum of five dollars he was persuaded to take us to Mrs. Robinson's and await our return. It took but fifteen minutes to reach the big red house in the woods, and Holmes was soon pounding impatiently at the front door. To my surprise and alarm, it was one of the jack pine twins. Laura, as I soon learned—who greeted us when the door at last swung open. She was wearing a becoming yet modest white dress, and there was no hint in her manner of the provocative pose she and her sister had adopted during our earlier visit.

"I should like to see Mrs. Robinson," said Holmes, stepping inside before the girl could protest. "Tell her, Laura, that Mr. Baker and Mr. Smith are here on a most pressing matter."

How Holmes knew that this was Laura rather than Dora was quite beyond me, and it was only later that I learned the secret— Laura's earlobes were pierced while those of her twin sister were not, a difference which Holmes, with his phenomenal powers of observation, had noted the first time he saw them.

In any event, Laura now told Holmes: "I am sorry, sir, but I cannot help you. You see, Mrs. Robinson is gone."

"Gone where?"

"I do not know, sir. But I think she may be gone for quite a while."

Holmes received this unwelcome news with a look of consternation. His eyes narrowed and he gave Laura a withering stare.

"You are lying," he said flatly. He then swept past the girl and went up the steps into the parlor, where he called for Mrs. Robinson repeatedly. There was no response.

"All right, where is she?" Holmes demanded, turning to face Laura, who had followed him up the steps. "I want an answer, Laura, and I want it now!" he said in a voice so loud, harsh and fearsome that Laura instantly broke out in tears, like a small child being scolded by her father.

"I am sorry, sir," she said between deep sobs, "but I don't know where the madam has gone."

It was at this moment, as a flood of tears streamed down Laura's long sad face, that I realized, for the first time, how very young this unfortunate girl was and how, under a different set of circumstances, she might have led a life far removed from her present depravity.

"Do not badger her, Holmes," I said. "She is but a child."

"She is old enough to be a whore," Holmes replied with a cruelty that astonished me, "and she will answer my question or face the consequences."

"She has answered to the best of her ability, and you will gain nothing by treating her so harshly," I said rather hotly. "You have gone beyond the bounds of decency, Holmes, and I will not tolerate it."

Holmes reacted with biting sarcasm. "My lands, Watson, but you are in a paternal mood today. Had I known you harbored such deep feelings for this 'child,' as you call her, I would not have interrupted your lovemaking some days ago."

As he spoke these sneering words, Holmes gave a disgusted shake of his head and walked away. Laura, whose crying had became uncontrollable, then fell to the floor. I rushed over to attend to her. The girl's ashen face and rapid but regular pulse left little doubt that she had fainted, but I was soon able to restore her to consciousness.

"Thank you, sir, you have been very kind," she said after I had helped her to a chair, where she sat stiffly and dabbed at her tears with a handkerchief. "And you have no reason to be."

"What do you mean?"

"You know, sir," she said, looking down at the floor and speaking so softly that her words were almost a whisper. "But I just want to tell you that what happened before, when we first met, wasn't my idea, nor Dora's either. Mrs. Robinson, she put us up to it, and she is not a woman to be argued with."

I could not doubt the sincerity of her words, and I assured her that I held no grudge regarding that unfortunate episode.

She lifted her head and smiled. "I will say it again, sir, you are very kind. It is not often men have been so with me."

As though to remind her of this sad fact, Holmes's voice—faint yet clear—could be heard from somewhere in the back of the house. He was still calling for Mrs. Robinson.

"I told him, she is not here," Laura said, quivering slightly at the sound of her tormentor's voice. I held her hand, which was as small and delicate as that of a child, and told her not to worry about Mr. Baker. I then inquired whether she was alone in the house, as we had seen no one else since our arrival.

"Dora is here, but she's been sleeping all day, which is what she does when she's been at her laudanum.[8] The rest of the girls went to town this morning on account of Mrs. Robinson gave everybody the day off. Only I didn't go because I didn't want to leave Dora all alone."

"I see. And I suppose Mrs. Robinson went with the others into town?"

Laura shook her head. "No, that is what I was trying to tell that horrible Mr. Baker. Mrs. Robinson usually stays here on Wednesdays to do her accounts and whatnot, but when I went to look for her this morning I couldn't find her. It's not like her just to go somewhere without telling anybody."

"She did not leave a note or other message?"

"Nothing. It is very strange, sir, since we are supposed to open at five o'clock tonight."

"She will not be back tonight or ever," said Holmes, who had evidently overheard Laura's remark as he came out of the hallway which led to Mrs. Robinson's private quarters. The girl shrank back at the sound of Holmes's voice and I felt her hand tighten around mine.

"Please, do not leave me," she said, in a tone so heartfelt and pitiful that no decent man could fail to be moved by it.

Holmes, however, no longer seemed to have any interest in Laura, and did not even look at her as he walked by us. "Come along, Watson," he said as he reached the stairs leading down to the foyer, "there is nothing for us here."

"I must go," I said, gently disengaging my hand from the girl's. "But I promise you, I shall come back as soon as I can in order to see to it that you and your sister, if she wishes, are removed from this vile and despicable place. You have my word upon that."

"Oh, thank you, sir," Laura said, a new tear glistening in one eye. She stood and gave me a kiss upon the cheek, as chaste and innocent an expression of affection as I have ever received. "I would very much like to become a respectable woman again."

"And you shall!" I said, resolved now that this poor child should have a better life than she had thus far known.

"Watson! Are you coming or am I to leave without you!" These words came from Holmes, of course, who stood atop the staircase in a pose of imperious disdain.

"I am coming," I said, though it was one of the few instances during our long friendship when I felt no real desire to follow Holmes. But I also knew I could not leave him now, no matter how abominably he had acted, and so I bade farewell to poor Laura and followed Holmes out the door.

We spoke not a word on the short ride back to Hinckley, and it was several hours before I learned from Holmes why we had left the house so quickly. For while I was engaged with Laura, Holmes had broken into Mrs. Robinson's room, only to discover that most of her clothes and other personal possessions were gone.

"And where do you suppose she is now?" I asked.

"If only I knew," Holmes replied with a rather forlorn shrug of his shoulders, "if only I knew. But I will tell you this, Watson. I have been a fool yet again."

Chapter Sixteen

"Watson! Are You All Right?"

❋

These comments regarding Mrs. Robinson's unforeseen departure came at midnight as Holmes and I sat in a ramshackle cabin beside a desolate swamp a few miles from Hinckley. As Holmes spoke, I was struggling to remain awake. The urge to sleep, however, had begun to overpower me despite the fact that my position—I sat upon the cabin's dirt floor, my back against a wall and my legs tucked up toward my chin—was hardly comfortable. Holmes had already volunteered to take the first watch of the night, and while I did not wish to leave him with no one to talk to, I inevitably found myself drifting away into the deep sleep of exhaustion . . .

❋

We had reached the cabin after a mysterious journey which was the culmination of a series of bizarre events initiated by Holmes.

First, he had insisted that we check out of the Morrison House at nine in the evening. The clerk, unused to customers departing at such an hour, naturally demanded that we pay for a full night's lodging. Holmes, to my surprise, made no objection, telling the clerk only that "a matter of some urgency" required our immediate attention elsewhere.

Next, Holmes without explanation instructed me to pack a single change of clothes and any other "absolute necessities," as he called them, into a small satchel. He did likewise, after which we carried the remainder of our luggage across the street to the St. Paul & Duluth station. There, after sending out another telegram to Hill (the contents of which were not revealed to me), Holmes told the agent to forward our bags to Pine City on the first available train, saying we would retrieve them "at our earliest convenience." Then, without another word, Holmes set off south along the St. Paul & Duluth tracks, all the while maintaining a high state of alertness.

When we reached the nearby juncture with the Eastern Minnesota tracks, Holmes turned to the west to follow that line. And so we trudged along the tracks through the darkness, which was alleviated somewhat by moonlight shining through the usual layer of smoke. Had anyone seen us, he undoubtedly would have concluded that Holmes and I were members of that peculiar breed of railway vagabonds known in America as hoboes.

I saw no one, however. For his part, Holmes maintained a watchful silence, repeatedly gazing out into the dark, scrubby woods along the track but giving no clue as to the nature of his concern. Nor was I in any mood to talk, for I still felt the sting of Holmes's cruel remarks, and equally cruel behavior, at Mrs. Robinson's.

After a walk of perhaps three miles, we came upon a fetid body of water along the south side of the tracks.[1] A lonely cabin sat at the far side of this noxious swamp, in a rock-strewn clearing that might once have been a farm field. The cabin—which leaned precariously to one side as though pushed off its foundation by some giant hand—was little better than a ruin, though hardly of the picturesque sort.

Even in its most pristine state, this forest hideaway could not have been a pleasant abode, for it was extremely small and crude, with none of the charm of the typical English cottage. The cabin had but two small windows to either side of the front door, and its simple gable roof, which had already begun to collapse, offered only a thin layer of tar paper as protection against the elements. Its occupant, whoever he may have been, had obviously left long ago, and the cabin—with its broken windows, unpainted clapboard walls and unhinged front door—conveyed an air of utter dilapidation and abandonment.

Nonetheless, Holmes turned toward this wretched ruin, at the same time uttering his first words in nearly an hour:

"We will spend the night here, Watson."

I made no attempt to disguise my incredulity. "Spend the night? That is perfectly ridiculous, Holmes."

"Not really," Holmes replied in an even voice. "The ridiculous is by its very definition the illogical. And there is nothing illogical about spending the night in this place, which I have reason to believe will provide us with a safe haven, if not necessarily the comforts of home."

"And what are we seeking haven from? I have seen or heard no one since we left town. Is there some invisible threat to which only you are privy? If so, please enlighten me."

My words were harsh, I admit, but I feared that Holmes had begun to lose his grip under the pressure of events. How else explain this crazed journey in the dead of night to an abandoned shack in the middle of an uninhabited tract of forest? My concern, I hasten to add, was not based merely on annoyance at Holmes's inexplicable behavior but rather on precedent.

Holmes's mind was a fine and intricate thing—a jeweled Swiss watch from the very hand of the God who created us all—and yet on one or two occasions I had seen the machinery go awry, and when it did, the results were extremely peculiar. His baffling conduct during the singular affair of the Etruscan grave robbery, a case which ended quite unsatisfactorily, is but one example in this regard.[2] Whether he had reached a similar point of delusion now I could not tell, but I determined to find out why he had insisted upon leading me to this desolate place.

"I think I am entitled to an explanation of why we have come here," I said as Holmes, using a small lamp, peered into the foul-smelling confines of the cabin, which proved to be empty save for a small wooden bench, an old broom, and several discarded tins of food.

Ignoring my question, Holmes stepped into the cabin and sat down on the bench, as silent as Buddha in the darkness. I stood in the doorway and watched as he got out his favorite pipe, filled the bowl with tobacco, lit it, and then inhaled the smoke with a contented sigh. Only then did he speak, and his words came as a revelation.

"First, my dear Watson, let me apologize for my behavior this evening. You were quite right, quite right indeed, in calling me to task at Mrs. Robinson's. I was naturally anxious to solicit every bit of information I could from poor Laura, but I fear that in doing so I somehow lost sight of the fundamental decencies. The milk of human kindness, I must confess, has never flowed strongly within me, and that is one reason why I value your friendship, Watson. You are the guardian of my conscience, and I know that I can always count on you to rein in the darker impulses of my nature. As for my conduct at Mrs. Robinson's, my only excuse is that I believed then, as I do now, that we are on the verge of a great catastrophe unless we can obtain conclusive proof of the Red Demon's identity as quickly as possible."

I had never heard Holmes speak in quite so open and frank a manner before, and I could not doubt his sincerity. Even so, I continued to wonder about our present situation, since Holmes had not as yet explained our sudden flight to the swamp.

"Your apology is accepted," I said, "and there is no need to trouble yourself with the matter any further. But I am still at a loss as to why we have come here."

"It is, as I said, a matter of safety," Holmes said amiably, taking another draw on his pipe. "You see, I have little doubt that the Red Demon knows we are closing in on him. The death of Thompson, the wounding and flight of LeGrande, the confession of One-eye Johnson, the apparent disappearance of, first, Mr. Chalmers and then Mrs. Robinson—all are part of a pattern which is now pointing in but one direction, toward the Red Demon.

"He realizes this, and he will resort to the most desperate measures to stop us from foiling his malevolent plans. And that, Watson, is why we left Hinckley this evening with such unseemly haste. I am convinced that the Red Demon has been watching us, waiting for the perfect opportunity to strike. We must not give him that chance!"

"And you believe we could not be safe in Hinckley?"

"Precisely. Equally important, I believe that our continued presence in Hinckley might have jeopardized other lives as well."

"What do you mean?"

Holmes shifted in his seat, and as he relit his pipe I saw his eyes, wild and intense, in the flickering light of the match. "What I mean, Watson, is that I believe the Red Demon might well have tried to burn down the Morrison House, with you and me inside. A hundred or more people might have perished in such a fire and I did not want that on my conscience. No, I think we are better off here, at least for the night."

"But how did you know about this place?"

"I saw it from the train on our way to Hinckley. It did not strike any particular chord at that time, but it came immediately to mind when I began considering a place of temporary refuge."

"I take it we are not to stay here long. After all, we have little food or water."

"Do not worry, Watson. A single night in this primitive accommodation should suffice. After I am certain that the Red Demon has lost our trail, we will move on to a more comfortable location. In the meantime, I suggest you take some rest. I will maintain a guard, though I doubt we have anything to fear."

The clarity and calmness of Holmes's demeanor was reassuring, and I could see that I had been wrong to attribute his earlier conduct to some form of temporary derangement. There could be no question that the Sherlock Holmes I had known and trusted for so long was in complete command of the situation, and thus reassured, I soon fell asleep.

❈

. . . I shall never forget the dream which came to me later that night. I was walking through a vast, dark and mysterious forest, beneath a peculiar orange-red sky. It was evening and the path ahead offered a prospect of profound gloom, for the great trees rising all around had somehow been stripped bare of their leaves and needles, leaving only stark black trunks and branches which rose in desolation from the ground. I remember looking down at the path and being astonished to see that it was ash white, as was all the earth around it.

Immediately, I began to feel a sensation of heat, which seemed to radiate up from the earth itself, as though the very gates of hell had opened beneath me. I felt a deep and growing terror. I began to run, hoping to escape this terrible world of white earth and black trees, but my legs had turned to stone and each breath was an agony. Then a great rolling ball of smoke poured out of the earth and enveloped me so suddenly that I had no time to flee.

Blind and disoriented, I fell to the ground and gasped for air. But there was none to be had, for the smoke was everywhere, like a white shroud of death. My lungs burned, my eyes watered, and then I heard a voice from another world:

"Watson!"

Where was it coming from? Who could it be? What did this disembodied voice want of me? I felt an abrupt movement, as though my body were being transported through space, and the smoke began to disappear. Curiously, I did not want the smoke to leave, for by some strange act of magic it had turned into a silky white siren, inviting me into its arms to partake of the long, dreamless slumber from which no man ever emerges.

"Watson! Are you all right?"

The voice, loud and insistent, roused me from my reveries. I opened my eyes, sure that I had crossed over into another and far better world, only to behold a sooty, blackened face that for an instant called to mind Beelzebub himself!

"My dear Watson," this strange visage said in a familiar voice. "I thought for a moment that I had lost you."

"Holmes. It is you!"

"Who did you think it was?" Holmes replied with a smile.

"The devil," I admitted groggily, for my mind was still somewhat tangled in the cobwebs of sleep.

Holmes, who obviously took my remark as a compliment, laughed and said: "I have always thought the devil must be a most interesting fellow, with a fine criminal type of mind, and perhaps one day I shall meet him. But I assure you, Watson, that when your time comes, it will be St. Peter and not the Prince of Darkness who shall greet you in the great beyond."

As my head began to clear, I became aware that I was lying on the ground, on my back, and that somewhere off to my left a great light was flickering. I also recalled Holmes's comment about almost losing me.

"I fear I am rather confused," I said. "What has happened and why am I here?"

"You will understand soon enough," said Holmes, helping me up to a sitting position so that I could see the light behind us.

A shocking sight greeted me, for the cabin where I had fallen asleep was now a giant torch. Angry flames poured out of the cabin's windows and door, shot up through its roof and assaulted its walls. The fire burned with such ferocity that I could feel its heat stinging my face, even though we were thirty yards or more from the inferno.

"My God, Holmes. How did it start?"

"I think that should be obvious," Holmes replied. "We have had a visit from the Red Demon."

❋

Since the air was calm and there were no trees near the cabin, the fire—deprived of new fuel—soon began to burn itself out. I watched with a mixture of dread and relief as the cabin became a heap of glowing ash, for had Holmes not come to my rescue, I surely would have perished. At the same time, I wondered how the fire could have been set with Holmes standing guard, and I listened eagerly to his explanation:

"It was all my fault, Watson. I was confident that we had not been followed here, and so I became careless. After you had fallen asleep, I sat for a while in the cabin, smoking my pipe and pondering our situation. You were sleeping with your usual sonorous gusto, and as I could see no reason to be concerned about your safety, I decided to go out for a short walk.

"The warm night air was pleasant and I walked back around the swamp toward the railroad tracks. Naturally, I inspected our surroundings closely before leaving. I saw or heard nothing. It was a walk of but a few minutes to the tracks, where to my surprise I saw a slow freight train coming along from the southwest, going toward Hinckley. Not wishing to be discovered, I took cover behind a small tree and watched as the train, which was quite long, passed by. This was nearly a fatal mistake.

"For no sooner had the train gone than a flicker of light across the swamp caught my attention. You may imagine the sudden anxiety that filled my heart when I saw that the cabin was on fire. The fire had obviously been ignited only moments before, since flames were visible on only one side of the cabin—the east side, opposite from where I knew you were sleeping. This fortunate accident, Watson, may have saved your life!

"The speed with which the blaze spread was quite phenomenal. When I first saw it, the flames were no higher or more menacing than those which might be seen in a small bonfire. But as I raced back to the cabin, praying that I would see you emerging from it at any moment, the fire grew with astonishing rapidity. From the side wall, the flames shot immediately to the roof, and then began making their lethal way along the front of the cabin. With each step I took, the fire seemed to take a step of its own until I felt I was in a race against death. I am certain it took me no more than two minutes to reach the cabin, but by that time the smoke and flames had already consumed half the structure.

"When I reached the door, I called your name but received no reply. Fearing you were injured, I went inside, for the flames were only beginning to reach the door, and there I found you. To my utter surprise, you were fast asleep, despite the fact that the smoke and heat from the fire were already quite intense."

"I have always been a sound sleeper," I acknowledged somewhat sheepishly. "Still, I cannot believe that the fire failed to awaken me."

Holmes smiled. "Your response is not as unbelievable as it may sound, my dear Watson. Fire is as often as not a stealthy assassin, creeping up upon the unsuspecting victim when he least expects it. I am aware of a number of recent fires in London in which the victims died quite peaceably in their sleep, suffocated by poisonous smoke. In any event, Watson, the rest of tonight's story is known to you. I managed to carry you from the cabin before the fire could do its deadly work. Had I arrived a few seconds later, I fear that the worst might have happened."

"You have saved my life, Holmes, for which I shall be eternally grateful."

"Think nothing of it. You would have done the same for me, I am sure. Besides, had I not been so singularly careless, your life would never have been put in jeopardy."

The flames had died away now, and we walked over to the smoldering remains of the cabin. Holmes circled the ruin, searching for clues as to how the Red Demon had done his work. Unfortunately, Holmes's lamp had been consumed in the fire, and he lacked any strong light with which to conduct his examination.

"Bah, it is hopeless," he finally said. "We have no good light, and the ground is too hard for footprints."

"But how do you suppose the Red Demon knew we were here?" I asked, thinking back to our flight from Hinckley and Holmes's precautions along the way.

"I have no good answer, other than to say that the Demon is obviously more clever than I had ever thought possible."

A disquieting thought now occurred to me. "If the Red Demon set this fire, Holmes, then he cannot be far away. Why, he may be watching us at this very moment, waiting for another opportunity to strike." I reached into my coat pocket and got hold of my revolver. "But this time, I shall be ready for him!"

Holmes responded to my display of resolve with a shake of his head. "You may put your pistol away, for the Red Demon is not here."

"How do you know that?"

"Because, Watson, I have no doubt that the Demon timed his assault very carefully. Remember the freight train I saw going to Hinckley? Well, you may be assured that the Demon, after trying to incinerate you, took the opportunity to board it. He is undoubtedly back in Hinckley by now. And even though the hour is late" — it was, I saw by my watch, nearly four in the morning — "that is now where we must go. Come along, Watson, we have a long walk ahead of us."

❉

Our return to Hinckley was accomplished in gloomy silence, for Holmes seemed preoccupied with his own thoughts and I did not wish to disturb him. Nonetheless, as we followed the tracks of

the Eastern Minnesota through the dark and empty countryside, I
wondered where the strange case of the Red Demon might lead us
next. As I turned over in my mind the events of the past week—for
it had been exactly seven days since our arrival in Hinckley—I
searched in vain for some unifying feature that might bring everything into clear focus.

Yet it seemed to me, as Holmes himself had remarked, that we
had been manipulated toward a series of discoveries, only to confront more questions with each answer we received. We had been
led from Mrs. Robinson to Thompson to Chalmers and finally to
LeGrande. All were pieces of a puzzle that, when fully assembled,
should have revealed to us an image of the malevolent genius
known as the Red Demon. Holmes, in fact, had said as much. But
where he claimed to see a pattern emerging from these disparate
pieces, I could discern nothing but a perfect blank.

After all, Thompson was dead, his secrets gone with him to the
grave. LeGrande, Chalmers and Mrs. Robinson were gone as well,
only their whereabouts remained unknown. Meanwhile, the Red
Demon—whoever he was—appeared to operate with impunity,
and I began to consider the possibility that Holmes might never
learn the villain's identity. This thought was a troubling one.

The attack at the cabin, in which my life was so nearly forfeited,
had clearly taken Holmes by surprise, and I feared that—for all of
his declarations of confidence—he himself was beginning to have
doubts. Still, I was not ready to accept the notion that any man
could, in the long run, outwit Holmes, and I determined to follow him to the very end of this mysterious affair, regardless of its
conclusion.

Such were the unhappy thoughts afflicting my mind when we
finally reached the outskirts of Hinckley shortly after five in the
morning. Though I was by this time greatly fatigued, and extremely
hungry, Holmes displayed his usual ferocious energy and it was all
I could to do to keep up with him. Holmes had given no hint of
our destination, and had he now stated his intention to dig a hole in
the ground and occupy it for the next fortnight, I should not have

been in the least surprised. As it was, his plans proved far less extreme.

"Keep your chin up, Watson," he said as we passed the juncture of the Eastern Minnesota and St. Paul & Duluth tracks, where several gas lamps illuminated the darkness. "We are almost there."

"And where is there?" I inquired wearily, noticing under the lights how sooty we had become in the fire.

"The St. Paul & Duluth station," said Holmes, turning north toward the depot two blocks away. "But first we must find a place to bathe, lest we be mistaken for chimney sweeps. I am sure there is a hotel nearby that can accommodate us. Then we shall rest for a few hours before boarding the morning train to Pine City."

"And what, pray tell, is in Pine City?"

"Why, our luggage, of course."

"I am aware of that," I said with some exasperation. "But what is it you expect to find in Pine City?"

Holmes's response was cryptic: "I expect to find absolutely nothing in Pine City, and that is why we must go there."

Chapter Seventeen

"He Began Ranting about the Railroads"

✶

We caught the train to Pine City without incident and were soon traveling south through yet another stretch of dreary, desiccated woodland. Settling into his seat, Holmes occupied himself by scribbling entries into the small notebook he always kept during the course of an investigation. After we had gone several miles, he paused long enough to remark that the morning seemed especially "smoky," an observation that did not overwhelm me with its perspicuity.

The haze that hung like a curtain of blue gauze in the sky was, in fact, no different from the smoke that had accosted us every day since our arrival in the pineries. Indeed, it seemed a more or less permanent thing, like the dampness of London or the arid heat of the Sahara. I had by now become so accustomed to this perpetual pall that I hardly noticed it, despite the pungent aroma of burned wood which infiltrated all my garments.

As Holmes showed no further interest in polite intercourse, I struck up a conversation with a traveler sitting across from us. He was a man of forty or so, with a jolly round face and ruddy cheeks, and he turned out to be an employee of the St. Paul & Duluth. His name was James Morton, and he was returning to St. Paul, where he worked in the railroad's dispatch office.

Since he seemed well posted on all matters relating to the operation of a modern railroad, a subject in which I have always taken some interest, our conversation proved most pleasant. As might be expected, Morton was especially informative on the topic of dispatching, pointing out the innumerable complexities involved in maintaining a reliable schedule over miles of track.

"Now, a lot of people think keeping a schedule is an easy thing," he noted, "but I will tell you, sir, there are a hundred ways — nay, make that a thousand — that matters can go wrong. Why, just last week, all hell — you will pardon my language, sir — all hell broke loose not two miles south of Pine City on account of a simple little fire."

Holmes, who had displayed a sphinxlike disregard of our conversation up to this moment, looked up from his notebook and bestowed an ingratiating smile upon Morton.

"A fire, you say. What sort of fire, Mr. Morton?"

"The common variety," Morton responded. "Some farmer had gotten careless, I imagine, while burning brush. Soon, he had a fine little blaze going. Now, you would think that in a time of drought such as this men would be careful, but that is not the case. Most of these farmers, if you ask me, are ignorant fools!"

"Indeed," said Holmes sympathetically. "And am I to take it that this particular fire spread to the tracks of the St. Paul & Duluth, with unfortunate results?"

"Oh, it spread all right. Burned a hundred yards of ties before the firemen got it under control. I am sure you can imagine the problems this caused. Trains were delayed all along the line while the damage was repaired. But the worst of it, sir, is the fact that every time a blaze breaks out anywhere within sight of a railroad track, who do you think is blamed?"

"The railroad?"

"Exactly. It is always the railroad which is accused, sir, regardless of the circumstances. Of course, all of our locomotives carry the finest spark arresters money can buy.[1] But this fact means nothing to those who view the railroad as a bottomless bag of money into which anyone with a grievance, however unfounded, can put his grasping hand. Hardly a day goes by when we are not sued for this or that. It is a disgrace!"

"Ah, it must indeed be a vexing problem," said Holmes, shaking his head in sympathy with Morton's complaint. "But the St. Paul & Duluth, I trust, takes a hard line in such matters."

Morton nodded. "Indeed we do, sir. Our lawyers do not give an inch and they seldom lose a case. Even so, the expense of defending so many frivolous actions is quite onerous."

"No doubt. But I suppose other railroads—such as your competitor, the Eastern Minnesota—face similar problems."

"I cannot deny that, though I suspect the Eastern gets sued less often than we do simply because everybody knows that James J. Hill is as hard a man as God ever made and will not part readily with his profits. Fact is, I don't know of anyone who's ever gotten a penny from the Eastern. I imagine that's why Hill is just about the richest man in the Northwest."

No sooner had Morton delivered this intriguing judgment upon our employer than the train whistle sounded and the scattered wooden buildings of Pine City came into view. A few minutes later, we bade farewell to Morton and stepped out onto the platform at the Pine City depot. I did not know it then, but Holmes was now ready for his final assault upon the Red Demon.

✳

As I review my notes from this time, I am struck by the abrupt change that overtook Holmes once we reached Pine City. During our week in Hinckley, when every day seemed to bring some thrilling new adventure, Holmes had often been tense and uneasy, like a sentry in the sight of enemy battalions. But now, removed from that unrestful village, he settled into a state of what can only be described as intense calm. It was as though all the physical energy he had expended over the past week had now been concentrated into pure thought, allowing the full extent of his genius to flower.

After our arrival in Pine City, we immediately reclaimed our baggage from the depot and walked across the street to the Brackett House, reputed to be the town's finest hotel. While this establishment was hardly of the luxurious variety, it was clean and quiet, and that is all Holmes wanted.

"I shall need time to think," he told me after we had settled into our rooms. "Allow no one to disturb me."

And so, for two hours, I sat in Holmes's room while he undertook his thinking. He lay upon the bed, his shirtsleeves rolled up, his eyes closed, his hands folded on his chest, his breathing so slow and relaxed he might have been asleep. Yet all the while, I knew, his great brain was at work, moving swiftly and surely through every aspect of the case, drawing inferences, making connections, identifying the significant and rejecting the irrelevant, until at last it had created an iron web of proof from which the Red Demon, for all of his malignant wiles, could never hope to escape.

At half past two, Holmes opened his eyes and sat up upon the bed "I have him!" he said, then added to my surprise: "Watson, I wish to thank you."

"For what?"

"For pointing me to the Red Demon. Without you and your friend Mr. Morton, I might never have seen the final avenue that must now be explored."

"How so?" I asked, since I had not detected anything of particular value in our brief conversation with Morton. Nor did I know what I had contributed to Holmes's newfound insight.

"You will find out soon enough, Watson. For this case is now a purely mechanical matter."

Although I pressed Holmes to explain himself, he declined to do so, and I knew it was hopeless in such circumstances to try to draw him out. My only recourse now was to assist him in whatever way I could as he drew closer to the Red Demon.

✳

For the next eight hours, I became a messenger, shuttling back and forth between the hotel and the St. Paul & Duluth depot so frequently that my footsteps undoubtedly left a furrow in the street. Each time I left Holmes I bore a message to be wired to Hill, and as often as not I returned with our employer's latest reply. How many telegrams came and went this way I cannot hope to remember, but the number of replies received by Holmes was eventually sufficient to form a small pile upon his bed.

Day became night and yet the flood of messages did not recede. The station agent in Pine City by now groaned at my every new appearance, and it was only by the steady application of silver dollars to his purse that he was persuaded to give Holmes's telegrams priority.

Holmes, meanwhile, was indefatigable, receiving each reply from Hill with anxious interest, voraciously consuming its contents and then scribbling off yet another message. What Hill thought of this barrage of messages I do not know, but he gave no hint of exasperation in his telegrams, perhaps sensing that Holmes was at last closing in on his quarry.

At half past ten I arrived back at the room with Hill's latest telegram, one that at first glance seemed to hold no special promise. I have it before me now, and as I look at the decoded message, I cannot help but shudder, for it turned out to be an invitation to a holocaust:

"Here are three more cases from legal dept., though quite old.

John Anderson et al. vs. Eastern Railway of Minnesota, St. Louis County District Court, Minn. Damage to property. Settled, 10-16-89. Bradford Cornell vs. Eastern Railway of Minnesota, Douglas County District Court, Wis. Unlawful death. Verdict for complainant, 3-19-91. Overturned on appeal. Donald Jackson et al. vs. Eastern Railway of Minnesota, Douglas County District Court, Wis. Unlawful taking of property. Verdict for defendant, 6-8-90. Do you wish to go back further? J. J. Hill."

Holmes, who was still sprawled out on the bed, scanned this wire as quickly as he had all the others. But instead of throwing it into the pile, which is what I expected him to do, he sprang to his feet and, without a word, opened the largest of his suitcases. He then began tossing out the contents as though in the grip of some uncontrollable compulsion. Apparel, toilet articles, notebooks, even his most prized magnifying glass, went flying. For a moment, I thought he had truly gone mad.

"What is it, Holmes? Have you lost something?"

My question was ignored. "Ah, here it is," he said, lifting a booklet from the bottom of the bag, which had now been all but emptied of its contents. The book, I could see, was a guide and schedule published by the Eastern Minnesota Railway.

Holmes rapidly thumbed through the book, a look of exhilaration animating his features. "Now, let me see, where are the maps? Ah yes, here they are. Douglas County. It must be along the northern end of the line, near Duluth, for that is where the Eastern Minnesota tracks pass through Wisconsin. Eureka! I have found it. Superior!"

This last word was uttered so triumphantly that one might have thought Holmes had stumbled upon the location of the Grail.

"What exactly have you found?"

He responded by reading a paragraph from the guide: "Superior, a busy port city on the lake of that name, is the seat of Douglas County, Wisconsin, and lies directly across St. Louis Bay from the city of Duluth, which is the northern terminus of the Eastern Railway of Minnesota."

"I will take your word for it, Holmes, that this is a significant piece of information, though I cannot imagine why."

His eyes shining with excitement, Holmes turned to me and said: "My dear Watson, 'significant' is a word entirely insufficient to describe what I have found. Don't you see? The haze that has surrounded us since we came to this bleak country has lifted and the path to the Red Demon lies clear before us. We need only follow it now!"

"Follow it? But where?"

"To Superior, Wisconsin. We shall be on the first train to that fair city in the morning."

❉

"Fair," as it turned out, was not a word that accurately described the city of Superior, which we reached at two o'clock on the afternoon of Friday, August 31. We had taken the morning St. Paul & Duluth train to Hinckley and then transferred to the Eastern Minnesota, arriving in Superior after a ride of nearly three hours through desolate and smoky forest lands.

Despite its high-sounding name, Superior was a rather grim place, its major architectural monuments consisting of docks, grain elevators and other industrial structures arrayed along the margin of the lake, which was all but invisible from much of the city. Even so, this low, flat and unpretty community did offer one charm, for on the afternoon of our arrival a dense fog had pushed in from the lake, instantly evaporating the heat of the day. This damp chill brought to mind London, and after suffering more than a week in the heat and haze of the pineries, I could not help but view this cooling mist as a kind of deliverance.

Holmes paid no heed to this climatic turn, other than to remark that the fog was a "decided nuisance" in view of our unfamiliarity with the city. Nonetheless, after leaving the Eastern Minnesota depot we soon reached our destination—a tidy brick building that announced itself as the Douglas County Courthouse. Here, upon suitable inquiries, we were directed to the clerk of court's office, where Holmes at last found the document which was to lead us to the Red Demon. It was one of the lawsuits—*Cornell vs. the Eastern Minnesota*—mentioned in the latest telegram from Hill, and it told a tragic story, which I have summarized below:

The complainant, Bradford Cornell, was a schoolteacher who lived with his wife in a small cottage on the outskirts of Superior in an area described as "well wooded." On the morning of July 19, 1890, Cornell had taken the train to Duluth, where he taught at the public high school. His wife, who was carrying a child at the time, remained at home. The day was extremely warm and dry, and small fires were already burning in the surrounding countryside, though none seemed to pose a serious threat.

However, at some point in the afternoon an intense fire began near the Eastern Minnesota tracks south of Superior and spread rapidly into the nearby woods. Cornell's cottage lay in the path of the blaze and soon caught fire, with his wife trapped inside. In a matter of minutes, the house was engulfed in flames. Cornell, returning from Duluth, happened to arrive home at the very height of the blaze and heard his wife's agonized screams for help.

Despite the smoke and flames, he was able to rescue his wife from the burning house. But she had already suffered "painful and disfiguring burns over most of her body," according to the lawsuit. She lingered in "unbearable pain" for over a month before dying at a hospital in Duluth. Attending physicians attempted to save her baby but the child was stillborn.

Cornell then sued the railway, contending that sparks from a locomotive "operated in a reckless and unsafe manner" had ignited the fatal fire. The Eastern Minnesota's attorneys, in response, argued that there was no evidence of negligence on the railroad's part and that it could not be held responsible for Mrs. Cornell's unfortunate death. A jury decided in Cornell's favor after trial and awarded him ten thousand dollars in damages. The railroad, however, immediately appealed and several months later the jury's verdict was thrown out by a higher court.

"It is a very sad story," I remarked to Holmes after we had finished examining the file. "But what does it have to do with the Red Demon?"

"Everything, I fear," said Holmes gravely. "Come along, Watson, time is of the essence. We must go to Duluth at once."

❄

Duluth, a bustling community of some thirty thousand souls, proved to be surprising in every respect—a city that had somehow taken root in a great rock garden by the shores of an inland sea. Its situation was picturesque in the extreme, for the entire city clung precariously to steep hills that rose from the cold blue lake. A grid of streets ascended these hills, which were studded with vast outcroppings of black rock, at grades so daunting that they reminded me of San Francisco.[2]

Yet as we rode across the only railroad bridge connecting Superior to Duluth, Holmes showed no interest in this magnificent prospect of land and water. His every thought was now focused upon the Red Demon, and had we been passing through the most scenic valley of Switzerland or the most romantic quarter of Paris I doubt he would have noticed.

Upon our arrival at the Duluth station, which was new and quite elaborate in the French manner, we received directions to the city's high school and proceeded there at once.[3] It was now after three in the afternoon, and Holmes was anxious to speak to the principal before the school day ended. But when we finally reached the school, located midway up one of the city's hills, we met with disappointment. A clerk informed us that the principal, whose name was George Grady, had left earlier to visit his mother in a community some miles away and would probably not return to Duluth until the following afternoon.

Greatly disappointed, Holmes then attempted to secure information from the clerk regarding Bradford Cornell. In particular, Holmes wished to see any photographs of Cornell. The clerk, however, proved to be an ignorant and uncooperative fellow, saying that he had never heard of Cornell and that, in any event, all such inquiries would have to be taken up with the principal. The conversation soon became heated, and I believe the clerk, who became rather impolite, might have taken a thrashing from Holmes had I not finally persuaded my friend to leave.

"I am sure we shall find Mr. Grady in the morning and that he will tell us all we need to know," I said to Holmes as we walked down the front steps of the school.

Holmes reacted to my reassurances with a look of withering scorn. "You do understand," he said, with such vehemence that I could see a small blood vessel throbbing in his forehead, "there is a great evil in the air, Watson. I can feel it as surely as I feel the beating of my heart. It is an evil that hangs over Hinckley like a shroud, and it is at once insidious and terrible, for it stems from the most implacable of all human motives—vengeance. We alone, we alone are in a position to stop this evil, and that is why we cannot suffer a moment's delay. We are in a race now, Watson, a race against time and the Red Demon, and if we lose it, then I fear that unimaginable horrors await us!"

❋

That night we took lodging at the Spalding Hotel, Duluth's newest and largest inn, though it quickly became apparent that Holmes would not enjoy a moment's rest.[4] He was agitated in the extreme and paced about his room, smoking endless pipefuls of tobacco and showing no interest in conversation. Nor would he consider dinner, so I dined alone in the hotel restaurant, where I chanced to meet several businessmen of the city.

These gentlemen were all boosters of the typical American type and talked excitedly of a new lode of iron ore discovered nearby that, in their opinion, was sure to make Duluth the seat of a great inland empire.[5] It was nearly nine by the time I returned to our quarters, only to find Holmes still in a state of ferocious unease and his room so rank with the stench of tobacco smoke that I was soon driven from it.

How he endured the night I do not know, but at six the next morning he awakened me with his usual indifference to the niceties of decorum.

"Open up, Watson," he shouted from the hallway.

I quickly dressed and opened the door, and there stood Holmes like a refugee from Bedlam—his clothes disheveled, his hair uncombed, his eyes locked in a feverish stare.

"What is the matter?" I said, for my friend's appearance was little short of alarming.

"Everything is the matter. The Demon has had yet another day to go about his work while we have done nothing. Nothing! Let us move along, Watson. I do not intend to waste more time."

Moments later, having been afforded no opportunity for breakfast, I followed Holmes out of the hotel and into the early morning sunshine. Holmes obviously had a destination in mind, for we at once turned west along the thoroughfare in front of the hotel and proceeded two blocks to a singular sight.

It was a funicular railway, similar to several I had seen in Europe, and it provided a direct if precipitous means of ascending one of the city's foremost hills.[6] A sign informed us that the first car of the day would leave at half past six, and so we had a wait of but a few minutes before boarding. Fifteen minutes later, we were at the top of the hill, which offered a magnificent prospect of the city and the glittering lake.

Holmes, of course, paid no heed to this charming scene. Instead, he directed my attention to a large wooden house with shingled walls which commanded a superb blufftop vantage point a few hundred yards from the funicular station.

"According to my inquiries at the hotel, that is Mr. George Grady's house," he said, "and if he has not yet returned, we shall camp there until he does."

"Camp" proved to be an appropriate choice of words, for Grady was not at home, nor was anyone else. And so, finding a place upon the front stoop, we sat, looking no doubt like a pair of vagrants awaiting a free meal. Grady, meanwhile, seemed in no hurry to return from his parental visit. Ten o'clock passed with no sign of him, as did noon (when I went to a nearby grocer's store to buy bread and cheese). An hour later, Grady had still not appeared, and I began to fear that our long wait might prove fruitless.

I was about to remark on this when a tall man with a bag slung over his shoulder emerged from the funicular station and walked toward us. When he reached the walk leading to the house, I prayed that he would turn in our direction. He did, his eyes meeting mine with a quizzical and somewhat apprehensive look.

"Is there something I can do for you gentlemen?" he asked.

"Ah, you must be Mr. Grady," Holmes said, standing up and extending his hand. "I hope you will not be alarmed, sir, if I tell you that you are just the man we have been waiting to see."

❋

Adopting a perfect American accent and speaking with his usual suavity, Holmes soon put Grady at ease. He explained that we were attorneys from Chicago and had come in search of Bradford Cornell to notify him of a legal settlement in his favor. Grady, after examining the card Holmes had proffered (where he had obtained this counterfeit I could only guess), invited us inside, where we took seats in the parlor and sipped on excellent tea.

"Well, your news comes as a surprise," said Grady, who was a man in his fifties, trim of figure and with the unmistakable glint of intelligence in his blue eyes. "I had thought poor Cornell lost his case on appeal."

"So it might have seemed," Holmes acknowledged, "but it was decided in our office to chance yet another appeal, and though the process has taken longer than expected—justice, as you know, Mr. Grady, can be a slow and cumbersome thing—we have at last prevailed. The sum of ten thousand dollars is now owed to Mr. Cornell, providing, of course, that we can locate the gentleman. Thus far, our efforts have proved fruitless, but we are hoping that you, as a former employer, might have heard from him. Any help you could provide would be most appreciated."

Grady gave a reluctant shake to his head. "I am sorry, but I have not heard a word from him since some months after the terrible incident at his home."

"I can only imagine what a shock to Mr. Cornell that must have been."

"Indeed it was, sir. He had been one of the finest teachers in our school system but after the death of his wife and child, well, I am afraid he fell quite to pieces. His behavior became extremely odd, to the point that he frightened the children."

"Odd in what way, if I may ask?"

"He began ranting about the railroads and how they were destroying the country, that sort of thing. Naturally, such talk could not be tolerated and I had no choice but to dismiss him."

"How sad," said Holmes, his voice fairly oozing sympathy. "How sad indeed. But tell me, what did Mr. Cornell teach?"

"Mathematics and philosophy. In addition, he was our drama teacher and staged the senior class play for us every year."

"An unusual combination."

"Yes, it was. But he was quite a brilliant man. He used to amuse the students, I recall, by having them devise ciphers and then solving them. He was very good at anything mathematical."

"But the unfortunate deaths of his wife and unborn child, as you said, unhinged him?"

"Absolutely. He was convinced that the railroad had caused the fire and he pursued his lawsuit with a vengeance. When he lost — or perhaps, I should say, when it appeared he had lost — he became very bitter. I was afraid, in fact, that he might resort to self-destruction."

Holmes nodded in commiseration. "Well, perhaps the settlement we have obtained on his behalf will at least offer some measure of satisfaction. But you say that you have not seen him in several years?"

"That is correct. I believe it was in August or early September of 1891 that the appeals court overturned the verdict in his favor. It was shortly thereafter that his behavior became unacceptable and he left. I have not seen him since."

"And you have had no correspondence from him either?"

"None."

"I see," said Holmes. "Well, Mr. Grady, you have been most helpful. Incidentally, would you by chance happen to have a photograph of Mr. Cornell? For some reason, our office does not possess one and it might be of assistance in our search."

Rubbing his chin, Grady considered this request. "A photograph. No, I—hold on! Just wait here a minute."

He left the room, returning moments later with a large quarto-sized book, which in gold-embossed letters bore the title *Black Bear Annual*.

"This is our senior-class yearbook for 1890," said Grady, thumbing rapidly through the book. "I know that Mr. Cornell is pictured here. Ah yes, here he is—on page sixty-six."

Holmes bent over to inspect the page, but gave no sign of recognition. He handed the book to me, and I could hardly hide my astonishment, for the man in the picture—the man Holmes obviously believed to be the Red Demon—was all too familiar!

"May we keep this book temporarily?" Holmes asked.

"Certainly," said Grady. "I have several copies."

Holmes tucked the volume under his arm. "Thank you. It shall be returned to you at the earliest possible time."

Grady nodded, shook our hands, and then offered a parting comment: "I was just thinking, Mr. Baker, how odd and ironic it is that you are here in search of Mr. Cornell, for his tragic story always occupies my mind on this particular day."

Holmes, who was halfway down the front steps, stopped as though struck by a bullet and spun around. "And what, pray tell, is so particular about this day?"

"Oh, I thought you would have known, sir. You see, it was exactly four years ago, on September 1, 1890, that Mrs. Cornell died, her poor child dying with her. It was as sad a scene as I have ever witnessed, for she suffered horribly to the very end. May God bless her!"

These words caused the blood to drain instantly from Holmes's face, and he turned and began running as fast as his long legs would carry him.

Chapter Eighteen

"My God, the Clouds Are on Fire!"

✳

As I sit at my writing desk, a thick fog swirling outside the windows of 221B Baker Street, I am haunted by fantastic images of that terrible day, September 1, 1894. These phantasms dance before me like the flames in a hearth, illuminating numerous incidents of heroism and disaster amid the cruel majesty of Nature's fury. I see a locomotive roaring through a deadly veil of black smoke, its occupants working feverishly to reach a doomed village . . . I see the agonized faces fleeing before a whirlwind of fire . . . I see Sherlock Holmes's look of astonishment as his deerstalker flies from his head and instantly ignites into flames . . . I see two gaunt figures upon a great burning trestle, locked in mortal combat while all around the very air seems to be on fire . . . But most of all, I see the twisted, charred bodies of the dead, lying like crushed black flowers in an eerie white wasteland of rubble and ash.

And now, as I turn to the concluding chapters of this story, which is surely the most tragic adventure of Sherlock Holmes's career, I pray that I shall at last be able to exorcise these demons of memory which have plagued me for so long.

✳

When Holmes sprinted from Grady's house, I followed as best I could and caught up with him at the funicular station.

"What is it, Holmes?" I panted, leaning against a pillar and struggling to regain my breath.

"We must return to Hinckley at once," Holmes declared. He peered anxiously down the incline in search of an oncoming car. "Today will be the day."

"The day?"

"The day of judgment, Watson, which the Red Demon spoke of in a letter to Mr. Hill. The exact words, as I recall, were: 'Now comes the day of judgment. Ruin shall rain down on you like the wrath of God. Day shall become night, the very air shall catch fire and the Eastern Minnesota shall be consumed.'"

Holmes's rendition of these words sent a chill down my spine. "And you believe the anniversary of the death of his wife and child will cause the Red Demon to act today?"

"I am sure of it," said Holmes, still staring down the track, where a car crept up the steep grade toward us. "G-dd--nit!" he said, the first time I had ever heard him utter that blasphemous expletive. "Why can't the car go faster?"

Once we reached the bottom of the hill, Holmes bolted from the car and dashed toward the Union Depot. As usual, I lagged behind. At the depot, which was crowded with afternoon travelers, Holmes went to the stationmaster's office and demanded to send a telegram to Hill immediately.

The stationmaster, a sour-looking man named Jorgenson, was obviously stunned by this highly irregular request. Yet Holmes's tone was so urgent and his manner so commanding that Jorgenson instantly complied. I have retained a copy of this fateful message, which read as follows: "Red Demon will strike today. Must have first available locomotive to Hinckley and clear track. Send warning there immediately. Lives at stake. John Baker."

I took a seat while we waited for a reply, but Holmes could hardly contain his impatience.

"Hurry up," he urged, hovering over Jorgenson and glowering at the silent key beneath his fingers. Suddenly, the key began to click. A message! Jorgenson scowled as he wrote it down.

"Well?" Holmes demanded. "Has Mr. Hill responded?"

"Not yet," said Jorgenson, "but I can tell you this: You won't be getting any messages through to Hinckley, at least not for a while. I have just gotten word that the lines there are down and all messages are being rerouted through St. Cloud."

Holmes froze when he heard these words. "Lines are down, you say? What has happened?"

"Don't know. Probably a fire in the woods. We've had reports of pretty heavy smoke in that area all morning."

Just then, the telegraph key came to life again. Holmes and I watched intently as Jorgenson jotted down the incoming message. When he had finished, he handed the wire to Holmes and said:

"Well, I'll be! Mr. Hill says you're to have a locomotive and engineer, no questions asked. It's a strange way to run a railroad if you ask me, but I guess that's the way it's going to be. All right then, come along. I'll get you that locomotive."

※

We rushed out to the train shed, where a passenger train was preparing to leave. Jorgenson found the conductor and explained the situation. The conductor's eyes opened wide in disbelief when he learned that his locomotive was about to be commandeered.

"But what will I tell the passengers?" the poor man said as Jorgenson showed him the telegram from Hill.

"Tell them whatever you want. Tell them that Jim Hill has gone crazy, for all I care. But they will just have to wait."

Holmes, meanwhile, was already striding toward the locomotive, where a worker in overalls was performing adjustments with a large wrench. As we approached the man, he turned around and I was surprised to see the fearless features of William Best.

"Well now," he said, setting down his wrench, "what in blazes do we have here?"

Before Holmes could reply, Jorgenson rushed up. "It is all right, Bill," he said, handing Best the telegram. "These men are to have your locomotive. Orders from Jim Hill himself."

Best read the wire, then a slight smile creased his face. "And just what are you and your friend intending to do with this locomotive, Mr. Baker? Take it across the Atlantic to England?"

"No," said Holmes calmly. "We intend to go to Hinckley at once and I am hoping that you will take us there."

"Is that a fact? And what is so g-dd--ned important in Hinckley that you must kidnap my train?"

Holmes fixed an intense gaze upon Best, who returned it without flinching. "I will not be coy with you, Mr. Best. I have reason to believe that at this very instant the entire community of Hinckley is in grave danger. You were correct in assuming that I was hired by Mr. Hill to investigate the fires which have struck the Eastern Minnesota. I now know who the culprit is, and I also know that it is not a member of your union or anyone connected with it. And as I am certain that this arsonist will attempt today to set his most dangerous fire yet, it is imperative that we reach Hinckley at once. I only pray to God that we will not be too late to prevent a great tragedy!"

Holmes paused and looked up at the idling locomotive, which throbbed and rumbled like an iron monster waiting to be unleashed. He then returned his gaze to Best, studying him the way a general might inspect his most decorated soldier. "I have been told, Mr. Best, that you are the finest engineer in the Northwest. I shall ask you now to prove it!"

Best took off his hat and wiped the perspiration from his brow, for the engine—even in its immobile state—cast off a tremendous amount of heat. He said: "I take it then, Mr. Baker, that you believe great danger may await us in Hinckley."

Holmes gave a solemn nod. "The telegraph lines are down and Hinckley is cut off from the world, so I can be absolutely certain of nothing. Yet I fear that an inferno may already be burning in the pineries around Hinckley."

"So you're saying that if we take old No. 125 here"—Best reached up and touched his gloved hand to the locomotive's hissing boiler—"and head off for Hinckley, we just might be going into the very fires of hell."

"It is possible," Holmes acknowledged.

Best grinned and wiped a cinder from his begrimed face. I shall never forget his next words: "Well, then, you are in luck, Mr. Baker, for if you are looking to go to hell, then by God you've found the man to take you there!"

"You are a champion, sir," said Holmes, grabbing Best's hand and shaking it so vigorously that I feared he might pull the poor man's arm off. "We must leave at once."

"I'll have to find my firemen first," Best said.

"There is no time," replied Holmes, climbing up into the cab of the locomotive. He motioned me to follow, then removed his coat and threw it to the ground. "Mr. Smith and I will shovel all the coal you can use."

❈

The locomotive and tender were soon disconnected from the rest of the train, and Best—with two blasts of his whistle—announced his intention to leave. He pushed a lever to the floor with his right hand, admitting steam into the cylinders, and then eased back on the throttle with his left.[1] The locomotive, emitting a great gasp as though relieved to be on its way, surged forward. I looked at my watch. It was two o'clock and Hinckley was seventy-two miles away.

"Start shoveling," Best said. "We'll need all the steam this old girl can use."

"How long to Hinckley?" Holmes asked. He was shoveling coal into the glowing firebox at a frantic pace, and the engine was already so noisy that he had to shout to be heard.

"All depends. We'll just see what she can do."

We could not make much time at first, for we had to proceed slowly across the bridge into Superior and wend our way through that city's maze of rail yards. Once we left the lake behind, the weather became extremely hot, and the blazing firebox in the cab only intensified our discomfort.[2] Holmes and I, who took turns shoveling at Best's command, were soon drenched in perspiration. Best, meanwhile, seemed immune to the suffocating heat, remarking only that it was "getting a trifle warm."

After we cleared the Superior yards, Best began to "pour on the steam," as the Americans say, and the locomotive responded with such a cacophonous mixture of clanging, hissing, roaring and shaking that I feared it would literally fly apart at any instant. The din in the cab was deafening, and my ears soon ached from the mad clamor of pounding metal and raging steam.

For the first thirty miles or so we fairly flew along, with no sign of fire in the woods. Light smoke hung in the air, but we thought little of it, since similar conditions had prevailed during our entire time in the pineries. But as we approached the village of Holyoke, an ominous change occurred, for the smoke began to thicken and darken as though we had suddenly passed into a great black cloud.[3] As visibility grew worse, we were forced to stop so Best could light the engine's headlamp.

Nonetheless, Holmes resisted any idea of slackening our pace. "We must go forward at all cost and as quickly as possible," he told Best.

"All right, Mr. Baker, I guess you're the conductor of this train," said Best as we lurched into motion again. "But we'll be running blind, and if the line's not cleared and there's another train up ahead, or if a bridge is down, then you'd best say your prayers because we'll be going to hell sooner rather than later!"

And so we sped through this eerie blanket of smoke, which rendered the atmosphere as dark as if the sun had been eclipsed. Here and there, the gloom lifted long enough for us to catch glimpses of the countryside, which rolled past in a brown blur. Word of our frantic race to Hinckley had obviously preceded us, for as we sped past several remote communities—Holyoke, Kerrick and Mansfield are among those I recall—townspeople gathered by the tracks and cheered us on with wild shouts.

Best, meanwhile, was master of the road, and no horseman ever controlled a thundering steed more expertly than Best manipulated his locomotive. The darkness in which we found ourselves did not affect him in the least. He knew by heart every curve, grade and bridge along our route and adjusted his speed to accommodate each new circumstance. More than once, as we approached a tight curve or narrow bridge in the gloom, I was certain that we would fly off the track and come to a deadly end, but Best somehow kept the racing locomotive on its rails.

Though the cab was crowded with dials, gauges, valves and similar devices, Best paid them no heed. Instead, he leaned constantly out his window, listening to the sound of the locomotive the way a physician might study a patient's breathing.

"Is something wrong?" I yelled. We were now twenty miles from Hinckley, and the smoke had lifted somewhat. I was in the fireman's seat on the left side of the engine while Holmes, whose energy seemed boundless, continued to feed the firebox.

"I'm just listening to my sweetheart here," Best shouted back. "Driving a locomotive's like playing the piano by ear, Mr. Smith. Sound is everything. Right now, the old girl's moaning and groaning but she'll be all right."

At the next instant, Best was seized with a look of stark terror. "Water," he screamed, pointing to a valve near my right hand. "Turn it. Turn it hard. Now!"

Without hesitation, I did as I was told, while Best stared apprehensively at a small glass gauge over the firebox. Then he let out a sigh of relief. "That was a near one," he said.

"What happened?"

"I've been running her on blue steam and I got careless. From now on, Mr. Smith, you keep an eye on that gauge and don't ever let the water drop out of sight."[4]

"What would happen then?" I shouted.

"Nothing, except that we'd all be blown to kingdom come."

How fast we were going I cannot say, though the sensation of speed was overwhelming. The locomotive seemed a living thing, a raging beast with an insatiable appetite for coal, and we rode it in the way an American cowboy might ride a "bucking bronco," hanging on for dear life. At one point, I looked out the cab window, feeling the blast of hot air on my face, and was mesmerized by the sight of the rods below me driving the locomotive's iron wheels. Back and forth they went, so rapidly that their motion was all but invisible, as though the devil's own hot breath were driving them. Only later did I learn from Best that on several stretches of straight track we had reached the unheard of speed of seventy miles an hour, which he had calculated by counting the number of telegraph poles we passed per minute.[5]

Yet even this frightening velocity was not adequate for Holmes, who as we neared the village of Sandstone paused from his backbreaking labors long enough to urge Best on to even greater speed. "We must go faster, faster," he cried, his eyes glowing as fiercely as the coals in the firebox.

Best shook his head. "There's no more to be had out of her, Mr. Baker. This old girl's a liver-splitter and if we go any faster she'll buck right off the track. Besides, the high bridge is coming up and we'd lose her for sure if we tempt fate there."

We had crossed this long, high trestle—which spanned the gorge of the Kettle River—on our way to Duluth, and I had remarked to Holmes then that it hardly seemed adequate to support the weight of a train. Now, as we came upon this structure once again in the dim smoke, its appearance was even less reassuring. It had the look of an enormous makeshift contraption, rising from a wide base and then narrowing as it climbed one hundred feet above the river in a maze of wooden cross ties and diagonal braces. The bridge culminated in a slender deck just wide enough to accommodate a single track.

Best told us normal speed on the bridge was four miles an hour but that he would get us across "a bit faster."

Once we were upon the bridge, I was forced to close my eyes after peering out the cab window and seeing nothing except the frothy green river rushing far below amid jagged slabs of rock.

"Looks like they're keeping busy down there," Best remarked, referring to workers in a large quarry at the bottom of the gorge that yielded a fine-grained sandstone from which the adjoining village had taken its name.[6]

I had no wish to view this scene, however, for I have always felt discomfort in the presence of heights. This sensation was intensified by the trembling I felt as the locomotive made its way across the bridge, and not until we reached firm ground did I feel comfortable. As we picked up speed again, I glanced back at the bridge, hoping that I would never have to cross it again.

Holmes, meanwhile, seemed obsessed with maintaining the engine's speed no matter how much labor it required. He had become a stoking machine, and though I offered time and again to spell him from his hot drudgery, he would not yield his place in front of the firebox. Shovelful after shovelful of coal he threw into the blazing box, his pace unstinting as we sped through Sandstone and began the final sprint to Hinckley.

Best was quite amazed by Holmes's performance. "For an English gentlemen, you shovel like the very devil," he said.

"That is because it is the devil I hope to catch," replied Holmes.

Holmes's performance did not surprise me, for he was capable of remarkable feats in times of crisis. Normally, he did not take much exercise, fearing it would only squander his energy.[7] Yet he always kept himself trim and fit, and I recall his commenting once that a good detective, like a good general, must always have "fresh reserves at hand." In Holmes's case, these reserves of energy were powering us to Hinckley, now but eight miles away. I looked at my watch. It was quarter past three.

Five minutes later, when we were but a few miles from our goal, the thick smoke unaccountably cleared and I began to entertain hopes that we might reach Hinckley before the Red Demon undertook his malevolent work. Holmes, too, appeared to take heart from the improved atmospheric conditions and he redoubled his efforts to keep the locomotive well stoked.

Then, as we rounded a slight curve, a sight so fantastic appeared before us that even now I can scarcely believe that I have lived to tell about it. Best was the first to see it, and his hand instinctively pushed forward on the throttle, so that the locomotive began to lose momentum.

"What is it? Why are we slowing down?" Holmes demanded.

In response, Best pointed up the tracks, toward Hinckley, and uttered words which caused Holmes to drop the shovelful of coal in his hands as though he had been struck by lightning.

"My God," said Best, "the clouds are on fire!"

❋

Our faithful engineer did not exaggerate. The sky to the west presented a perfect image of Armageddon, for a roaring storm of fire raged across the heavens, creating a spectacle at once sublime and awful. Athwart this angry scarlet firmament, sheets of flame leaped like dancing devils before a vast rolling cloud of smoke. But the most astonishing sight of all was the whirling column of fire at the center of this immense conflagration. The whole fury of the storm seemed to concentrate upon this gigantic vortex, which reached to the highest vault of the heavens.[8]

So transfixed was Best by this distant spectacle that he allowed the engine to come to a halt.

Holmes's grim determination to reach Hinckley, however, did

not waver, while I had already determined that whatever fate held in store this day, I would remain at Holmes's side.

"We must go forward, Mr. Best," Holmes said, looking at the onrushing firestorm as coolly as he might contemplate an afternoon thunder shower, "no matter what may lie ahead."

"I see what lies ahead, Mr. Baker, and that is an early grave for all of us. But if today is the day I die, then I do not propose to do so with my back to the enemy. All right, gentlemen, sing your last songs and say your last prayers, for it is to hell we are going and nothing will stop us now!"

He opened up the throttle and the locomotive sprang back to life. Then Best sounded his whistle, its plaintive call echoing through the thick smoke which once again began to envelop us. And so, through deepening darkness, we rode the last few miles to Hinckley and our final confrontation with the Red Demon.

Chapter Nineteen

"You Are Mad!"

✴

The scenes of pandemonium which greeted us when we reached Hinckley, at half past three, are almost beyond description. A red sea of fire, billowing and frothing in the woods to the west, was rushing toward the town, and terrified masses of people ran wildly in the streets, fleeing for their lives. Men clutching their belongings, women with babes in their arms, children clinging to favorite toys, terrified horses and cattle—all streamed toward us we approached the Eastern Minnesota depot. The lifeboat they were seeking in this raging ocean of flames was another Eastern Minnesota train, with five passenger cars, that apparently had arrived moments before.

"Lord almighty," said Best, halting our engine on a siding beside the passenger train. "The world has caught fire!"

Best was hardly exaggerating, for the great whirlwind of flame we had seen a few miles from Hinckley was now poised to make its final assault upon the village, and no human agency had the power to quell its monstrous appetite. Brilliant fireballs, borne on howling winds, served as the inferno's vanguard, streaking through the smoky sky like comets. I saw one of these missiles strike a man as he fled, and in an instant his body exploded in fire as if it had been soaked in kerosene. Flailing his arms, the poor man managed just two more steps before he slumped to the ground in a blazing heap. He did not move again.

Meanwhile, a deadly rain of cinders, scraps of wood and other burning objects fell from the heavens, igniting small fires everywhere. Houses and other buildings were already ablaze, and they did not seem to burn so much as melt, their thin clapboard walls peeling away so rapidly that the contents of rooms could be seen as the hungry flames consumed them. As these awful scenes unfolded before me, I began to feel as though I had fallen into a lurid dream, and it was only with the utmost effort that I fought my own instinct to flee this maelstrom of death and destruction.

Yet Holmes, who possessed a singular ability to ignore the larger circumstances of reality while focusing on the particulars of the moment, seemed barely to notice the conflagration raging all about us. The Red Demon was his only concern.

"He will be here," said Holmes, donning his deerstalker despite the fierce heat. "I know he will be here because he will wish to see with his own eyes the work of destruction he has wrought. And I shall find him if it is the last thing I do on this earth. Mr. Smith, I should like to have your pistol."

I handed him my Colt, which he tucked into his waistband before leaping down from the locomotive cab. Looking back up at me, he said: "Stay here and assist Mr. Best in whatever way you can. I shall be back."

"But Holmes—"

"The name is Baker," he said with a smile. "Do not worry, my dear friend. This affair is now between the Red Demon and myself, and it shall end soon enough, one way or the other."

"But the whole town is burning," I protested. "There is nothing to be done. We must leave at once or perish."

"As I said, I shall be back. But if I do not return, then your first priority must be to save yourself."

"But, Holmes—"

My words were futile, for in an instant he was gone. Just before he disappeared across the tracks into the swirling black smoke, I saw his cap fly off in a gust of wind and instantly ignite, as though by spontaneous combustion. At that moment I wondered, for the first time, whether I would ever see him again.

I turned to Best, who was talking with the conductor of the passenger train beside us. "What are we to do now?" I asked, for Holmes's departure had unnerved me.

"We are to form up a combination train with those boxcars yonder"—Best pointed to four empty cars parked farther down the siding—"and get as many people on board as we can. Then we must try to make it back to Duluth. But we are in for a hot time of it, I will tell you that. Where has Mr. Baker gone?"

"In search of a demon," I said.

Best laughed and shook his head. "A demon? Well, Mr. Smith, since we appear to have made it to hell, finding Beelzebub himself would be easy enough, I should think."

❋

With Holmes away on his own, my only duty lay in assisting Best and the other railroad men who were working frantically to load survivors onto the train. I learned from Best that the passenger train next to us was the Eastern Minnesota's No. 4, which had left Duluth at noon. The plan which Best and the crew from the No. 4 had agreed upon was quite complicated, due to the fact that the Eastern Minnesota's roundhouse—where engines could be turned—was already in the grip of the fire.

The plan was this: While the passenger cars were being loaded with refugees, the engineer of the No. 4 would uncouple, switch to a parallel track, connect to the freight cars and then back up to recouple with the passenger cars. Next, Best would couple his locomotive to the other end of the train, thereby providing engines at front and back. All told, this combination train would have eight cars, enough to carry hundreds of people away to safety. However, Best was quick to note the singular disadvantage of this arrangement, which was that both locomotives would have to face south even though the train would go north.

"We'll have to back up all the way to Duluth, but there's no other way," he said, gesturing toward the crimson wall of fire sweeping in from the west and south. "We'd never reach the roundhouse and live to tell about it."

With two blasts from his whistle, Best started the locomotive forward again and I stoked the firebox as we moved down toward the front of the passenger train. All the while, the people of Hinckley continued their mad rush through the streets, the fire literally nipping at their heels. Everything seemed to be ablaze—buildings, sidewalks, rail ties, even the water tower from which the train crews had replenished their tanks.

The fire itself, visible through an ever thickening blanket of foul black smoke, had become a kind of trickster. Sometimes it galloped forward, shooting out tongues of flame, like a huge dragon eager to consume everything in its path. At other times, it seemed to move more languidly, almost reluctantly, as though wishing to give the masses who fled before it a fair chance of escape. But there could be no question that the town's utter destruction was only minutes away.

One question preoccupied me as I peered into the smoke and heard the roar of the fire and the agonized screams of those caught in its terrible grasp. Where was Holmes? I began to fear the worst. Was this, I wondered, to be the end after all? Was the indomitable Sherlock Holmes to perish in this godforsaken place? The thought was too painful to bear, and I decided that if Holmes was to die, then I should at least have the courtesy to die with him.

"I must go after Mr. Baker," I said to Best as we backed toward the passenger train and prepared to couple with it. The flames were now so close that I had the sensation of being at the door of a giant oven. "I must find him."

Best's response was not what I expected. Anger flashing in his eyes, he grabbed my arm with a grip so powerful that I gave an involuntary cry of pain. "You will do no such thing," he said. "Our only job now is to get as many people into this train as we can and then run for our lives. I will not have you committing suicide, Mr. Smith. I need your help and I expect you to do your duty. Now, more coal, and make it quick."

He was right, of course. My duty was to the living, not the dead. Holmes himself had said as much in his final words to me.

"Very well," I told Best. "I shall do my duty, but I fear that my friend is in grave danger and needs my help."

"Mr. Baker decided to run off and he'll have to live, or die, with that decision," said Best, releasing my arm. "In any case, there's nothing to be done about it. We will have the devil's own time saving ourselves, least of all your friend."

Best was right again, for the flames encircling us continued to grow in power and intensity as our engine was at last coupled with the passenger cars. I now began to believe that we all might die in the conflagration, and though I did not wish to lose my life I also felt no fear at the prospect, as life without Holmes hardly seemed worth the endeavor.

Such were my desolate musings when I heard, above the roaring din of the inferno, two piercing whistle blasts—the signal for departure—from the front engine of our newly formed train. I leaned out the cabin window and scanned the smoky gloom, searching for the face of Sherlock Holmes among the desperate crowds still rushing toward the train. But he was not there.

❄

I expected Best to release his air brake and send us on our way, but he did not do so. Instead, he kept one hand firmly on the brake lever. Moments later, two more whistle blasts came from the other engine. Again, Best refused to release the brake.

"What is wrong?" I asked.

"We must wait," he said, looking out toward the street in front of the depot, where panicked masses were still struggling to reach the train. "We must save as many as we can."

I have known many capable men in my life, men able to meet any crisis with resolve, but Best on this day displayed such coolness as I had never seen before. The heat was now so intense, and the smoke so thick, that I could scarcely breathe, and only by keeping a wetted handkerchief around my mouth was I able to keep from succumbing. And yet Best stood firm, his hand never leaving the brake. Meanwhile, stragglers continued to emerge out of the smoke and climb gratefully aboard the train.

Suddenly, four men—their faces contorted and their eyes wild with desperation—jumped on the front of the engine and shouted at Best to set the train into motion. "Back up! Back up!" one of them cried, "or we will all be burned to death!"

"Boys, do not get excited," Best responded calmly. "We are all right yet."

I was not so sure. The flames had now reached the depot and every building within view of the tracks, and it seemed as though any additional delay could not help but prove fatal.

One of the trainmen, who came rushing back from the front engine, was of a similar mind. "We must go, Bill," he shouted, "or Mr. Barry says he will pull the coupling pin and leave."[1]

Best looked down at the man and said simply: "I guess not."

Soon, yet another member of the train crew delivered the same ultimatum, but Best refused to yield. Again and again, the whistle screamed from the front engine. And again and again Best held his ground, all the while motioning to the people still in the streets to board the train.

A woman, her clothes burned off and her long hair singed to a deep black, could now be seen crawling out of the smoke. "For God's sake, hold the train!" she wailed, and though I feared we were all doomed, I helped her into the nearest passenger car.

When I returned to the locomotive, Best—for the first and only time during that fateful day—revealed how terribly his decision to hold the train had weighed upon his mind.

"This is the hardest place I ever stood in, Mr. Smith," he said, one hand still resting on the brake. "Good God, do you think I will sacrifice the train at last?"

As he spoke these plaintive words, he stared toward the white-hot whirlwind of fire in which all of Hinckley was being devoured. No living thing was in view. All that could be seen were the burning skeletons of buildings and the grotesque, twisted bodies of the dead—men, women, children, and all manner of livestock—lying like obscene debris in the streets.

I told Best that we had no choice but to leave. "We cannot stay a moment longer. You have done all that any man could do."

Best, who was standing on the steps of the engine, took one last look around, nodded, and with an expression of deep sadness climbed back up into his seat. He then released the air brake. The train, with its precious cargo of dazed survivors, seemed to take a deep breath before it lurched backward, toward Duluth and safety, whistles sounding against the deep-throated roar of the pursuing inferno. As we began to move, I saw, coming up the tracks toward us, a solitary figure, bent over at the waist, head wrapped in a white cloth, yet running as smoothly and swiftly as a greyhound on the hunt. Cinders and burning debris rained down upon this lonely runner, and fireballs crashed all around him, but on he came, seemingly impervious to whatever assaults the conflagration could muster. And in that instant, I knew who he must be.

"Holmes, Holmes," I shouted, forgetting momentarily his assumed name. "Keep coming, and I will grab you!"

I leaned out of the cab and extended my hand as Holmes drew closer. Though the train was accelerating, its speed was as yet no match for that of Holmes, who with a final burst drew beside the cab. I caught his hand and fairly floated him up into the locomotive, such was the excitement I felt at that moment.

"My God, are you all right?" I asked, for Holmes's clothes were so dark with soot that he resembled a poor Welsh collier. His breath came in long, choking gasps.

Removing the damp cloth from his head, he took several gulps of air before shaking his head. "I am not all right, for I have not found him." He paused, the whites of his eyes looking like bright pieces of china against his blackened face. "But I have every reason to believe that the Red Demon is aboard this train!"

❉

As we backed away from Hinckley, I saw several people emerge from the blazing town and run toward the train, waving their arms frantically and beckoning us to stop. Best, who had stared death in the face numerous times this day, could not bear to look at these pathetic creatures, who were condemned to die as surely as if they had been brought up on the gallows.

"G-dd--n," he said, turning his head away, "but we cannot stop now."

And so it was, amid continuing scenes of ruin and death, that we retreated from what seemed to be the very gates of hell on earth. Soon thereafter, Holmes told his story.

Upon leaving us, he had gone first to the Eastern Minnesota depot, thinking someone there might be of assistance. The depot, however, was abandoned and had already caught fire. Holmes then went into town, hoping to find someone who had seen the Red Demon, since the villain was a person known in Hinckley. But the people Holmes found were in such a state of fright and hysteria that he could gain no useful information. By this time, the whole village was ablaze and Holmes realized that he could not stay long. Nonetheless, he continued along the streets, dodging fireballs and struggling to find his way through the blinding smoke. Then he had a stroke of luck.

A young clerk from the Morrison House, whom we had seen several times during our stay, was attempting to lead his prized stallion down the street, but the horse reared up in a fright and ran away after knocking the man to the ground. Holmes, who had witnessed the incident, helped the young man to his feet and then inquired whether he had seen a certain individual from the community. The clerk said he had indeed seen this person, not five minutes before, running toward the Eastern Minnesota depot. Holmes offered to go with the clerk in that direction, but the young man—insisting that he must find his horse—went toward the other end of town. Holmes never saw him again.

"Naturally, I endeavored to return to the depot as quickly as possible," Holmes said over the roar of the locomotive, "but certain impediments presented themselves, and I was forced to take a wide detour to avoid the worst of the fire. Fortunately, you were still here when I arrived back at the depot."

"You have Mr. Best to thank for that," I said, explaining how that worthy man had held the train to the very last minute.

Holmes made a slight bow in Best's direction and said: "You have my deepest gratitude, sir."

"It wasn't you I was waiting for," Best responded with his usual candor, "but I am glad enough to see that you made it."

"Tell me," said Holmes, "will we stop in Sandstone?"

"If we make it. There are thirteen bridges between here and there, Mr. Smith, and if any of them is burned out, then we are probably done for. That is, if the fire doesn't get us first."

Best's caveat was well taken, for we were hardly out of danger. The woods to either side of the track were already within the fire's eager grasp, and the wind blew with the force of a typhoon. Several small trestles over which we passed were also on fire, as were the wooden ties on many sections of the track. Nonetheless, our sturdy iron ark did not fail us, and the farther we got from Hinckley the more confident I became that we would survive our terrible ordeal by fire.

Yet what I remember most of our perilous run to Sandstone is Holmes's expression as he sat beside me in the fireman's seat while I continued to stoke coal. Resting one elbow out the window, he stared ahead into the smoke and fire with a look that sent chills down my spine. Never before had I seen from my friend such a look—the cold, dead stare of the executioner. Sandstone, I knew, would be the place where Holmes and the Red Demon would meet.

❊

When we reached Sandstone, which had not yet experienced the awful onslaught of the main fire, Holmes leaped down from the engine as soon as the train came to a stop. The atmosphere was already heavy with smoke, and the station platform was crowded with gawkers as well as passengers who poured out of the train in hopes of getting a breath of fresh air.

Word of the fire in Hinckley was circulated at once, and yet—to my astonishment—no one from Sandstone tried to board the train. Nor could any residents of the village be persuaded to do so, for they seemed to think that the fire could never reach them. As I looked at their stolid, uncomprehending faces, I realized to my horror that many of them would soon die.[2] But there was nothing I could do to save them, for our business was now with the Red Demon.

I followed Holmes as he ran alongside the train, fighting the crowds while he looked for the only face which now interested him. But the large number of people, the smoke, and the confusion of the situation made the task extremely difficult.

"Where is he, Watson, where the devil is he?" Holmes said over and over again as he went from car to car.

"Perhaps he has run away, to continue his deadly mischief elsewhere."

Holmes, who was stepping up into the vestibule of one of the cars, suddenly froze.

"Watson," he said, spinning around and dropping back down to the ground, "you are at times a perfect genius. Come along, quickly, for I believe I know where we shall find the Demon!"

"Where?"

Holmes's only response was to begin sprinting up the track, past the lead engine of the train and out toward the eastern edge of town. As I turned to pursue him, I noticed an ominous glow flickering in the woods to the west—a certain sign that the great fire would soon be upon us.

The heavy smoke, which made breathing a torture, and my extreme exhaustion soon caused me to fall far behind Holmes, whose endurance in this trying situation was nothing less than phenomenal. Still, I continued along as best I could, stopping occasionally to regain my wind.

As I followed the tracks around a gentle curve, I found myself at one end of the towering wooden trestle over the Kettle River. A shack, presumably used by the bridge's watchman, stood off to one side, though there was no sign of its occupant. The bridge itself was largely hidden in clouds of swirling black smoke, but I did glimpse a solitary figure walking on the track near the center of the span. Almost instantly, however, the smoke again thickened and the figure vanished, like a thing seen in a dream. Thinking it might be the watchman, I was about to call out when, to my surprise, Sherlock Holmes emerged from the door of the watchman's shack, my pistol in his hand.

※

"Have you seen him?" Holmes asked, his face a grim mask.

"The watchman?"

Holmes shook his head. "No, Watson, the watchman is here." He stepped back from the door to reveal a man lying on the floor, blood flowing from a horrible gash to his head.

I started toward the man but Holmes stopped me. "There is nothing you can do for him, Watson. He is dead."

"Good God! What happened?"

"It is the Red Demon's work, I am sure. Now, did you see anyone as you approached? The smoke was so heavy when I arrived that I could see little of the bridge. But if the Demon has gone out upon it, then he can have only one purpose in mind."

I told Holmes of the figure I had seen moments before.

"It is as I feared," said Holmes in a steely voice. "He intends to destroy the bridge so that no one can escape the conflagration of his making. Well, he shall have to contend with me first!"

"What do you intend to do?"

"I intend to kill him," said Holmes matter-of-factly, "or to die in the effort."

"And I shall gladly be at your side."

"No, my dear friend, that cannot be. You must stay here to watch for the train. If you do not hear from me before the train arrives at the bridge, then you must stop it at all costs. There may then at least be some possibility of getting people safely down to the river."

"But how will I know—?"

"I will fire two shots to indicate that all is well," Holmes said, anticipating my question.

"But Holmes—"

"It must be this way," he said, stepping out onto the bridge. As Holmes vanished into the swirling smoke, I found myself thinking of another murky gorge, far away, where the Falls of Reichenbach plunge amid tumultuous sprays of mist and foam. And I could only pray that, once again, Holmes would prevail.

❋

The next few minutes seemed an eternity. I stood by the shack, staring out across the bridge, hoping to catch sight of Holmes. But the smoke, which seemed to grow thicker with every passing second, would not permit it. Nor did I hear the two shots that might have put my mind to rest. Meanwhile, the red glow off to the west was becoming more pronounced, and I had little doubt that the fire, its voracious appetite fed by the vast expanses of "slash" and waste trees that lay between Hinckley and Sandstone, would arrive shortly. This in turn meant that the train must also be on its way at any moment, since Best and the other railroad men would not want to face the fury of the flames a second time.

And then I heard it—a long whistle blast, followed quickly by another. The train was leaving Sandstone, coming toward the bridge! My anxiety was now acute. Should I hold my position, as Holmes had told me, to warn the train crew of danger on the bridge? Or should I go to Holmes's aid, thereby jeopardizing the hundreds aboard the train?

It was not a decision easily made, and the world may justly censor me for it, but I realized that, no matter what terrible fate might befall the train, I could not bear the thought of having failed my friend in a time of need. And so, I abandoned my post and walked out on the bridge.

A narrow walkway of wooden planks ran alongside the bridge's single track, but I did not use it due to my fear of heights. Instead, I kept as far from the sides of the bridge as possible, which required me to walk down the track. The smoke was now so dense that I could scarcely see my hands in front of my face. But it had not yet settled all the way into the gorge, so that I occasionally caught a dizzying glimpse of the river far below.

As this view made me weak with vertigo, I determined to keep a level gaze and to banish all thoughts from my mind regarding the precarious construction and tormenting height of the structure. Cinders and other small burning objects had already begun to mix with the smoke, and with each step I took the wind grew stronger, until I was forced to stoop over in order to keep my balance.

On I went, hoping at every step to see my friend's familiar face, yet finding only more smoke and fire. Meanwhile, I had lost all orientation, for nothing was visible through the smoke, and I felt strangely removed from the earth, as though I had been transported into some dark, formless corner of the empyrean.

My mind, however, was preoccupied with earthly matters. What had happened to Holmes? Had he and the Red Demon already reached the far side of the bridge? Or had one or both already plunged into the chasm below, a fate that would have meant certain death? The smoke held no answers, and so I forged ahead, not knowing whether I had reached the midpoint of the bridge.

Then came a sound that chilled my soul—the plaintive wail of a locomotive whistle, so close that it seemed the train must be but a few feet away in the smoke. What if the bridge had been sabotaged, as Holmes feared? Had I doomed hundreds to die because of my selfish concern for the fate of one man?

The thought made me sick at heart, and I suddenly found myself unable to move, paralyzed with doubt. To this day, I do not know what I would have done next had I not heard, coming from somewhere up ahead on the bridge, another sound above the roar of the wind. What was it? I strained to hear, my every nerve tensed, but at first I could detect nothing save the noisy stirring of the air. But the wind, as though aware of my desperate circumstances, died down for an instant, and I heard the sound again. This time, it was unmistakable. Voices!

Though I could not hear the voices clearly enough to identify them, I was certain who the speakers must be. Had Holmes cornered the Red Demon at last? Or was Holmes himself in dire jeopardy? Just as Napoleon taught his soldiers to always go toward the sound of the guns, so I shed my paralysis and moved toward the sound of the voices, all the while praying that I would find Holmes in command of the situation. But as I crept forward through the smoke, the bridge began to tremble and groan. Then came a low rumbling noise followed by another whistle blast. The train was on the bridge!

What happened over the next few moments remains as clear and perfectly formed in my mind as if it had occurred only yesterday, and I shall describe the sequence of events as precisely as possible. I remember first the disembodied voices in the smoke, growing louder and more strident the nearer I approached.

Holmes's voice was the first I could identify. "You are mad!" he said.

"Am I?" came the taunting reply, in a voice that I also recognized. "What is so mad, Mr. Holmes, about seeking justice from those ruthless plutocrats who prey on the blood and sweat of other men so that they can have their fine hats and fancy carriages and lavish mansions? And what of a society that will stand by and watch the killing of a woman and child in their own home and then protect the wealthy men who did it? Is not such a society mad and should it not be destroyed like the vile and pernicious thing it is?"

I now discerned a pair of figures standing atop the bridge, no more than ten yards ahead, yet only dimly visible on account of the smoke. I could not see, however, their faces, nor could I tell which held dominance over the other. Then, once again, I heard Holmes's distinctive voice:

"And so, in order to avenge two deaths, you would kill hundreds of innocent people?"

Said the other voice, that of the Red Demon: "There are lessons that can be written only in blood, Mr. Holmes. This society is sick and corrupt and it can only be cleansed with a purifying flame. Then a new order will grow from the ashes."

The shaking and creaking of the bridge now became more pronounced, as did the rumble of the advancing train, which I feared might burst out of the smoke at any instant and throw me to my death. With no other reasonable choice before me, I made the desperate decision to rush forward, even though I knew not whether Holmes held a pistol to the Red Demon or vice versa.

"Holmes," I shouted, running ahead into the blinding smoke, "the train—"

As I did so, I lost my footing, for there was some sort of liquid drenching the bridge's wooden members. I slipped and fell forward, catching my ankle between two of the rail ties. Still, I had gotten close enough to see Holmes and his nemesis. Holmes had his back toward me and held a pistol. The Demon, his hands raised over his head, was farther up the track, facing me. An ax and a large can lay near his feet.

When I made my clumsy appearance, Holmes spun around to look at the source of the commotion. In that instant, the Demon, with a deep growl that seemed to spring from some savage place in his soul, sprang upon Holmes, who raised his pistol but was unable to fire off a shot before the weapon was knocked from his hand and went clattering into the gorge. I tried to assist Holmes but my ankle was so tightly wedged that I could not twist it free. And so I could do nothing but lie on my side and watch as Holmes and his nemesis engaged in a titanic struggle atop the bridge.

Holmes was, despite his lanky frame, a man of sinewy strength and a superb boxer.[3] But he was no match for the Red Demon, who seemed to possess almost superhuman power. As they fell wrestling to the bridge deck, the Demon gained the topmost position, from which he tried to choke the life out of Holmes, all the while pushing him closer to the edge of the bridge and the certain death beyond.

I could do nothing to help Holmes during this desperate struggle, for despite frantic efforts on my part, I could not dislodge my ankle. But I could feel the vibrations on the bridge become stronger and hear the rumble of the approaching train grow ever louder. I resigned myself to die, and yet my only thought was whether Holmes might somehow survive.

And then, as I looked upon what I thought would be my last sight on earth, Holmes—with a powerful thrust of his legs—pushed the Demon away. But as he fell back, the villain landed near the double-headed ax, with which he presumably had planned to do his work of sabotage. His hand settled on this wicked tool and a malevolent grin spread across his contorted features. Standing up, the ax lifted over one shoulder, he loomed over Holmes, who had just regained his feet.

"I shall cut you to pieces," he said, raising the ax high above his head to make his final, lethal strike.

"I think not," said Holmes, whose presence of mind in moments of crisis had always been extraordinary. Seizing the large container I had seen before, Holmes splashed its contents onto the Demon's face and torso. The Demon struggled back, bellowing like a wounded animal, and then I saw a burning object fly out of Holmes's hand. It struck the madman in the chest and his upper body became a blazing torch, the flesh melting almost instantly from his face and hands. He dropped the ax and gave out a terrible scream, a shriek of agony so intense that it seemed to emanate from the deepest circle of hell. Stumbling backward, his face a grotesque burning mask, the Demon let out one last cry before he plunged off the bridge and fell soundlessly into the gorge below.

❋

No sooner was this lurid spectacle over than the noise of the approaching train became thunderous.

"Save yourself," I shouted to Holmes, who had gotten back up to his feet.

But Holmes never hesitated. He picked up the ax, which had fallen on the track, and with one mighty blow severed the tie that held my ankle. And then, as I looked up and saw the locomotive and its tender erupt out of the smoke, he yanked me onto the walkway beside the track. With a deafening roar, the lead locomotive sped past, its drive wheels coming so close to my face that I was spattered with hot grease. The passenger and freight cars, crammed with their precious human cargo, followed. Best's locomotive brought up the rear of the train.

A look of amazement appeared on that noble engineer's face when he saw us. He signaled with his whistle and the train came to a stop at the far end of the bridge. We ran through the smoke and climbed aboard.

"I take it that you did not hear the two shots I fired," said Holmes once we were safely in the cab of the locomotive, where a very frightened looking lad of eighteen or so had been commandeered to serve as Best's fireman.

"I heard nothing. The wind must have played tricks. I did not know what to do other than come to your assistance."

Holmes smiled, and to my eternal surprise, gave me a hug. "Well, it is all over now, my friend, but it was a near thing. Mr. Mortimer's lighter, you will be pleased to know, was our salvation. I think it only fitting that this humble object, stolen from poor Mortimer's lifeless body, proved to be the Demon's undoing. There is justice in this world after all!"

I could hardly take issue with this sentiment. Still, one question troubled me: "I am curious, Holmes. What would you have done with the Demon had I not blundered onto the scene?"

Holmes's reply came without hesitation: "I would have invited him to jump off the bridge."

"Do you really think he would have done so?"

"What do you think?" Holmes responded.

I looked into Holmes's eyes and saw in them no uncertainty, no pity, no mercy.

"He would have jumped," I said.

❋

As the locomotive picked up steam again, I gazed back at the bridge and saw a deep angry glow through the smoke. Then I heard several small explosions.

"The kerosene," said Holmes. "That is what the Demon had in the can. He doused it all over the bridge. I imagine a spark from one of the locomotives has now ignited it."

The bridge, we were later to learn, collapsed shortly after our crossing and crashed into the gorge. And there, amid the debris, searchers would in a few days find the charred body of one Bradford Cornell, the Red Demon, better known to the people of Hinckley as Benjamin Cain, local agent of the Eastern Minnesota Railway.

Chapter Twenty

"The Greatest Failure
of My Career"

❋

"I do not doubt," said Sherlock Holmes, "that Bradford Cornell will forever occupy a notorious place in the annals of criminal infamy. He was supremely ruthless and diabolically clever, and he made of his private hell a public graveyard for hundreds of innocents. I pray the world shall never see his like again. Now, as to the matter of how this monster was finally brought to justice, I would first call your attention to . . ."

So began my friend's final commentary on the singular case of the Red Demon, delivered to the only three people—myself, James J. Hill and J. G. Pyle—who had reason to know the terrible truth of the matter. We were gathered in the study of Hill's mansion on a cold and windy night, a fire blazing in the hearth and a sullen rain pounding at the windows. Would that this torrent had come a week sooner!

It had, in fact, been seven days since the great tragedy

in Hinckley, and I was anxious to hear Holmes's account, for I hoped that by speaking about the case he might find surcease from the despondency into which he had fallen. From the moment of our arrival in Duluth on Best's refugee train, Holmes had been preoccupied by news of the fire, convinced that quicker action on his part might have averted the tragedy. He read the newspapers avidly, and as the death toll mounted—within a few days it reached four hundred, a number almost beyond imagining—Holmes's spirits sank accordingly, until I feared for his sanity.[1]

"It is all my fault, my fault," he muttered over and over, becoming so agitated that I was forced to administer sedatives to allow him to sleep.

While Holmes nursed his pointless remorse, refusing to leave our hotel room even for meals, I went to work. The injured from Hinckley and other communities soon began pouring into the hospitals in Duluth, and as a doctor my duty lay in providing what aid I could to these unfortunates. Never before had I seen so many burned and scarred human beings, and even now their dreadful cries—especially those of the orphaned children, wailing for their lost parents—echo in my memory.

One benefit of this work, however, was that it brought me in touch with Laura Olson (for that, I learned, was her full name). I found her by chance in a ward at one of Duluth's hospitals, where she was recovering from minor burns. She had survived the fire by hiding in a well behind Mrs. Robinson's house, which was destroyed. Her sister, Dora, unfortunately, was among those feared dead.[2] We had a tearful reunion and I renewed my promise to help Laura find a more decent life.

My volunteer work also resulted in attention from the press, for I was interviewed at the hospital by Miss Nellie Bly, the famous New York newspaper correspondent. Naturally, I could not give her my real name, and as it turned out my comments were never included in her celebrated account of the fire.[3]

After a week's time, the citizens of Duluth had organized so effectively to assist the fire survivors that I saw no further need of my services. Moreover, my concern for Holmes's welfare was growing. He had gone days without eating, and his eyes had acquired the gaunt, haggard look of a man dispossessed of his senses. Still, he continued to peruse the newspapers, lingering over the lists of the dead, which by the fourth day after the fire included the name of Benjamin Cain.

Fortunately, a story appeared the next day which buoyed his spirits, for it provided irrefutable evidence that his efforts had not been in vain. The article, in the *Duluth News Tribune*, recounted the tale of a Sandstone man who had fled to the bottom of the Kettle River gorge as the conflagration approached. This survivor, a Swede by the name of Anderson, described the collapse of the bridge moments after Best's train passed over it:

> Some of the bridge timbers were already burning when the train made its perilous crossing, Anderson reported. Miraculously, the structure held under the weight of the train and the hundreds of refugees whose very lives depended on its safe passage. But no sooner had the rear engine cleared the bridge than the demons of fire, cheated of their opportunity to inflict yet more human misery, rose up in vengeance. The bridge was now their target and they did their awful work with astonishing speed. The great wooden trestle, pride of the Eastern Minnesota Railway, was but kindling in the face of such a ferocious assault, and as Anderson watched in horror the flames spread to every part of the structure until, with a terrible roar, it collapsed into the rushing waters one hundred feet below.
>
> Anderson said he cannot doubt that had the train been on the bridge at that instant, all aboard would have perished, so precipitous was the collapse. By the same token, had the train arrived a few moments later, when the bridge was a ruin at the bottom of the gorge, it is equally doubtful that anyone aboard would have survived, for the flames

were by then so intense that no living thing could have resisted their voracious appetite for destruction.

"God smiled on those people," said the brave Anderson, who is recovering from burns to his legs at St. Luke's Hospital in this city. Indeed, Anderson's account is cause for wonder at the mysterious hand of fate, which preserved so many aboard the fleeing train while claiming the lives of countless others who sought but could not find a place of refuge in the holocaust.

"I trust you will now admit that you accomplished something after all," I told Holmes. "Hundreds more might have died had you not been on the bridge when you were."

"It is true, I suppose," Holmes acknowledged, rising from his bed and putting on his shoes for the first time in days. "You have been right, Watson, to keep busy, for work is always the best anodyne. I shall be a burden upon you no longer. We have done here what we could, no more and no less, and it is time now to begin our long journey home. First, however, I should like something to eat, for I find that my appetite is returning."

From that moment forward, Holmes's mood improved, and he was in decent, if not high, spirits when we left Duluth on September 8 to make our final report to Hill. Our return to St. Paul was of necessity accomplished on the St. Paul & Duluth line, since the Eastern Minnesota's connection to the Twin Cities had been severed by the destruction of the high bridge, which was not repaired until some weeks later.[4]

Although my memories of the fire were still vivid, nothing prepared me for the extent of the devastation which presented itself as our train approached Hinckley. Where once forests had stretched to the horizon, there was now a desert of white ash in which the black stumps of trees stood like eerie sentinels guarding a wasteland. Hinckley itself was gone, and only building foundations and the ruins of the town's school—built of brick—testified to the community's former existence.

When we reached the remains of Hinckley, I discovered that our train was crowded with excursionists anxious to obtain a view of the devastation and collect charred souvenirs from the ruins. These human vultures were more than I could tolerate, and I had sharp words with several of them before Holmes intervened.[5]

"It is not worth your time, Watson. The human animal is not always a pleasant creature to contemplate, but we cannot change the facts of nature or the irresistible force of curiosity."

Holmes was otherwise quiet, gazing out at the devastation with a rather forlorn look but offering no comment. It was six in the evening when we reached St. Paul, where our friend Pyle greeted us warmly at the depot. A short carriage ride brought us to Hill's mansion, and there, after dinner, Sherlock Holmes held us spellbound with the story of how he had found the Red Demon.

※

He began by calling our attention to the letters received by Hill: "These peculiar missives raised an obvious question: Why did the Demon engage a woman, whom we now know to have been Mrs. Robinson, to write all but the last of them? Several possibilities occurred to me. Perhaps the Demon was somehow incapacitated and could not write. Perhaps he was illiterate and required help composing the letters. But there was another—and far more obvious— possibility. Perhaps the Demon did not write the letters himself because he feared his handwriting might prove familiar to Mr. Hill or someone else at the railroad."

"Good God, I never thought of that," Hill admitted. "And yet, as you say, it is quite obvious."

Holmes smiled and lit his pipe. "I mention this only as a possibility, of course. With Cornell dead and with Mrs. Robinson's whereabouts a mystery, we may never know the exact nature of their relationship. However, it should be obvious that Cornell, in his role as the trusted station agent Benjamin Cain, was required to write numerous documents every day. And since this entire affair shows him to have been a man of extraordinary guile, I see no reason why he would not have taken the precaution of ensuring that his handwriting could not be traced."

"Then your suspicions must have been directed at Cornell, or perhaps I should say Cain, at once," said Pyle, "since he was the Eastern Minnesota's most prominent employee in Hinckley."

"To be sure, I kept him in mind, but in the beginning he was hardly the sole suspect. Best might also have had reason to disguise his handwriting in such a situation, as might any number of other people in Hinckley who dealt regularly with the railroad. Initially, therefore, Cain—as I shall call him for the time being—was only one of several suspects. However, he soon moved to a more prominent position on my list."

"And why was that?" inquired Hill.

"First, there was the matter of the black rose petal. I saw it in the flower arrangement on his table on the night Watson and I arrived in Hinckley."

"I did not notice it," I said.

"Nor, I am sure, did Cain. But as you will recall, Watson, we also saw black roses in Mrs. Robinson's quarters. The lady even mentioned that she cultivated them. Now, I cannot believe that Hinckley is full of black rose fanciers, and I thus deduced that the petal in Cain's room must have come from Mrs. Robinson."

"Then you caught him in a lie!" I said, perhaps too enthusiastically. "For I remember Cain telling us that Mrs. Robinson's activities were anathema to him as a Christian. But if you already knew then that Cain was the Red Demon, why—"

"—didn't I act more quickly?" said Holmes, finishing my question. "For the simple reason, Watson, that I knew no such thing. The rose petal hardly demonstrated Cain's guilt. A visitor—Angus Hay, for example, who often played cards with Cain—could have planted the petal in order to cast suspicion on the station agent, though it would have been, I admit, an extremely subtle clue.

"But assuming that Cain himself had obtained the rose petal from Mrs. Robinson, what did this prove? Nothing, except that he had been less than forthcoming about his relationship with the madam. This came as no great surprise to me. The world is full of men who profess outrage over brothels in public while patronizing them in private. No, the black rose suggested hypocrisy on Cain's part but was hardly evidence of conspiracy.

"Still, my suspicions regarding Cain had been aroused at this point. I became even more suspicious when Mrs. Robinson, during our interview with her, remarked upon our supposed employment by *The Times* of London."

"Why should that have made you more suspicious?" Pyle asked.

Holmes, who had been pacing in front of the fireplace, paused to lean again the mantle, so that firelight flickered across his face. "For this reason, Mr. Pyle. When we arrived in Hinckley, I mentioned our supposed connection with *The Times* to only two people—Hay and Cain. Naturally, I concluded that one of these gentlemen had been in contact with Mrs. Robinson prior to our visit with her. While I could not rule out Hay as the culprit, Cain seemed the more likely candidate in view of subsequent events. His hand in the matter became especially obvious when the attempt was made to murder Watson and myself at the Big Pine Camp."

I was now confused. "Really, Holmes, I do not follow your logic. It was LeGrande who tried to assassinate us, not Cain."

"True, LeGrande was the chosen agent of destruction, but the fact that we had been identified as a threat to the Red Demon, and therefore marked for extermination, clearly suggested that Cain was somehow involved in the affair."

Pyle shook his head. "I fear you have lost me as well, Mr. Holmes. I do not see how you inferred Cain's involvement."

Demonstrating the keen intelligence which had made him the master of a vast inland empire, Hill provided the answer. "The point is: Why would the Demon have marked Mr. Holmes and Dr. Watson for death unless he knew their real identities and purpose? But if he knew, how did he know? Am I correct?"

Holmes responded with a nod toward Hill. "Should you ever

take up a career as a consulting detective, Mr. Hill, I am confident you would enjoy as much success as you have in railroading. You have indeed put your finger on the central question. How were Watson and I found out so quickly? Here again, there were several possibilities. Perhaps something we said or did had inadvertently revealed our true identities. Perhaps someone in Mr. Hill's employ — Mr. Pyle, for example — had alerted the Demon to our presence. Perhaps — "

Pyle bridled at this suggestion. "I cannot believe, Mr. Holmes, that you could ever think such a thing!"

"Do not be alarmed, sir. It is my responsibility to think many things, not all of which are pleasant. You may be assured that I did not for a moment believe you to be the guilty party. Rather, I came to a more logical conclusion, which was that we were found out because our telegraphic messages were being read."

"But you used the Great Northern's cipher," Hill protested. "I have been assured that it is unbreakable."

"I fear that no cipher is unbreakable, Mr. Hill, for what one mind can conceive, another mind — if clever enough — can unravel. And, of course, we now know that cryptography was Cain's hobby, so much so that he enjoyed demonstrating his skill to his students. The Great Northern's cipher is a simple substitution code, and as such could be readily broken by someone of Cain's ability. Remember also that, as a station agent, he sent and received hundreds of coded telegrams. I am sure he spent many nights studying these messages and that a detailed knowledge of the code was the fruit of his labors. He thus knew from the day of our arrival in Hinckley who we were and what our mission was."

I felt compelled to make an objection. "But there was at least one other person who might have had easy access to our telegrams."

"Angus Hay," Holmes said with a nod. "You have made a good point, Watson, and I must confess that when I learned of Hay's skill with the telegraph key, I began to have second thoughts. But I soon satisfied myself that he could not be the Red Demon."

"And how were you able to reach such a conclusion?" I asked.

"That will be explained in good time, Watson. Suffice it to say that I became convinced, based upon all the evidence at hand, that Cain was the man decoding our telegrams."

It was now Pyle's turn to raise an objection. "But if you knew, Mr. Holmes, that Cain was reading your messages, why didn't you confront him? Surely, this was conclusive evidence that he must be the Demon."

"I think not," said Hill, who had followed Holmes's every word with intense interest. "It merely indicated, I should think, that Cain was somehow involved in the matter."

"Precisely," said Holmes, who moved to the window, where the rain continued its relentless battering. "Keep in mind, gentlemen, that telegraphers are notoriously susceptible to bribery because they are privileged to know all manner of private information. As a result, my first thought was that Cain might merely be passing on information to the Demon in return for money.

"Also remember that at this stage there were, besides Cain, several other logical suspects — Best, the union agitator; LeGrande, the woodsman said to bear a grudge against Mr. Hill; Thompson, the corrupt marshal; Corbett, who presented himself as our savior but whose background and character were odd, to say the least; the mysterious lumberman, Bartlett Chalmers; the madam with much to hide, Mrs. Robinson; and, of course, Hay, the newspaperman who seemed to know so much about the dark side of life in Hinckley. However, as time went by, I was able to eliminate the first four as suspects."

"And how did you accomplish that?" inquired Hill.

"It was largely a matter of observation and analysis. In Best's case, I saw at once that his character did not fit that of the Red Demon. There was something so blunt and straightforward in Best's manner that I could not envision him scheming for months and years to accomplish some secretive end. No, I believe that if William Best harbored some grudge against you, Mr. Hill, he would come straight at you, in broad daylight, and settle the matter with his fists. The devious way was not for him."

Hill gave out a hearty laugh. "Your judgment is sound in that respect, Mr. Holmes, for precisely such a thing happened this spring during the strike on the Eastern Minnesota, when Best and I nearly came to blows."

"I agree with your judgment regarding Best," Pyle said, "but what of LeGrande? Why did he not remain a suspect? After all, it was he who murdered my friend Mortimer in cold blood."

"Indeed it was," said Holmes. "Yet LeGrande, I saw at once, lacked the intelligence to be the Red Demon. He is merely a thug, and as such was used by Cain to do his dirty work. The same is true of Thompson. As to how these two ruffians came into Cain's employ, the answer may never be known, unless LeGrande finally reappears from the woods."

"I understand he has not been seen since the fire and is presumed dead," said Pyle.

"His demise would be no loss to civilization," I noted, remembering how close he had come to murdering Holmes and me.

"I should prefer him alive," countered Holmes, "since he could answer many questions regarding this case. In any event, I suspect that, as Cain drew up his elaborate scheme of revenge, he searched for brutal yet easily manipulated allies to serve his sinister purposes. As I shall explain later, part of Cain's malignant genius was his ability to find others to act on his behalf, while shielding himself from suspicion."

Pyle said: "Before you go on, Mr. Holmes, can you tell me why Cain had his henchmen kill Mr. Mortimer?"

"I can only speculate, but I believe Mr. Mortimer discovered something, or was about to discover something, which might have jeopardized Cain's plans. And so he had to be silenced forever. Unfortunately, the precise motive for his murder may never be known."

"You should know that Thomas Mortimer was a very fine man," said Pyle, "who left behind a wife and two children."

"So I have heard. I trust they are being provided for."

"They are," said Hill. "Mrs. Mortimer and her children will

want for nothing as long as they live. I shall see to that. It is the least I can do. But I must say, Mr. Holmes, I am surprised to learn that even my friend Boston Corbett was a suspect in your mind. After all, he saved your life."

"Indeed he did, and I shall be eternally grateful to him. But you must admit that Corbett is a most unusual character, and until I could confirm his story—after all, who would have believed that he had shot John Wilkes Booth?—I maintained a skeptical posture. However, I was soon able to satisfy myself, by means of telegrams to St. Paul, that Corbett was in your service and that he could be trusted in every respect despite his eccentricities. I only wish he were here now so I could thank him again. Has any word come as to his whereabouts?"

Hill sighed and shook his head. "I fear not. My only hope is that he survived the fire and has now disappeared back into the countryside, as he is wont to do. Yet I believe that we would have heard from him by now if all were well."

The thought that poor Corbett might be lying somewhere dead in the burned-out wilderness cast a pall over the conversation. Pyle finally interrupted the silence with a question.

"I should like to return to the matter of Cain's ability to read coded telegrams. I understand now why this did not of itself prove he was the Red Demon. What I don't understand is why you didn't use a new code to prevent your messages from being deciphered."

Holmes had anticipated the question and his response was revealing. "Naturally, I considered the idea. But I concluded that a sudden change of code would only serve to alert Cain, and presumably the Red Demon, of my suspicions. In some respects, it was useful to know that he was following our plans. For example, when Thompson agreed to meet us at the gravel pit, I made certain to mention the time and place of our rendezvous in a telegram to Mr. Hill. I knew that the Demon, apprised of this information, would attempt a second ambush. Instead, Watson and I, with help from Corbett, staged an ambush of our own, with notable results.

"In other circumstances, however, I took precautions, as Mr. Pyle has suggested. The rather frantic trip which Watson and I made to Pine City is a case in point. I insisted that we go there because I wished to send telegrams from a place where our messages would not be exposed to Cain's prying eyes."

"I must admit, the suddenness of the trip did strike me as rather odd," I said.

"For which I apologize. But I saw no other choice. And as it turned out, Cain's discovery of our identity was the key to unlocking the case."

"How so?"

Holmes stared out the window, as though searching for an answer in the rain-drenched darkness. "Let me put it to you this way, Watson. It was only when he learned who we were that Cain decided to murder us. He then set about, by means of a series of subtle clues, to lure us to an ambush at the Big Pine Camp. Yet had he simply ignored us, and kept to his secret plans, I am not sure we would ever have found him out.

"All of which brings me to the most brilliant feature of his scheme—the manner in which he disguised his true identity from almost everyone, including the henchmen who did his bidding. And that is where the mysterious Mr. Chalmers enters the picture."

"He is indeed mysterious," agreed Hill, "for until you brought his name to my attention, I had never heard of the man. And that is odd, because I pride myself on knowing all of the important lumbermen in the Hinckley area."

Returning to his place in front of the fire, Holmes relit his pipe with a glowing coal. "The fact of the matter, Mr. Hill, is that no one seems to know Chalmers. I made numerous inquiries in Hinckley, and sent out many telegrams, in hopes of tracking down the elusive lumberman. But these efforts were to no avail, and so I finally came to a rather remarkable conclusion."

Holmes's next words caught us by surprise: "The reason no one seems to know Bartlett Chalmers is that he does not exist."

"That cannot be!" I remonstrated, believing that Holmes was now playing one of his infernal games. "I talked with him. He is as real as you or I!"

"Ah, my dear Watson, you misunderstand. I do not claim that the man you talked with in the dining room of the Morrison House is a phantasm of your imagination. I merely said that Bartlett Chalmers does not exist."

"What do you mean?" asked Hill sharply.

"What I mean is that the obese, perspiring, and—pay special heed to this—gloved man Watson met was in fact Bradford Cornell, alias Benjamin Cain, alias the Red Demon."

※

"My God," I said. "It hardly seems possible. But how did he manage to disguise himself so well?"

"The disguise was easy enough for a man of Cain's attainments. Remember that he taught drama at the high school in Duluth and was thus familiar with costumes. Some padding about the waist, heavy facial makeup, a wig, the proper clothes, and, *voilà*, Cain becomes Chalmers. But there was one thing he could not readily conceal—the burns on his hands.

"As you will recall, I noticed these burns during our interview with Cain, for as I have observed many times, the hands tell you everything about a man. Cain no doubt sustained the burns, which obviously were from an old injury, while carrying his wife from their burning home. Yet he claimed to us that the injury had occurred only recently when he fought the fire at the depot—a fire, of course, which he set.

"In his role as Chalmers, Cain naturally saw the need to disguise his burned hands so as to be assured he would not be unmasked. And that is why he wore gloves, despite the heat. His burns would have been difficult to cover cosmetically because the hands are used so much that any makeup might have worn off at an inopportune time. Gloves were therefore Cain's most reliable means of disguise. Unfortunately, this rather obvious ploy did not occur to me until the night of the incident at the gravel pit, when I found an old pair of gloves near the river. This somehow triggered a connection."

Holmes paused and turned to me: "And here, Watson, might be a convenient place to answer your question as to how I eliminated Angus Hay as a suspect. I did so by examining his hands."

The bizarre incident in which Holmes had grabbed Hay's hands now came to mind, and I saw at last why Holmes had acted so peculiarly. "You were looking for burns," I said.

"Precisely," said Holmes. "It was, I fear, a rather crude bit of business, but I had to be certain. And once I satisfied myself that Hay's hands showed absolutely no evidence of scarring, I knew he was not our man. As for Hay's rather hostile behavior toward us that afternoon, I think it can be explained by his friendship with Cain. I suspect that Cain, by means of subtle insinuations, convinced Hay that we were not to be trusted. He may even have suggested to Hay that we were not, in fact, who we claimed to be. I also suggest that it was Cain who supplied Hay with the information regarding the 'mystery woman' seen at Thompson's house on the night of his murder."

I now took a moment to enlighten Pyle and Hill about the singular episode with Hay, since they were not familiar with the incident and had found Holmes's remarks quite puzzling.

"So you simply grabbed the poor fellow's hands," said Hill with a wide grin. "I wager he was surprised."

"I believe," said Holmes drily, "that he thought me to be a lunatic, an idea, I might add, to which my good friend Watson has also subscribed on occasion."

"Why Holmes, I never—"

"Hush, Watson, hush," said Holmes. "There is no need to apologize when no offense has been given."

Fortunately, Pyle now stepped in to return our conversation to the more important matter of Benjamin Cain's conduct: "Mr. Holmes, I am curious about one point. Why would Cain go to all the trouble of creating another identity for himself? What purpose could such a charade serve?"

"His purpose was to insulate himself from suspicion," replied Holmes, who had resumed his pacing. "Cain was a master manipulator, and Chalmers was his greatest creation. I have no doubt that it was in his role as Chalmers that Cain recruited LeGrande and Thompson. And if either were here today, they would be surprised, I imagine, to discover that Cain—whom they probably knew only as a local railroad agent—was in fact the Red Demon. If anyone knew who Cain really was, it would have been Mrs. Robinson, but I fear we shall not hear from her again."

"Surely the Pinkertons will find her," I interjected. "Mr. Hill has told me that they are already on her trail."

"Then they will find her grave," declared Holmes. "The Red Demon killed Mortimer and Thompson because they knew too much. Why should we assume Mrs. Robinson's fate was any different?"

※

Holmes next went on to describe how our chance conversation with James Morton during the train ride to Pine City had led at last to the Red Demon's identity.

"Until that moment, I had assumed that the Demon's motive stemmed from a recent event, such as the railroad strike. But when Mr. Morton informed us how frequently the railroads are sued over injuries both real and imagined, it occurred to me that the Demon's hatred of Mr. Hill might have been spawned by some personal tragedy.

"I also recalled the scene Watson and I had witnessed near the St. Paul depot, when a little girl fell beneath a train and was horribly mutilated. What if something similar had happened to a member of the Demon's family and he had found no justice, or at least no satisfaction, in the courts? Might not such an incident have triggered the ferocious enmity so apparent in his letters? With that in mind, I began telegraphic inquiries into past lawsuits against the Eastern Minnesota."

"But how did you know what to look for?" Hill asked. "There are upward of fifty lawsuits a year filed against the Eastern Minnesota, many of which claim some dreadful injury."

"That was indeed a problem, but I pinned my hopes on a singular feature of this case—the fact that Benjamin Cain and Bartlett Chalmers, whom I by then believed to be one and the same, possessed identical initials. Was it possible, I wondered, that both were aliases for yet a third person with the same initials?

"Thus, when I learned of the lawsuit involving Bradford Cornell and that it arose from a fire occurring on a July 19, the same date as that of the first fire set in Hinckley, I concluded that the existence of three such names with identical initials must be more than coincidence. The rest of the story you know. When I finally obtained a photograph of Cornell in Duluth, there could be no doubt that he was Benjamin Cain and that he must therefore be the Red Demon."

"But if Cornell hated Mr. Hill so much, why didn't he simply attempt to assassinate him?" asked Pyle. "Why undertake such an elaborate and lengthy scheme of revenge? And, above all, why kill four hundred innocent people to strike back at one man?"

Holmes bowed his head and said softly: "I do not have the answers, Mr. Pyle. I have only theories, for the toxin that poisoned Cornell and turned him into a monster of cruelty is beyond all human analysis. But I suspect that Cornell, as he plotted his awful revenge, became angry at the whole world. Seized by his own bleak hatred, he lost all human ties and his heart grew as cold and silent as stone. That is the only explanation I can offer.

"As to why he did not try to kill Mr. Hill, I am inclined to think that he sought a worse fate for the man he had come to hate. His goal was to ruin Mr. Hill, financially and in every other way before the eyes of the world. From Cornell's depraved perspective, death would have been too easy a fate for Mr. Hill."

With these chilling words, Holmes seemed ready to conclude his account. There was, however, one aspect of the case that continued to puzzle me.

I said: "But what of the fire at the cabin in which you came to my rescue? I am still at a loss as to how Cornell followed us there and was able to set the fire despite your precautions."

Holmes rubbed his chin and smiled. "I am rather embarrassed to admit it, Watson, but I started that fire."

I have received many surprises from Sherlock Holmes during our long association, but none was quite as shocking as this revelation. "You? Good God, Holmes, why?"

"It was purely a scientific exercise. You see, I have failed to mention one other circumstance which led me to suspect Cain. I am speaking of his account of the fire at the depot. He told us, as you will remember, that he was awakened by the smell of smoke at four in the morning and went outside to investigate, where he found a fire burning. Yet when I examined the scene, it was apparent that the blaze had been a very small one — far too small, in my judgment, to have awakened Cain. Fire is an insidious thing. It stalks its victims quietly, and hardly a day goes by when the London newspapers fail to report on some poor wretch who has been overcome by smoke in his bedroom.

"Still, I wished to test how a sleeping man would respond to smoke. And so, while you were asleep, Watson, I set the cabin on fire and watched your response. Your reaction, I believe, was quite typical, which is to say that had I not awakened you and pulled you from the cabin, you might well have perished. I concluded from this little experiment that Cain's story was quite unbelievable. I should have told all of this to you earlier, Watson, but I quite frankly hoped that you would forget about the entire matter and thus spare me this belated confession. And now I can only hope that you are not angry with me."

"It is a well-known scientific fact that guinea pigs do not anger easily," I said, and there was laughter all around.

✳

Holmes was now finished with his account, and Mr. Hill took the floor. As he stood before the hearth, his massive brow set off by the glow of the fire, it was easy to see how he had come to be a leader of men who had bent the world with the iron rod of his will. His presence was intimidating, and when he spoke, his words were forceful and succinct.

"I intend to make but three points and then we shall all be done with this unfortunate business, in which so many have suffered so needlessly. First, I am convinced that no purpose would be served by making the true nature of what occurred in Hinckley known to the general public. It would not be good for the Eastern Minnesota, which would inevitably be blamed for Cornell's wrongdoing, nor would it profit the people of Hinckley to know that a madman caused them such sorrow. Cornell deserves nothing but oblivion for his evil deeds, and oblivion he shall have! I expect that no one in this room shall ever speak of what happened in Hinckley. Do you agree to that, Mr. Holmes?"

"I do," said Holmes without hesitation. "I have no wish, nor does Mr. Watson, to share this tragic adventure with the world at large. You may count upon our discretion."

"Good. Mr. Pyle, I know, can also be relied upon. The only other person who had detailed knowledge of the affair is Mr. Best, and I have already communicated with him. He has received a substantial reward for his services, as well as a promotion to become engineer of my private train, and I am confident that he will keep his silence."[6]

"I am pleased to hear you speak so highly of Mr. Best," said Holmes, "for whatever good we were able to accomplish was due in large measure to his courage and skill."

"I agree," said Hill. "Now, as to the second point, I wish to inform Dr. Watson that, at his request, arrangements have been made to admit a young woman named Laura Olson to the Visitation Academy in St. Paul. Her tuition and boarding expenses will be paid. Upon her graduation, she will be placed as a servant in my home and will receive such other assistance as she may need to lead a respectable life."

Mr. Hill's generosity left me speechless. "I do not know what to say," I finally blurted out, "but God will bless you, Mr. Hill, for helping this poor child."

"I have never made it a point to rely upon God's blessing but I hope your prediction proves true," said Hill with a smile. He then reached into his vest pocket and removed an envelope.

"And now we come to the final point," he said, handing the envelope to Holmes. "Please open it."

Holmes did so, and found within a cashier's check, made out in his name, for the sum of fifty thousand American dollars.

"You have earned it," said Hill. "I am convinced that no one else could have found the Red Demon."

Holmes examined the check—the largest, I am sure, that he had ever received—and then attempted to hand it back to Hill.

"I cannot accept this," he said in a firm but quiet voice, "for I regard this case as the greatest failure of my career."

"Nonsense," said Hill, refusing to take the check. "I will not hear of it."

I, too, remonstrated with Holmes. "How can you account the case a failure when your actions saved hundreds of lives?"

"I concur," said Hill. "You were hired to find the Red Demon and you did so. I can think of no money I have ever spent that was better spent than this."

"You were magnificent, Mr. Holmes," added Pyle. "Had it not been for your efforts, the Red Demon might at this very moment be plotting some new outrage."

I had seldom seen Holmes change his mind, but he did so now. "Very well," he told Hill, "I accept your check."

He then shook Hill's hand and did likewise with Pyle. "And now, if Mr. Pyle will be so good as to provide a carriage, I believe

Dr. Watson and I can still catch the late train to Chicago and points east. It is time for us to go home. And I hope that you will not take offense if I remark that it is my fervent hope that I shall never again set foot in Minnesota."

These words proved ironic, for Holmes could not know that little more than a year later we would return to St. Paul to confront the bizarre mystery of the spectral head in the ice palace—a case which was to produce one of the most brilliant and astonishing solutions of his career.[7]

✸

On October 4, 1894, readers of the *St. Paul Pioneer Press* were astonished to learn that an anonymous English benefactor had contributed the sum of fifty thousand dollars to the fire relief effort in Hinckley. The newspaper said a letter from London accompanying the donation specified only that the money be used "to feed the hungry, shelter the homeless and provide all possible assistance to those caught in the deadly grip of the Red Demon."[8]

"I Shall Never Forget Our Afternoon Together"

✳

Upon our return to London, which was accomplished without incident, Holmes threw himself into his work and would tolerate no talk of our tragic adventure in the Minnesota pineries. But one day in early November, shortly before he became involved in the curious case of young Willoughby Smith's murder, a letter arrived which brought the Red Demon once again to our attention.[1]

Mrs. Hudson had carried up the mail that morning, and when I reached the last letter in the pile I experienced a shock of recognition. It was not the envelope's return address—there was none, in fact—which produced this effect but rather an unmistakable aroma of perfume. Jicky!

I called over Holmes, who had been busy examining several suspected banknote forgeries with a powerful lens. His eyebrows arched in surprise when he caught a whiff of the scent.

"It appears that Mrs. Robinson has survived after all," he said, sounding more mortified than pleased by this news. "Well, go on, Watson, open it. Much as it pains me to revisit this matter, I suppose we must hear the lady's tale."

The letter, which bore a Chicago postmark and was written in Mrs. Robinson's distinctive hand, read as follows:

Dear Mr. Holmes,

I hope this letter finds you and Dr. Watson well after your long journey back from Minnesota. I am writing to you because I wish to state, for the record, what I know of the recent, tragic events in Hinckley. You, of course, are the world's foremost consulting detective, and I have no doubt that you already know much of what I am about to reveal. Still, there may be a few minor points upon which I can enlighten you.

Let me begin by saying that my heart is burdened with sorrow over the loss of life which occurred. I assure you that had I known of Mr. Cain's intentions, I would have done my utmost to stop him. But as you must realize by now, he was quite mad, and no one—not even you, Mr. Holmes—was able to forestall the horrific dénouement of his plans.

I first met Benjamin Cain, as he called himself, in the spring of 1893, shortly after he had assumed his duties as stationmaster for the Eastern Minnesota Railway. Like many men of Hinckley, he patronized my establishment. But I saw at once that he was different from the usual run of men with whom I came in contact. He had a fine mind, and he understood the evils of the cruel and unjust society in which we live. We became lovers.

Though he was a very private man, he gradually opened his heart to me, and one evening, after we had expressed our love for each other in the usual way between a man and a woman, he told me his story. By now, I should imagine, you know that his true name was Bradford Cornell and that he had suffered grievously at the hands of James J. Hill and his accursed railroad.

A thirst for revenge burned within him, and at first he was content to satisfy it by means of simple thievery. I feel no compunction in saying that I abetted these plans, since I have always believed that Hill and his kind are themselves nothing more than thieves, who plunder from the masses to advance their own fortunes. Mr. Cain was quite brilliant in the schemes he devised — "kickbacks" on lumber shipments, theft of timber from land owned by Hill or his friends, and even simple embezzlement of railroad funds.

In time, however, Mr. Cain's hatred of Hill grew to such depths that it began to go beyond all reason. He then conceived his scheme to set fires to destroy railroad property, just as the fire caused by Hill's railroad had destroyed his family. I argued against this course of action, fearing the loss of innocent lives, but Mr. Cain would hear no dissent. Moreover, his manner soon became so violent and obsessive that I began to fear for my own life.

It was only under such duress that I wrote the letters to Hill, as Mr. Cain feared his own handwriting might prove too familiar. I suppose, too, that I was still in love, and a woman in that condition will sometimes let her heart cloud the better sense of her mind. Still, I thought the chances of detection slight — until Thomas Mortimer arrived.

After spending several days in a vain search for information, Mortimer came to my house for an evening of carnal recreation (for which, I am sure, Hill unknowingly footed the bill). While engaged in his amorous pursuits, Mortimer happened to come across a note I had written to one of the girls in my employ. He questioned the girl at once and then left, indicating that he would return the next day to speak with me.

The girl came to me immediately with her story, and I

then mentioned the matter to Mr. Cain, who assured me he would "take care" of it. I assumed that he meant to bribe Mortimer into silence, and it was only later that I learned he had ordered the poor man to be murdered by his henchmen, LeGrande and Thompson.

Naturally, I was appalled and told Mr. Cain so. His response was to threaten me with instant death if I uttered a word to anyone about what had happened. He also began to rave about what he called "the final holocaust," which he said—I recall his exact words—would be "a thing of purifying beauty." You may imagine the terror which I felt. I pleaded with him to end his violent campaign against the railroad, but he was insensible to any form of persuasion.

Your appearance in Hinckley, Mr. Holmes, only added to my uneasiness. Mr. Cain, of course, learned of your identity at once, for he was quite adept at reading the Great Northern's supposedly secret cipher. When you came to my house, I could only assume that you, like Mortimer, had somehow learned of my role in the affair. I suppose I might have told you the truth then, but my fear of Mr. Cain was such that I dared not take that step.

Your questions that day, and your transparent attempts to secure a sample of my handwriting, left no doubt that I had been found out. I knew then that I had to act to preserve my own interests. This was not easy. I am but a weak woman and like all of my sex I am inclined to go where my heart leads me. For, after all that had happened, I still loved Mr. Cain. But while love is a wonderful thing, I have found through hard experience that it is a mistake to take it to extremes. I therefore determined that my best course of action would be to leave Mr. Cain, and Hinckley, and start a new life elsewhere.

With travel in mind, I went to the Eastern Minnesota depot one afternoon, where I encountered you and Dr. Watson. Since I did not wish to talk to Mr. Cain for obvious reasons, I spoke with Best, the engineer, with whom I confirmed certain information regarding railroad schedules. My initial plan was to board a freight train from Hinckley to St. Paul, since I suspected you would track my movements if I left town by more conventional means. But when I met you at the depot, I feared my plan might be compromised, so I decided upon another alternative.

Meanwhile, I had other difficulties to contend with. Thompson, unbeknownst to me, had apparently decided to "cash in" before the situation became too hot by claiming the reward which, I learned only later, you had so cleverly dangled before him. LeGrande, who was little better than a brute, somehow got wind of the marshal's plans and the two of them had a terrible row at my house one evening, since both coveted the money. I feared, of course, that their arguing would soon lead one or the other of them to talk and thus compromise my position.

Another problem confronted me as well. It involved certain incriminating documents which had fallen into the hands of Thompson, whose abilities—modest as they were—included a talent for blackmail. While he and LeGrande were quarreling, I decided on a bold stratagem. I slipped away that night and, using a key I had duplicated earlier, gained entry to the marshal's house.

Thompson was a man of rather limited imagination, and it was easy enough to find where he had secreted his little treasure trove. I found what I was looking for and left the house, though as I walked away you can imagine my surprise when I saw you and Dr. Watson lurking in the bushes nearby. This discovery reaffirmed my plan to leave Hinckley at once. Of course, I did not know that Mr. Cain, having apparently discovered that the marshal was about to "spill the beans," would soon commit his second act of murder.

The next morning, after telling the girls I was going to

town, I engaged a friend (for a substantial amount of money) to take me by carriage to Spooner, Wisconsin.[2] It was a wearisome journey, to be sure, but unavoidable. Once in Spooner, I was able to make train connections directly to Chicago while bypassing St. Paul, where I knew your agents would be on the alert. I traveled under an assumed name and wore a plain but not unattractive wig which effectively disguised my appearance.

It was only after I arrived in Chicago that I learned of the tragedy in Hinckley. I do not know whether Mr. Cain intended to create so great an inferno, but the atmospheric conditions apparently were such that a gigantic blaze was inevitable.[3] There is much more I could tell you about my relationship with Mr. Cain but I believe I have taken up enough of your valuable time already.

Let me conclude by saying that I have now assumed a new identity and a new line of work in a rather remote place. Any attempt to trace my whereabouts, I assure you, will prove futile, as I have taken numerous precautions. I am truly sorry for what happened in Hinckley. It was indeed a great tragedy, the product of one man's madness but also of the terrible times in which we live. I remain confident that a new order will one day come out of the ruins of our corrupt civilization. Still, my sojourn in Hinckley did provide me with an opportunity to meet the great Sherlock Holmes, and I shall never forget our afternoon together.

Sincerely,

Mary Robinson.

When I had finished reading this extraordinary document, Holmes went to the window and gazed out over the ceaseless commotion of Baker Street. "A remarkable letter," he said. "Disingenuous in the extreme, full of evasions and half-truths, yet utterly brilliant in the way in which it absolves Mrs. Robinson of responsibility for the tragedy in the pineries. She has the rarest kind of female mind—one that is at once intuitive and yet utterly realistic about the hard truth of the world—and I do not doubt that she will succeed in whatever new venture she has embarked upon."

"We should send a copy of this letter to Mr. Hill, at once," I suggested. "Perhaps the Pinkertons will find it useful."

Holmes turned around and slowly shook his head. "No, Watson, there is no point to it. The Pinkertons will not find her. She was too clever for me and she will be too clever for them. Her letter, it seems to me, is a suitable coda for this tragic case. But it is over now and I do not wish to listen to its awful music of destruction any longer. Now, come along. Let us have lunch and turn our thoughts to whatever intriguing little puzzles the good criminals of London may provide for us today."

※

As it turned out, one final note remained to be played. It sounded a week later, when a telegram from Hill informed us that a party of hunters had come across the remains of two bodies near the burned-out Big Pine Camp. One was that of a huge man who could not have been anyone other than Jean Baptiste LeGrande. There was a single bullet hole in the middle of his forehead. The other corpse, still gripping a rifle in one hand, was identified as that of Boston Corbett.

"Do you suppose Corbett and LeGrande fought to the death before the fire overtook them?" I asked Holmes.

"I do not know," he replied, "but I shall always think that such was the case."

The news of Corbett's death left Holmes greatly saddened and he kept to his room all that day. The next morning, however, he sent the sum of fifty pounds to Hinckley. Identifying himself as "an anonymous friend of the deceased," Holmes directed that the money be used "to erect a suitable gravestone for the late Thomas (Boston) Corbett, soldier, woodsman and implacable enemy of all assassins."[4]

Notes

✳

Introduction

1. The James J. Hill mansion, at 240 Summit Avenue in St. Paul, was completed in 1891. Peabody and Stearns of Boston were the principal architects of the thirty-six-room house, which is in the Richardsonian Romanesque style. Hill lived in the mansion until his death, at age seventy-seven, in 1916. To this day, the house remains the largest private dwelling in St. Paul.

2. The other "treasures" in the safe include a number of documents that, if ever published, will provide startling new details on Hill's personal life.

3. There are numerous accounts of the Hinckley fire. The best modern book on the subject is Grace Stageberg Swenson, *From the Ashes: The Story of the Hinckley Fire of 1894* (Stillwater, Minn.: Croixside Press, 1978; St. Cloud, Minn.: North Star Press, 1988, 1994). Understandably, none of these standard histories of the fire mentions the role of Holmes and Watson, whose presence in Hinckley would not be known until the publication of this book.

4. Larry Millett, "Seeing Red: The Dispute over Three Early Versions of *A Study in Scarlet*," *The Watson Journal* 6 (Spring 1978): 16–28.

5. Larry Millett, *Truth amid Fiction: Authenticating the Manuscripts of John H. Watson, M.D.* (St. Paul, Minn.: privately printed, 1990).

6. The Eynsford Mills, founded about 1755, remain in operation today.

7. Readers interested in learning more about the Koh-I-Noor may consult Henry Petroski, *The Pencil: A History of Design and Circumstance* (New York: Alfred A. Knopf, 1990).

8. The standard account of Hill's life and career is Albro Martin, *James J. Hill and the Opening of the Northwest* (New York: Oxford University Press, 1976; St. Paul: Minnesota Historical Society Press, 1991).

9. This book has been edited to bring the text into conformity with modern American spelling and usage but otherwise stands exactly as written by Dr. Watson.

Chapter 1

1. Watson is referring, of course, to *The Times* of London.

2. This is the only known mention of an adventure that, like so many others casually cited by Watson, does not appear to have ever been committed to paper. St. John's Wood is a residential neighborhood of London not far from Baker Street.

3. Joseph G. Pyle was connected with James J. Hill for many years, first as editor of the Hill-owned St. Paul *Daily Globe* and later as a member of his personal staff. Pyle wrote the first biography of Hill, a two-volume work published in 1916, the year of Hill's death. It appears from Watson's account that Pyle also worked as a kind of agent-at-large for Hill in matters involving the Great Northern Railway, which was organized in 1889 by combining a number of lines. Its successor company, still in operation today, is the Burlington Northern Santa Fe Railroad.

4. Victoria Station, to which Pyle refers, was the terminus of the London, Chatham and Dover Railway, among others.

5. The Great Northern's transcontinental route, linking St. Paul to Seattle, was completed in January 1893.

6. The Eastern Minnesota Railway, a branch of the Great Northern, was organized in 1887. Its line from Hinckley to Duluth was completed two years later.

7. Watson is referring here to the assassination of President Sadi Carnot of France on June 24, 1894, in Lyons. The assassin, Santo Caserio, was an Italian anarchist.

8. The strike mentioned by Holmes involved Eugene Debs's American Railway Union and came in response to industry-wide wage cuts brought on by a depressed economy. The strike hit the Great Northern and its subsidiary lines, including the Eastern Minnesota, in the spring of 1894. However, both sides agreed to arbitration, and the walkout was short-lived.

9. This monograph, one of at least ten Holmes is known to have written, has apparently been lost.

10. The *Lucania* and its sister ship, the *Campania*, were launched by the Cunard Line in 1893 and were the finest ocean liners of their time. The *Lucania*, which could carry over eighteen hundred passengers at a top speed of twenty-two knots, set a record for the Atlantic crossing in 1894, going from New York to Ireland in less than five and a half days. Hill himself is known to have taken the *Lucania* to Europe at least once, in 1896.

Chapter 2

1. Holmes's remarks here are eerily prophetic, since it was an iceberg that sank the fabled *Titanic* on its maiden voyage across the Atlantic in 1912.

2. Holmes often conducted research at the London Library in St. James's Square. Lomax, first name unknown, was a sub-librarian there. He is also mentioned in one other case, "The Adventure of the Illustrious Client," which dates from 1902.

3. The Pennsylvania Special made its inaugural run in 1887 and was the first American passenger train to include lounge and library-buffet cars in addition to the usual Pullman sleepers.

4. The Pennsylvania's ferry terminal at Jersey City, completed in 1892, handled all of the railroad's passenger traffic into and out of New York City. Not until the construction of a tunnel beneath the Hudson River and the opening of Pennsylvania Station in Manhattan in 1910 were the railroad's passengers at last able to enter and depart from New York City directly.

5. Horseshoe Curve, just west of Altoona, Pa., was built in 1854 to carry trains up and over 2,161-foot-high Allegheny Mountain at a modest 1.8 percent grade. The curve, which remains in use today by Conrail trains, is now a National Historic Landmark.

6. This would have been the old Chicago Union Station, built in 1871 at the northeast corner of Canal and Adams streets. It was razed in 1923 after completion of the present Union Station.

7. London's first underground train line, the Metropolitan, opened in 1862 with coal-burning engines that often made travel in the tunnels "abominable," to use Watson's word. Watson mentions London's underground in two other stories, "The Red-Headed League" and "The Adventure of the Bruce-Partington Plans." Electric streetcars first appeared in St. Paul in 1890.

8. Hill and his wife, Mary, had nine children — six girls and three boys. Gertrude was the second-youngest member of the clan and would have been ten years old in 1894.

9. Timber cruisers were skilled woodsmen sent out by logging companies to find and estimate the value of standing timber. They were also sometimes called "estimators" or "land lookers."

10. Curiously, Holmes left no known monograph on the subject of handwriting, but it can be supposed that he was a pioneer in the science of graphology.

11. Like so many other cases mentioned in passing by Watson, this one was never published and so it is not known how Holmes's acute sense of smell contributed to the mystery's solution.

12. In *The Hound of the Baskervilles*, Watson noted that Holmes was familiar with seventy-five kinds of perfume, an indication of just how sensitive and discriminating his sense of smell was.

Chapter 3

1. The first Holmes adventure to appear in an American magazine was "The Sign of the Four," which was published by *Lippincott's Magazine* in its February 1890 issue. Other stories were soon published in *McClure's Magazine* and *Harper's Weekly*, both popular American periodicals of their time.

2. Hill, in fact, had a great many English "acquaintances," most notably Sir George Stephen, later Lord Mount Stephen, a Canadian financier whose successes in business earned him an English peerage. Stephen worked with Hill on a variety of projects, and Hill made his first visit to London, in 1892, to visit Stephen. It is possible that Stephen may even have recommended Holmes to Hill, although no evidence exists to support this theory.

3. Holmes's expertise as a cryptographer is well known and was most brilliantly demonstrated in 1898 in the "Adventure of the Dancing Men." It is also known that Holmes published a monograph on cryptography some time prior to 1898, although no mention of it is made here.

4. The building that housed Schuneman's, constructed in 1890–91, was at the northwest corner of Sixth and Wabasha streets in downtown St. Paul. Watson's description of it is quite accurate in all the particulars. The building was demolished in 1964.

5. Irene Adler, of course, was *the* woman in Sherlock Holmes's life. An opera singer born in New Jersey, she outwitted the great detective in "A Scandal in Bohemia," one of the most famous of Holmes's early adventures.

6. Jicky perfume was introduced by Guerlain, one of the most celebrated of the French perfume makers, in 1889. It is recognized today as the first modern perfume because it made use of synthetic oils and new techniques for extracting floral essences. The perfume was named after a favorite nephew of Aimé Guerlain, who developed the scent. Holmes, incidentally, was quite correct in analyzing the composition of the perfume. Its ingredients include rosewood, bergamot and basil in addition to the lavender, lemon, rosemary and sandal that Holmes noted.

7. The Ryan Hotel, at Sixth and Robert streets in St. Paul, was for many years that city's most popular inn. Built in 1885 at a cost of one million dollars, the seven-story Victorian Gothic structure was, as Watson rightly noted, similar

in style to the huge St. Pancras (or Midland) Hotel, erected in London in 1871. The Ryan Hotel was demolished in 1962.

8. Train-pedestrian accidents were, as Pyle noted, shockingly common in the nineteenth century, in part because trackage was so extensive but also because so many trains crossed streets at grade. In Chicago, quite possibly the world leader in this kind of accident, as many as 430 people a year were killed by trains during the 1890s.

9. The stone arch bridge Holmes and Watson crossed was built in 1883 and still stands, although it is now used by pedestrians rather than trains.

10. Minneapolis was indeed the world's foremost flour-milling city in the 1890s, producing over ten million barrels a year.

11. Pyle's prediction was accurate, for the Minnesota pineries were all but exhausted by 1920. However, he was wrong in assuming that farms would replace the pine forests, since most of the cutover land proved ill-suited to agriculture.

Chapter 4

1. The Baldwin Locomotive Works of Philadelphia were founded in 1831 by a jeweler named Matthias Baldwin. By 1900, the firm—which built engines for railroads all over the world—was the largest locomotive manufacturer in the United States.

2. The "American type" locomotive to which Holmes refers here was the most common of all American steam locomotives from about 1840 to 1900. Its 4-4-0 wheel arrangement (four small wheels at the front of the engine, four large drive wheels toward the rear center, and no wheels at the far rear) was particularly well suited to the rough condition of most track in the nineteenth century. Locomotives of this type were also popular because of their reliability and ease of maintenance. "Tractive force," also known as "tractive effort," is the force, measured in pounds, that a locomotive exerts on its driving wheels. The "adhesion ratio" is obtained by dividing the weight of a locomotive's driving wheels by its tractive force. The 3.8 ratio cited by Best means that the weight of his locomotive's driving wheels, called the "weight on drivers," was about 46,300 pounds. Holmes could have learned about these measurements by consulting any good locomotive technical manual of the time.

3. Holmes was accustomed to fasting and his eating habits in Hinckley were indeed an aberration, as Watson noted. In fact, in "The Adventure of the Mazarin Stone," which took place in 1903, Holmes went so far as to observe that "faculties become refined when you starve them."

Chapter 5

1. The first American book edition of *The Sign of the Four*, the second of Watson's four novels about Sherlock Holmes, appeared in 1893, three years after its initial American publication in *Lippincott's Magazine*.

2. Holmes is referring here to the Greek gods of sleep and dreams, respectively.

Chapter 6

1. "Swampers" were loggers whose job was to cut the branches off trees after they had been felled.

2. Holmes's expertise in analyzing the human hand is well known. He even authored a monograph on the subject, which is mentioned by Watson in *The Sign of the Four*.

3. A "scaler" was the man who estimated the number of board feet of lumber in a log.

4. These three firms were among the largest doing business in the Minnesota pineries in the 1890s. But it was Frederick Weyerhaeuser's array of interconnected companies that eventually came to dominate the logging industry.

5. Watson, alas, never committed the Huddleston case to print, and this is the only known mention of it.

6. This is another of those tantalizing cases that Watson never saw fit to publish.

7. The two women mentioned by Watson were both celebrated, and quite calculating, murderers. Constance Kent was a sixteen-year-old English girl who murdered her three-year-old half brother in 1860. Suspected of the crime, she covered her tracks brilliantly and won her release following a court hearing. Four years later, however, she confessed and eventually served twenty years in prison. Catherine Wilson was a London nurse who poisoned at least seven elderly victims after she had convinced them to make out their wills in her favor. She never showed any remorse for her crimes and was hanged in 1862 as a crowd of twenty thousand people looked on.

Chapter 7

1. A "log mark" was a logo—either a set of initials or a symbol—stamped into the end of a log to identify its owner. Such marks were used when logs from several companies were sent down river at the same time.

2. Presumably, the book referred to here is Marx and Engels's *Communist Manifesto*, a slim volume published in 1848.

3. The subject of Watson's wives—there may have been at least three between 1886 and 1902—has long troubled Sherlockian scholars. What is clear here is

that Watson is referring to Mary (née Morstan) Watson, whom he met and wooed during the adventure of *The Sign of the Four* in 1888. Mary Watson died some time between 1891 and the spring of 1894, when Watson's "sad bereavement" is mentioned in "The Adventure of the Empty House."

Chapter 8

1. "Baking a batch of rolls" was a slang term for sexual intercourse used by prostitutes in the lumber camps.

2. Watson is using the word "intercourse" here in the sense of an interchange of feelings and ideas. Given his situation, however, it must be accounted a poor choice of words.

3. Gustave Doré (1832–1883) was a French illustrator known for his fantastic imagination. Among Doré's most famous illustrations were those for an 1861 edition of Dante's *Inferno*.

Chapter 9

1. Pine City became the county seat of Pine County in the early 1870s. By 1894, it had one thousand or so residents, which made it about the same size as Hinckley.

2. Watson first mentioned the amazing gaps in Holmes's knowledge in *A Study in Scarlet*, noting there that the peerless detective "was ignorant of the Copernican Theory and of the composition of the Solar System. That any civilized human being in this nineteenth century should not be aware that the earth travelled round the sun appeared to be to me such an extraordinary fact that I could hardly realize it."

Chapter 10

1. "Stag pants," also known as "malones," were heavy wool pants worn by lumberjacks during the winter logging season and were prized for their ability to shed water. That Holmes would actually have worn such heavy trousers during the heat of summer is doubtful, and he may simply have used the term "stag pants" to impress Watson with his command of lumberjack lingo.

2. There are at least a dozen known adventures in which Holmes resorted to disguises of one sort or another. He sometimes went to extremes in this regard. For example, in "The Adventure of Charles Augustus Milverton," Holmes—disguised as a plumber—became engaged to a housemaid.

3. The Spanish Armada, to which Watson refers, sailed in 1588.

4. About one thousand members of what is now known as the Mille Lacs band of the Ojibway lived in the woodlands around Hinckley in the 1890s. Today, the band owns a prospering gambling casino on the edge of town.

Chapter 11

1. The term "wanigan" has many meanings and many variant spellings in logging parlance, but in this case it refers to a camp store, where lumberjacks could buy food, clothes and other supplies at cost. A business office was often part of the wanigan as well.

2. A "jill-poker" in lumberjack lingo was a slow or lazy fellow.

3. Natty Bumppo was the frontier scout who served as the hero of James Fenimore Cooper's epic Leather-Stocking novels, the most famous of which is probably *The Last of the Mohicans* (1826). It is a bit surprising that Watson, who generally does not seem to have been a great reader of fiction, would have been familiar with the character.

4. Corbett's claim to having shot John Wilkes Booth is disputed, but there is no question that he was on the scene when Lincoln's assassin was cornered by a detachment of Union troops and shot to death on April 26, 1865. Corbett was a member of the 16th New York Cavalry, which surrounded the barn near Bowling Green, Virginia, where Booth was found hiding twelve days after the president's assassination. Corbett claimed afterward that he shot Booth, although other sources believe Booth committed suicide. In any event, Corbett received a $1,650 reward—an item he seems to have forgotten in his complaint to Watson about the nation's ingratitude.

5. Holmes's description of this implement, a variation of the so-called "cant hook" loggers used on land, is accurate. It was named after Joseph Peavey of Maine, who invented it in 1858. Lumberjacks also referred to it by a number of other names, including "peewee," "crooked steal," and "Quebec choker." The peavey's handle was usually anywhere from four to six feet long.

6. Here is what is known about Corbett, based on the scant biographical information available. Born Thomas P. Corbett in England in 1832, he emigrated to the United States at age seven and later went by the first name of Boston. At some point he "got religion" and became an itinerant preacher. He volunteered for the Union army at the outbreak of the Civil War, but—as he told Watson—was soon captured by the Confederates and sent off to the infamous Andersonville Prison in Georgia. He was eventually paroled, however, and served in the Union army until the end of the war. After the Booth episode, he moved to Kansas, where he farmed for many years before securing a position as an assistant doorkeeper at the state capitol. But one day in 1887, after hearing what he considered to be blasphemous remarks, he went berserk and began waving a pistol. He was then declared insane—a fact not mentioned to Watson—and sent to an asylum in Topeka. However, he escaped in 1888 (whether this escape was indeed "miraculous" is questionable) and somehow found his way to Hinckley. How he became acquainted with Hill is unknown,

but Corbett apparently had a reputation as an expert marksman, and that may be why Hill hired him to watch over Holmes and Watson.

7. Corbett, according to some sources, was self-castrated, which would explain the high-pitched voice noted by Watson.

8. Lumberjacks did indeed have a distinctive language of their own. A "Michigan jumper" was a lumberjack who frequently changed camps, perhaps to stay ahead of his bad reputation. A "go-devil" was a two-pronged wooden sled, much like a travois, used for hauling logs. The "robber's stick" was a hardwood ruler used to estimate the number of board feet of lumber in a log or tree.

Chapter 12

1. This was a large square, laid out in 1761, at the south end of Baker Street. It was only a few blocks from the flat where Holmes and Watson resided.

2. Although Hinckley had no telephones in 1894, they were already common in larger cities like St. Paul, and Hill undoubtedly had a telephone at home. Interestingly, this is Watson's earliest mention of the telephone in one of his narratives. Prior to the discovery of this manuscript, the first Holmes case in which the telephone was known to play a part was "The Adventure of the Retired Colourman," which appeared in 1927 but concerned events occurring in 1898.

Chapter 13

1. Holmes is known to have resorted to breaking and entering at least three times during his career. In 1898, in "The Adventure of the Retired Colourman," he broke into a murderer's house in order to secure evidence, later telling Watson: "Burglary has always been an alternative profession, had I cared to adopt it, and I have little doubt that I should have come to the front." The next year, he and Watson broke into a blackmailer's home and burgled his safe in order to prevent him from making a woman his next victim. This episode, related in "The Adventure of Charles Augustus Milverton," is the source of Holmes's famous remark that "I have always had an idea that I would have made a highly efficient criminal." The great detective's last known burgling occurred in 1902 in "The Adventure of the Illustrious Client."

2. Watson remarked in "The Cardboard Box" that "my term of service in India had trained me to stand heat better than cold."

3. The weapon Watson carried was most likely one of the so-called "new-line" single-action pocket revolvers manufactured from about 1873 to 1890 by the famed Colt Firearms Co. of Hartford, Conn. This five-shot revolver came in a variety of calibers and barrel lengths, but Watson probably was armed with either the .41- or .38-caliber model, since the smaller versions were often considered women's weapons (the .32-caliber, in fact, was called the Ladies' Colt).

This, incidentally, is the only Holmes adventure in which the kind of revolver used by Watson is identified.

4. Watson remarked elsewhere upon Holmes's superb eyesight at night. In "The Adventure of Charles Augustus Milverton," he wrote: "Holmes had remarkable powers, carefully cultivated, of seeing in the dark." Unfortunately, Watson did not say what sort of "cultivation" had enabled Holmes to accomplish this optical feat.

5. This, of course, is a reference to the gigantic dog, its face and mouth coated with phosphorus, that played such a terrifying role in perhaps the greatest Holmes adventure of all, *The Hound of the Baskervilles*. It is odd that Watson should mention it here, however, since the adventure, which occurred in 1888, was not published until 1901.

6. This reference leaves no doubt that Watson completed the manuscript of "Sherlock Holmes and the Red Demon" some time in 1896. He probably sent it to Hill shortly thereafter.

Chapter 14

1. A "pencil pusher," in loggers' parlance, was a clerk. The "swindle stick"—known by a variety of other, equally colorful names—was a hardwood ruler used by a "scaler" to estimate the number of board feet of lumber in a log or tree.

2. To say that a lumberman "logged on section thirty-seven" was to accuse him of being a timber thief, since the standard American township has only thirty-six sections.

3. In Victorian times, there was great fear of being buried alive. As a result, coffins were sometimes equipped with bells, so that in the event of premature burial, the occupant of the coffin could signal that he or she was still among the living. Edgar Allan Poe immortalized such a device in his 1844 short story, "The Premature Burial." In this story, Poe wrote of a "large bell, the rope of which [extended] through a hole in the coffin, and so [was] fastened to one of the hands of the corpse."

4. A "deadhead" was a water-soaked log that would sink to the bottom of a lake or river.

5. Watson is referring to a worker at the Brennan Lumber Mill, which was Hinckley's largest employer in 1894. The mill was only a few hundred yards west of the spot along the river where Holmes found the glove.

6. The story of this fabulous gem is related by Watson in "The Adventure of the Blue Carbuncle," first published in 1892 but describing events that had occurred about four years earlier.

Chapter 15

1. A "road monkey," one of the more lowly figures in the hierarchy of the lumber camp, was assigned the job of keeping logging roads in good condition. A "swamper" trimmed limbs off trees after they had been cut down. The term was also used to describe a man who cleared roads. The smallpox mentioned here is a reference to "logger's smallpox," which was not a disease but a set of scars inflicted by spiked boots during a fight. "Frog," of course, is a derogatory term that was used to describe a French-Canadian.

2. Sherlockian scholars have argued for years over whether Holmes, who mentions his experiences as a student in several stories, attended Oxford University or its rival, Cambridge. This provides the first definitive evidence that he was at Oxford (probably in the early 1870s), although some scholars believe Holmes also attended Cambridge some years later.

3. Holmes's cat, presumably, was named after C. Auguste Dupin, a French detective introduced by Edgar Allan Poe in his famous story "The Murders in the Rue Morgue," which appeared in 1841. Dupin also was featured in two other Poe stories, "The Mystery of Marie Roget" (1842) and "The Purloined Letter" (1845).

4. High Street is one of the main thoroughfares in the historic center of Oxford.

5. This would have been Dr. D. W. Cowan, one of three physicians who practiced in Hinckley in 1894. Interestingly, one of the other doctors in town was a woman, Inez Legg.

6. This is yet another case that Watson never published. Scafell Pike, located in the Lake District north of Liverpool, is the highest point in England, with an elevation of 3,210 feet.

7. The last headline is a reference to a type of horse-drawn, steam-powered fire engine manufactured by the Waterous Co. of St. Paul. These engines, capable of pumping about 350 gallons of water a minute, were purchased by many small communities in Minnesota in the 1890s.

8. Laudanum, a tincture of opium, was widely used as a painkiller and all-purpose drug around the turn of the century. It was especially popular with women.

Chapter 16

1. The exact location of the swamp described by Watson is difficult to pinpoint today because many of the small wetlands once found in Pine County have been drained or altered. The best guess is that the swamp was somewhere in section 33 of Hinckley Township, along what are now the tracks of the Burlington Northern Santa Fe Railroad.

2. This case, like so many others mentioned by Watson, was never published, and the exact nature of Holmes's "baffling conduct" remains a mystery. However, the tone of Watson's remarks here, and his reference to the case's "unsat-

isfactory" conclusion, leave little doubt that Holmes botched the investigation. Although no date is assigned to the case of the Etruscan grave robbery, it may well have taken place in the late 1880s, a period during which Holmes was using cocaine. At least one published adventure from 1888, "The Yellow Face," shows that Holmes was not in the best of form, and it is tempting to think that the Etruscan affair occurred at about the same time, when extensive drug use may have dulled the detective's normal acumen.

Chapter 17

1. Spark arresters were netlike devices placed in a locomotive's smokestack and designed to keep sparks from escaping and thereby causing fires along the track. However, not all locomotives of the time were equipped with such devices, and fires caused by passing trains were quite common.

2. Some Sherlockian scholars have long suspected that Watson visited America as a young man, and the reference here to San Francisco, while not conclusive, certainly suggests that this was the case.

3. The Duluth Union Depot, completed in 1892, was in fact quite new when Holmes and Watson saw it. Watson's comment regarding the depot's "French manner" is appropriate, for the structure's château style was based on French Norman prototypes. The depot still stands but is now used as a museum.

4. The Spalding Hotel, at West Fifth and Superior streets in Duluth, opened in 1889 and was, as Watson described it, the city's finest hotel at that time. The seven-story structure, which had more than two hundred rooms, was torn down in 1963.

5. The "new lode of iron ore" mentioned by Watson is, of course, the fabled Mesabi Range, discovered in the timbered hills north of Duluth in 1890. But it was not until 1893 that the first shipment of ore from the Mesabi left Duluth.

6. The "funicular" or "incline" railway described so ably by Watson was built in 1891 along West Seventh Street in Duluth. It was more than half a mile long and rose 509 feet. Like many other incline railways of this period in the United States, it was designed by Samuel Diescher of Pittsburgh and used a system of two counterweighted cars pulled by steam-powered cables. The Duluth incline remained in operation until 1939, when it was demolished.

Chapter 18

1. The lever Best used to start the locomotive is called the power reverse lever. Besides controlling the locomotive's direction, this lever determines when steam will be admitted to the cylinders during piston strokes. The lever is usually fully engaged when starting the locomotive, so as to provide maximum power, and is then gradually pulled back—a process known as "hooking up"—as the engine gains speed. A good engineer will use the power lever skill-

fully in order to achieve the most economical use of steam while the locomotive is in motion.

2. It is not known exactly how hot it was in Hinckley on the day of the fire, but Watson's reference to "extreme" heat is borne out by the historic record. For example, the town of Collegeville, not far west of Hinckley, reached ninety-five degrees on September 1, 1894 — nearly a record for so late in the season — with a maximum humidity of twenty-eight percent. The conditions, in other words, were perfect for wildfire, especially after the summer-long drought in the region.

3. Holyoke, twenty-nine miles from Superior, is in Minnesota, a few miles west of the Wisconsin border.

4. "Running on blue steam" meant that Best was keeping water in the locomotive's boiler to an absolute minimum in order to maintain the highest possible speed. The danger in this was that if water levels in the boiler became too low, internal parts would begin to melt and the boiler would explode.

5. Seventy miles an hour was indeed impressive, especially along a branch line like the Eastern Minnesota in a relatively small locomotive like Best's 4-4-0 American type. However, larger locomotives on better track were capable of much greater speeds. In May of 1893, for instance, a New York Central locomotive — No. 999 — attained a speed of 112.5 miles an hour during a one-mile test run. But along a line like the Eastern Minnesota, such dazzling speeds were unheard of. The normal run from Duluth to Hinckley in 1894 required two and a half hours, an average speed of about twenty-nine miles an hour. Top speed during the trip probably did not exceed forty miles an hour.

6. Watson does not mention that Hill had a major interest in these quarries, from which stone was shipped throughout the Great Northern's vast territory. The Great Northern's massive office building in St. Paul, completed not long before Hill died, made extensive use of Kettle River stone, as did a number of the railroad's depots. The stone is no longer quarried today.

7. In "The Yellow Face," an adventure published in 1893, Watson offered similar sentiments regarding Holmes's approach to exercise: "Sherlock Holmes was a man who seldom took exercise for exercise's sake. Few men were capable of greater muscular effort . . . but he looked upon aimless bodily exertion as a waste of energy, and he seldom bestirred himself save where there was some professional object to be served."

8. The "whirling column" that Watson describes so dramatically was the convection column of the Hinckley firestorm. All fires have such rotating columns of smoke and gas that function almost like a flue. In the case of the Hinckley fire, this column — sometimes likened to a reverse tornado — may have reached thirty thousand or more feet into the atmosphere.

Chapter 19

1. This would have been Edward Barry, engineer of the Eastern Minnesota passenger train to which Best had linked his locomotive.

2. Watson is correct in stating that no one from Sandstone boarded the train, despite word of the horrors in Hinckley just eight miles away. When the fire swept through Sandstone less than an hour later, after the train had left, at least forty people in the town died and scores of others were injured.

3. Watson mentions in *A Study in Scarlet* that Holmes was an "excellent singlestick player, boxer, and swordsman." In another story, "The *Gloria Scott*," Holmes himself remarked that his only athletic interests while a college student were "fencing and boxing."

Chapter 20

1. The final coroner's report on the fire listed 418 dead, of whom 248 came from Hinckley. However, some sources believe the actual death toll may have exceeded 500, including Native Americans and isolated woodsmen whose bodies were never found. The fire, one of the most lethal of its kind in American history, consumed 480 square miles of forest before it burned out on the evening of September 1.

2. Hiding in a well was no guarantee of safety during the fire. Although some people did indeed survive in this way, many others perished when they were suffocated by poisonous smoke and gases. In one grisly instance, eighteen disintegrating corpses were pulled from a dry well on a farm near Sandstone two days after the fire. The dead included nine members of one family.

3. Nellie Bly, just twenty-six years old but already a star reporter for the *New York World*, arrived in Hinckley a few days after the fire. As Watson indicates, her itinerary included a stop in Duluth, where she interviewed fire victims. Her account of the catastrophe appeared in the *World* on September 9. Bly first became famous in 1890 when she circumnavigated the globe in seventy-two days, thereby eclipsing the record of the fictional Phileas Fogg in Jules Verne's *Around the World in Eighty Days*.

4. The high bridge, with a new central span, reopened for traffic on September 18. However, Hill was so unhappy with the pace of the work that at one point he went to Sandstone to personally supervise the repair crews, whose performance he termed "disgraceful."

5. Thousands of sightseers did in fact converge on the fire scene, and the railroads even provided special trains for this purpose. In Hinckley, unwanted visitors became such a problem that a vigilante committee was formed to discourage people from making off with "souvenirs" from the fire.

6. Best did keep his silence, for he made no mention of Holmes and Watson in several newspaper interviews after the fire. Unfortunately, Best never re-

ceived proper credit for his heroic actions on the day of the holocaust, and nothing is known about his subsequent career with the Eastern Minnesota.

7. What a tantalizing clue Watson has left here! Unfortunately, no record of this case has been located, in either Hill's or Watson's papers. Nonetheless, it is possible to make some inferences based on the known history of ice palaces in St. Paul. Several large ice palaces were built in the city near the end of the nineteenth century. The first was erected in 1886. Others followed in 1887, 1888, and, most significant as far as Holmes and Watson are concerned, 1896. The palaces were normally built in January. Thus, Watson's remark that he and Holmes returned to St. Paul "little more than a year later" suggests they must have been in St. Paul in January of 1896, when that year's palace—the last built in St. Paul in the nineteenth century—was completed. It can only be hoped that Watson's account of "the bizarre mystery of the spectral head in the ice palace" (assuming that he committed the adventure to paper) will one day be found.

8. Holmes gave nothing away with his final reference to the Red Demon, since this name was widely used at the time as a metaphor for fire in general.

Epilogue

1. This case was recounted by Watson in "The Adventure of the Golden Pince-Nez," first published in 1904.

2. Spooner, Wisconsin, is about fifty miles southeast of Hinckley. From Spooner, Mrs. Robinson would have been able to reach Chicago by rail in several different ways without going through St. Paul.

3. Mrs. Robinson's statement regarding "atmospheric conditions" is correct. The hot, dry and windy weather was perfect for a forest fire. There is evidence, in fact, that the blaze which destroyed Hinckley began as two separate fires that united just before reaching the town. While Cornell undoubtedly set one of these fires, it will never be known whether he started the other one as well.

4. Although Boston Corbett did indeed perish in the fire, as Watson reported, it is not known whether the monument ordered by Holmes was ever erected. There is certainly no trace of it in Hinckley's Memorial Cemetery, where more than two hundred victims of the fire are buried.

Author's Note

❄

Although "Sherlock Holmes and the Red Demon" is a work of fiction, much of it is based on historic fact. To begin with, there is the Hinckley fire, which did indeed claim more than four hundred lives on September 1, 1894. My description of this lethal event is generally accurate, though of course no Englishmen by the names of Holmes and Watson were in the middle of it. I based my concluding chapters on numerous eyewitness accounts of the fire as well as a large secondary literature that has grown up over the years.

To this day, no one knows how the fire started, but it is interesting to note that in December of 1894 a report submitted by the state of Minnesota's Pine Land Investigation Committee charged that the blaze was set by thieves "to cover up their stealing of timber on state lands." That allegation, however, was never substantiated with any convincing evidence. What can be said with certainty is that the Hinckley conflagration was a disaster waiting to happen